# LORDS *of* DESIRE

# LORDS
## *of*
# DESIRE

**VIRGINIA HENLEY**
**SALLY MacKENZIE**
**VICTORIA DAHL**
**KRISTI ASTOR**

KENSINGTON PUBLISHING CORP.
http://www.kensingtonbooks.com

KENSINGTON BOOKS are published by

Kensington Publishing Corp.
119 West 40th Street
New York, NY 10018

All Kensington titles, imprints, and distributed lines are available at special quantity discounts for bulk purchases for sales
promotion, premiums, fund-raising, educational, or institu-
tional use.

Special book excerpts or customized printings can also be created to fit specific needs. For details, write or phone the office
of the Kensington Special Sales Manager: Kensington Publishing Corp., 119 West 40th Street, New York, NY 10018. Attn.:
Special Sales Department. Phone: 1-800-221-2647.

Kensington and the K logo Reg. U.S. Pat. & TM Off.

ISBN-13: 978-0-7582-2966-3
ISBN-10: 0-7582-2966-6

First trade paperback printing: February 2009
First mass market printing: June 2010
10  9  8  7  6  5  4  3  2  1

Printed in the United States of America

# CONTENTS

# SMUGGLER'S LAIR

# VIRGINIA HENLEY

# The Smuggler's Song
*Rudyard Kipling*

If you wake at midnight, and hear a horse's feet,
Don't go drawing back the blind, or looking in the street,
Them that asks no questions isn't told a lie.
Watch the wall, my darling, while the Gentlemen go by!

    Five-and-twenty ponies, trotting through the dark,
    Brandy for the Parson, 'Baccy for the Clerk;
    Laces for a lady; letters for a spy,
    And watch the wall, my darling, while the Gentlemen go
      by!

Running round the woodlump if you chance to find
Little barrels, roped and tarred, all full of brandy-wine;
Don't you shout to come and look, nor take 'em for your
    play;
Put the brushwood back again, and they'll be gone next
    day.

If you see the stable-door setting open wide;
If you see a tired horse lying down inside;
If your mother mends a coat cut about and tore;
If the lining's wet and warm, don't you ask no more!

If you meet King George's men, dressed in blue and red,
You be careful what you say, and mindful what is said.
If they call you "pretty maid," and chuck you 'neath the
    chin,
Don't you tell where no one is, nor yet where no one's
    been!

Knocks and footsteps round the house, whiles after dark,
You've no call for running out till the housedogs bark.

Trusty's here, and Pincher's here, and see how dumb they
    lie,
They don't fret to follow when the Gentlemen go by!

If you do as you've been told, likely there's a chance
You'll be given a dainty doll, all the way from France,
With a cap of Valenciennes, and a velvet hood,
A present from the Gentlemen, along o' being good!

    Five-and-twenty ponies trotting through the dark,
    Brandy for the Parson, 'Baccy for the Clerk.
    Them that asks no questions isn't told a lie,
    Watch the wall, my darling, while the Gentlemen go
        by!

# PROLOGUE

As dawn began to lighten the sky, the naked female immersed breast-high in the River Rother relished the feel of the cool water on her skin. The forbidden indulgence filled her with a sense of freedom she seldom experienced in the restricted, narrow life she led. Victoria knew she must end her swim and return home to the priory before she was discovered.

She took one last, lingering look at the medieval castle of Bodiam and went very still. From atop one of its high towers, a dark figure watched her. Silhouetted against the gray sky, the black-clad male remained motionless and Victoria shivered as gooseflesh crept up her arms. The ancient castle, neglected for decades, had been unoccupied for the past few years.

*How long has he been watching me?* Her thought was followed by another, even more chilling: *How many times has he spied on me from the high tower?* Victoria swam in the Rother twice a week at dawn when she professed to be at church. Her pulse raced madly. *He knows my secret!* She closed her eyes in panic. *How long before Mother learns of my deception?* When she opened her eyes, the figure was gone.

"It was a trick of the light. I only imagined him," she murmured with bone-softening relief.

With pounding heart, Victoria slipped from the water and retrieved her clothes from their hiding place. She pulled on her drawers, dress, and shoes, wrapped her dark cloak about her, and quickly walked the mile that brought her to the priory gardens. She hurried into the shed and donned the stockings that she had earlier stuffed into her pocket, then pulled back her wet hair, plaited it tightly, and pinned it into a bun at the nape of her neck. She tied on her bonnet, picked up her prayer book—a present from her late father, the Right Reverend Thomas Carswell—and proceeded with dignified, measured steps into the house. When she reached the haven of her bedchamber, Victoria let out a long, shuddering sigh of relief.

"I imagined him!" she whispered. But vision or no, she sensed deep in her bones that she would encounter him again.

# CHAPTER 1

"A dinner invitation from *Mad Jack's* nephew?" Victoria asked with prim disdain.

"The gentleman's name was Captain John Fuller," Lady Carswell said repressively. "Wherever did you hear such a vulgar sobriquet? Surely not from one of the history books in which you constantly thrust your nose? John Fuller was a Captain in the Sussex Light Infantry and a respected Member of Parliament for four years."

"Yes, Mama." Victoria reluctantly closed her book. *Anyone who fritters away a fortune building follies and is buried sitting up wearing a top hat has earned the nickname Mad Jack!*

"His wealth came from manufacturing cannon for the Royal Navy."

*Undoubtedly a big noise!* Victoria hid her amusement.

"His nephew, Sir Peregrine Palmer Fuller, inherited everything."

"*Peregrine?* The name alone invites ridicule," Victoria declared.

"That is quite enough. Young ladies should be seen and not heard. Your manners are appalling. A far higher standard of gentility is expected from a clergyman's daughter. Since our year's formal mourning period has been over for months, I shall accept the invitation. Obviously the gentleman wishes to form a connection with us because of our reputation for respectability."

*Why else would he invite us to dinner?* It was obvious he wanted to distance himself from Mad Jack's eccentricity by cultivating the rigidly moral, straitlaced Lady Edwina, widow of the Right Reverend Thomas Carswell, and her spinster daughter.

"I'd rather decline, Mama," Victoria said with daring.

"The dinner is to be held at Bodiam Castle."

*"Bodiam?"* Victoria gave her mother her full attention. The medieval castle was one of her passions. Constructed in the fourteenth century in the reign of Edward III, one of England's great Plantagenet kings, the magnificent castle on the river had been built to protect the Rother Valley from French raids.

Victoria's interest in Bodiam had been sparked when the main gates were suddenly replaced. That was a decade ago, when she was seven, and though it had lain neglected ever since, she had fallen in love with the romantic, moated castle with its high towers and battlemented ramparts.

"Did Mad Jack . . . I beg your pardon, Mama . . . did Captain John Fuller own Bodiam Castle?"

"Yes, and now it is owned by his nephew, Sir Peregrine Palmer Fuller. What possible objection could you have?"

"None. None whatsoever." *I've longed to go inside Bodiam Castle since I was a child—this is the opportunity of a lifetime!*

Victoria appraised her reflection in her cheval glass. Her dark hair was pulled back into a neat bun at her nape and only a tiny white frill around its high neck relieved the plainness of her long-sleeved mauve cambric dress. As she pinned on her jet mourning brooch, she was satisfied that her mother could find no fault with her appearance tonight. She noticed with pleasure that her eyes matched the shade of her gown exactly. Victoria smiled at her reflection and murmured, "Vanity, thy name is woman!"

Downstairs, her brother Edmund stood in the front hall waiting patiently for his mother and sister. He wore his clerical collar and a black suit. He had become the Reverend of the Hawkhurst parish church after his father died, which enabled the Carswells to keep possession of the priory. Victoria suspected her mother had planned it that way by insisting Edmund follow in his father's footsteps, despite the fact that he felt no calling. Edmund's nature was too gentle to go against his mother's wishes, but he was complicit in guarding Victoria's shortcomings and remained silent about his sister's absence from church services in the early morning.

Edwina, garbed in her best bombazine, finally appeared and gave her daughter a thorough inspection. "Tonight, Victoria, do not speak until you are spoken to. You must use a deferential tone and manner, as becomes a young unmarried lady. Remember to be prim and proper at all times and, above all, keep your lashes lowered. It is improper to look directly into a gentleman's face, and it will help conceal the strange color of your eyes."

Edmund held his sister's cloak and squeezed her shoulders to take the sting from their mother's words and comfort her.

Victoria raised her dark lashes to reveal the full impact of her pale violet eyes, then lowered one eyelid in a solemn wink.

Since the Carswells could no longer afford a driver,

Edmund drove their carriage the short distance to Bodiam. As they went over the narrow bridge that led across the moat, Victoria saw that the gate moved up and down like a portcullis and she silently thanked Mad Jack for duplicating the original medieval apparatus. She glanced down into the moat and saw water lilies, closed now that it was eventide, and she thrilled at the reflection of the moon upon the water. Mist was floating in from the river, adding to the otherworldly atmosphere that felt timeless. *Tonight, the shadows make it look as it did centuries ago.*

Lit torches flared in the courtyard, leading the way to the stables and revealing a large grassy quadrangle. *This is the castle bailey.* A stableman came forward to take care of their horse and carriage and Victoria wished he'd been wearing livery.

A servant met them at the door and led the way through what must have been the Great Hall, then he ushered them into a smaller adjacent chamber furnished as a dining room.

Victoria stared wide-eyed at the high stone walls, the arched timbered ceiling, and the ancient chandelier that held myriad blazing candles. She thought she heard the faint echo of voices and imagined they were sounds floating from the past of people who had inhabited Bodiam over the centuries. *I wish it were mine!*

The servant took the ladies' cloaks and told them that their host would be with them directly. A uniformed female servant stood unobtrusively against the wall and Victoria noted the fatuous look of approval on her mother's face because the maid had been stationed there in deference to the ladies. *Sir Peregrine must revere propriety as much as Mother does.*

When their host arrived, Edwina rushed forward to meet him, while her daughter hung back. Victoria had formed a picture of what a man called Peregrine would look like, but all her preconceived notions now shattered into a thousand shards. His presence was compelling; the back of her neck began to prickle. The man was dark, his build powerful, his face strong, and his manner hinted of dominance.

*He's at least thirty. He makes Edmund seem like a boy.*

"Lady Edwina, I am delighted to make your acquaintance." He took her hand. The quick bow of his head, though polite, was not obsequious.

"Sir Peregrine, this is my son, Reverend Edmund Carswell."

"I'm pleased you could come, Reverend."

"And my daughter, the Honorable Victoria Carswell."

Victoria cringed. Her mother had no right to be addressed as *Lady Edwina*, nor claim her daughter to be *Honorable*. Nonetheless, since it added to her consequence, she did so without a blush.

"Mistress Carswell, I welcome you to Bodiam."

Victoria did not offer her hand. With downcast eyes, she sketched a ghost of a curtsy.

"I named my daughter after a royal princess, never dreaming that one day Victoria would become our beloved queen."

"Sherry or port, Lady Edwina?"

"Good heavens, neither. Carswell ladies do not drink wine, but I have no objection to you gentlemen indulging."

Their host poured two glasses of port from a decanter on the sideboard and handed one to Edmund. He raised his own glass and said politely, "To the ladies."

Victoria stood quietly with clasped hands and downcast eyes, while Edwina proceeded to monopolize the conversation. "I see we are your sole guests tonight, Sir Peregrine. It is wise to be selective. Moral rectitude and respectability are desirable qualities not shared by

everyone, I fear. You may be assured that I have taught
my children the virtues of decency and decorum."

"It is clear you extol convention," he said smoothly.

Edwina took it as a compliment.

*He is mocking her!* Every instinct told her that Sir Peregrine was the dark figure she had glimpsed atop the
high tower. Though Victoria longed to give him a set-
down, she remained passive with downcast eyes. She
was secure in the knowledge that the plain girl in the
prim dress, with her hair in a severe bun, bore no resemblance to the naked nymph in the River Rother.

When they sat down to dinner, their host gallantly
held Edwina's chair and Victoria was glad that he apparently found her invisible. She hid her amusement
when she tasted the soup and found it was liberally
laced with cream and sherry.

"May I inquire what you do for pleasure, Reverend?"

"Tory's passion is history and mine is painting, Sir."

Edwina almost choked on her soup. She pressed her
lips together and reprimanded, "*Passion* is an unsuit-
able word in mixed company, Edmund, and I prefer
you call your sister Victoria. Life is not for pleasure; it is
for duty and obedience."

*You do not believe that, do you, Tory? Meekness does not sit
well with you. I warrant that Tory and passion go hand in
hand. When I first walked into the room, I thought there had
been a mistake. I was convinced you were not the same female
I followed to the priory.* Peregrine smiled. *Your disguise is
clever, quite cunning enough to deceive the venerable Edwina,
and artful enough to give you a false sense of security.*

"I have always discouraged my son from painting,"
Edwina confided. "People with artistic natures are in-
variably unstable. Fortunately, Edmund shows no apti-
tude."

Victoria's dark lashes flew up. "His paintings of Bodiam Castle are magnificent!" An awkward silence descended and she quickly lowered her lashes.

As the soup plates were removed and the game course placed before his guests, Peregrine sat bemused behind his mask of indifference. *Her eyes are the color of pale violets in the snow. All shades of purple denote passion. I know your secrets, Tory!* "If you love history, Bodiam must fascinate you. I invite you to come one day and explore the castle."

"Thank you," Victoria murmured. *He's using Bodiam as bait. He's fully aware how tempting it is. He wants me to return for a tour so he can control me, but I prefer to see it now!*

Tory ate most of her food, then placed her linen napkin on the table. "Please excuse me." She moved her chair back and arose.

Peregrine stood politely and signaled the maid. The uniformed woman curtsied to Victoria and led her from the room. The host resumed his seat and after a moment spoke to Edwina in a confidential manner. "I am most impressed with your daughter, madam. She has a modest, self-effacing demeanor that appeals."

Edwina simpered with pride. "Victoria is a most biddable girl. My insistence upon impeccable behavior has resulted in virtue and chastity, which, though exceedingly rare, are only right and proper in a maiden."

"I would like your permission to pay my addresses to her."

"Sir Peregrine, I would be delighted. You do us great honor."

When Victoria and the maid came to a stone staircase, Tory spoke up firmly. "I prefer to manage on my own, thank you."

"Very good, Miss. I'll just wait here."

Tory ran lightly up the steps, turned, and went down a long passageway that looked neglected. She passed occasional brackets holding rush lights that seemed to illuminate wisps of fog that had crept inside. There were a couple of narrow openings in the stone walls, but the pitch-black rooms beyond held no temptation. Victoria shuddered and then she heard music. Drawn by the sounds of instruments and laughter, she found herself walking along what could only be described as a minstrels' gallery.

She looked down in amazement at a group of people who had obviously gathered for a party. "It's a fancy-dress ball!" The men wore powdered wigs, satin breeches, and brilliantly hued brocaded vests and coats. It was the women, however, who drew Victoria's eye. Their wigs were adorned with jeweled ostrich feathers; their gowns were not only beautiful but also extremely risqué, designed to deliberately display the women's upthrust breasts.

Tory was shocked, yet for one moment she pictured herself in such a glorious gown. The scene below was exactly as it would have been a century ago in Georgian times. As she watched, she realized their behavior was beyond vulgar as they openly flirted and touched each other in inappropriate places.

Her shock slowly turned to anger. "That brute Fuller is throwing a party. His dinner invitation to the Reverend's family is a clever subterfuge to cover up the licentious goings-on at Bodiam. I warrant he cannot wait to be rid of us!"

Her anger made her feel dizzy and she put a hand to her head to steady herself. Victoria turned away from the revelers below and went back the way she had come. She became slightly disoriented and it was a few minutes before she found herself in the familiar passageway that had led her to this part of the castle. Finally, with thudding heart, she located the stone staircase and descended the steps. The maid awaited her as she had promised, and the pair returned to the dining room.

Sir Peregrine and Edmund rose to their feet until she was seated, and Victoria saw they had awaited her return before dessert was served. "I'm so sorry," she murmured.

"Not at all," their host said smoothly.

The dessert was trifle, Victoria's favorite. Perversely, she didn't want any. Without raising her lashes, she spoke to her mother. "I'm afraid I have a dreadful headache." It wasn't a total lie; she did feel strangely light-headed.

Edwina pursed her lips. "Manners, Victoria, manners!"

*Manners? Swine have none!*

"If Mistress Carswell has a headache, I insist you take her home immediately. I hope we can have dinner again soon."

*There, you swine! I knew you'd find a way to be rid of us.* Though she had invented the headache so she could leave, she laid the blame squarely at his door.

As Sir Peregrine accompanied them through the neglected Great Hall to the front entrance, he gave his polite attention to Edwina's incessant stream of words. Victoria took the opportunity to study the dark male who towered beside them. She saw that he had a birthmark that slanted down his cheek from ear to chin. He had tried to cover it by growing fashionable sideburn whiskers, but all they did was emphasize his dangerous, rakish look.

Sir Peregrine took Edwina's cloak from the servant and helped her into it. He did not extend the same courtesy to Victoria. A shiver ran down her back when she thought of his hands touching her. She did not know if she felt relief or disappointment.

On the short carriage ride home, Victoria apologized for leaving the room during dinner, but the outrage she expected from her mother did not come.

"Your absence gave Sir Peregrine and I the opportunity to speak freely and come to an understanding," Edwina declared.

"About me?" Tory asked in shocked disbelief.

"We'll speak of it in the morning, when your headache is gone."

Her mother bade her good night and went upstairs, but Victoria waited for Edmund to come from the stable. With a finger to her lips, she beckoned her brother into the parlor.

"When I left the table, what exactly did Mother and Fuller say about me?"

"Our host told Mother he was most impressed with you, and that your modest, self-effacing demeanor appealed to him."

"I did play the part rather well. What did Mother say?"

"She said you were a biddable girl, then told him your virtue and chastity were only right and proper in a maiden."

Tory covered her mouth so her laughter wouldn't bubble out.

"Sir Peregrine asked if he could pay his addresses to you."

Her laughter turned to dismay. "Damnation, I played my part *too* well!"

"Mother said she would be delighted and honored."

"Hell and Furies! I should never have left the room to go exploring. Still, if I hadn't, I'd never have known the dissolute devil was throwing a party in another part of the castle. The guests wore Georgian costumes and the atmosphere was *bawdy.*"

Her brother looked at her oddly. "Are you sure?"

"I'm not daft, Edmund. I know what I saw. Why do you think he got rid of us so quickly?"

"We left because of your headache."

"I don't have a headache!"

"Good night, Tory." Female logic was too much for him.

It took a long time for Tory to fall asleep. Sir Peregrine Palmer Fuller was not the nonentity she had expected. On the contrary, the man was extremely compelling. She was highly offended that he wished to forge an association with her as a stratagem to acquire respectability in the eyes of the people of Hawkhurst. Before she met him, she assumed he desired the social connection to distance himself from Mad Jack's reputation, but now she knew it was to cover his own dissolute activities.

*I shall decline every invitation!*

As she drifted to the edge of sleep, she fancied herself in an elegant ballroom wearing a gown with scandalous *décolletage.* She flirted outrageously from behind her fan as she decided which of a dozen escorts to favor with a dance. She raised her lashes and looked full into the eyes of a dark man, with a powerful build and a strong face, whose manner had more than a hint of dominance.

# CHAPTER 2

"A note has been delivered from Sir Peregrine Fuller addressed to the Honorable Victoria Carswell. If it is an invitation to view Bodiam in daylight, as I expect, Edmund may chaperone you." Edwina handed her daughter the letter with every intention of reading it once the seal was broken.

"If it is an invitation to Bodiam, I shall decline it." Tory was in the library, where she was allowed to spend an hour each afternoon. She set her book down and opened the letter.

"You selfish girl! You will do no such discourteous thing. This is the first gentleman of means who has shown any interest in you. Spinsters and beggars cannot be choosers and you could soon be both if we do not find you a suitable match." Edwina plucked the invitation from Tory's fingers and read it. "For the benefit of your family, you will accept with grace and gratitude."

"Yes, Mama," Victoria acquiesced quietly.

"What are you reading?"

"It's a history of Sussex."

Edwina swooped upon the book and confiscated it.

As she scanned the pages, she gasped with horror. "It is a book about smugglers and criminal activities. Surely you didn't find this book on the shelves of your father's library?"

"Yes, it's one of Father's history books. Smuggling was rampant along the Sussex coast in the last century."

"'Tis no fit subject for a lady!" Edwina threw it on the fire. "Do something productive. . . . Reply to Sir Peregrine's invitation."

The moment her mother closed the library door, Tory snatched up the poker and, with her heart in her mouth, prodded the book from the flames onto the tiled hearth. She stomped out the smoldering edges and cleaned up the bits of charred paper with pan and brush.

*This book is precious. A century ago, the people here in Hawkhurst were up to their necks in smuggling. When the export of wool was illegal, Sussex men secretly shipped wool to Calais. After that they smuggled in brandy from France, tea from India, and silks from China. How romantic and exciting it must have been to go on a smuggling run!*

Tory hid the book behind a religious treatise on the top shelf and sighed with resignation as her eye fell on the invitation. She sat down at the desk, took a sheet of parchment, and dipped the pen in the inkwell. Mutiny stirred in her soul. Though she longed to explore Bodiam Castle, she was determined to discourage Fuller from seeking an alliance with her. She threw down the pen.

*I shall answer Sir Peregrine in person. That way I can visit Bodiam, refuse his invitation, and squelch, once and for all, any pretended interest the conniving swine has in me.*

Victoria folded the invitation and slipped it into her silk bag. She put on her cloak, firmly tied the black ribbons of her bonnet beneath her chin, and slipped out the priory's back door. As she walked along a footpath that led to the castle, Tory took delight in the profusion of Canterbury bells, larkspur, and wild roses that bloomed in the hedgerows. As she crossed the narrow bridge and looked down into the moat, the white, purple, and pink shades of the water lilies filled her with joy.

When she pulled on a ship's bell beside the portcullis, a servant appeared and raised the gate. He looked at her askance, so she said blithely, "I'm here at Sir Peregrine's invitation."

Tory followed the man to the Great Hall; he took her cloak and bonnet and asked her to wait. The minute she was alone she walked the perimeter of the chamber, taking in every dank detail. It had a sadly neglected air; its high windows were dirty and broken, with some even boarded up. It lacked furnishings of any sort and its gaping, empty fireplaces were blackened with soot. The wooden dais had splintered boards. Decay from disuse was apparent everywhere.

"Mistress Carswell, what a delightful surprise."

Tory whirled about at the sound of the deep, masculine voice.

He waved his hand. "Bodiam is in deplorable condition, I'm afraid. All needs to be repaired and refurbished."

"That will take a deal of tender loving care, not to mention a fortune, Sir Peregrine."

His dark eyes lit with amusement. "Fortunately, I have both."

"You also have—"

He held up his hand. "Please allow me to show you more hospitality than Bodiam's Great Hall affords. I have only refurbished a couple of small chambers. Let us repair to my sitting room." He led the way and Victoria followed to a small chamber adjacent to the dining room they had used two days ago. Its stone walls were hung with tapestries, the flagstones were covered by a deep-piled carpet, and comfortable brocaded chairs and settees were arranged in front of a small stone fireplace.

"You were saying?" he prompted.

Tory lifted her chin. "You also have bald-faced effrontery."

His dark eyes glittered. "I warrant you are about to explain."

"The only possible reason you can have for inviting my family to dinner and wishing to pay your addresses to me is to lend yourself a veneer of respectability. You believe an alliance with the straitlaced daughter of the Right Reverend Thomas Carswell will provide a smoke screen for your profligate pleasures." She paused for dramatic effect, then delivered the coup de grâce. "Sorry to disappoint you, Sir Peregrine, but I am neither prim nor proper!"

His mouth curved. "In that case, have some sherry."

"I'll have port," she said defiantly.

He poured two glasses and handed her one. "Do sit and tell me what profligate activities you have discovered."

Tory took a chair and, to give her the courage she would need, took a large gulp of port. A red rose bloomed in her breast and she liked the warm feeling the wine produced.

"Dinner with the Carswells the other night was a ruse. You couldn't wait to be rid of us so you could join the bawdy guests you'd invited to your masquerade ball. When I excused myself, I went exploring and discovered the dissolute gathering."

His dark eyebrows drew together for a moment and then he grabbed her hand. "Show me," he ordered.

She clutched her wine with one hand and pulled her other one from his. "You don't believe I discovered your secret party. Follow me, I'll soon show you."

Tory ascended the staircase with Fuller towering at her side. She turned and went down the long passageway. In the dim light of day it looked even more neglected. At first Tory couldn't find the place she sought, but by retracing her steps and turning in a different direction, they came upon the minstrels' gallery.

"The party was down there. I saw them clearly from here."

He seemed intrigued. "You actually *saw* them? I've heard music, but I've never seen anyone."

"Of course I *saw* them! Surely you're not trying to fob them off as ghosts?" she scoffed. She looked down at the empty chamber below and was amazed at how different it now seemed. The deserted room looked dingy and dilapidated. Without the glittering guests and the light of myriad candles the chamber appeared desolate.

"Can you describe the guests' costumes?"

"I most certainly can. They wore Georgian dress. The men were in powdered wigs and satin knee breeches. The ladies, and I use the term lightly, wore exquisite jewels and their gowns exposed their . . . charms . . . in an explicit and provocative way. Their behavior was beyond risqué, it was downright bawdy."

"Fascinating!"

Tory stared at him for a moment and then her innate honesty came to the fore. "I admit I found it most fascinating." She drained her wineglass. "I also admit I would have preferred the masquerade ball to the staid dinner invitation."

"That doesn't surprise me in the least, coming from a young woman who disguises herself as a water sprite."

Tory's mouth fell open. "How did you know it was me?"

"The first time I saw you, I followed you to the priory."

"Why?"

"I was completely enchanted."

"How many times have you watched me?"

"Half a dozen." He smiled into her eyes. "My enchantment shoots large holes in your theory that I am interested in an alliance because of your respectability. I quite agree that there is nothing prim and proper about you, Tory Carswell."

"Then why are you interested in me?"

"You are beautiful, audacious, uninhibited, and unawakened as yet; therein lies your fatal attraction."

"Well, I'll be damned!"

His mouth curved. "Not for swimming naked, you won't."

Her eyes sparkled. "Mother wouldn't agree."

"There is something infinitely familiar about you, Victoria, as if we have met before—perhaps in another time, another place."

"And perhaps you have inherited Mad Jack's eccentricity!"

"Touché!" He threw back his head and laughed. "I think we would deal well together. We have a mutual love of history, we share a fascination for Bodiam Castle, and we are not above thumbing our noses at society. Will you allow me to court you?"

"Court me with a view to marriage?"

"Of course."

"Marriage that endows me with all your worldly goods?"

He smiled knowingly. "You covet Bodiam."

She smiled back. "I do indeed, especially when you dangle it before me as bait."

He reached out and gently brushed her cheek with his fingertips. "Then your answer is yes?"

Tory shivered at his touch. She felt breathless and filled with excitement. *He thinks me audacious!* She swayed toward him, then caught herself before they could indulge in anything as daring and impulsive as a kiss. "I will give you my answer after I have fully explored the castle."

His arm swept out in a magnanimous gesture. "Be my guest."

Victoria couldn't believe her good fortune. It seemed the attractive devil who owned Bodiam was half in love with her because he'd watched her from one of his castle's high towers, cavorting naked in the River Rother.

Her blood sang with anticipation as she walked through the ancient chambers, exploring every nook, arch, and cranny, every artifact left behind by previous generations, no matter its sorry condition. She sensed intangible remnants left floating in the very air like dust motes. She spun around, dancing a solitary waltz, and let her head fall back as she gazed up at the vaulted ceiling. "I *love* this castle!"

Tory was eager to explore Bodiam's towers. The castle had a round tower at each of its four corners and square ones midway between. She was traversing a long passageway that led to a round tower, when suddenly she heard a faint noise of padding feet behind her. She turned, fully expecting to see a dog. Her eyes widened in shocked disbelief. "It's a leopard!"

She started to run, her heart pounding with fear. She glanced back, hoping she had been mistaken, but she was gripped with terror when she saw the large spotted cat was now chasing her. She reached the end of the passageway and in desperation began to climb the spiral staircase of the round tower. She could hear the animal gaining on her and ran faster and faster. Her silk bag slipped from her fingers as she frantically hoisted up her skirts so she would not trip. Her breath was exhausted and she had a painful stitch in her side when she saw a door up ahead. Hope plummeted as she realized she had reached the tower's summit. "Please let it be unlocked!" she beseeched heaven.

Tory lifted the latch and pushed hard. The heavy oak door swung open. She stumbled through it, slammed it shut, and leaned back against it, weak with relief and gasping for breath.

"Who the devil are *you* and what the hellfire are you doing here?" a deep masculine voice demanded.

Victoria found herself in a luxuriously appointed chamber at the top of the round tower. "Peregrine, is that you?" she asked breathlessly. "There's a *leopard* outside this door!"

He advanced toward her. "The leopard lives here. It's your identity that is in question."

Tory stared at the man who looked like Sir Peregrine and yet he was somehow different. *Perhaps it's his brother.* "You are wearing a wig," she blurted.

His hand swept off the powdered wig and negligently tossed it onto a gilt chair. His own black hair fell to his shoulders. "And you are wearing the ugliest garment I've ever seen."

Tory looked down at her gray cambric dress with its leg-of-mutton sleeves and was highly offended.

"You are extremely rude!"

"Rude, crude, and tattooed," he affirmed. "What is your name?"

She lifted her chin. "I am Victoria Carswell."

*"Carswell?"* He spat the name as if it were an abomination. "If you're Thomas Carswell's offspring, you're here to spy on me."

"My father, the Right Reverend Thomas Carswell, is deceased."

"Reverend? You must think me simple in the head! He's the bloody customs officer who just gibbeted George Chapman on the village green."

*Oh heavens, the man is mad . . . it must run in the family.* Tory backed away from him. *They keep him locked up here in the tower.*

He picked up a sword and took a threatening step toward her. "D'you know the fate of a spy is imprisonment, or worse, wench?"

"Please . . . I was merely exploring the castle. . . . I'm not a spy."

He bowed gallantly. "Ah. In that case, feel free to leave."

She moved toward the door and remembered the leopard.

He gave her a wicked grin. "Exactly."

"You cannot keep me here," she gasped.

"I can." He flourished the sword. "You might as well make yourself comfortable." He swept her with a critical glance. "If we are to dwell together, I must rid you of your offensive garb." With a deft flick of his wrist, the slim blade of his sword swished through the air and slashed her dress from neck to hem.

Tory screamed, then stared in dismay as the gray cambric parted to reveal her corset and drawers. "You lecherous swine!"

The wicked grin returned. "Lord Hawkhurst, at your service."

The name was familiar to Victoria from the history books she read. The town of Hawkhurst had been named after the noble lord who had owned Bodiam Castle a century ago. *Could it possibly be? No, I'm just being fanciful!*

"Why d'you wear your hair screwed into a knob?"

Her hand moved to her head. "It's a bun."

"It's bloody ugly." He set aside his sword. "Here, let me help you." He took hold of her leg-of-mutton sleeves and pulled off her dress. Then he took the pins from her hair and it came tumbling down in a silken mass that curled about her shoulders.

Tory flew at him and tried to scratch his insolent face.

He took firm hold of her wrists and appraised her with bold black eyes. "By God, wench, you are quite a showy piece."

"Wench? My name is Victoria—I was named for the queen!"

He let go of her wrists. "The queen's name is Caroline."

"Caroline was King George the Second's wife."

"*Is* King George's wife," he corrected.

"Queen Caroline has been dead for almost a century. This is the year of our lord, eighteen thirty-seven."

"*Seventeen* thirty-seven, you ignorant wench."

*If that is true, I am from a hundred years in your future, and you are from a hundred years in my past.*

"Don't call me *wench*. My name is Victoria."

"A hideous name."

"I quite agree. I much prefer Tory."

"You called me Peregrine when you came in. How did you know? It's a name I detest; I changed it to Falcon years ago."

*Falcon . . . what a lovely, romantic name.* "It quite suits you, Lord Hawkhurst."

Her glance traveled from his frilled lawn shirt to his tight black breeches that did little to hide his masculine bulge. *You are quite convinced you are a Georgian gentleman and you are certainly dressed like a Georgian. I wonder if this is a dream?*

"Now that we have dispensed with the formalities, confess what you're really doing here."

"I've fallen in love with Bodiam Castle. I came to explore."

His bold stare was insolent. "You look quite fetching in those—"

"Drawers."

His stare turned into a wicked leer. "I'm going to enjoy keeping you captive."

*This isn't a dream; it's more like a fantasy. Perhaps I've conjured him from my imagination. Lord Hawkhurst . . . Falcon . . . finds me attractive. He thinks I'm a showy piece and wants to seduce me.* Common sense came to her rescue. *Stop it, Victoria . . . that's just wishful thinking!*

He went to the door, opened it, and called, "Mr. Burke."

Tory, who had fully expected the leopard to rush in, let out a relieved breath. In a few moments a servant, wearing powdered wig and livery, entered the chamber. She saw him eye her drawers.

"I didn't know you had a guest, milord."

"Someone the cat dragged in. By necessity, she'll be staying a while. We'll have dinner up here tonight, Mr. Burke."

Tory seized the opportunity. "Mr. Burke, my name is Victoria Carswell. Lord Hawkhurst thinks he can keep me captive here, but that is impossible. I live at the priory and I must return home. You can see it from the window—I'll show you."

Victoria went to the north window of the tower and looked toward the town of Hawkhurst, but all she could see was forest. Her brows drew together. "I can't see the priory, but you must know it. It's on the edge of town, next to the parish church."

"Let's humor her, Mr. Burke. Come up to the parapet, Tory; you'll have  an unimpeded view for miles." Hawkhurst drew back a curtain, opened a door, and climbed steps that led to the tower roof. Tory and the servant followed him.

She gazed out across the treetops, perplexed that no

roads or buildings of the town were visible, not even the church spire. "Where is Hawkhurst?" she asked.

"The village is over there. You can just make out the Oak and Ivy, half a mile this side of the village."

"The Oak and Ivy Inn? I read about that in my history book." *That's where the smugglers used to meet.* Tory walked to the crenellated wall and gazed out in every direction. "Good heavens, there's a sailing ship moored in the river!"

"It's mine," Hawkhurst said matter-of-factly.

Tory had read about Lord Hawkhurst's ship. It was a two-masted brigantine capable of great speed, and she remembered its name.

*This cannot be happening.* She reached out to the wall to steady herself. She felt the rough stone beneath her fingers and knew it was real. "What is the name of your ship?"

"The *Seacock.*"

Tory's hand went to her head and she felt herself slipping down into oblivion.

# CHAPTER 3

"Where am I?" Tory felt strangely disoriented.

"You're in my bed."

She looked up into the bold black eyes of Falcon Hawk-hurst and remembered everything. *Somehow, I've gone back in time and there's nothing I can do about it.* Tory suddenly laughed. *Perhaps there's nothing I want to do about it!*

"Why are you laughing, wench?"

"Because I'm your captive." *The air is charged with danger and excitement and I've never felt freer in my life!* She reached out and traced her fingertips down his cheek. "You don't have a birthmark."

He took hold of her fingers and removed them from his face. "If you touch me intimately, there will be consequences."

She changed the subject quickly. "Do I smell food?"

"Mr. Burke brought our dinner. I suppose I must feed you."

The tip of her tongue licked her top lip in an unconscious, provocative gesture. "I'm starving," she murmured.

"Shall we dine in bed?"

"Cheeky swine! Do you enjoy deluding yourself?"

"Not as much as you enjoy being a cocktease."

Tory gasped at the shocking word he used. She had never heard it before in her life, but she knew it was wicked, and she knew exactly what it meant.

"Victoria, you are actually blushing. Ladies of my acquaintance never blush." Falcon was intrigued.

"Do you even *know* any ladies?"

His dark eyes searched her face. "I do now, it seems."

She threw back the covers. "Though it's most unladylike to dine in my underlinen, 'tis entirely your fault."

"I don't mind in the least. I find your undergarments quaint."

He led her to a small table, held a gilt chair for her, and then sat down opposite her. He lifted a heavy silver cover, carved the bird, and, without consulting her, piled her plate with food. He poured them wine and started to eat. "Now tell me who you really are and why you are here."

"I really am Victoria Carswell. My father, who was Reverend of the Hawkhurst parish church, died eighteen months ago. Bodiam has been empty for years and has fallen into sad disrepair."

Falcon listened without interrupting, fascinated by her tale.

"A gentleman by the name of Sir Peregrine Palmer Fuller recently inherited the castle and invited me to dinner. He told me his intention was marriage. Because he knows how much I love Bodiam, he gave me permission to explore it. I have a great affinity with this castle and I was thoroughly enjoying myself, sensing the lingering impressions left behind by previous inhabitants. I was walking down a long passageway when I heard something padding behind me. I turned to look and saw a leopard! I was terrified and ran frantically up the spiral tower staircase trying to escape. I opened the door and there you were."

"And here we are." He raised his glass in a mocking salute.

She took a deep breath and plunged in. "I believe the leopard chased me into the past. I ran from Victorian times back into the Georgian era, a distance of a hundred years."

"You speak as if you believe it with a passion."

Tory blushed again. "I feel everything with a passion, though I have learned to mask it."

"Why would you want to mask it?"

"It's not proper for a respectable lady to show emotion. It's not even proper to *have* emotions, especially not passionate ones."

"Passion is the greatest and rarest emotion to experience." His eyes examined her face. "The things I say keep you in a perpetual blush, and I find it intriguing. Perhaps we *are* from two different worlds."

She nodded. "You think me your captive, but I'm not sure I want to escape. My world is rather repressive. Your world is so much more stimulating than mine."

"How is it different?" he asked, bemused.

"My world is morally strict and rigid. Everything enjoyable is considered a sin. My mother is so straitlaced, she worships at the altar of respectability. I am restricted to the point of suffocation." Tory was struck by a sudden thought. "Did you give a party a few days ago, Lord Hawkhurst?"

"I did," he acknowledged.

"I saw it! I watched from the minstrels' gallery! I thought it was a masquerade because everyone was in Georgian dress! Oh, don't you see, that night I came back in time for just a moment. I had a tantalizing taste of the banquet that was to come."

"Your metaphor has me half convinced," he drawled. Falcon made no effort to hide his amusement. "Tell me more."

"I coveted the gorgeous gowns and the ladies' jewels, but I was shocked at their licentious behavior and the bawdy atmosphere."

"I suppose through an innocent's eyes it would seem rather ribald. Since you've come back in time, you might as well experience one of my affairs."

"You think I'm deranged. . . . You're humoring me."

*And enjoying every mad moment.* "Then you must humor me."

"I've nothing to wear to one of your . . . affairs." She felt her cheeks warming. She knew he'd used the word *affair* deliberately.

"That's easily remedied. There's a wardrobe full of feminine attire in the chamber below this one. Belonged to my . . . sister." He substituted the word *sister* for *mistress.* "The baggage prefers London to Sussex and slung her hook. That's a sailors' term."

*I thought it was a pirates' term.*

"That is most generous. May I get something to wear now?"

"Absolutely not. I want you to strut about in your drawers and stays this evening. They fascinate me." *You fascinate me.*

*The bold devil knows I'm at a disadvantage in my underclothes and thinks me easier to control. He still suspects I'm spying on him; therefore there must be something he is trying to conceal.*

They heard the scratching on the door at the same time. "That must be Pandora." He walked to the door to open it.

"Pandora?" she asked warily.

"My leopard. Don't fret, she's gentle as a pussy, so long as I'm here, of course."

Tory ran back to the bed and climbed up on it. With her heart in her mouth, she watched Falcon open the door. In strolled the leopard, carrying something in its mouth.

Falcon scratched the big cat behind her ear and she affectionately rubbed herself against his leg. "What's this?" he asked, taking a small silk bag from the leopard's mouth.

"That's mine," Tory said breathlessly.

"Pandora is perfectly safe." He handed Tory the embroidered bag and held out his hand. "Come down and I'll introduce you."

She clutched her bag with one hand and grasped his with the other. Never taking her eyes from the leopard, she allowed Falcon to help her climb down from the bed. She stood rigid while Pandora first sniffed at her, then licked her hand with a rough tongue. Some of her fear evaporated, but a healthy wariness remained. "How did you come to own a leopard?"

"I was opening crates of tea, a cargo I acquired from an East Indiaman. I lifted the lid of a box, and there she was. She was only a kit at the time, young enough to train. It amused me to teach her to be a *watchcat*. The name Pandora suggested itself."

"Unbelievable," she murmured.

"Rather like your story," he drawled.

Tory watched the leopard stretch its length on the carpet and when it began to purr, her apprehension lessened. She opened the drawstrings of her bag and took out the folded note. "Here is my invitation from Sir Peregrine."

He took the paper and read it. It was dated 17 August 1837. It was addressed to the Honorable Victoria Carswell at the priory, Hawkhurst, Sussex. It extended an invitation for the lady to visit Bodiam and explore the castle in daylight. It was signed *Sir Peregrine Palmer Fuller.*

"It's a rather curious invitation. The day and month are correct, but the year is off by a hundred. There are other similarities—this is Bodiam Castle and my family name is Palmer."

"Your name is Peregrine Palmer? Then obviously you must be Sir Peregrine Palmer Fuller's ancestor!"

"Obviously," he said dryly.

She ignored his mocking tone. "Your resemblance is uncanny. He, too, is darkly handsome, with a strong face, powerful build and a compelling, dominant manner. Though you seem far more cynical."

Her description amused him. "Mea culpa—I am indeed a cynic. Is this Fuller your lover?"

"Absolutely not!" She felt herself blushing. "I told you his intentions were honorable."

"Then we are not alike. We're different as chalk from cheese."

Her blush deepened. "Yes, you are far coarser!"

"Flattery, begod!"

"You are a devil!"

Hawkhurst grinned knowingly. "And that excites you, Mistress Prim and Proper."

Her chin went up in defiance. "I'm not so prim and proper. All summer I've swum naked at dawn in the River Rother."

His glittering eyes narrowed. "Females don't swim."

"Perhaps they didn't a hundred years ago. That was long before the Prince Regent popularized Brighton and bathing machines—things you wouldn't know about," she taunted.

"If that thing you were wearing when you arrived is an example of how fashions have advanced, I'm thankful I'm a Georgian."

"You can mock all you want, Lord Bloody Hawkhurst, but the fact remains that I have come back in time one hundred years."

"If that is the game you wish to play, I will partner you."

She ignored his innuendo, then her eyes widened. "Oh, I just remembered. I think I have some coins in my bag."

"I'm quite a connoisseur of coins," he drawled.

Tory pulled out three pennies and inspected them. Two were William IV coins, but the third was new, minted for Victoria's coronation. It bore the queen's head and it was dated 1837. "There you are . . . proof positive!"

Falcon took the coin she thrust at him and looked at it with amused skepticism. "It's copper. Pennies are made of silver."

"Not in my day and age. Look at the date."

He read the date and gave her a quizzical glance. Then he tossed the coin into the air, caught it on the back of his hand, and covered it with his fingers. "Call it. Heads, you can have your way and I'll believe everything you say." He winked. "Tails, I'll have my way."

"Georgians were—are obsessed with gambling."

"Among other things," he said with a leer. "Call it."

"Heads," she said decisively.

"Heads it is," he said ruefully, "and here's me longing for tail." When she neither laughed nor blushed, he realized the coarse jest was lost on her.

"Speaking of swimming, Pandora likes to cool herself in the moat at dusk on these warm summer nights."

The large feline stretched and got to her feet.

"She knows it's that time. Would you like to come?"

"She's very beautiful. . . . I'd like to watch her." Tory looked down at her underclothes and hesitated. Then the corners of her mouth lifted. "Since this is a lewd and licentious age, why should I let my dishabille stop me from enjoying myself?"

His brow arched. "Is it exciting for a repressed female to step back in time to an age that is lewd and licentious?"

She gave him a saucy glance. "Not quite as exciting as it must be for a lewd and licentious male to encounter a chaste female."

"That would be a novelty," he drawled. Then he gave

her an admiring glance. "Your rejoinders are clever. They show wit."

She felt inordinately pleased at the compliment. "I've never been allowed to say them out loud before."

"Feel free to indulge in whatever gives you pleasure—no matter how outrageous." He grinned wickedly and took her hand. "Come."

When he opened the tower chamber door, the sleek feline silently slipped through and they followed her down the spiral stairs. Now that Tory was no longer blinded by fear, she saw through an open door that there was an elegant chamber below his, furnished for a lady, and she saw another room below that before they reached the ground floor.

They went outside and walked along a stone balcony. Pandora's leap was a graceful arc of supple sinew. The moment she plunged into the water, some waterfowl rose in alarm, flew toward the river, and were swallowed by the shadows of twilight. As Victoria watched the magnificent creature glide through the water, stained by the last glimmer of a wine sunset, the exquisite beauty of the scene touched her soul. *I'll remember this forever.*

Falcon covered her hand where it rested on the balustrade. "Will you let me see you swim sometime?"

Victoria drew in a swift breath and looked up into his black eyes. The amusement was gone, replaced by a haunting intensity. "Yes, if it will give you pleasure, my lord."

"To be enjoyed to the full, pleasure must be shared."

She gazed up at him and realized the truth of his words. She felt the warmth of his powerful fingers seep into her hand and surge up her arm; she felt her pulse-beat merge with his. *Perhaps that's why I came here, so we could share pleasure.* For the first time in her life, Tory felt the exquisite stirring of desire.

Pandora emerged from the moat unnoticed until a

shower of water droplets cascaded over them as the leopard shook herself. Their laughter broke the spell of the intimate moment they shared, and Falcon led the way back up to the chamber atop the round tower.

He lit the candles in the wall brackets, bathing the room in a warm glow. "Alas, my time is promised elsewhere tonight. You may take my bed until a chamber can be plenished for you tomorrow. That is, of course, if you decide to stay."

She searched his face. "I thought I was your captive."

"It would be difficult to keep a captive who wished to return to her own time." He took an iron key from the drawer of a bedside table and offered it to her. "If you choose to stay, lock the door when I leave for your own protection."

Tory stared at the key on his open palm, then raised her eyes to his, trying to discern his thoughts. In the fathomless depths she saw secrets, never to be told, but she also saw desire. She reached out and took the key.

Once she was alone, Tory explored the chamber. She sniffed the glass decanters on a side table. Two held wine, but the third she suspected was forbidden French brandy. In the bedside table she discovered aromatic tobacco, a pipe, and flints. She connected the smell with the memory of her father, yet she had never seen him smoke. Hidden knowledge floating from the past made her smile. *Mother forbade the pleasure, so he indulged in secret.*

She looked at the items on his desk. It held sheets of paper, a silver inkwell, several feather quills, red wax, and a gold seal ring carved to stamp the imprint of a peregrine falcon. Tory was almost sure she had seen it on Falcon's little finger earlier. She tried on the ring, traced the raptor's outline with her fingertip, and felt a frisson of yearning for she knew not what.

She opened the desk drawer and saw a long leather box. She lifted the lid and saw that it was a case designed to hold a pair of pistols. She touched the velvet indentations and realized Falcon must have the pistols with him. The other item in the desk was a book. Tory sat down, opened it, and turned the pages. It was a ledger with a list of names that were common in Sussex. The symbols and numbers after each name were a cipher of some sort that she didn't understand. There was a section at the back of the ledger that listed more noble-sounding names along with their titles.

Victoria put the book back and yawned. She longed to explore the chamber beneath this one, but the thought of a prowling Pandora stopped her. The wide bed beckoned, so she snuffed all the candles save one, removed her shoes and stockings, loosened the strings of her corset, and slipped between the sheets.

Though she lay still, her mind began to race. She relived everything that had happened to her in this incredible day. Thoughts and emotions she had never before experienced chased each other in ever-widening circles, producing a myriad of questions that could only be answered by drawing one conclusion: *She had traveled back in time one hundred years.*

Tory finally realized she was far too restless to sleep. She threw aside the covers and climbed from the bed. She was filled with a compelling urge to go outside in the cool night air, and felt an irresistible force drawing her up on the roof.

There was no moon tonight and the sky was like black velvet. She walked slowly around the crenellated wall, breathing deeply. She could smell the sea, but could see nothing in the vast blackness. Suddenly, she saw a light through the trees. It was gone in an instant, like a lamp being shuttered. She listened intently, but all she heard was the faint hoot of an owl.

When another owl answered, the hairs on the nape of her neck stood up and she shivered with excitement.

She had read about it in the history book about Sussex only this morning. "*Owling* is the signal device used by smugglers!"

Victoria stood still as a statue, watching for the least glimmer of another light, listening for any noise that disturbed the still night air. The hoots of the owls gradually became fainter, then stopped altogether. After an hour she became aware of the cold stone beneath her bare feet and, chilled, she sought the warmth of the bed below.

Soon, she drifted into a dream. She felt powerful arms slide around her and was drawn to a man's chest, hard with muscle. She stiffened instinctively and whispered, "No!"

She felt his arms tighten, felt his lips brush her ear.

"You decided to stay."

"Yes."

"You left the door unlocked."

"Falcon." She sighed with pleasure and clung to the dream.

When morning light filtered into the chamber, Victoria stirred in the lovely warm cocoon. She did not need to open her eyes to know where she was. She was filled with a delicious, languorous feeling from her toes to her fingertips. Her mouth curved into a smile and with a slight sense of reluctance she lifted her lashes.

Her eyes widened in shock. Her back was cushioned against a hard male body. Her full ripe breast, freed from the confines of her corset, rested in a man's cupped hand. He was wearing a gold seal ring on his finger. His forearm bore the tattoo of a raptor in flight.

"Lord Hawkhurst!"

Victoria felt the male body stir.

"That would be me."

# CHAPTER 4

Tory removed his hand from her breast and turned to confront him.

He gathered her close and held her fast to prevent her escaping from the bed. "I like it better when you call me Falcon."

"Raptor!"

"Never! Well, hardly ever," he amended. "I'd much rather woo you to a giving mood." His glance surveyed her breasts with appreciation, then he slowly raised his eyes to her mouth. "How can I resist your deliberate temptation?"

"Deliberate?" Her breasts rose and fell with her indignation.

"Did I not give you the key?"

Tory could not deny it.

"Do you recall my warning?"

She remembered his words exactly. *If you choose to stay, lock the door when I leave for your own protection.*

"Exactly," he said softly. "You have a sweetness about you that I've never encountered before." His eyes caressed her face. "I hazard a guess that it is a result of chaste innocence."

"All unwed females are chaste," she protested.

"Perhaps in your time, Victoria; certainly not in mine. I thirst to taste your sweetness; hunger to awaken you." He brushed a dark tendril from her temple and it curled about his fingers.

*His touch is gentle and . . . seductive.* She realized he was no longer holding her captive, yet she made no move to escape. She had the same thought she'd had last night when he touched her. *Perhaps that's why I came here—*

He finished the thought for her. "So we could share pleasure."

"Falcon." She knew he would kiss her and she lifted her mouth and opened her lips in breathless anticipation. When his mouth touched hers, she wanted the contact to last forever. The first slow, melting kiss led to another and then to a dozen; all were achingly perfect. When his lips touched the corners of her mouth and moved down against her throat, whispering seductive words against her skin, desire lit a forbidden fire in her blood.

He withdrew his hungry mouth so he could look at her and savor her first arousal. When she became aware that he was naked, he sensed her yearning. Slowly, he pulled the laces from her corset and removed it, and then he undid her drawers and slid them off. He dipped his head to her breast and felt the delicious thrust of her nipple against his tongue.

Tory entwined her arms about his neck and arched her breast into his teasing mouth, loving the sensations he aroused in her body. When his tongue feathered over her skin, kissing the soft, satiny flesh beneath her breasts, she cried out with pleasure.

He moved over her, captured her naked thighs between his knees, and gazed down at her with eyes that were black with passion. He dipped his head and the tip of his tongue circled her navel, then he went lower, pursed his lips, and blew on the dark tendrils that covered her mons. The vibrations were so titillating, Tory wanted to scream. When he thrust his tongue into her honeyed sheath, she did scream. She threaded her fingers into his long black hair, holding him captive while he devoured her. She thrashed her head from side to side on the feather pillow. "Falcon! Falcon!" Gauging her climax exactly, he thrust deep and she dissolved in liquid tremors.

He stretched himself beside her, gazing at her intently, watching her eyes turn dreamy, her body become languid and soft with surfeit. Initiating her in the first delicate mysteries of her own sexuality gave him infinite pleasure. Falcon smiled. He knew there was more to come. So much more.

Tory floated back to awareness and lifted her lashes. She had suddenly developed a curiosity about the body of the male who shared her bed. She drew the sheet down and gazed at his nakedness. Her cheeks blushed pink at her own boldness. She reached out her hand and traced the muscles of his wide shoulders and broad chest. She felt the crisp black hairs that covered his upper torso and marveled at his sun-bronzed skin. Her eyes moved lower and she watched avidly as his shaft lengthened and hardened and stood out rigidly from his body. With great daring she reached out with tentative fingers.

"Don't touch my cock!" He tried to smile to soften his words, but his face was hard with need. "If you touched me now, I would ravish you and you would hate me." He drew in a deep breath to gain control. "For a little while, I want to keep you the way you are, virgin, innocent, only half awakened, and yearning for fulfillment. Victoria, you are every man's dream."

· * * *

*This chamber is every woman's dream.* Victoria, sitting in a slipper bath decorated with hand-painted roses, glanced around the room. Its walls were hung with tapestries depicting medieval ladies and mythical beasts in wooded settings. There was a wide, velvet-curtained bed, a deep-piled carpet, an elaborate dressing table, and, best of all, a huge mirrored wardrobe, filled with feminine garments.

An hour before, Falcon had carried her to the chamber below his, where breakfast and a bath awaited, and left her with the words, *I'll be gone for a couple of days on business. If there's anything you need, Mr. Burke will be happy to oblige.*

*He didn't need to ask if I'd be here when he got back—the cocksure devil knows I want to stay.* Tory laughed with delight. *I never would have dared think such a word before I met Falcon. He has freed me from all my constraints.* She thought of her corset and wiped away a tear of mirth.

Victoria climbed from the bath, wrapped herself in a thirsty towel, and opened the wardrobe. The colors and textures were a feast for the eyes and she couldn't resist touching the infinite variety of fabrics. She selected a pair of pink stays and was amazed to see that they lifted her breasts, but were not designed to cover them. Though she searched, there were no drawers to be found. *Is it possible that Georgian ladies wore nothing beneath their skirts? How frightful.* The corners of her mouth lifted. *How delightful!* She pulled on a pair of flesh-pink stockings and fastened them with ribbon garters adorned with rosebuds. Tory surveyed her reflection in the mirror. She knew the undergarment that left her breasts and bum bare was purposely designed to titillate the male of the species, and she also knew she had never looked nor felt more alluring in her life.

She took quite a while to pick a dress because they

were all impractical. The frivolous concoctions were
more suited to evening than daytime, but finally she
chose a pink and green striped taffeta with ruffled
sleeves tied with ribbons. Its full skirt, nipped waist, and
low-cut neckline made her feel deliciously feminine.
She sat down at the dressing table and examined the
array of face creams, rouge, and maquillage. She put on
pink lip-rouge, darkened her brows, and could not resist a black silk beauty spot in the shape of a half-moon
that she placed at the tip of her right cheekbone. Then
she picked up a dainty fan and posed like a practiced
coquette, trained in the use of artifice.

"Why on earth did women allow respectability to become the mode? It took all the fun out of our lives!"

Tory looked from the window and saw that Lord
Hawkhurst's ship was gone. She wished with all her
heart that she was sailing with him and vowed that the
next time he boarded the *Seacock,* she would join him.
She heard a knock and opened the door to find a pair
of young male servants in livery who had come to
empty and clean her bath. She surmised that Pandora
was not roaming about loose and decided this was a
good time to explore. *This is my golden opportunity to see
Bodiam Castle as it was a hundred years back in time.*

As she walked the passages and wandered through the
high-vaulted chambers, her admiration for Hawkhurst
grew by leaps and bounds. He had lavished love and de-
votion on Bodiam by restoring and maintaining the medieval castle as it was originally designed. Though the
furniture in the rooms of his own tower was Georgian,
the rest of the castle furnishings and fixtures were from
the 14th century to match the architecture.

Tory walked into the vast kitchen, where heat radi-
ated from its enormous fireplaces. The flagstone floors
and long wooden worktables were scrubbed spotless,
and scores of cooking utensils hung from iron racks.

The air was redolent with roasting meat and piquant, exotic spices. She spotted Mr. Burke, who was addressing the kitchen staff. "I've been exploring the castle. It's the most fascinating place I've ever seen."

Burke introduced her to the cooks, scullery maids, and kitchen boys. The females bobbed her curtsies and called her "milady." The young males simply stared.

"Come, I'll show you the rest of it," Burke offered. "I was just giving them the menu for Thursday's entertainment."

Excitement and anticipation bubbled up inside her. "Does Lord Hawkhurst entertain every Thursday?"

"Nay, only as the mood takes him. He's not a man of rigid habits—more influenced by the moon and the tides than the calendar, milady."

Victoria sighed, knowing the romanticism only added to her infatuation. They entered a large chamber with a polished stone floor and dozens of elaborate brackets holding scores of unlit candles. There was a dais at one end and gaming tables at the other. She knew she'd seen this room before and glanced up at the minstrels' gallery. "This is where he entertains."

Burke nodded and led her through an archway and down a narrow stone passage. "This leads to the oldest section of the castle. It originally housed soldiers garrisoned at Bodiam to defend the coast from French attack. Now it houses the crew of the *Seacock*."

She sighed inwardly. *They're all off on an adventure.*

There was a round tower at the next corner, but its heavy oaken door was padlocked. A few yards farther along, however, were open steps that led down. "Does Bodiam have dungeons?" Tory asked.

"Nay, those are water stairs. In times past, boats from the Rother were rowed right under the castle."

"Oh, just like the Tower of London. Prisoners were

taken through the Traitors' Gate that way." She shuddered, imagining haunted spirits from a lot further back than a mere hundred years.

A half hour later, as they entered one of the square towers, Victoria gasped with delight as she found herself surrounded by books. "Falcon has a library! You may leave me here Mr. Burke, these books will keep me amused for a month or more."

"Very good, milady, though I'm amazed you can read."

It was brought home to her how blessed she was to have had a modern education. She found a book about Sir Francis Drake. *A seaman like Hawkhurst would be drawn to Drake, but I love the parts about Queen Elizabeth.* She found a few volumes of Shakespeare and chose *Othello;* her father had a copy of *Macbeth* that she'd read in secret. Tory picked out a book that chronicled diary excerpts by Samuel Pepys, written in the time of Charles II. It described the plague and the Great Fire of London in vivid detail. She gathered up the books and took them to her chamber. Reading would make the evenings go faster while Falcon was away.

Something awoke Victoria from a dream. Her chamber was shrouded in darkness and she could see nothing, but her ears were alert for sounds. *There it is again—I didn't imagine it.* The heavy thudding came from a distant part of the castle. She sat up in bed and when she swung her feet to the floor it almost felt like she could feel vibrations. She doubted that the thick stone walls of a castle could tremble and realized it was an echo that reverberated on the still night air. She went to the north window and looked out into the darkness. There was no moon and she sensed that it was long past midnight.

She crossed to the south window and drew in a swift breath. *There's a light in the tower! That's the one I passed yesterday that had a padlock on the door.*

She stood at the window for the better part of an hour hearing the echo of low thuds and when the tower went dark she remained where she was. She saw nothing but blackness, but soon she heard the sound of waves lapping against stone. She looked down into the moat and knew something unseen moved through the water.

When all was silent, her imagination began to paint vivid, dramatic pictures in her head. *I wager when dawn lights the sky, I'll see that the* Seacock *is back.* She crossed to the door and listened. Only silence met her ears, but somehow she sensed the moment when Falcon Hawkhurst stole past to his chamber above.

"Will you stay abed all day, wench?"

Tory looked up into bold black eyes. "Ah, the Master of Bodiam has returned. Perhaps I should have fled while I had my chance."

He cocked a dark, mocking brow. "And miss my entertainment tonight? Not bloody likely. Wild horses couldn't drag you away."

*You look remarkably well rested for a man who was stowing contraband all night.* "You're right, of course. I'm looking forward to tonight's affair."

"Good. Chastity is its own punishment," he teased.

Her cheeks bloomed rosy. "I didn't mean—"

Pandora stalked in, picked up Tory's slipper, and turned to leave.

"Come back, you sneak thief," Falcon ordered.

Tory laughed. "I warrant it runs in the family."

He ignored the innuendo and retrieved the slipper. He noted the book on her bedside table. "Reading in bed is far too passive for a lively lady like you. I'll see what I can do to change your habits." He winked. "Wear something spectacular tonight."

Sitting at her dressing table, Victoria turned at the sound of her chamber door opening. Her eyes widened at the satin-clad figure. "I would never have recognized you—your elegance borders on foppery, milord."

An attendant followed him into the room, carrying a box and a bag of flour. The young man flourished a muslin cape, and at a nod from Hawkhurst, draped it about Tory's shoulders.

"Claude is my coiffeur; he's here to powder your hair."

"Put flour on my hair? I think not!"

Falcon's eyes crinkled at the corners. "I didn't think so. Then it will have to be a wig. You cannot go down naked. Brunettes are decidedly démodé."

Tory looked at the wigs that adorned her dressing table. "I'll wear this one with the curl that falls over the shoulder."

Claude brushed her long hair into a topknot and pinned it. Then he dropped the wig into the box, drenched it with flour, gave it a good shake, and fitted it over her dark tresses. He opened a drawer in the table, selected a bejeweled feather ornament, and fastened it into the white curls. "Voilà!"

"Claude can help you with your makeup," Falcon suggested.

Tory eyed him critically. "Did he help you with yours? I've never seen a man wear powder before. I'll do my own, thank you." She touched her eyelids with kohl, rouged her cheeks, and painted her lips. She took a large puff and powdered her face and her breasts. Then she chose a heart-shaped black silk patch and placed it beside her mouth. Victoria threw off the muslin cape and stood up. "What do you think?"

The amusement left Falcon's eyes as he stared at the vision before him. Her stays pushed her curves up and out. The bodice of the lavender silk confection did not quite cover her pink nipples. "I think your breasts are exposed."

"Oh, good. I've decided to take the girls out for an airing."

"I think I prefer Mistress Prim and Proper."

She picked up a fan and made a moue with her lips. "I'm willing to wager I can change your mind before the night's over, my lord."

"I have no doubt of it." He held out his arm and escorted her down to the entertainment.

Their arrival caused a stir among the guests and Tory surmised that people always reacted this way to Lord Hawkhurst, no matter who was on his arm. All the candles were lighted and her gaze traveled from the musicians on the dais to the gaming tables already in use by the habitual gamblers.

"Allow me to introduce you to our venerable customs officer, Thomas Carswell."

Tory was jolted out of her excited reverie. *Hawkhurst has deliberately led me to this man to gauge our reactions.*

"Carswell, this is Victoria . . . Palmer, my young sister."

The man eyed her breasts avidly. "Such a pleasure, my dear lady. I would be honored if you'd save me the first galliard."

Hawkhurst thumped the customs officer on the back. "Damned good job you're doing, Carswell. Bringing thieving scum to justice is a crucial task, though often thankless. Be assured that I and everyone here owes you a debt of gratitude."

"I try to do my duty, your lordship." Carswell, a

brutish looking man, tried to appear humble and failed.

Falcon led Tory across the room to a table filled with refreshments. "My suspicion was wrong. The customs officer is clearly not your father. Swine though he is, Carswell would hardly be sexually attracted to his own daughter."

"You were testing me, you devil! Everything I've told you is the absolute truth."

He grinned down at her. "I believe you; thousands wouldn't."

Three females, all insatiably curious, hurried to join them.

"Lady Goodwood, Lady Firle, Lady Sackville . . . m'sister, Tory," he said negligently.

Tory immediately recognized the noble names from the journal.

Lady Firle stroked her fan along Falcon's arm. "Darling, are you sure you have no French wine hidden away?"

He took her fingers to his lips. "If I had, I'd keep it for myself, Joan. Try the gin, I'm told it provokes lust."

"I'll gladly share a glass of blue ruin with you, darling. Just keep it away from Lord Firle," she cautioned dryly.

Lady Sackville narrowed her eyes. "I warrant gin's not the only thing you'd gladly share with Falcon."

Joan laughed. "What makes you think I haven't, Lavinia?"

"If you had, your look would be more content and less rabid."

"You should know, Lavinia," Lady Goodwood drawled.

*They're having a catfight over him.* Tory accepted a glass of cider from a footman and almost choked on its powerful effect.

"Careful, m'dear, it's as potent as your brother," Joan warned.

Carswell came to claim his dance. The galliard was a favorite and all the ladies eagerly sought partners. The laughter became raucous and it didn't matter that Tory missed a few steps. She was breathless when the dance ended. The musicians played a slow pavane, and she was glad that everyone left the floor. Carswell returned her to her "brother."

"Your eyes followed me all around the room. Were you afraid I'd disgrace myself?"

"Yes, I thought your titties would fall out of your bodice."

"In this crowd I'd have lots of help putting them back in."

"They wouldn't dream of touching the precious objects without a formal introduction, so come and meet them."

Victoria met government officials, a magistrate, and various lords from Rye and Hastings. Some of the nobles she met were from the next county of Kent. The guests were far more interested in drink, cards, and gossip than they were in dancing. The one exception was the captain of the Sussex Militia.

"Any arrests this week, Captain Drudge?"

"There was another sighting of the phantom ship two nights back prowling the coast for prey, your lordship."

"Superstition is rife in coastal villages. If you had a crown for every phantom ship reported, you'd be a wealthy man, captain."

"She's no phantom, she's just familiar with these waters. I'll be ready for her at the next dark of the moon."

"Excellent! Keep your sword to hand, Drudge."

Falcon led Tory to the card tables and handed her a couple of gold crowns. "Here, go mad."

Tory had never gambled in her life, but now that she had money she wasn't going to pass up the opportunity to indulge. She didn't dare throw dice; she chose a card game instead. Eventually she lost everything, but she resolutely pushed away the feeling of guilt that seemed bound and determined to have its way with her.

It must have been around midnight when she saw Mr. Burke at the chamber's entrance. She saw him nod once at Falcon, then quietly leave. Victoria knew it was a signal. Thoughts chased through her mind as she pondered the things that went on at Bodiam. Though her conclusions seemed far-fetched, she felt as if some sixth sense revealed the castle's secrets to her. It wasn't long after that the party broke up and the guests began to depart.

She stood beside Lord Hawkhurst at Bodiam's front entrance, as they watched the drivers bring the carriages from the grass quadrangle to pick up their noble masters.

When the last coach went beneath the portcullis, Falcon took Tory's hand. "Are you ready to collect your wager?"

# CHAPTER 5

Victoria's provocative words from earlier in the evening flew back to her and suddenly she felt shy.

Falcon toyed with the curl on her bare shoulder. "I cannot wait to rid you of such artifice. You have a natural beauty transcending that of any lady of my acquaintance."

"Brunettes are démodé, my lord."

"I have superlative taste."

"Your red high heels attest to it."

Falcon's mouth twitched. Tory used humor as a shield when she felt vulnerable. He drew her arm through his and led her through the castle to the foot of the round tower. He bent his head and murmured, "I think I'll tan your arse for that remark, wench. I'll give you five second's head start."

Tory whooped and was off in a flash, her shyness forgotten. Falcon soon caught up, but he stayed one step behind. He slipped a bold hand beneath her petticoat. His questing fingers slid up her leg and stole a garter. She felt her stocking slide to her ankle. This only made her run faster. She did not stop at her chamber, but ran up to his and burst through the door, laughing with triumph.

He bowed in defeat. "You win! I concede I am a figure of fun."

"Ha! I have you beat hands down. Take a look at this—I'm wearing a bloody birdcage!" Tory hoisted up her skirt and petticoat to reveal the short hooped pannier made of reed, which did indeed cage her hips. She had forgotten, however, that she was not wearing drawers and that one stocking pooled about her ankle.

Falcon shook his head gravely. "It's enough to frighten the pigeons from Bodiam's eaves."

"Cheeky devil!" She kicked her foot and the slipper and stocking flew off. She turned and ran, intending to put the bed between them. She didn't make it. He caught her and tumbled her to the bed. Her wig came off and her dark hair spilled over her bare shoulders as they rolled together, laughing like children.

"Let me relieve you of your misery." Falcon removed her gown and petticoat, unfastened the hooped panniers and then her stays. "I'll let you keep on the stocking and garter to preserve your modesty." As he gazed down at her, the amusement left his eyes and was replaced by a look of tender possessiveness.

"But how will you preserve yours?"

"I have no modesty."

"Good. I shall enjoy watching you undress." She gathered up her strewn-about clothes and put them on a chair, then she sat down cross-legged on the bed.

Falcon removed his wig, washed the powder from his face, and combed his fingers through his long, black hair. He took off his satin brocade jacket and vest, then stripped off his silk shirt. He kicked off his shoes, removed his white stockings, and divested himself of the satin knee breeches. "We are slaves to fashion. I take little pleasure in looking like an effete popinjay."

"Enjoy it while you can. A hundred years from now you will be garbed in black, or, if you're particularly frivolous, dark gray."

"Will I?" he asked quizzically. As he approached the bed, she lowered her eyes shyly. "Look at me, Tory."

She raised her lashes and felt her pulse begin to race. His body was lithe and lean, his muscular torso powerful. He joined her on the bed and ranged himself over her in the dominant position, bracing himself on his palms. When she saw the falcon tattoos on his forearms, a frisson of excitement rippled from her breasts to her belly. He worshipped her with his eyes, his glance roaming over her possessively like a hot flame. His overt maleness made her feel seductively feminine. She entwined her arms about his neck and lifted her mouth to his. She opened her lips for his ravishing and the deep thrust of his tongue made her arch her body against his in wanton invitation.

Falcon kept an iron control on his desire. His erection was hard and throbbing, but he knew Tory was not yet ready. He wanted her at the peak of arousal, so that her pleasure would vanquish any pain. His lips hovered at the corner of her mouth above the beauty spot. "Guard your heart, my beauty, I am about to steal it." He plunged his tongue into her honey-drenched mouth, imitating what he longed to do with his cock. When she arched restlessly against him, he slipped his hand between her legs to stroke and play among the silken curls. He slid a finger into her tight sheath and caressed her tiny bud until she became wet and gasped in a fever of need. "Falcon, please!"

He placed the head of his phallus against her cleft and, bracing his weight on his arms, thrust firmly until he was buried deep within. She cried out and clung to him fiercely. She was so hot and tight, he felt scalded. Though it was silken torment, he held perfectly still until she became used to the fullness inside her. When he was sure she was ready, he began to thrust slowly. The hot, sliding friction made her close sleekly around him. She was sweet as wild honey and the brush of her thighs against his inflamed his dark, erotic passion until he was reeling with need.

Tory savored his fullness inside her and longed to feel the weight of his body. His masculine smell coupled with the sensual rhythm of his thrusts sent her arousal soaring. He was the Falcon and she let him take her higher and higher. She reached a peak of pleasure so intense she did not think she could bear more and she bit his shoulder in a frenzy of passion.

Falcon felt a surging wave of desire he could not control. He went taut, then suddenly the night exploded into a million fragments, fusing the couple together in love, bathing them in liquid tremors; they floated together on a sea of bliss. She clung to him sweetly, limp from the loving. He rolled with her until she lay on top, languid, replete, and deliciously warm. He feathered his fingers through her wildly disheveled hair and felt her lips against his chest. Then his arms enfolded her possessively.

After a long, quiet time, Tory raised her head, looked into his eyes, and whispered, "*Now* I am ready to collect my wager." He had made a woman of her and she was imbued with confidence. She believed they had reached a level of intimacy where it would be difficult for him to refuse her anything.

He cocked a dark, indulgent brow. "What do you desire?"

"Take me with you on your next smuggling run!"

A denial sprang to his lips, but he did not utter it. Instead, he looked incredulous. "Tory, your imagination soars without boundaries. I am a staunch advocate of law and order. Among my guests tonight were a customs officer, a magistrate, various government officials, and the captain of the militia."

"And right under their noses you passed contraband to your noble guests. When all was safely stowed in the carriages, Mr. Burke signaled you."

He pulled her down to him. "Violet-eyed witch. Now I shall have to kill you." He kissed her instead.

"Take me on a run!"

His arms tightened. "I would not expose you to danger."

"If the danger is so great, why do you do it?"

"Danger excites me."

"Then we are two of a kind." Her eyes glittered. "If you won't take me, I may as well go back to my own time."

"Blackmail won't work, sweetheart, but I'm particularly vulnerable to bribery."

"You black-eyed devil." She slid both her hands down between their bodies. "Then bribery it is, milord." She rolled his hardening cock between her palms.


As they finished breakfast, Falcon asked, "Do you ride?"

"Father taught me to ride when I was a child, but all we have now at the priory is a carriage horse."

"Pandora likes to hunt in Ashdown Forest. If you ride astride, you can come with us. Mr. Burke will find you some britches."

Within the hour an excited Tory stood in front of the mirror dressed as a boy. The britches and jacket must have belonged to a young servant, but she didn't care. She tucked in the shirt, tied her hair back with a ribbon, and shouted up the stairs, "Ready!"

The leopard paced outside the stable while Falcon saddled two mounts. His own was a black mare with a deep chest and sturdy legs; hers was a dark brown pony.

Tory mounted without his help. "I thought you would ride a more showy animal."

"You think me vain!" He flashed white teeth. "I don't deny it, but I put expedience before vanity. Bess has endurance and speed; your pony is sure-footed."

The moment they emerged from the stable, Pandora loped off toward the forest. The leopard spotted a hare and disappeared into the trees. Falcon did not follow her; he trotted beneath the thick green canopy for more than a mile until he came to a well-hidden path. "Do you think you could ride through here in the dark, my love?"

*He's testing me for a smuggling run!* "I know I could."

He winked at her. "Try to keep up with me." He took off without warning, taking the twists and turns with practiced ease. Tory gripped the reins and touched her heels to the pony's flanks. In truth all she had to do was keep her seat and keep her head low; her mount knew the way.

When she caught up, he asked, "Which way is the castle?"

She hesitated, unsure.

"Then how would you get to the safety of Bodiam?"

"If I were lost, I'd give the pony its head."

His grin was a leer. "Beauty and brains, a heady combination."

Tory heard the distant cry of an animal, quickly cut off. She guessed what it was and went pale. "I don't enjoy blood sport."

"Make no mistake, smuggling is a blood sport."

"Men's blood I can stomach."

"Spoken with bravado."

Falcon gave a trilling whistle and shortly Pandora joined them. They returned to Bodiam at a leisurely pace and as they climbed the stairs of the tower, he asked, "Did your mount suit you?"

"Yes. I wish he were mine."

"Wish granted. Keep those clothes handy if you want to come on the run tonight."

*"Tonight?"* Her pulse began to race.

"It has to be at the dark of the moon. Are you game?"

Tory nodded eagerly.

"Good, I'll get you a slouch hat. Have a rest this afternoon."

Everything was different at night. Black shadows loomed everywhere in the darkness, exaggerating the size and distorting the shape of trees and dwellings. As she trotted beside Falcon, she was thankful her pony did not shy. The very air felt eerie and charged with peril. She became aware that, one by one, other riders fell in behind them. She copied Falcon and did not turn to look. *I wonder if he has his pistols with him? Of course he does— everyone will be armed.* Tory shivered.

They rode in silence at a slow, steady pace, the muffled hooves of their mounts making little sound. Tory sensed they rode west and she knew by the sound and the smell when they reached the sea. A mile or so farther brought them to a vast marsh. Without hesitation their mounts trotted into the reedy saltwater and were soon up to their hocks.

When Falcon dismounted, she followed suit, and, as she turned, she was amazed to see scores of dark figures that numbered about eighty. The men searched the marsh for barrels and wooden crates, hoisted them onto their animals' backs, secured the cargo with ropes, and left as silently as they had arrived.

Falcon picked up two wooden crates and secured them to Bess, then he slung a brace of small barrels across the pony's back and signaled Tory with his thumb to mount. Back in the saddle, they fell into line behind the other riders.

*This must be Romney Marsh. This cargo has been dropped off a merchant vessel from a foreign port. Will we take it to Bodiam?* They rode for more than an hour. Cold and wet, Tory found the journey tedious. Only the danger made it exciting.

They skirted a cemetery, which some of the riders entered. She followed Falcon into a stand of trees and realized they were in Ashdown Forest. Soon they were on a path and rode in single file for miles. When they reached the northern edge, the riders dismounted and dropped their cargo amid the cover of the trees. Falcon lifted the barrels from her pony and bent to whisper in Tory's ear. "Home."

Tory gave her pony its head, sensing it would find the shortest way through vast Ashdown Forest to its snug Bodiam stable. When she got to her own chamber, Mr. Burke sent the servants with hot bathwater. By the time she had wrapped herself in a velvet bed robe, Falcon arrived and beckoned her upstairs.

He poured them each a tot of French brandy and while she took a tentative sniff and then a sip, he stripped off his wet clothes. "You're doing it the right way. First you inhale the fragrant fumes, then you hold it on your tongue to savor its fine flavor. When you swallow, it will warm the cockles of your heart."

He padded naked across the room and stretched out before the fire. "Come and be warm, love."

She sat down beside him and took another swallow. "It feels like a bloodred rose is blooming in my breast."

"The potent warmth will soon spread through your veins like a river of fire." He cocked an inquisitive brow. "So, what did you think of your first run, my beauty?"

"I expected it to be great fun, but after the anticipation wore off, I realized it was tedious work. Only the danger made it exciting. My curiosity's sated and I'm not eager to go again."

"That's the reaction I was hoping for. If I'd told you, you wouldn't have believed me—you had to experience it for yourself."

"It's a larger operation than I thought and covers a wider area. When the goods are dropped at the far side of Ashdown Forest, they must be picked up by others and delivered to wealthy noble customers, perhaps as far away as Penshurst."

Falcon sipped his brandy. "And from Penshurst to London."

"I don't understand why you do it. The excitement must have palled long ago." She thought of the noble names listed in the back of the journal. "Why put yourself in danger to save your wealthy friends from paying import taxes?"

Falcon laughed. "I don't do it for them. The villagers of Hawkhurst would starve eking out a living by fishing alone."

"Ah, the names listed in the front of your journal." Tory rubbed a taut muscle in her back. "What was the name of the 'phantom ship' that dropped the contraband in Romney Marsh?"

"The *Seacock*," he said quietly.

Tory's eyes widened. *You took the* Seacock *out to raid the cargo of a French merchant vessel.* "Falcon Hawkhurst, you are not just a smuggler, you are a pirate!"

He smiled into her eyes, slipped the robe from her shoulders, and bade her lie prone before the fire. Then, with long, slow, sensuous strokes, he began to massage her back and buttocks. The thrilling thought of a pirate's hands caressing her naked flesh made her want to scream with excitement. Before he was done, Tory thought her very bones would melt with pleasure.

He turned her onto her back and proceeded to work his magic on the rest of her body. Her lush breasts spilled into his possessive hands and he brought his lips down to hers in a demanding kiss that was primal and savage.

His mouth tasted of brandy and it sent her senses reeling. She wrapped her legs tightly around his back and heat leaped between them as he impaled her with a hot, driving thrust. She was wildly intoxicated by the brandy and the potent maleness of the reckless devil who was making love to her.

It was too intense to last long and all too soon they were both crying out their pleasure. He gathered her close and held her against his heart until her body softened. Falcon watched her eyes close and felt her body grow limp in his arms as she drifted into sleep. A need to protect her now mingled with his desire to possess her. "Don't leave me, Victoria."

When Tory awoke, she was in Falcon's bed, but she was alone. The last thing she remembered was being held in his arms before the fire. *When I fell asleep he carried me to bed.*

She knew she was losing her heart to this man, yet in the cool light of day, what she had learned about him last night brought her conscience into conflict. Hawkhurst was noble and altruistic regarding the welfare of the less privileged families of the area, and Tory had no problem with them smuggling contraband. Piracy was another matter. Fiction portrayed it as adventure, but the reality was often bloody and brutal. The words he had uttered came winging back to her: *Danger excites me.*

She now realized with dismay it was the sheer, reckless danger of life-or-death risks that held Falcon in thrall. *He is a buccaneer who boards vessels and plunders cargo.* The crates of tea from the East Indiaman where he'd found Pandora came to mind. *The* Seacock *is fitted with a row of cannon and its master carries a brace of pistols.*

Tory dressed and sat down before the mirror to brush her hair. Her mind went back over what the history books had recorded of Lord Hawkhurst of Bodiam Castle. His ship was named, but no mention had been made of piracy or even smuggling. *I'm letting my imagination run amok. Most likely Falcon never sank a ship or killed anyone.* Tory decided to give him the benefit of the doubt.

She smiled into the mirror and admitted she was head over heels with the bold devil. She had been ruled by rigid morals all her life and refused to allow a strait-laced upbringing to deprive her of the pleasure Falcon brought her. It felt so much more romantic to let her heart rule her head.

The sun was high and Tory decided to take her book down to the grassy quadrangle. A serving woman brought out her lunch and Tory realized Mr. Burke had been instructed to take care of her needs. In the early afternoon she saw Falcon ride beneath the portcullis. *He's returning from God only knows what nefarious business.*

He dismounted and dropped down on the grass beside her. "It occurs to me that you haven't received your share of spoils. Come to my ship and choose your reward," he invited.

Tory hesitated. The *Seacock* was the wicked instrument of his iniquity. She swept her conscience aside and smiled into his eyes. His ship was too sinfully tempting to resist. *Admit the truth and shame the Devil, Victoria. It is Falcon Hawkhurst who is too sinfully tempting.*

He lifted Tory into the saddle and mounted Bess behind her. They left Bodiam and rode along the bank of the River Rother until they reached the *Seacock.* He held her hand tightly as they traversed the narrow gangplank, then he lifted her over the rail.

Tory's face lit with eager curiosity as her gaze swept from the brigantine's rigging to its well-scrubbed deck. Her eyes purposely avoided the rows of cannon. Below, she took in the cabin's rich mahogany and polished brass. Falcon lit a lantern and took her into the hold. It smelled of tar and tea and piquant spices she could not name. He removed a false panel and led her into a space that held a cabinet and some trunks.

Falcon unlocked the cabinet doors and pulled out a drawer. Gold and silver necklaces, bracelets, rings, and earbobs, many set with precious jewels, glittered in the lamplight. As Tory gazed with appreciation, he lifted a trunk lid and revealed its contents. She drew in her breath and reached out to touch the bolts of exquisite silk, shot through with shining threads.

"The choice is yours, Victoria."

Without hesitation her fingers sought the pale green silk with silver threads. "I've never seen anything as lovely in my life."

He handed her the bolt of silk. "Its loveliness pales beside yours." He closed the lid and moved to the cabinet. He took out a pair of carved jade earrings. "You must have these, too. They match perfectly. Both your beauty and your taste are exotic."

"Thank you, Falcon, for the gifts and the compliment." She looked down at the exquisite objects and a bubble of joyous laughter escaped. "And they say the wages of sin are death!"

He led the way back up on deck. "You promised to swim for me. The warm afternoons of August will soon give way to the cool autumn days of September."

"Will you swim with me, milord?"

"I will, milady." He immediately began to throw off his clothes.

Tory set down her presents, removed her dress and petticoat, and draped them to protect the delicate gifts of silk and jade. By this time, Falcon was naked and, not to be outdone, Tory stripped off her drawers and stays. She followed him as he strode to the bridge. He raised his arms and launched himself into the air, diving down to the water like a sea hawk. He surfaced laughing and flung the wet hair from his eyes. "Your turn!"

Tory, rooted to the spot, was overwhelmed by the height. "I can't. I don't know how to dive. . . . I'm afraid!"

"Darling . . . don't be afraid. If you can't dive, then jump. . . . I'm here to catch you."

She stared down, striving to banish her apprehension. She wasn't afraid of the water, only the height. She gathered her courage, focused her attention on Falcon, and made her decision to place her trust in him. She shut her eyes and jumped.

The water closed over her head as her body plunged deep. As she started to come up, she felt a moment's panic as the river's current threatened to carry her away. She surfaced like a cork, bobbing on the water. To her great relief, Falcon's powerful arms were there, keeping her safe as he had promised. Together they swam in a wide arc around the *Seacock*. *He has taught me to take risks. It makes life so much sweeter.*

# CHAPTER 6

"When are you hosting your next entertainment? I need time to finish my new gown." Pandora lay at Victoria's feet, demonstrating that the pair of females had grown quite used to each other.

"You can actually sew? Is there no end to your accomplishments, my beauty?" Falcon asked with amusement as he sat at his desk, marking symbols against the names in his journal.

"Your guests will be agog when they see me in the green silk. I shall set the fashion with my risqué Grecian design."

"The jade earrings you're wearing and the silk are from China."

She shook her head to make the jade earbobs swing. "Since I haven't the faintest notion how females dress in China, I shall sew a Grecian robe that bares one shoulder. When is the party?"

Falcon consulted a chart that showed the lunar tides. "I need a couple of moonless nights or at least nights when moonrise occurs in the late hours." A visit to the Mermaid Tavern in Rye had supplied him with a list of vessels that would be bringing cargo to the Cinque Ports for the next month.

He pored over the chart, knowing a merchant ship was due to dock in the Port of Winchelsey in five days. "How about a week from today? I'll send out the usual invitations."

Tory drew in a swift breath as she felt cold fingers touch her heart. She had been thinking of enjoyment only; she had forgotten that Falcon mixed business with pleasure. Fear of risks he would take and dread of deeds he might commit made her temper flare. "Why do you have to be so calculating? Why does everything in your life have to be illicit?"

His dark eyes studied her for long moments. "I give you free rein to do whatever you wish. Can you not extend me the same courtesy, mistress?"

"I am not insanely reckless! Come to think of it, madness runs in your bloodline."

"Ah yes, claiming to have traveled through time is perfectly normal," he drawled.

She jumped up. "You mocking swine. Go to the devil!" When Tory shouted, the hairs along Pandora's neck stood on end and the leopard growled in her throat. Tory threw Hawkhurst a furious glance. "Now see what you've done!" She stalked from the room.

The lovers avoided each other for the next forty-eight hours, yet both found that the time apart seemed endless. To Victoria, the days and nights estranged from Falcon were joyless. To Hawkhurst they were unendurable. He held out until the third night, but when the hour grew late, his patience snapped.

Falcon's mood was dangerous as he descended to her chamber. He had every intention of breaking down the door if it was locked against him. To his surprise, it swung open when he tested it. A smile of satisfaction curved his mouth. *She's been hoping I would come for her.*

The room was in darkness and when he lit the candles and saw the empty bed, the complacent smile was wiped away. His heart constricted. *She's left me. . . . She's gone back to her own time!* He felt bereft. Sharing things with Tory had given him deep pleasure and brought new meaning to his life. He refused to accept her loss. "Come back to me, Victoria," he demanded. His glance swept about the chamber and he noticed that the books were gone from the bedside table. A tiny glimmer of hope lit in his heart and he clung to it fiercely as he descended the stairs of the round tower and made his way to the small library. He flung open the door and it crashed against the wall.

Tory gasped. "I . . . I couldn't sleep. . . . I was getting a book." The undisguised look of relief on Falcon's face revealed to her what he had feared and her heart softened toward him. "I was never angry with you. My temper flared to mask my fear for your safety." *And my dread of your committing shameful deeds.* She quickly shoved the book she'd been reading back on the shelf. It was about shipwrecks caused by accident or by foul deliberation.

"I want no gulf between us, Tory. I've always been a solitary man—I never knew what I was missing until you came into my life."

She went to him and raised her face to his. "Thank you, Falcon. I feel exactly the same way. Sharing your life fills me with wonder and joy. And I do appreciate the freedom you offer me—my existence was so restricted before. I shall try my utmost to return the favor."

He wrapped his arms about her and grinned. "That was our first quarrel."

"We feel things so passionately, I doubt it will be our last."

"Passionate?" He bit her ear. "I'll show you passionate." She laughed, and wriggled from his embrace. She had the urge to run for the sheer pleasure of having him chase her and catch her. Perhaps if she used feminine, subtle persuasion, she could keep him from his piracy.

That night after their mating, Falcon held her for hours while they talked. He told her about his childhood, his sailing adventures to foreign lands, and the time he'd spent in London at the Royal Court. Tory entertained him with stories of how she escaped from the confines of her narrow life by the clever use of ploys, tricks, and deceptions that often needed the compliance of her brother, Edmund. The part where she used the garden shed to put on her stockings, screw her hair into a bun, cram on a black bonnet, pick up her prayer book, and put a pious look on her face had Falcon roaring with laughter.

They slept in spoon fashion; his powerful body curved about her back, his arm anchoring her to him possessively. As Tory drifted into sleep she hoped that tomorrow night she would be able to keep him attached to her by an invisible thread that would stay him from his dangerous roving.

When Tory awoke she was alone. She wasn't too concerned because he always arose early and usually broke his fast in Bodiam's Great Hall with the other castle inhabitants, including his crew. Just to make certain he hadn't left, she went to the desk and pulled open the drawer. She let out a long breath when she saw his pistols were still in their case. She ran her fingers along the twelve-inch barrels, fascinated that such beautiful objects were meant for a deadly purpose. She heard the chamber door open behind her and spun round guiltily. Quite used to being caught in compromising situations and talking herself out of them, she spoke a half-truth. "Falcon, I was admiring your pistols. Would you teach me how to use them?"

"I admit I enjoy tutoring you in pleasurable pursuits, but I'm not sure shooting qualifies as such. I assumed guns would be offensive to you."

"I prefer to think of them as defensive."

He came to the desk and lifted the weapons from their case. "This is a pair of naval officer's belt pistols. The barrels and mountings are made of brass, which resists the corrosion of salt water. These are matched and have left- and right-hand locks."

"Isn't it usual to have your name or initials engraved on the polished butt caps?" she puzzled. "These say 'James Freeman.'"

"That's the maker's name." He winked. "Expedience before vanity. I want no identifying marks on my lethal weapons."

She felt a chill and purposely ignored it. "You are the best tutor I've ever had. I shall strive to be a model pupil, milord."

From behind a false panel, he opened a cupboard she didn't know about and extracted a small barrel of gunpowder. He offered Pandora a small leather pouch, which she carried in her mouth. "Come, then; I warrant target practice is never time wasted."

On the grass quadrangle in the courtyard, Falcon set out two metal brackets that each held a square candle, which he then lit. "Twenty paces is far enough for a beginner, I think."

"That's the accepted distance between duelists when they turn and fire."

He gave her a quizzical glance as they strode down the field. "Duels are fought with swords and rapiers, Tory. I've fought enough. Hellfire, don't tell me men challenge each other with guns in your time? Where's the honor in that?"

She was about to ask Falcon about the duels he'd

fought, but bit her lip. She didn't want to know if he'd killed anyone.

He opened the barrel of gunpowder and took out a flask with a small spout. Then he took the pouch from Pandora's mouth and fished out a lead ball. He gave Tory an empty pistol to hold and loaded the other. "Watch carefully. Keep it at half cock until you're ready to shoot." He put the pistol down, took the one she'd been holding and loaded it the same way, then picked up the other one. "Now you fully cock, aim, and pull the trigger."

Tory jumped as the powder exploded with a bang and both candle flames were snuffed. "You are a superb marksman!"

He shook his head. "They didn't go out at the same instant. My left hand is slower on the trigger."

"But you aimed two pistols at once, at two different targets. I am in awe, Falcon Hawkhurst."

"Are you game to try it? I'll go and light the candles."

"No need. I won't even hit the candle, let alone a flame. And I can't handle two guns at the same time."

He handed her the pistol with the right-hand lock. "Load it the way I showed you and don't forget to keep it half-cocked until you are ready."

"Are you sure it won't go off at half cock? Isn't that where the expression comes from?"

He gave her a wicked grin. "It is a belt pistol. If it went off it would literally mean half cock."

"You are making me laugh to distract me. Behave yourself." Tory had no trouble loading, unlocking, or aiming. The snag came when she fired the weapon and landed on her derriere. "I wasn't expecting that." She dusted off her bottom. "Let me try again."

Exercising infinite patience, Falcon encouraged and instructed her in the use of firearms the entire morning. Only when her lead ball hit the castle and chipped the ancient stone did Victoria throw up her hands in defeat. Falcon gave the pistols to Mr. Burke, who was watching the target practice, to clean and reload.

To Hawkhurst, the morning had been a great diversion. It was a new experience to have a female for a friend, especially one who was willing to share his interests and not just his bed. "Let's go for a ride. We can stop at the Oak and Ivy, then I'll show you the village. You haven't seen it in daylight."

The inn, about a half mile from Hawkhurst, fascinated Tory. Its doorstep was worn down from all the feet that had entered over the years. Downstairs were four snug rooms with rough-hewn trestle tables and benches. Each had a large fireplace with a spit for roasting haunches of meat. The mellow light came from candles mounted on ancient oxcart wheels. Barrels of ale were stacked against the walls and the air was redolent of smoke, cooking smells, hops, and malt.

"An honor, yer lordship, how can I serve ye?"

"A dozen oysters and a pint of ale. M'sister will have the same, and a pint for your good self, Harry."

When the food arrived, Tory looked askance at the raw oysters sitting on their shells.

"What's the matter, love? Don't you like them?"

"Only men eat oysters raw. Ladies like their crustaceans decently fried, but I'll try anything once," she said gamely.

Falcon picked up a shell. "Swallow the oyster and wash it down with a swig of ale . . . like so."

Victoria mimicked what he did, including wiping her mouth with the back of her hand. The first few went down easily, but at the sixth she couldn't suppress a shudder.

Falcon laughed and finished them off. "What are friends for?"

Harry came to replenish Falcon's ale. "Bring us some winkles."

"Winkles?" Tory was disconcerted. "My mother would never approve of anything so vulgar and low class as eating winkles."

"She wouldn't approve of your strutting about in your drawers either, but it proved to be great fun. Eating winkles is a pleasure not to be denied."

When the miniscule shellfish arrived, Tory took the pin, stabbed the winkle, pulled it from its tiny case, and popped it into her mouth. She rolled her eyes with pleasure. "Delicious!"

Falcon gave her a suggestive wink. "*You* are delicious."

"Stop that, I'm supposed to be your sister," she said laughing.

They finished off their meal with bowls of mutton and barley stew and bread fresh from the oven, then they rode into the village of Hawkhurst, which was three miles from Bodiam.

Tory gazed about avidly. "Neither the priory nor the parish church have been built yet, though there is a cemetery."

"Graveyard," Falcon corrected. "Bodiam Church is on the hill."

"The village is much smaller than the Hawkhurst I know, but it is endearingly rustic and surrounded by the same lovely rolling hills that I've walked all my life. Thank you for bringing me."

On the ride back to the castle, Victoria was busy planning her strategy to keep Falcon at Bodiam for the night. "You are such a good tutor. How would you like to teach me the dice game of hazard?"

"I'll teach you games, all of them hazardous," he promised. Falcon helped her dismount and told her he was taking Bess to the smithy to get her reshod. "I enjoyed your company today. I'll see you tonight, sweetheart. We'll find out if oysters really are an aphrodisiac."

Hawkhurst usually ate the evening meal with his men and seldom sought his chamber before nine, so Victoria planned accordingly. At the appointed time, she made sure she was reclining in her slipper bath with her hair spilling over the edge and cascading to the carpet in a dark waterfall. Her back was facing the door, which she had purposely left open. When she heard his step she lifted a slim leg and let the sponge trickle water down it. The bath drew him like a lodestone.

"Let me do that." His deep voice sent shivers up her spine. Without turning to look at him, she said, "I'll give you the sponge if you teach me to play hazard."

He knelt down beside the tub and took the dice from his pocket. "The sponge is the stake. I throw the dice to establish a *main* point." He rolled the dice. "The *main* point is seven. Now I throw again to establish a *chance* point. I'm out if I roll a two, three, or twelve." He cast again. "I rolled a *nick,* so I win!"

He reached for the sponge.

She hung onto it. "A *nick* is when you roll eleven?"

"Only if the *main* point is a seven."

She gave him the sponge. "I surrender. I warrant you make your own rules, Falcon Hawkhurst."

"I reckon I do, Mistress Cocktease." He held the sponge up high so that water trickled onto her breasts and formed droplets that clung to her nipples. He licked off the drops and laughed as the tips of her breasts hardened into tiny spears. "I believe I made my point."

Tory reached out and ran her finger down the length of the bulge in his breeches. "So you did, and here's the evidence."

He grabbed her and lifted her from the water. "Just the way I like you, wet and wild."

She struggled in his arms, laughing as the water soaked his clothes. "You promised to teach me to play hazard. Put me down, I insist upon my turn casting the dice!"

Reluctantly, he set her feet to the carpet and watched her reach for her robe. "Games are supposed to be fun."

"I'll come up to your chamber and be wet and wild," she paused and licked her lips, "if I lose, of course."

He made a grab for her and she danced away and ran upstairs. She sat cross-legged on the bed and he handed her the dice. "Explain this *nick* thing again. I understand how to get a *main* point." She cast the dice and rolled an eight.

"You haven't set the stake."

"I have. I shall reveal it only if I win."

As Falcon removed his wet clothes, he explained that only a twelve or another eight would give her a *nick*.

She shook the dice and cast them. "Double six. I win!"

Falcon, amused and completely naked, took a step toward her. "Now you must reveal your secret desire."

She hesitated for only a heartbeat. "I want you to stay with me all night. . . . I don't want you to leave."

He stood still and the amusement left his eyes. "I cannot," he said quietly. Falcon selected black garments and began to dress.

Tory picked up the dice and flung them at him. "You bloody pirate. Don't you dare go roving!"

He took off his seal ring and put it on the desk as if he hadn't heard her.

She stood up on the bed. "If you go, I won't be here when you come back. And don't bother looking for me in the library!"

He ignored her completely and for a moment she wondered if she were invisible. Then she remembered what he'd once said: *Blackmail won't work, sweetheart, but I'm particularly vulnerable to bribery.* She realized with a sinking heart that tonight neither bribery nor all the blissful delights of Elysium would entice him to stay.

# CHAPTER 7

"Up anchor!" Hawkhurst waited for silence as the anchor chain was pulled up through the hawsehole. He knew he must court caution tonight. He was well aware that Captain Drudge and his militiamen would be on the lookout for a marauding ship in coastal waters.

"When we get to the mouth of the Rother, we'll drop anchor in the hidden cove. We'll take the longboat and row out to the *Boulogne*. I'll take only seven," he pointed to the men he wanted. "The rest of the crew should be ready to run back up the river on the tide, whether we're here in time or not."

Hawkhurst took the *Seacock's* wheel and guided her silently down the River Rother. When they got to Rye Bay he ordered, "Ready the longboat!" and turned the wheel over to the first mate.

The boat, fitted with grappling irons, was lowered into the water and Falcon was first down the rope ladder. He set his cutlass beside him and took his place at an oar along with the other seven. With the riding lights of the merchant vessel to guide them, they pulled alongside in less than an hour.

Hawkhurst was always first to swing across from the *Seacock* to the ship they were invading and tonight was no exception, as he flung his grappling hook, grabbed his cutlass, and shinnied up the thick rope. He swung his legs over the rail and before his boots hit the deck he got the surprise of his life.

"Fuck!" Hawkhurst saw the dark figure cross the deck with raised sword and knew it was Drudge. He parried the thrust hard, but as the weapon flew from his opponent's hand, he felt it slice into his cheek. Knowing his men would not be far behind, he alerted them to the danger. "Back! Retreat now!"

He was over the side in a flash and jumped from the rope into the rocking boat. He held it steady until the four men who were climbing grappling ropes made it back down. "Man the oars!" *Thank Christ I had the presence of mind to keep the* Seacock *hidden. They were expecting a ship and had the cannon ready to blow us out of the water. Our longboat surprised them as much as Drudge surprised me.* "God rot the bastard!"

"Go and rot, Falcon Hawkhurst!" Victoria paced the chamber. As she passed the mirror, she caught a glimpse of her worried face and knew that her anger paled beside her fear for Falcon's safety.

She went to the window, hoping against hope that she would see the *Seacock* moored in the river. The brigantine was gone and her heart filled with dread that Falcon was off marauding another vessel. She heard the echo of his words when they'd taken Pandora into the forest to hunt: *Make no mistake; smuggling is a blood sport.* Tory knew a pirate risked a hundredfold more danger than a smuggler.

She wished she could take back the angry words she'd

thrown at him. Her threats were empty; she would never leave Falcon of her own volition. The hours until he returned would drag endlessly and Tory knew she must do something to keep her imagination from running riot. She picked up a book and began to read, but when she reached the end of the chapter, she realized she had not comprehended one word. She forced her mind to think of something pleasant and thought of the upcoming party. Then she remembered that she hadn't finished sewing her dress.

She went to her own chamber to retrieve the material and the needles and thread that Mr. Burke had provided. She took them upstairs, knowing she would feel more comforted in Falcon's tower room. Handling the exquisite jade silk brought a soothing sense of serenity. As she focused on the needle, sewing the hem with tiny stitches, a peaceful calm descended.

Victoria finished the gown and couldn't wait to try it on to gauge its effect. She heard footsteps on the tower stairs and her hope soared because Falcon had returned early. Her eyes widened with alarm as she watched him drag himself through the door. She quickly set aside the dress she'd been sewing and ran toward him.

Mr. Burke hovered behind him, ready to catch him if he fell. The look of grave concern on his face told her that Falcon had been injured. Then she saw the blood on his cheek and saw him stagger. She dragged a chair forward and Falcon sank down on it. "Mr. Burke, fetch me hot water to cleanse his wound."

Burke hurried off to do her bidding and she dropped to her knees before Falcon to examine his face. The blood was welling from the slash wound and dripping onto his black shirt. When Tory helped him remove it, she became aware that the shirt was soaked with his blood. He had lost far more than she first realized.

His mouth curved. "You're still here."

"Of course I'm here. Where the hell else would I be?" Her heart hammered as she ran to the bed and grabbed a bolster case. She wiped his chest, which was dripping with blood. She was terrified that she would find another wound. "Press this to your face."

As the white cloth turned red, he assured her he had no other injuries. "It's just a scratch, Tory. Don't be upset."

Mr. Burke arrived with hot water and towels.

"I'm thirsty. Get me some ale, Mr. Burke."

Tory washed the blood from Falcon's neck and his ear, then she tenderly bathed the wound as he drained the tankard of ale. She sat back on her heels, alarm marring her delicate features. "It won't stop on its own. I'm going to have to stitch it."

"I'm so glad you can sew, sweetheart."

"Pour him some brandy, Mr. Burke." Victoria picked up a needle and, in spite of her shaking hands, managed to thread it. She came back and waited until he drained the glass. "Get him some more."

She handed Falcon a clean linen towel. "I'll start at the top. Press this firmly to your cheek." As she pushed the needle through the gaping flap of flesh she felt the pain in her heart. Falcon barely flinched as she proceeded to stitch his skin together from his temple, down in front of his ear, all the way to his jaw. The minute she was finished, she fed him the brandy.

She stared at her handiwork and shook her head in despair. "You'll have a scar."

"That won't bother an ugly devil like me." He tried to smile, but it hurt too much.

Tory pulled off his boots. "Can you make it to the bed?"

He nodded and carefully got to his feet. "My knees are as weak as wet linen." He walked slowly to the bed and sank down gratefully. "Thank you, Mr. Burke. I appreciate your help."

Burke picked up the bloody shirt, towels, and water. "Good night, my lord. I leave you in good hands."

With Falcon's help, Tory managed to divest him of his breeches. She spread a clean linen towel over his pillow and he laid the left, uninjured side of his face against it, then closed his eyes.

Victoria snuffed some of the candles. She undressed and slipped beneath the covers, trying not to jostle the bed.

Falcon reached out for her hands and held them possessively. "I love you, Tory."

A lump came into her throat. She knew his words were not prompted by gratitude; they came from his heart.

They both had a restless night. Whenever he dozed off and turned on his right side, the pain awakened him. Tory checked his wound often and brought him drinks to quench his raging thirst. By morning he had regained most of his strength. When he kissed her, she placed her hand against his other cheek and was relieved that he hadn't developed a fever.

"We'll have to cancel the party. It was Captain Drudge's blade that did this. If he sees my wound he'll immediately suspect me. Though calling off the entertainment could also arouse suspicion."

"Don't cancel it—just send word that it is to be a masquerade. Everyone will wear a mask and none will be the wiser."

"Ingenious!"

"No, it's simply expedient."

"The ladies will love the idea of wearing costumes and masks, but what about the men?"

"They'll voice a token grumble, but privately enjoy indulging a fantasy. We'd all like to be someone else for a few hours."

"Delusions of grandeur—there'll be a plethora of royalty."

"And you should be no exception. I suggest you go as King Charles II, since you have an abundance of long black hair. We could curl it into lovelocks that fall forward across your cheeks. With a mustache and an eye mask, most of your face would be hidden."

"Your suggestion has possibilities. Charles always charmed the ladies. Of course you'll wear your Grecian gown and be a goddess."

"Not just any goddess. I shall be *Diana,* Goddess of the Hunt."

*Diana was a Roman goddess, but I won't spoil her fun.* "They'll be so busy looking at you, they won't notice me."

Tory slipped from the bed and bowed. "I shall make certain of it, *Your Majesty.*"

"I should breakfast with the men to let them know I survived," he said dryly and threw back the covers.

"Was anyone else wounded?"

"No, I ordered a quick retreat."

Tory refrained from asking further questions. She didn't want to know the grisly details of what he and his crew had been up to. "I'll go to the woods and gather some of our most common Sussex herb, tormentil. It helps heal wounds and fade scars."

Falcon sat up and winced. "The very name makes me shudder."

She gave him a saucy wink. "I'll make you shudder."

Late the following afternoon, Victoria sat Falcon at her dressing table to examine his wound. "I don't dare remove your stitches. It's too soon—the last thing we want is blood everywhere. I'll cover it with maquillage."

He cocked his left eyebrow. "Aren't you the wench who objects to men wearing powder?"

"Guilty as charged, but a masquerade is an exception." With gentle fingers she applied a liberal amount of tinted paste over the stitched wound. When she was satisfied that both cheeks looked almost the same, she stuck the curling iron into the fire. "I'm going to do your hair. We won't need the services of Claude. I've read all about Charles Stuart's lovelocks."

She had to heat the iron more than once. When she was done, Falcon stared at his reflection. "Good God, even Claude wouldn't give me ringlets!"

"Lovelocks," she corrected. "Don't complain about them being uneven; the right side is supposed to be longer than the left." Tory took a pair of scissors and cut a long strand from her own black hair. "This is for your mustache, but I won't attach it until just before you go down tonight. Do you have your costume?"

"I have a lace shirt, black satin knee breeches, tall leather boots, and a wide-brimmed hat. I have many brocade coats and vests; since you're the expert, what color do you suggest?"

"Charles preferred dark colors to add to his majesty. Now I must see to my own costume. I need silver ribbon and I believe there's a hideous gown in the wardrobe that will supply my needs."

Two hours later, Victoria went up to Falcon's chamber, wearing her jade silk gown that draped across one shoulder. She had crisscrossed silver ribbon about her breasts and waist à la Grecian style. With the curling iron she had fashioned her dark hair into a myriad of curls and tendrils and allowed them to cascade over silver ribbon. She had sewn an eye mask from the green silk material and she was wearing her carved jade earbobs.

"You look regal as a goddess and ethereal as a wood nymph at the same time, my beauty. The way your toga clings to your curves will guarantee you the center of attention. I wish I could have supplied you with a silver bow and arrow to perfect your costume."

Tory smiled her secret smile. "I have an accessory that will draw every eye. Let me help you with your coat, Your Gracious Majesty, then I shall glue on your mustache."

"It's bloody cruel to try to make me laugh." Falcon had chosen black brocade embroidered with gold.

Tory touched up his scar and painstakingly affixed the thin mustache that stretched across his top lip and partway across his cheeks. With the black silk eye mask in place, he looked convincingly saturnine. When he donned his cavalier hat she declared him perfect.

Falcon bowed and held out his arm. "Shall we go down, my beauty?"

They began to descend the stairs, then Tory drew him into her chamber. "One final touch." She pulled his black curls forward to conceal his scar. Then she took a royal purple ostrich feather from a powdered wig, pinned it to his hat, and curved it down across his right cheek. Their eyes met and they knew they were playing for high stakes. *Fortune favors the bold.*

Tory stepped back and blew Falcon a kiss. "Go down and greet your guests, my love. I intend to make a grand entrance."

Hawkhurst arrived at the same time as his four earliest guests. As he had predicted, Lord Sackville and elderly Lord Firle were both dressed as King George, complete with white wigs, powdered faces, and star-and-garter decorations draped across their chests. *Not much of a stretch.*

The ladies' costumes, however, were quite out of character. Lavinia was masquerading as a shepherdess and Joan a nun. Falcon murmured to Lady Firle, "You have a sly humor, Joan."

"Charles, darling, if you'd like a religious experience, join me in the confessional!"

"Washing away my sins would take all night, my dear."

Lord and Lady Goodwood arrived next. She was gowned as Queen Eleanor of Aquitaine, complete with crown, and Lavinia and Joan both seethed that she was royalty while they were mere commoners.

Hawkhurst was amused that his noble guests were early, proving their eagerness to role-play. The government officials, including the customs officer and the magistrate, were late arrivals, revealing their lack of enthusiasm for frivolity. Falcon's tension mounted as he awaited Drudge. The first few minutes would be a test. He must allay any suspicion the captain might harbor.

The large chamber was filled and many were dancing to show off their costumes when Drudge arrived. He was dressed as a sea captain and Hawkhurst felt his neck prickle a warning. "Captain, let me see if I can rustle up some navy grog."

Drudge's eyes narrowed as he scrutinized King Charles Stuart. "Two nights ago, I set a trap aboard the *Boulogne* for the marauding devils who are fast becoming the scourge of the Sussex coast. I believe I wounded their leader."

"You shot one of them? Good work, captain. What about their ship? Did you sink it? I thought I heard cannon fire that night."

"We sighted no ship, my lord."

"Marauders without a ship?"

"They rowed out from shore in a boat."

"You fired cannon at a fishing boat and missed?"

"The crew of the *Boulogne* fired the cannon, Lord Hawkhurst. I was armed with only my sword."

Suddenly, a female screamed and others gasped with alarm. Then a hush descended as all eyes turned toward the arched doorway. The goddess of the hunt made her grand entrance into the chamber. A leopard on a long, silver ribbon stalked before her.

All the guests, of course, had heard rumors of Pandora, Hawkhurst's pet leopard, but none had expected to come face-to-face with the beast. They backed away as Victoria slowly walked around the perimeter of the room. She made a deep curtsy to King Charles and then without a word she arose and departed. A babble of excited voices filled the chamber, drowning out the music.

"I'll take that drink now, my lord," Drudge declared. His voice revealed his inner agitation. "Make it a double."

*Tory deliberately made herself the center of attention. She did it for me . . . and just at the right moment.*

By the time the captain of the militia had finished his drink, Victoria returned without her hunting companion. She walked directly up to Drudge and gave him a radiant smile. "Captain, I cannot resist a man in a uniform. How would you like to play with me tonight? Cards or dice . . . whatever you desire." Her glance lowered to his breeches and she smiled her secret smile.

At that moment Thomas Carswell came up, removed his black hood, and asked her to dance. She saw the look of rivalry that the militia captain and the customs officer exchanged and decided to intensify the enmity. "Captain, I so love to dance. I'm sure you won't mind waiting for me. Save me a seat at the gaming table."

Carswell led Tory onto the dance floor. "You are an extremely courageous young lady to handle a leopard."

Tory saw that Carswell was dressed as a hangman. She wondered if it was a veiled threat and decided to issue one of her own. "Pandora is quite gentle, but only with family members, of course. She guards us fiercely and would attack if either Falcon or I were ever threatened."

When the dance ended, Tory invited Carswell to the card table. She sat between the two rivals, who were now openly scowling at each other. "I shouldn't play. . . . I've overspent my allowance and my brother will be furious if I lose any more of his money."

"It would be my pleasure to cover your losses, Mistress Palmer."

"How very gallant of you, Captain Drudge." Tory picked up her cards and gave her attention to Thomas Carswell. "I warrant your job as customs officer was far more lucrative when the export of wool was illegal. I understand that port officials were offered bribes. Now that the French can get their wool from Ireland without problems, bribery has become rare."

Carswell stiffened. "Bribery is nonexistent, Mistress Palmer, now that I am in charge."

*You mean the smugglers are so well organized, they don't need to grease your palm.* "Such authority—it makes a lady weak just thinking about it. I feel very protected sitting between two upright pillars of law and order whose morals are incorruptible."

Tory lost an ample amount of Carswell's money and then, to be scrupulously fair, she began to lose Drudge's silver.

When the party was over, Falcon slipped a possessive arm around Tory and drew her close as they ascended the tower staircase to their chamber. "I hereby declare your suggestion of a masquerade a resounding success. You came down from Olympus to mingle with mere

mortals tonight, my love, and kept my enemies well occupied."

She gave him a seductive glance. "I serve at the pleasure of His Majesty the King."

# CHAPTER 8

"How would you like to go for a sail aboard the *Seacock*?"

"Falcon, I'd love it above all things!" Tory then had second thoughts. *What if he's going roving?* She had just removed the stitches from his cheek and applied tormentil.

He placed his fingers beneath her chin and lifted her face. "Banish that look of anxiety, sweetheart; we sail for pleasure, not business, and sea air helps to heal wounds."

Tory smiled. "Where will we go?"

"The Strait of Dover is most pleasant for sailing, providing we go before the autumn gales start to blow."

"It sounds wonderful! When shall we leave?"

One of the things he found so exciting about her was how ready and eager she was for adventure on a moment's notice. "Tomorrow, if you can be packed and ready. You'll need warm garments, no diaphanous gowns. It can be brisk on the sunniest days. I'll lend you one of my wool cloaks to wrap up in."

Tory opened his wardrobe. "May I have this dark

blue one? I'd better shorten it and take up the hem or I'll be tripping and falling overboard."

"I would dive in and rescue you, my love. You must know I couldn't live without you."

Victoria sighed. "I love you, Falcon Hawkhurst."

The following day, Tory stood at the rail of the *Seacock* as it glided down the River Rother toward the coast. She was filled with excitement as the breeze ruffled her hair and she breathed in the salt tang of the sea air as if it were the elixir of life.

When the ship reached the sea and moved into the strait, Falcon beckoned her to come up to the forecastle, where he stood at the *Seacock's* wheel. "Look back, Tory. Those are the chalk cliffs of Dover that give the strait its name."

"I've been atop the cliffs, looking out to sea, but I've never seen them from this vista. They are quite breathtaking."

"It's comforting to know they still stand sentinel a hundred years hence." He grinned. "Do you suffer from mal de mer?"

"I'm not sure. I've never sailed before."

"If you start to feel queasy, I have ginger wine in my cabin."

Tory let her head fall back so she could watch the sailors in the rigging as they unfurled the sails. Her hair flew about in wild disarray. Terns and gulls screamed and dipped around the tall mast and the sound of the ship's bow cutting through the waves set up a rhythm she could feel in her blood.

Falcon turned the wheel over to his first mate and took Tory on a walk around the deck. "You have to get your sea legs. It's a matter of balance; match your gait to the ship's roll." They laughed together. "You stagger like a drunken sailor."

They enjoyed a lunch of prawns and curried rice and, to be on the safe side, Tory tried the ginger wine. "I like spicy things."

Falcon stole a kiss and rolled his eyes. "Me, too."

In the afternoon, they went back up to the forecastle and Falcon took over the ship's wheel. "How would you like to sail the *Seacock*?"

"Will you show me how?" Excitement glittered in her eyes.

"Such a willing pupil!" he teased. "Come, take the wheel." His strong brown hands covered hers. "To keep a ship on a steady course is not difficult once you learn the secret. You must feel the wind on the back of your head. Never let it come past your right or left cheek."

Tory did as he instructed and glanced up at him over her shoulder. "Is that all?" she asked in disbelief.

He whispered in her ear, "As simple as making love, once someone has taught you its secrets."

She felt his hard body brush against her buttocks and desire flared up in her and raced through her blood like wildfire. When he pulled her back against him, he shuddered with need and pressed his lips to the nape of her neck.

Falcon summoned his first mate to take over the wheel and he swept Tory into his arms and carried her below to his cabin. The next two hours were filled with delicious, potent lovemaking as they unleashed the fierce desire that had been building all day.

He wrapped her in the warm wool cloak before they went back up on deck. He found her a seat facing west on a great coil of ship's rope. "There should be a magnificent sunset. You'll have a front-row seat. In the next two hours you'll see the clouds turn fuchsia, edged with brilliant gold. Then the sky will be washed with magenta as the sun starts to slowly sink. When it touches the water, it will disappear rapidly as if the sea is swallowing it."

She turned to look at him and something caught her eye. "Is that land I see in the distance?"

"Mmm, I warrant it's the coastline of France." He changed the subject. "I'd better go and take my turn at the wheel."

In two hours, when the sea had swallowed the ball of fire, the sky was completely dark. The wind seemed to have lessened and Tory carefully made her way to the forecastle. "Ahoy there, mate!"

"Come on up and watch the stars come out, sweetheart."

She climbed the stairs and Falcon slipped an arm around her. She raised her eyes to the heavens and gazed in awe. The sky had turned to black velvet with a million sparkling diamonds scattered across it. It was the sort of night that made her believe in the reality of intangible realms, when she *knew* that nothing was impossible. Tory sighed happily. "I'll remember this always."

"Down anchor!" Falcon's order shattered her reverie. "Since the wind has dropped we might as well ride out the night in this sheltered cove. We'll join the crew in the galley for dinner."

Before they went belowdecks she saw a light on the shore. "Is that a French village?"

"Cap Griz Nez, not really a village, just a few farmhouses."

"You've been here before."

"It's the closest point to England and a safe haven."

In the galley Falcon and Tory sat at a long table for a very informal meal. The crewmen were more than a little rough around the edges, but Tory never stopped laughing at the jibes they tossed at one another. She tasted rum for the first time and was quite tipsy by the time Falcon put her to bed.

Just before midnight, when he was sure his companion was sound asleep, Hawkhurst slipped from the berth and silently quit the cabin. Within minutes the longboat was lowered and in just over an hour it was being rowed back to the *Seacock* with a cargo of a dozen crates wrapped in oilskins.

Tory was roused from sleep by the movement of the ship. She opened her eyes, saw that it was morning, and knew they were under way. Falcon opened the cabin door and sat down on the berth.

"The rum had its way with you. How's your head this morning?"

"Was I very drunk?"

"Legless!" He grinned.

"I must have slept it off. Amazingly, I feel fine. What on earth is that divine smell? The air is thick with it. Oh, I know, it's chocolate!"

Falcon gave her a quizzical glance. "You're familiar with it?"

"It's one of my favorite things to drink."

His brows drew together in consternation, then he banished the frown. "So much for my surprise."

Tory put her head on one side to study him, then realization dawned. "Surprise, my arse! You think well on your feet, Lord Bloody Hawkhurst. You came for a contraband cargo of chocolate and intend to smuggle it past the customs officials."

He looked outraged at her suspicion. "I have no such intention." Then he winked. "We have to ditch it before we let the customs officer come aboard the *Seahawk*."

Tory gasped. "But what about the smell of chocolate?"

His arms swept around her and he drew her close. "Your first instinct is to protect me and my ship, in spite of the fact that I tried to deceive you. You are my dearest coconspirator. Don't worry about the smell. The *Seacock* is prepared."

"I only overlook your deceit because I adore chocolate."

"Nay, you accept me with all my flaws because it's *me* you adore, not chocolate."

"Cocksure devil!"

"Did you know chocolate comes from the seedpods of the cacao tree in Portuguese Guinea near the equator? They must be fermented, then shipped to Portugal, where they are dried and roasted. I have a standing order every year with a Cap Griz Nez merchant for a dozen sacks of cacao beans."

"Their journey from the equator to Bodiam is as exotic and miraculous as mine from Victorian times."

"'Tis for exactly the same purpose—to give pleasure."

"Let me look at your scar." She brushed his hair back. "The angry redness has faded. It will be invisible on a dark and moonless night," she teased.

"I suggest dry biscuits and ginger wine to keep your stomach on an even keel. If you come on deck, wear the warm cloak. There's been a sea change; the wind's brisk and the swells are high."

It was dusk before the Dover cliffs came into view and Hawkhurst took advantage of the northeast wind to carry the ship southwest. The crew dropped the cargo near Romney, where the crates would be carried into the salt marsh on the tide. He then took the *Seahawk* back out to sea and once more let the wind take her. Then he turned so his ship could sail into Rye from the opposite direction.

Down in the hold, his first mate opened a heated barrel of tar. The acrid odor obliterated any trace of the chocolate fragrance. Falcon dropped anchor at the Rye

Bay Customs House, swung over the rail, and hailed one of Carswell's men. He followed Hawkhurst aboard and they took a lantern below for a cursory inspection of the hold. When they emerged, Carswell was standing on the deck.

"You're too late, Tom. I've already bribed your man here." Falcon winked. "For a bottle of French brandy he turned over his cutlass and offered to throw in his sister."

Carswell didn't laugh. "I must perform my duty, Lord Hawkhurst. Have you any goods to declare?"

"Not a herring." He handed him the lantern and jerked his thumb toward the hold. "Be my guest. Speaking of sisters, I took mine for a sail to the Isle of Wight yesterday before the autumn gales threaten. Lord Carisbrooke invited us to the castle. Confidentially, he's looking for a bride, but Tory isn't keen."

"Good evening, Mr. Carswell." Victoria had put off her cloak to catch his eye. "You conduct yourself with such authority, sir, it quite takes my breath away. May I accompany you while you inspect the ship?"

"Mistress Palmer, it would be an honor." He held the lantern high and moved toward the hold. "Mind your step, my dear."

On the stairs she took his arm and held it tightly as if she were afraid of falling. "Ugh, why do ships always smell of tar?"

"Ship's timbers are caulked with tar to keep them waterproof. 'Tis a necessary evil, I'm afraid."

"Like customs officers," she said sweetly.

"We are necessary, but hardly evil, my dear."

She threw him a mischievous glance. "I'm teasing you, Thomas." Tory went back up the steps ahead of him, affording him a generous glimpse of her trim ankles. "Goodnight, Mr. Carswell. Falcon, do hurry and haul up the anchor, I'm freezing to death."

"Good night, Carswell. Your vigilance is commendable." Falcon picked up Tory's cloak and draped it about her shoulders. "And your cockteasing is shameless," he murmured.

Tory stood at the ship's rail as it glided up the river and docked close by the castle. Relief washed over her that they were home safe, yet she knew marauding and smuggling were in Falcon's blood. How long would it be before he'd be off roving again?

Victoria didn't have long to wait. The following night, after they watched Pandora swim beneath the light of the waning moon, and they returned to their tower chamber, she became alarmed when she saw Falcon change into dark clothes and remove his seal ring.

"You cannot go for the chocolate tonight. The moon is out and there is no cloud cover."

"Sweetheart, it's not a smuggling run through Ashdown Forest. The cacao beans are destined for Bodiam. It will only take six of us to transport the entire dozen crates. Besides, there's a low mist coming in from the sea that will give us cover at the marsh."

"If it's only for Bodiam, why the devil didn't you simply pay the excise tax on the bloody cacao?"

He winked. "Contraband chocolate tastes so much sweeter."

"Moonlight is an omen—omens are ominous. Don't go."

"You are full of portents tonight, like a pagan dryad reading her rune stones. I prefer to read my tide tables. If it makes you feel better, Tory, I'll take my pistols."

*That makes me feel worse!* "I'm coming with you."

She went to the wardrobe to get the boy's garments she'd worn when she'd gone to the Romney Marsh before.

"To prove how little risk there is, I'll agree to take you along." He loaded his pistols and when she was dressed he held one out. "Don't forget to fully cock before you shoot." Falcon stuck his weapon in his belt and with bravado she copied him.

He took a signaling lantern up to the battlements and waited patiently until he got his reply. He came back down, wrapped Tory in the wool cloak she'd shortened, and pulled a hat down over her eyes. "Don't move farther away from me than pissing distance."

They left Bodiam and rode at a measured pace toward the village. Tonight nothing seemed to loom out of the blackness as it had the last time. The trees and buildings did not appear ominous; they were merely dark shadows touched by silver.

Once again riders fell in behind them, but Tory knew there were only a few, perhaps four by the sound of the muffled hooves. As they approached the sea, the rising mist swirled about their horses' hocks and when they reached the marsh, the tide was so low, the animals' hooves hardly made a splash.

*The fog will make it difficult to find the crates.* Tory refused to become alarmed, even though she realized the small number of boxes might be hard to locate in the vast marsh.

She saw two riders dismount and each lifted a pair of oilskin crates. When the others did the same, she realized that Falcon must have wisely roped the boxes together so that the tide need make only one deposit. Falcon dismounted and hooked two crates to Bess's ropes, then he counted the boxes to make sure they had all twelve and gave the men a thumbs-up.

Tory was relieved that the operation had taken such a short time and that her pony didn't need to be burdened tonight. They fell in line behind the other riders and left the marsh. She thought she heard the sound of hooves behind her in the distance, but when she turned she saw that the sea mist had risen to shroud everything. At the same moment she looked back, Falcon firmly took hold of her reins and led her into a line of trees. *He heard it, too!*

He did not quicken their pace, but held at a steady gait. Tory strained her ears to pick up the drum of hoof-beats, but all she could hear was the thunder of her own heartbeat. She noticed that the tree trunks were now closer together and knew Falcon had moved inland from the coast and had made his way into the forest.

Her eyelashes were covered with drops of mist and when she licked her lips, she tasted fear. Falcon let go of her reins and gestured for her to ride in front of him. Victoria shivered.

Suddenly, a shot rang out and the explosion made her almost jump out of her skin. She quickly covered her mouth to keep in the scream that was fighting to escape. Falcon stopped, turned in the saddle, cocked his pistol, and fired into the fog. An answering shot came almost instantaneously.

Tory's every instinct told her to bolt; instead she followed a bold impulse and drew the pistol from her belt. Her hand shook like a leaf, so in a flash she passed the pistol to Falcon, whose eager fingers seemed to be waiting for it. He cocked it, fired, and shouted, *"Go!"*

In less than a minute he was beside her and had taken her reins into his control. Falcon led Bess and the pony out of the trees so they could gallop hell for leather. *Either his ball hit its mark, or we've outridden them.*

Tory found nothing exciting about their ordeal. She had never been more afraid in her life. She had no idea where she was and placed all her trust in Falcon. She silently prayed that their mounts would get them back to the castle without stumbling.

At Bodiam the portcullis was up and they rode straight through. Within minutes all the men who'd gone on the run arrived. Without dismounting, Falcon ordered, "Drop your crates into the moat."

It suddenly occurred to Tory that one man was missing.

"Any sign of Dick?" Falcon asked tersely.

All four riders shook their heads. Falcon nodded and they left. "Tory, fetch Mr. Burke."

*Something has gone wrong. The man called Dick has been shot or taken.* Tory dismounted and ran to the castle to get Burke. When they returned, Falcon was inside the stable, where a groom had unloaded the pair of crates from Bess. Falcon stood leaning against his horse. Tory's heart began to race; instinctively she knew the trouble was much closer to home. "Falcon!"

He held up his hand to stop her questions and smiled at Mr. Burke. "I'm afraid you are going to have to help me, my friend."

That Hawkhurst needed help from anyone and worse, that he was asking for it, sent Victoria into a panic. *God Almighty, what's wrong?* Though every instinct screamed denial, she knew what was wrong. It had happened when he had made her ride ahead of him to shield her. *Falcon has been shot!*

# CHAPTER 9

Tory relieved Falcon of the pistols and Mr. Burke placed Falcon's arm around his neck to take most of his weight. When they reached the tower, Burke picked him up and carried him all the way to his chamber. He sat Falcon down on a wooden chair and knelt to remove his boots.

Tory set the pistols on his desk, threw off her cloak, and moved toward Falcon on unsteady legs. He helped her to remove his doublet, then, with tremulous hands, she took off his black shirt. She let out a long relieved breath when she saw no wound on his chest and no blood.

Falcon smiled to lend her courage. "I'm sorry, love. I took a ball." He gestured toward his back.

Burke was already at the door. "I'll get hot water."

Victoria was terrified to look at Falcon's back, but she had no choice. She lowered her lashes to mask her fear and moved behind him. High and just to the left of the center of his back, a black hole bubbled and oozed blood. *How in the name of God did you ride like the wind and manage to stay upright in the saddle?* "You must be in agony," she murmured.

He shook his head and smiled.

"It hurts when you speak!"

Again, he shook his head. "When I breathe."

"We'll get the ball out!" The words were to reassure herself as much as Falcon. She poured some brandy and held it to his lips. He managed to swallow some and she saw the gratitude in his eyes. She took his pulse. Though it was a bit rapid, it was strong.

"It missed your heart, Falcon," she assured him.

Mr. Burke returned with a bowl of scalding water, some clean linen towels, and a long metal instrument. She immediately knew it was to probe Falcon's wound for the lead ball.

She took the towels and spread them on the bed, then she and Mr. Burke helped Falcon move from the chair to lie prone on the bed. Burke gripped the instrument firmly and as gently as he could, inserted it into the frothing wound. She was appalled at how far it went in. Falcon did not cry out, but he coughed.

Mr. Burke groped about with the instrument, listening carefully for it to strike metal. Neither of them heard anything. "His heartbeat is strong," she assured Burke.

After a long drawn-out minute, Burke shook his head. Tory glanced fearfully at Falcon's face and saw that he had passed out. She blotted up the blood that was running more freely now. "Would you like me to try?"

"Yes—do it while he's unconscious. I cannot locate the ball."

She took the impaling instrument in her hand and by sheer dint of will forced herself to stop trembling. "Forgive me," she whispered and slowly inserted the probe to gently explore the wound. Her heart was in her mouth as she held her breath and continued the search. In spite of Tory's best effort, it was in vain. She shook her head at Mr. Burke, who took the instrument from her. She closed her eyes and tears seeped out from beneath her lashes.

Falcon coughed and it made him regain consciousness. They saw blood on his lips and both she and Burke instantly realized he would fare better in an upright position.

With tender hands they rolled him onto his right side and then propped him up with bolsters and pillows. Tory wadded up a linen towel and slipped it between the bubbling wound and the pillows.

"You couldn't get the ball." Falcon covered her hand and spoke slowly so he wouldn't cough. "It tore into my lung."

"Falcon, no!"

He waved away her protest. "If Drudge caught Dick, the game may be up. The captain may be on his way here."

"I'll go down and delay him if he comes." Burke took the bloody towels and the probe and Falcon's doublet and shirt.

After he left, Tory stripped off her boy's clothes and put on her corset and drawers. She put on her jade earbobs because she felt naked without them. Then she came back to the bed and bathed Falcon's face and wiped the blood from his lips. Her heart was in her eyes. "What can I do to ease your suffering?"

He shook his head and said simply, "Just love me."

"Oh, Falcon, I do. I love you with all my heart and soul."

Pandora pushed open the chamber door and came to investigate what was wrong. The leopard dropped a small leather pouch on the foot of the bed and moved to Falcon's side.

Tory opened the pouch. "It holds gold coins."

"She guards a hidden treasure." His breath was labored and he continued slowly, "I want you to have it."

"No! It's your treasure." She wiped his mouth and couldn't hide her panic.

"Get me a handkerchief, I'll do that."

She brought a linen handkerchief and tucked it into his hand.

"They're solid gold reales I marauded from a Spanish galleon. There's a large iron chest of them." He began to cough again.

"Did you sink the galleon, Falcon?" she asked with dread.

He shook his head. "She sank on her return voyage, though."

Pandora moved to the door and began to growl in her throat. Her tail began to lash from side to side.

"Someone's coming. Someone who's a threat," Tory cried.

Falcon gestured toward the door that led to the ramparts. Tory called the leopard and locked her outside where she would be safe on the roof. He then gestured for Tory to get into bed. Almost overcome with fear, she obeyed him.

They heard voices coming from the tower staircase. Mr. Burke was protesting loudly that Drudge had no authority and was intruding. The captain of the militia insisted he had every authority when he suspected a crime had been committed.

Mr. Burke opened the chamber door. "I'm sorry, Your Lordship."

Drudge stared with bulging eyes at the couple in the bed.

Falcon, reclining against a bolster, drawled, "Our secret's out. The captain has discovered you are not my sister." He coughed and dabbed his lips with the handkerchief.

"Captain Drudge, what in the name of heaven are you doing?" Victoria blushed up to her eyebrows.

"We shot a smuggler . . . perhaps more than one. I lost one of my militiamen."

Falcon raised an aristocratic eyebrow, as if to say, "What the devil does that have to do with me?"

"I suspected they were bringing contraband to Bodiam."

"You suspected wrong. Good night, Drudge."

The captain backed out and Mr. Burke firmly closed the door.

"Oh God, he suspects you, Falcon!"

"That's rather moot." He coughed and she jumped out of bed.

"Please don't say that. Don't give up," she pleaded.

"I'm a realist. . . . Don't be upset." He coughed again.

"Don't talk; it makes you worse." She heard Pandora scratch at the door and opened it for her. The leopard stalked about with raised hackles, then when she found Drudge gone, she calmed.

In a short time, Mr. Burke returned. "The captain has left. I pointedly reminded him you had friends in high places, my lord, and that you valued your privacy above all things. I doubt he'll be back tonight." He spoke to Tory. "Call me if you need me."

He was almost out the door when Tory picked up her boy's clothes and followed him. "I think you'd better burn these." She went out with him and closed the door. "Mr. Burke, I'm afraid. Falcon is talking like he's going to die!"

Burke looked at her with compassion in his eyes. "My

dear, he *is* going to die. His lung has collapsed; that's why his wound was bubbling air. He is slowly hemorrhaging. In a few hours, it will fill with blood, and, sadly he won't be able to survive."

Tory found she could not speak, but she nodded her understanding. She went back to the bed and pulled up a chair. On the inside she was a seething mass of fear, dread, and panic. *How will I bear it? What in the name of God am I going to do without him?* Firmly, she pushed aside all thought of the future. She had him for the next hours and that time was infinitely precious. She calmed and showed him only serenity and love.

Falcon closed his eyes and seemed to sleep, but his breathing was labored and occasionally he gasped for air. Tory's gaze never left his face. She memorized every line: the shape of his raven-wing eyebrows, his straight nose and flaring nostrils, the laugh lines around his dark eyes. She studied the scar that stretched from in front of his ear to his jaw. It had healed well and when she thought of how stoic he'd been while she stitched it, the lump in her throat threatened to choke her.

Sometime in the long, dark hours between midnight and dawn, Falcon stirred and had a coughing spell. When it was over, he asked for his ring. He patted the bed and she knew he wanted her to lie next to him. Tory carefully slipped under the covers and propped herself against the pillows, facing him. She clasped his hand possessively and tried to put his ring on his finger.

"You made a long journey, Tory. Thank you for coming to me."

She squeezed his hand. "You taught me that life is joyful. I've cherished every single moment."

He struggled for breath. "You proved there is no such thing as time. Keep my seal ring. I'll find you again, Tory."

She slipped the gold ring onto her thumb. "I won't let you go, Falcon."

He gasped and she had to listen very closely to his words. "Love is more powerful than death. I'll find you no matter where you are."

"I'll be right here, Falcon. Always. You are my soul mate."

The lovers spent the next hours touching, but not talking. The silence was broken only by Falcon's gasps for breath.

As dawn began to lighten the sky he gripped her hand. "Tory . . . you . . . are . . . going . . . to . . . have . . . to . . . let . . . me . . . go. . . ."

*I cannot! I cannot!* She drew in a shuddering breath. *Think about him, not yourself, Tory.* She leaned over and kissed his brow. "Au revoir, darling."

Her eyes flooded with unshed tears, blurring his face. Falcon drew his last shuddering breath and her tears overflowed and ran down her cheeks in rivulets of sorrow.

Tory's mind drifted away to a happier time, to a place where her heart didn't ache and she wasn't alone. She had no idea how long she remained in a suspended state, but Pandora got to her feet and began to growl deep in her throat.

Tory sprang from the bed and approached the door. The voices on the stairs told her that Captain Drudge was back. *I must convince him that Falcon was neither pirate nor smuggler. Lord Hawkhurst's noble reputation must not be smeared!*

Before she could open the chamber door, it was thrown open and she backed away as she saw Mr. Burke, Captain Drudge, and a militiaman on the threshold. Tory's eyes flew to Mr. Burke's. "Falcon's gone."

"Lord Hawkhurst is deceased. Show some respect, Drudge!" Mr. Burke demanded grimly.

"Good God, I suspected him all along. It was my bullet that killed him," Drudge declared.

"Nay!" Victoria denied. "Lord Hawkhurst was giving me target practice. I accidentally shot him with his own pistol."

Drudge turned to his man. "Arrest the whore!" Both pushed past Mr. Burke and came into the chamber, their purpose clear.

Pandora lashed her tail and crouched. Then she launched herself at Drudge's throat and sank in her fangs. Tory screamed and rushed toward the door that led up to the ramparts. She flew through the door and slammed it shut. Within a minute she realized that she had trapped herself up on the tower roof. She ran to the wall, looked down, and shuddered.

She couldn't go back. They would arrest her for Falcon's murder and likely Drudge's as well. Tory knew she was cornered; she had absolutely nowhere to go.

All at once she heard Falcon's voice. "Tory, jump!"

With trembling limbs she climbed onto the crenellated wall, but she was rooted to the spot, overwhelmed by the height.

Falcon's voice came again. "Darling . . . don't be afraid."

She wasn't afraid of the water, only the height.

"If you can't dive, then jump," Falcon urged.

Tory gathered her courage, focused her attention on the thought of Falcon, and made her decision to place her trust in him, as she had always done before. She closed her eyes and jumped.

The water of the moat closed over her head as her body plunged deep. She experienced an odd, out-of-body sensation and wondered if the impact had killed her. Tory felt strangely ambivalent. *Without Falcon, do I even want to live?*

# CHAPTER 10

Peregrine Fuller was standing atop Bodiam's round tower as he did every morning at this hour. The girl he had asked to marry him had disappeared more than a month ago. It seemed she had vanished while visiting his castle of Bodiam.

The entire town of Hawkhurst had searched for her in Ashdown Forest and along the banks of the River Rother, fearing she'd had an accident. She had been gone so long without a trace that rumor had it Victoria Carswell had run away. Her mother, however, had different ideas and had charged Sir Peregrine with her disappearance.

None felt the loss more acutely than Fuller. Though he'd had no hand in it, he felt guilty by association since she'd gone missing while visiting Bodiam. He harbored a fear that she had run off rather than accept his proposal of marriage. Each morning he stood atop the tower to look down at the river where he had first seen the water sprite bathing naked.

*Splendor of God, I think that's Victoria!*

Fuller ran down the spiral staircase at full speed,

flung open the door that led out to the stone balcony, and without even kicking off his boots, he dove into the moat.

Her arms and her hair were floating out from her body when he grabbed hold of her and his heart filled with joy that he had finally found her alive.

She wrapped her arms tightly around his neck and the ecstatic look on her face told him how happy she was to be rescued. "Falcon, you are alive!"

Tory clung to him sweetly as he towed her to the balcony and passed her up to his waiting manservant. Peregrine climbed from the moat and took Tory in his arms. He carried her up the spiral staircase and though her body was limp and her eyes closed, he knew she was breathing and that she would recover. He laid her gently down on the bed and turned to his man. "Go to the church and get Mistress Carswell's brother Edmund."

Though Peregrine knew he should send word to Victoria's mother, there was so much rancor between them that he chose to communicate with Tory's brother instead. When his man left, Sir Peregrine stripped off her wet corset, wrapped her in his velvet bed robe, and then removed her wet drawers. He pulled back the covers and put her into the bed.

Tory opened her eyes, heaved a huge sigh of relief, and smiled.

"Are you feeling all right?" He was worried about her mental state. "You called me Falcon."

She stuck up her thumb that held his gold seal ring and laughed. "That's your name, Lord Hawkhurst."

Sir Peregrine's brow creased. "I have an identical ring bearing the image of a peregrine falcon." He lifted his hand to show her. "Where did you get yours?"

"You gave it to me. After you were shot. Don't you remember?"

The furrows in his forehead deepened. "Victoria,

how did you come to be in the moat this morning? Do you remember? Everyone has been searching for you for a month. I've sent for Edmund."

Tory stared at him aghast. "God in Heaven, you are not Falcon, you are Peregrine. I've come back in time!" She turned her face into her pillow and began to sob.

Sir Peregrine felt alarmed. The things she said didn't quite make sense. When he dived into the moat to save her, she had seemed ecstatic, but now she seemed overwhelmed with grief. Her sorrow touched his heart. He had no idea what was wrong, but more than anything he wanted Victoria to be happy. He took dry garments from his wardrobe and went below to change from his soggy clothes. When he returned she was still crying.

Eventually she stopped sobbing. She lifted her face from the pillow and gave him a withering glance.

"Something's wrong. Can you tell me what it is?" he asked.

"I don't want you to be *Peregrine*! I want you to be *Falcon*!" she cried passionately.

"I'll be Falcon if you wish it. The name is interchangeable."

"Don't patronize me, Sir."

He was saved from having to make a reply when he heard footsteps on the stairs. He opened the chamber door to admit his manservant with Victoria Carswell's brother on his heels.

"You've found her. Heaven be praised." Edmund strode to the bed, took his sister's hand, and brushed the wet hair from her brow. "Tory, are you all right? Where on earth have you been?"

A lump came into her throat at the sight of her brother's face. It reflected love and relief in equal measure.

"I went back a hundred years in time, Edmund. It

was unbelievable! I traveled back to 1737 when Falcon, Lord Hawkhurst, owned Bodiam Castle."

Edmund glanced at Sir Peregrine with alarm. "She's had some sort of a shock, I believe. We had better get the doctor."

"Yes, I agree completely, Reverend Carswell. I held off sending for him until you got here." He turned to his servant. "Mr. de Burgh, would you kindly take a note to Doctor Cowper?"

"De Burgh?" Tory stared at the servant. "Isn't that French for Burke?" she asked.

"Yes, de Burgh is Norman French. In English it is Burke."

"Do you remember me, Mr. Burke?"

"Of course, Miss Carswell. We met when you visited Bodiam Castle on two occasions in September."

Tory shook her head in exasperation. *Why can't I make them understand?* "Do you see these exotic Chinese jade earrings? Falcon gave them to me. His sailing ship was the *Seacock*."

She saw her brother and Sir Peregrine exchange another look. "I know I am asking you to suspend your belief in all that's rational, but I did go back in time. That's where I've been for a month. Bodiam Castle was magnificent a hundred years ago. Every chamber was furnished with as many authentic artifacts as when it was originally built in the fourteenth century. Don't you see I am the only one who has the knowledge to restore the castle?"

"Well, wherever you've been, Tory, I'm glad you are back," Edmund declared. "I must go and tell Mother that you are safe."

Victoria sighed. "Yes, of course you must. Would you bring some of my clothes? I don't have anything to wear."

"I didn't realize. I will accompany Mother. . . . You'll need a buffer against her inevitable outrage, I'm afraid."

"Edmund, you are a dear brother, but I am not afraid of Mother. Not anymore. Her values and mine are not the same. Actually, they never have been. I'll face her and answer all her questions. Perhaps it's wicked of me, but I'm rather looking forward to it."

Edmund left to apprise their mother of the situation and Mr. de Burgh went to fetch the doctor. Alone with Sir Peregrine, Victoria stared at him, comparing him with Falcon. He was the same age and had the same powerful build. Their dark eyes and hair were indistinguishable. His looks were almost identical to Falcon's and Tory resented him for it.

She lowered her lashes to mask her true feelings. "Thank you for helping me. Since I disappeared on the day I visited Bodiam, it must have been disquieting for you, to say the least."

His dark eyes searched her face. "How did you come to be in the castle moat this morning?"

"I jumped from the round tower."

"My tower?"

Tory raised her lashes. "It was Falcon's tower."

"It is over sixty feet high," he pointed out.

"Yes, I was afraid to jump, but Falcon promised to catch me."

"I see."

*It was you who were there for me. Though I don't want to admit it, you and Falcon are the same man.*

"Why don't you rest until the doctor arrives?"

"Thank you." She watched him leave and close the chamber door. Her glance traveled around the room. The furnishings were not the same, although his wardrobe and his desk occupied the same places that Falcon's had. She raised her arm and sniffed the sleeve of the velvet robe. His evocative male scent was identical and her heart ached at the poignant memento.

Her mind drifted off to that other time; looking back, it seemed mystical and yet it had been so real, she could still taste it and smell it. Her emotions were bittersweet, for she sensed that she would never be able to go back again.

Tory's mind gradually came back to the present time. She got out of bed and observed herself in the looking glass. Her hair was a dreadful mess, so she picked up a towel from the washstand and began to rub it through her long, dark tresses. When she heard voices on the stairs she dropped the towel and hurried back to bed. She heard a polite knock and called, "Come in."

Sir Peregrine entered, along with Dr. Cowper and a young female servant. The maid was the one who had been in attendance at dinner the night Victoria had been invited to dine at Bodiam.

Tory made up her mind in an instant. *The only person I want to convince that I've been back in time is Sir Peregrine. Since I stand no chance of convincing anyone else, I won't even try.*

Dr. Cowper stood beside the bed and looked down at her. "Mistress Carswell, how are you feeling, my dear?"

"I am a little weary, doctor, but otherwise I feel quite well."

Cowper lifted her eyelids, then asked her to open her mouth so he could look down her throat. "No bangs or scrapes to complain of?" When she shook her head, he took his stethoscope from his bag and listened to her chest. "Breathe deeply, please." He bade her turn around and listened to her back while he tapped it.

The doctor put away his instrument. "I can find no physical symptoms of illness. Your health seems excellent, my dear." He cleared his throat. "Have you any idea where you have been for the last month, Mistress Carswell?"

Tory smiled at the doctor. "I'm sorry, I can't remember."

"Ah yes. I've heard of cases like this, though I've never encountered anyone with such a memory loss before. Sir Peregrine pulled you from the moat this morning. Are you sure you recall nothing before that moment?"

She looked at him trustingly, with wide eyes. "The last thing I recall is being at Bodiam Castle." She glanced at Sir Peregrine and saw his shrewd eyes watching her. *He knows exactly what I'm doing, but he's too gallant to call me a liar.*

They heard voices outside the chamber and all recognized the bell-like tones of Edwina Carswell. Mr. de Burgh opened the door and cast an apologetic look at Sir Peregrine.

"Lady Carswell, do come in," Fuller invited.

Of course she was already in before the invitation left his lips. The long-suffering young reverend brought up the rear carrying a wicker basket that held some of his sister's garments.

"In the name of all that is decent and holy, I demand to know where you have been, Victoria!"

"Do you, Mother?"

Edwina elbowed Dr. Cowper aside. "What are you doing in Sir Peregrine Fuller's bed?"

Tory's glance swept the chamber. "I seem to be holding court."

"I will not suffer insolence from a daughter who has brought disgrace upon her family."

The doctor spoke up. "Mistress Carswell is not herself at the moment. She is abed because I have prescribed rest."

"Doctor Cowper, I demand that you examine my

daughter to ascertain if she is still a maiden. I suspect she has been in this castle for the past month with the connivance of Fuller. If he has taken advantage of her innocence, I demand satisfaction."

Victoria blushed deep pink. "Mother, how could you humiliate me like this before everyone?"

"Humiliate? I am the one who has been humiliated and shamed by your scandalous behavior, you young strumpet! Examine her immediately, doctor."

Sir Peregrine stepped between Edwina and the doctor. "That will not be necessary, madam. I have every intention of asking Victoria to marry me. There will be no scandal unless you make one, *Lady* Carswell."

"Humph, an offer of *marriage* is the only decent thing you can do. Keeping her at Bodiam Castle naked, without a stitch of clothing for a month! I cannot imagine what has gone on here."

"Can you not, Mother?"

Edwina turned to her son. "Edmund, you will marry them now."

Tory said, "He will not. I have not consented to a marriage."

"But you will . . . you *must*," Edwina declared emphatically.

"Must I, indeed? This is a private matter between Sir Peregrine and me. I think I'll take the doctor's advice and rest now. Goodbye, Mother. Thank you for bringing my clothes, Edmund."

After they left, Tory stayed in bed for an hour, but her thoughts were running in circles, with the past crowding out the present. She felt a compulsion to get on with her future, but the siren song of the past called to her. She reminded herself that there really was no past, present, and future—they were all one. If she held on to this idea she'd be able to embrace all three.

She got out of bed and called for a bath. She washed

her hair and wrapped her head in a towel, then she opened the wicker basket of clothes that Edmund had brought. As she lifted out each garment she became dismayed that she had ever worn such unflattering dresses. Finally the dismay turned to laughter. *Who on earth dictates the clothes that Victorian women wear? Surely it's not the young queen?* The high, frilled necklines, leg-of-mutton sleeves, and voluminous skirts covered every inch of skin beneath the chin that a female possessed. Even the colors were either dark or drab, which only added to her amusement. *Every garment I own serves as a horrible example of what not to wear!*

She chose the dress that was the least offensive shade. It was the pale mauve cambric she had worn the first time she'd come to the castle and it gave her pleasure only because it matched the color of her eyes. She took her brush from the basket and stroked her dark hair until it crackled. She smiled at her reflection as she remembered what Falcon had said the first time he saw her: *Why d'you wear your hair screwed into a knob?* Tory tossed her tresses over her shoulder. *No more knobs for me, Falcon my love!*

Tory could not resist going up the steps and out onto the tower roof. Right away she could see that Ashdown Forest had been cut back from where it was a hundred years ago and the sprawling town of Hawkhurst was no longer a village. She walked across to the river side of the castle and saw the Rother had changed little.

She gazed down into the moat. It was a long way down and she marveled at the courage she had summoned to make the jump. She suddenly realized that this was where Sir Peregrine must have been standing this morning when he saw her in the moat.

*I stood here, too, with no escape but the water below. How curious—we must have occupied the same space at the same time. I know we are inextricably connected, but can I make him believe?* Victoria smiled her secret smile. Teaching Peregrine that he was Falcon would be the challenge of a lifetime.

She felt his presence before she saw him. He came toward her across the crenellated roof. "I am delighted to see you have recovered, Mistress Carswell."

"My name is Tory, as well you know." She swept out her hand. "Ashdown Forest is wearing her brilliant autumn colors. It is no wonder you like to stand atop this tower. The view is breathtaking." She pointed to the river. "That's where the *Seacock* was moored."

"I have imagined it often. Did you know that the ship's bell beside the portcullis is the *Seacock's* bell? It came into the foundry one day as scrap metal and I rescued it."

"That's amazing . . . yet not amazing. Did you know that Lord Hawkhurst's name was Peregrine Palmer?"

"Since I am Peregrine Palmer Fuller, he was obviously my ancestor."

"Falcon is much more than your ancestor. . . . He is you, and you are he. His soul has been reborn in you. Do you believe that such a thing could be possible?"

He looked at her for a long time. "I like to think I have an open mind. I believe it is no more amazing to be born twice than to be born once."

"Your gold ring . . . how long have you had it?"

He looked at his hand. "I had it made about ten years ago. A peregrine falcon seemed to be an apt symbol for a seal ring."

Tory raised her hand and lifted her thumb so that they could compare the gold rings. "The two are identical, not only in design but also in size. Do you not find that curious?"

"It is indeed a coincidence."

"I do not believe in coincidence. Rather I believe that you once owned the ring I am wearing and something compelled you to recreate it. Our past shapes our present."

"Since I am passionate about history, I believe it to be true that our past can shape our present."

"Except there is no past, present, or future; they are all one."

"That is an interesting concept that most would find difficult to imagine."

"But not difficult for you, Sir Peregrine."

He smiled and changed the subject. "Are you hungry, Victoria?"

"Yes. Lunch is a most welcome suggestion."

He took her down to the dining room and seated her across from him. He poured her wine, then carved some slices from a cold leg of lamb and allowed her to choose her own vegetables.

"Do you remember the raw oysters, followed by winkles when we dined at . . . I'm so sorry, that was Falcon. I can't separate you."

"Did he look so much like me?" Peregrine asked, bemused.

"You are physically identical, but he was often lewd and occasionally rather coarse, and reckless beyond measure."

"You don't think me capable of lewdness or recklessness?"

"Perhaps all men are capable of such things, but I would hope not every day and night of your life," she teased.

"You will have to get to know me better to learn the answer."

"Tell me, do you own a matched pair of officer's belt pistols?"

His eyebrows arched in surprise. "How did you know?"

Tory shrugged. "I thought you might. When we've

finished lunch, I'd like to show you something in the courtyard."

"You know more of Bodiam Castle's secrets than I know."

"I warrant I do and perhaps I know *your* secrets, too."

Amusement danced in his eyes; Tory knew he enjoyed her company.

After lunch, the pair strolled out to the grassy quadrangle that was the castle courtyard. "One day I asked Falcon if he would teach me how to shoot. He brought me out here for target practice. He was a marvelous shot and put out the flames of two candles at twenty paces. He gave me his right-handed pistol and warned me of the dangers of going off half-cocked. I was hopeless, though I tried many times. I gave up when my lead ball hit the castle wall and chipped one of the stones. Let me show you the spot . . . it's right over here."

Sir Peregrine ran his fingers across the rough stone. "I never noticed it before, but it looks like it was done with a ball."

"Yes. When it happened, I knew it would be there for all time."

He grinned at her. "Did you leave anything else behind, Tory?"

*Apart from my virginity?* "The day before I left, we dropped some wooden cases wrapped in oilskins into the moat. They contained cacao beans that were grown in Portuguese Guinea. That was a hundred years ago. They've likely disintegrated by now."

"Most probably," he agreed. "You shivered. Let's go inside, you need a warm cloak today."

"Edmund didn't bring me a cloak, which is just as well. The garments he did bring are all hideous."

"I think the dress you are wearing is most fetching."

"Falcon would have found it *retching!* Female fashions in 1737 were absolutely exquisite. I'm certainly going to miss the clothes. The chamber below yours in the round tower was furnished for a woman and its wardrobe was crammed with gowns and female frippery. He told me they belonged to his sister, but of course I knew they had belonged to a mistress who had *slung her hook.*"

"The things you say fascinate me, Victoria. Let's go up and you can show me the chamber."

They went inside and climbed the spiral staircase of the round tower. The chamber she had thought of as *hers* was empty now, save for dust and cobwebs.

"The walls were covered with medieval tapestries that depicted mythical beasts. I had a huge curtained bed, a mirrored wardrobe and even a slipper bath that was hand-painted with roses."

Sir Peregrine took two steps that brought him close to her. "We could re-create the chamber, if it would give you pleasure."

His closeness made her feel breathless. "That is certainly within the realm of possibility."

"What are these secrets you hinted that you know about me?"

She put her head on one side and glanced up. "Though I have never seen you without your shirt, I warrant you have tattoos."

His dark eyes widened. "Would you like to see me without my shirt, Tory?"

She caught her breath. "That's not necessary. You have peregrine falcons tattooed on your forearms."

"Damn, everything you say lends credence to your story of going back in time. Yet how can such a thing be possible?"

She looked up at him and raised her fingers to stroke the birthmark on his cheek. "When I first met Falcon, his cheek was unmarred. Later, he received a sword slash that opened his cheek from ear to chin. I was the one who stitched it. I knew it would leave a livid scar, but it did not detract from his looks."

He captured her hand, holding her fingers against his cheek and looked into her eyes. "You fell in love with him, didn't you, Victoria?"

"Falcon was a pirate and a smuggler. . . . How could I not fall in love?" she whispered.

Peregrine bent his head and brushed his lips against hers. Then his mouth took complete possession and he kissed her passionately, unleashing the desire that had been riding him since the day weeks ago when he had first glimpsed the water nymph.

# CHAPTER 11

Tory closed her eyes and felt the kiss all the way to her toes. She was in Falcon's arms, pressed close against Falcon's heart, her mouth fused to his so perfectly, she wanted it to last forever. When she could think as well as feel, she was reluctant to open her eyes for fear the spell would be broken. She summoned the courage and lifted her lashes.

*He is still Falcon!* Her heart swelled at the realization that physically Falcon and Peregrine were the same man. Their touch, taste, and scent were thrillingly identical. His dark eyes looked deeply into hers and it seemed as if their souls touched. *We've known each other forever.*

"We haven't just met recently, Tory. I feel as if we have known each other intimately for years."

She smiled happily. "I feel that way, too."

"Good. Come upstairs, we have much to discuss and many decisions to make."

When they arrived in his chamber, Peregrine sat her down before the fire and took the other chair.

"Tell me honestly, do you believe the things I've been

telling you? Do you think it possible you are Falcon, Lord Hawkhurst?"

"The honest answer is: I don't know. Tell me about him."

"He told me that one day he was unpacking a shipment of tea he'd taken from an East Indiaman. He lifted the lid of one of the boxes and there to his amazement was a leopard kit. He decided to call her—"

Peregrine held up his hand to stay her words as a long forgotten memory stirred his imagination. "Pandora . . . he called her Pandora, I think."

"You *do* remember! Oh, this is wonderful!"

Peregrine shook his head. "It could have been a lucky guess. Everyone knows the mythological story of Pandora's box."

"Think hard. . . . do you remember having a leopard for a pet?"

"From the dim recesses of the past, I can vaguely picture her."

"In what setting do you see her?" she asked quickly.

"Swimming in the moat."

"Exactly! She did it every night at sunset."

"This Falcon was rather a flamboyant character. You said he was a pirate and a smuggler. Did such things not trouble you?"

"Not the smuggling. He didn't do it for his own benefit. He did it for the villagers of Hawkhurst, who were poor fishermen. They lived a hand-to-mouth existence and the money they made from their midnight treks with contraband made their lives easier."

"So, he had a compassionate heart for those less fortunate than himself. But what about his pirating?"

"It troubled me constantly. I begged him not to go and tried my damnedest to keep him at Bodiam on moonless nights. But it was in his blood. He craved the marauding and couldn't help himself."

"Yet in the history books no such lawless deeds were attributed to Lord Hawkhurst of Bodiam."

"Isn't that amazing? Captain Drudge, head of the militia, suspected him, but when he came to arrest him, Falcon was already dead from a bullet that had torn into his lung the day before. When Drudge ordered his man to arrest me, Pandora lunged at the captain and I warrant she tore out his throat.

"Lord Hawkhurst had a loyal manservant called Mr. Burke. I know he would do his utmost to see that no scandal was attached to Falcon. Burke was most efficient and completely trustworthy."

Peregrine scrutinized her face. "So Falcon died?"

Victoria spoke softly. "He died slowly, losing more and more of his essence. Death was a thief that moved into our chamber and there was nothing we could do about it. It ate away at my heart. At first I prayed that he would not die, but he suffered so much that before the night was over, I began to pray that he would."

"So your only escape was to jump from the tower?"

Tory nodded. "It was either death or travel back to my own time. I don't remember choosing. In fact, it didn't much matter to me. I didn't want to live without Falcon."

"So Fate chose for you and I am very glad that you came back."

"You believe my story?"

"A part of me believes you. That isn't of paramount importance, though. You are here and what happens next is what is vital."

Tory leaned forward to emphasize her words. "Just before he died, Falcon said: *Love is more powerful than death. I'll find you no matter where you are.*"

"If he had not died, you would not have come back, would you?"

"No. I would have stayed with him forever."

"So, Victoria, you *need* me to be Falcon?"

"I *know* you are Falcon!"

"If I were not," he held up his hand and added, "just for argument's sake, would you consider marrying me?"

"I *would* consider marrying you, Peregrine, because in my heart I am sure you are Falcon."

His smile held a trace of regret. "That isn't the answer I hoped for, but I will accept it, Tory." His eyes again searched her face. "You are not agreeing to my proposal because your mother said that you must, are you?"

"There are no scandalous accusations Mother could throw at me that would induce me to wed a man I did not wish to marry. I am also accepting because I believe with all my heart that you have a *tendre* for me. Whether you come to believe you are Falcon or not, I am sure we are well suited to each other, Sir Peregrine."

"Falcon is a far more masculine name than Peregrine."

"But he, too, was christened Peregrine."

"Yes, but he had the courage to change it."

"Would you like me to call you Falcon?" she asked eagerly. "It would please me above all things."

"Then by all means address me as Falcon. I'm sure I could easily become accustomed to such a romantic name."

"You truly are open minded." *We are halfway home, Falcon, my love!*

"I have much to take care of . . . a ring, for one thing. I want you to be wearing my betrothal ring before you return home."

Tory sighed. "Must I return home, Falcon?"

"I'd much prefer to keep you with me, if you are willing."

Tory threw him a saucy look. "I'm willing and eager. We need to become intimately acquainted."

Falcon swept her into his arms and brushed his burning lips against her temple. "Lord God, how you make me quiver."

"Let's be married soon. I'd like my brother Edmund to perform the ceremony."

"That would be perfect. You had a marvelous adventure, Tory, but the last hours were heartrending for you. We'll marry whenever you feel up to it. I'll be back soon—rest while I'm gone."

Sir Peregrine went downstairs and asked Mr. de Burgh to help him find a rope and a grappling iron. They found them in the stables, and then Peregrine led the way to the moat. "Let's drag along here. I'm searching for some oilskin-covered crates."

He and de Burgh took turns dragging the grappling iron, but their search seemed in vain. Then suddenly the iron hook caught on something that lay deep on the bottom and it took both of them to haul it up. Fuller knelt down to examine their find. The oilskin was intact, but when he cut it open with his knife, the wooden crate had fallen in upon itself and rotted along with its contents. It was impossible to identify what the oilskin had held by looking at the crumbled mass, but the aroma that rose up was unmistakable. The smell was indisputably chocolate.

"Thank you, de Burgh. I'm going into town for a while." Peregrine needed to be alone. He wasn't often given to introspection, but he had a lot to think about and much self-searching to do. Victoria was convinced that he had lived before at Bodiam Castle, a hundred years ago. *I am starting to believe such a thing is possible. Am I losing my grip on reality?*

He saddled Bess, rode beneath the portcullis, and headed toward Ashdown Forest. The trees had turned color but had not yet shed their leaves and the golden canopy above him captured and held a mystic sense of timelessness because it had looked the same for centuries. He knew the secret paths through the forest so well that he often imagined he'd ridden them on moonless nights to smuggle contraband tobacco and brandy.

He could imitate the hoot of the owls perfectly and whenever he did it, long-forgotten memories stirred in the deep recesses of what? His imagination? His heart? His soul?

The impressions that came to him most vividly were those of Victoria. Deep in his bones he was sure he had known her before, in another time, yet in this same place. They had laughed together, ridden together, sailed together, and they shared a passion for Bodiam.

When she had gone missing, Peregrine had assumed she had run off to London. Life with her mother was extremely restricting and he thought she had taken the risk for a chance at freedom. It had saddened him that she had felt she needed to escape from him also. His heart overflowed with joy now that she had returned and he knew he must not risk losing her again.

*I truly feel as if I loved her before. Nay, I never stopped loving her. . . . I love her still. She thinks of me as Falcon. . . . Am I ready to admit that I think of myself as Falcon?*

A hare crossed his path and for a brief instant he wondered if it were a magical shape shifter sent by the Celtic goddess Brigantia. He smiled, knowing he'd read about it in a book of myths. *Tory would enjoy that book; I must find it for her.*

His mind moved on to another book he'd read and words that the wise Solomon had said formed clearly in his mind: *The thing that has been is the thing that shall be; and the thing that is done is that which shall be done: There is nothing new under the sun.*

He thought about how Falcon had died. Apparently, a lead ball had torn into his lung and he had suffered a painful death. A few times in his life, during particularly cold winters, Peregrine had come down with pleurisy. Liquid gathering in the lung made it difficult to breathe and brought on coughing. The pain was often excruciating. *We have too much in common not to be the same man.*

He threw back his head and laughed. *I entered the forest as Peregrine and I shall leave it as Falcon.* He turned Bess around and rode toward the Port of Hastings, where he knew there was a fine goldsmith's shop.

Falcon knew which ring he would chose for his bride the moment he saw it. The emerald surrounded by diamonds stood out from the other rings as if they were set with glass. It was expensive and he bargained hard with the goldsmith for a price he deemed fair. Then he headed home to Bodiam Castle and the woman he loved.

Tory was watching for him from the tower windows. The moment she saw him she ran down the spiral staircase to greet him. "I'm so glad you are back; I missed you."

"What a lovely homecoming. Will you always welcome me home so eagerly?" He placed his fingers under her chin and raised her face so he could look into her eyes. "Will you call me Falcon?"

Her smile was radiant. "Oh, I will, I will!"

"I smell food. Are you hungry?"

"Ravenous," she declared happily.

"Then let's go and eat. I warrant that appetites should be satisfied whenever possible."

"There are many different kinds of appetites. It would be rather decadent to satisfy them all."

He cocked a dark eyebrow. "I can only try, sweetheart."

Tory blushed. Anticipation for the night that was yet to come filled her with excitement.

Hands clasped, they made their way to the dining room, where a fire had been laid. Brilliant autumn leaves stood in a large pewter jug on one side of the hearth, and a cast-iron holder stacked with logs sat on the other.

Falcon poured them port wine. "Perhaps you prefer French brandy?" he teased.

"Since it's no longer illegal, I don't. Contraband always tastes sweeter."

"Taking risks makes life sweeter."

"Damnation, we are birds of a feather!"

"A falcon and a dove?"

"That would make you a predator and me your prey. I would prefer to be something small and beautiful like a merlin."

"Merlin is most apt. You have cast a magic spell on me."

"I believe we each have a spiritual core."

"More and more you make me aware that we share a psychic resonance."

Falcon carved a wood duck with chestnut dressing and let Tory serve herself with roast potatoes, leeks, and braised carrots.

"This wine gravy is divine. Is Mr. de Burgh a French chef?"

"Bodiam's majordomo is a man of all trades. He has made life considerably more comfortable for a bachelor like myself."

"Mr. Burke was indispensable to Falcon in the last century. Perhaps he has always served the owner of Bodiam Castle since it was built in King Edward's time."

"You make me think all things are possible, Tory." He came around the table and pulled her into his lap. "Even that you will become my wife." He took the ring from his pocket and held it out to her on his palm. "I bought you a betrothal ring."

Tory's eyes were like stars as she looked at it and then at Falcon. She held out her finger so he could slip it on. "An emerald—how did you know my favorite color is green? It's a perfect fit." She touched his cheek. "*We* are a perfect fit."

He covered her hand with his. "I have *always* been self-conscious about my birthmark. Yet it doesn't seem to offend you."

"It endears you to me. I wish you didn't have it, but I'm the one who stitched your cheek back together when you were wounded."

"You have a long memory," he teased.

"But it is infallible," she declared. "It was preordained that we should meet. We, who love Bodiam Castle so much, were chosen to restore it to its original magnificence. I cannot wait to get started. . . . It will be a labor of love for both of us."

Falcon changed the subject. "Where would you like to go for your honeymoon, sweetheart?"

"Why to London, of course. We'll scour all the antique shops and warehouses searching out ancient treasures for Bodiam." She slid off his knee and took his hand. "Come, I'll take you on a tour and try to describe how everything was a hundred years ago."

Somewhat reluctantly, he followed her lead as she swept up the staircase and took him down the long passageway that led them to the minstrels' gallery. "See how dilapidated this railing is? In fact it's quite dangerous. Once, it was exquisitely carved, polished black oak. We will have to employ a wood-carver to duplicate the oak leaves and clusters of acorns. The balcony was draped with gold velvet and the chairs for the musicians were all high-backed with padded seats." She smiled at Falcon. "This was where I first glimpsed the Georgians being entertained at Bodiam.

"The floor of the ballroom down there was highly polished and there were half-a-dozen chandeliers that held myriad candles. The light was reflected by scores of crystals that dangled from the candleholders." Tory sighed. "It's such a sorry mess of dust and cobwebs, but we'll restore it to its original beauty in no time.

"There were buffet tables at this end for the guests' food and drink, and at the far end were gaming tables for card and dice games. Georgians were addicted to gambling, but I have to admit I quite enjoyed the risk involved, especially when I wasn't wagering my own money."

"Falcon was unfailingly generous with you, was he?"

"Not only Falcon. All the gentlemen were anxious to garner my favor." She rolled her eyes. "Falcon told them I was his sister."

"Well, I'm glad he . . . I . . . tried to protect your reputation."

"Come, I want to show you the library." She took his hand and urged him to follow through the archway and down the stone passage. "Down there is where the crew of the *Seacock* were accommodated. That's the oldest part of Bodiam, where the soldiers were originally garrisoned."

"I've only been in that section of the castle once. It needs so much renovation, I am intimidated by such a large undertaking."

"Liar, I warrant naught intimidates you." Tory looked about her uncertainly. "There are so many square towers, I'm not sure this is the right one. Falcon had his library on the ground floor of a square tower. It wasn't large, but it was extremely cozy."

"Down this passage is where I found some books stacked. I added my own to what was already here, but there are no shelves."

When they entered the chamber, Falcon lit a torch on the wall. The light fell on stacks of old books. Tory was distressed. "Heavens above, these books are rotting away. This is where we will start," she said decisively.

Falcon took her hands. "Tory, I'm afraid I have a confession to make. There isn't enough money left to refurbish Bodiam. When you disappeared, I thought you were gone for good. The idea of restoring the castle to its original condition without you at my side lost all its appeal. The heart went out of it for me. I spent at least half the money and I've made commitments for the other half that cannot be rescinded."

Tory looked at him as if she didn't comprehend what he was saying. "What do you mean, there's no money to refurbish Bodiam?"

"Exactly what I say. Oh, I have enough money for us to live comfortably, but restoring Bodiam will have to wait a few years."

"You frittered away a fortune in one short month?"

"I didn't fritter—"

"You devil! Apparently you inherited more than the castle from Mad Jack Fuller, you also inherited his insanity! For years he wasted his money building follies and other extravagant whims that earned him the well-deserved nickname *Mad Jack*. Now you are following in his footsteps!

"Bodiam Castle is an ancient treasure that came into your hands with a sacred trust attached. How can you have squandered the means that were heaven-sent to restore a part of English history? You are a careless, thoughtless devil! How could you, Falcon?" she cried passionately, pounding her fists into his chest.

He seized her hands. "You little hellcat, stop it!"

Tory wrenched her hands from his and folded her arms across her chest in a posture of defiant anger.

He gazed at her, unable to mask his regret. "It is clear that Bodiam means far more to you than I do, Victoria. How naive I was to think you were marrying me for love."

"I did love you!" she cried.

"Yes, but you love Bodiam Castle more."

"You asked me to marry you under false pretenses," she charged. "Your confession about the disappearance of the fortune you inherited should have preceded your proposal."

"I warrant I didn't tell you because I feared your refusal. Finally, my conscience wouldn't allow me to keep you in ignorance."

"A damned good thing your conscience began to prick you, Sir Peregrine, before you bedded me!"

He stiffened. "I think we have insulted each other quite enough for one night, Mistress Carswell."

"Indeed. Kindly have the portcullis raised. I cannot remain here a moment longer." Tory tossed her hair back over her shoulder and turned on her heel. *Don't cry! Don't you dare to cry, Victoria Carswell!*

# CHAPTER 12

"Well, young madam, it's about time you returned home. Are you married yet?" Edwina demanded, the moment her daughter stepped through the door of the priory.

"Hello, Mother. I'm so sorry to have caused you so much worry over the last month."

"Worry I can handle; I've been a martyr to worry all my life. 'Tis the *shame* that is difficult for me to bear. All will be whispering that you have been living in sin. Your father, God rest his soul, must be spinning in his grave."

"I cannot control the way people think. I am sorry for the scandal I have caused."

"No, you cannot control scandal, but you can diminish it by joining Sir Peregrine Fuller in holy matrimony. When is the wedding to be, Victoria?"

"We have no plans, Mother."

Edwina's look of shock would have seemed comical, had Tory found anything funny in her situation.

"Oh, my dear, is that an engagement ring I see on your finger?"

Tory glanced down at the lovely emerald and diamond ring she had forgotten all about. She decided not to disabuse her mother of the notion that it was a betrothal ring. At least it would buy her time tonight and allow her to escape to her own bedchamber.

They both heard Edmund open the front door of the priory.

"Victoria is home and you will be happy to know that your sister is betrothed to Sir Peregrine Fuller." She turned to her daughter but did not lower her voice. "Poor Edmund, it cannot have been easy for a man of the church to hold up his head under the shameful circumstances of his sister's disappearance."

*You are an expert at fostering feelings of guilt, Mother. Even though Father smoked in secret I warrant he was racked with guilt.*

Edmund was alarmed at how pale Tory looked. "Are you feeling all right? Shouldn't you be in bed after such an exhausting day?"

"I am tired, though I hate to admit it. I think I'll go up."

Edmund held out a supporting arm and Tory gratefully leaned against him and they headed toward the stairs. "Good night, Mother. I'll try to answer all your questions tomorrow."

As the siblings climbed the stairs, Edmund asked kindly, "This morning you were insisting that you had been back in time a hundred years. Have you banished all your strange thoughts now that you have returned to normal, Tory?"

"I don't suppose I'll ever be completely free of strange thoughts, and what the devil is *normal,* I'd like to know?"

He opened her chamber door for her. "Here you are—just as you left it. Get a good night's rest, Tory. Sweet dreams."

She closed the door and sagged against it, drained of

energy. Her thoughts were in disarray, her emotions were in turmoil, and her happiness lay in shards all about her. "Splendor of God, how am I going to face the future without Falcon?"

She did not bother lighting a candle. As she undressed, her hands began to shake from fatigue. She put on a fresh nightgown and slipped into bed. Victoria lay on her back staring up into the darkness. Her mind and her body felt strangely numb.

Her thoughts slowly began to form coherently. Minutely, she went over the things she and Falcon had said to each other that had made her temper flare and compelled her to walk out on him.

*It is clear that Bodiam means far more to you than I do, Victoria. How naive I was to think you were marrying me for love.*

"I did love you," she cried. *Yes, but you love Bodiam Castle more.*

"Is his accusation true? Do I love Bodiam Castle more than I love Falcon?" she whispered.

The answer came back immediately. "Falcon means more to me than life. It is true that I love Bodiam and long to restore it to its original magnificence, but I would love Falcon even if he were penniless and had no bloody castle!"

*Splendor of God, I never even gave him a chance to explain. He tried to tell me that he didn't squander the money, but I was in such a self-righteous fury, I refused to listen.*

"It's his bloody money, Tory. The man can do whatever he wants with it. It is absolutely none of your business!"

She sat up in bed, wrapped her arms around her knees, and regretted with all her heart the things she had said. *I must go and ask him to forgive me.* She threw back the covers. *I cannot go running to Bodiam Castle at this time of night just to assuage my conscience. And what if he refused to let me in? What if he no longer wants me? I'll go to-morrow. In daylight the things I said won't seem so dark and ugly.*

As Victoria waited for the castle's portcullis to be raised, her hand brushed over the ship's bell that had belonged to the *Seacock*. She would cherish forever her memories of sailing to France aboard the brigantine. She sighed and thanked the man on the gate. Then she straightened her shoulders, gathered her courage, and walked in the front door of Bodiam.

"Good morning, Mistress Carswell. Allow me to take your cloak and I'll tell Sir Peregrine he has a visitor."

"Thank you, Mr. de Burgh."

Beneath her cape Tory was wearing a gray wool dress. Its design was similar to the one that Falcon had slashed to ribbons because it was the *ugliest garment he'd ever seen*. She smiled, remembering how outraged she had felt at the time, but it had given her the chance to strut about in her corset and drawers, something that had done wonders for her female self-confidence.

De Burgh did not return. Instead, it was Falcon who came to greet her. "Victoria, I hope you've had a change of heart?"

"Oh, Falcon, I have!" She ran into his open arms. "I'm so sorry for the things I said last night."

"Hush, we'll have untold arguments over the next hundred years. It will keep our life from becoming dull as ditchwater."

"Let's go upstairs. I must apologize to lift the heavy load of guilt from me."

"There'll be no guilt between us, love; not today, not ever."

When they arrived at Falcon's chamber atop the round tower, Tory stood contritely before him. "I searched my heart and can solemnly vow that I love you more than Bodiam. My love for you is boundless, even if you become penniless and own no castle."

He took her hands. "I should have told you about the money before I asked you to marry me, Tory."

"It's really none of my business what you do with your money, Falcon. It was shameless of me to feel furious about it."

"I like it when you are shameless." He reached up and took the pins from her hair so that it fell in soft waves about her shoulders. "That's better." He threaded his fingers into the dark, silken mass. "I hate it when you screw it into a knob."

Tory smiled her secret smile. *Those were the exact words Falcon used a hundred years ago.*

"Come and sit down. I want to tell you about the money."

She sat before the fire and Falcon took the chair opposite. "Last month there was a terrible tragedy off the coast. The *Thames,* an East Indiaman, was shipwrecked and went down with all hands. It affected me profoundly and I felt compelled to do something to avert these disasters. A new East Indiaman had just been launched and I equipped it with lifeboats with some of the money I inherited."

Victoria's eyes widened with admiration and Falcon held up his hand. "When you told me I used to be a pirate and a marauder, it suddenly dawned on me why the shipwreck affected me so intensely. I warrant I was compelled to make up for some of the barbaric things I did in my past life."

Tears threatened but she held them at bay. "It was the right thing to do, Falcon. I admire your generosity."

"Later, when I thought you had gone and would never come back, I decided to put the money Jack left me to good use. The people of Hawkhurst live a hand-to-mouth existence for the most part. Fishing is a dangerous occupation and the pay is pitiful. I own so much fertile land here at Bodiam, a hundred acres or more, so I donated it to the townspeople of Hawkhurst.

"I researched a crop that would be lucrative. I decided on hops. I have committed thousands of pounds for hop vines that will be delivered and planted in the spring."

"That is a brilliant idea! You have always helped the people of Hawkhurst supplement their meager existence. Now you will do it with something that is not illegal."

He grimaced. "Do you think you can bear a reformed reprobate?"

Tory's smile was mischievous. "I doubt you will ever be completely reformed. Recklessness is in your blood."

"I'll need a partner in crime. Any volunteers?"

"How about Tory Palmer Fuller? I warrant the name suits me."


"With this ring I thee wed, with my body I thee honor, and with all my worldly goods I thee endow." Falcon slid a wide gold band on Victoria's finger.

*Falcon has just endowed me with Bodiam. Never in my wildest dreams did I ever think to live in a castle, especially one as magnificent as Bodiam. It is a grave responsibility to be a keeper of the castle.*

"Those whom God hath joined together let no man put asunder." Reverend Edmund Carswell smiled down at his beloved sister. "Forasmuch as Peregrine and Victoria have consented together in holy wedlock, and have witnessed the same before God and this company, and thereto have given and pledged their troth either to other, and have declared the same by giving and receiving of a ring, and by joining of hands; I pronounce that they be man and wife together, in the Name of the Father, and of the Son, and of the Holy Ghost. Amen."

Behind her, Tory heard her mother sniffle back tears. *Most likely they are tears of relief that I am wed, after causing so much gossip.* She hid a smile as she remembered the fierce battle she had had a week ago when she had decided on pale green silk for her wedding dress. Her mother had insisted she follow the fashion set by young Queen Victoria, who always wore maidenly white.

"White is a symbol of purity, and I can hardly claim that after residing at Bodiam for a month. I believe *living in sin* was the phrase you used, Mother."

Falcon bent his head and kissed his bride's brow and Tory's thoughts came winging back to the present.

Victoria's brother Edmund solemnized the private evening ceremony at his Hawkhurst parish church. Her brother had also given her away, and Mr. de Burgh had acted as witness.

Outside the church, Tory bade her mother goodbye, then Falcon helped her into their carriage and de Burgh drove them back to the castle along a path that was lined with the cheering people of Hawkhurst. "Everyone seems to know about the wedding."

Falcon put his arm about her and drew her close. "Of course they know—I shouted my love from Bodiam's highest tower."

She laughed up at him. "I believe you—thousands wouldn't."

The carriage stopped at the front door of the castle and Falcon lifted his bride high against his heart and carried her over the threshold. He didn't put her down, but instead carried her along the passage that led to their round tower.

Suddenly Tory felt shy, and tried to mask it with humor. "You'd best not try to carry me up all these stairs, milord. You'll need to muster your strength for the jousting."

"Your words paint a very rude picture of a man riding with a stiff pole before him." Falcon set her feet to the floor. "I think I'll tan your arse for that remark, wench. I'll give you five seconds' head start."

Tory let out a whoop, her shyness forgotten. She picked up her skirts and ran like the wind. "You devil! That's exactly what you said to me before, but once you hiked my skirts you decided against beating me to a jelly."

"I warrant I was filled with awe."

"I warrant you were filled with lust."

He caught her before she reached the door. He swept her up in his arms and once again carried her over a threshold. He bit her ear. "It's been so bloody long, I forget!"

Her face was radiant. "It's been too long."

Falcon set her feet to the carpet, but kept a tight hold on her hand. He urged her up the stairs that led to the crenellated roof. Then he pulled her to the center of the tower, threw back his head, and shouted, "I love this woman!"

Tory laughed with delight. "You are a madman!"

"It runs in the blood."

His arms wrapped around her and she leaned back against him, gazing up at the stars. "This is our eternity, Falcon."

"That's how long I shall love you."

"There's no moon tonight. Are you sure you don't want to go roving?"

"I'm sure. There is no place I would rather spend this night than in my own bed."

"I believe you." She rubbed her bum against his thighs. "You have the hard evidence to prove it!"

"You are a saucy wench, Tory Palmer Fuller, but of

course that's the reason I wed you. Let's go down, I can no longer wait to see you again in your corset and drawers."

"Anticipation is an aphrodisiac," she teased.

Back in their chamber they found their bridal supper awaiting them. Falcon picked up a raw oyster and winked. "Speaking of aphrodisiacs—"

"I think I can resist."

"More for me," he teased.

Tory investigated the silver dish that was being heated by a spirit lamp. It held delicious melted Brie cheese and she dipped in a toast point and took a bite. "This is ambrosia."

"Food for the gods. Tonight I feel like a god."

"Do you remember when I went to your masquerade as a goddess?"

He raised a dark brow. "Did you wear green?"

"I did! Falcon gave me some green silk shot through with silver threads. I loved it so much. . . . That's the reason I chose green today."

"It's your color, my beauty. You should always wear green."

"Can you afford to indulge me with silk dresses?"

"I'm not exactly a pauper, Tory."

"You will be when I get through with you," she teased.

Tory tasted the crab with melted shallot butter then sampled the beef brisket with red wine gravy. "It all tastes divine, but I can't wait for the dessert."

"Me neither," Falcon said with a wicked leer. He put some fruit trifle in a small porcelain dish, picked up a spoon, and moved around the table. He lifted Tory into his lap and fed her trifle alternated with kisses. "Mmm, you taste of pears, almonds, and cream cake, an irresistible combination."

They quickly lost interest in the food as Falcon began

to undress his bride. He admired her corset and drawers, but his fingers soon began to unfasten the strings so that her luscious breasts spilled into his hands. It wasn't long before her drawers followed the corset and his lips caressed every inch of her warm, satiny skin.

Tory began to unfasten his shirt. "I want to see your tattoos," she whispered as she helped divest him of his garments. When they were both nude, he clasped her tenderly in his arms and quoted from the Song of Solomon: *"Let her kiss me with the kisses of her mouth . . . your lips are like a thread of scarlet . . . honey and milk are under your tongue . . . your navel is like a round goblet."*

The Song of Solomon seemed most apt for a reverend's daughter, so Victoria began where he stopped. *"His cheeks are as a bed of spices . . . his belly as bright ivory overlaid with sapphires . . . his legs are as pillars of marble."*

Falcon carried her to the bed. Tory's pulse beat wildly; her eyes feasted on the raptors displayed on his powerful forearms as he pulled the velvet curtains so they were enclosed in their own private world. *It seems like forever since he made love to me, then when I thought I had lost him to death, I feared I would never feel his arms about me again.* "Love me, Falcon!"

He kissed her for a full hour, then played with her hair and her body for another hour before he made love to her. He enjoyed the love play as much as she did. Finally, he thrust into her silken sheath and the throbbing fullness inside her set her whole body a-shiver. She loved his powerful maleness. Everything about him was hard as rock—his arms, his chest, his thighs, all corded with solid muscle. When his shudder came, it was so intense it entered her and she shuddered also, becoming one with him.

Falcon held her for a full hour after the loving, savoring the afterglow, whispering tender love words, enjoying the way she clung to him, pressing her lips against his throat. "My heart overflows with love for you, Tory."

Finally, he watched as she drifted into sleep, her arms entwined about his neck as if she wanted to be sure he would not disappear again. He smiled into the darkness, completely content. *We are soul mates forever.*

The next morning Tory lay supine, cradled between Falcon's legs while they talked. "The money we would spend going to London for a honeymoon trip would be better spent on Bodiam, I've decided. London in winter isn't very appealing. Let's put it off until next year."

"Are you sure, love? I thought you wanted a new wardrobe."

"I can design the dresses myself and have a Hawkhurst sewing woman make the clothes."

"This practical side of you is something new to me," he teased.

"Wait until you see my domesticated side. I have the whole week planned. I want all the servants to help me clean the cobwebs and dust from every area of the castle. All the flagstone floors of the chambers and corridors must be mopped. I even have a job for you."

"Ah, I suspected there would be a bloody fly in the ointment."

"I'll put you in charge of the high windows. Any that are broken or cracked must be replaced; the rest washed with vinegar."

"God help me, you issue orders like a sergeant major."

"Well, I am the mistress of Bodiam."

"Aye, and I am still the master. Let me prove it to you." He rolled her beneath him and took possession of her mouth. Tory dissolved into laughter and allowed him to have his way with her.

Two hours later, Victoria led a mop-and-bucket brigade

through the chambers of the top floor, since they were the ones that had been most neglected.

The following day, Victoria and the castle staff cleaned the next floor down and the day after that they tackled the main floor chambers of Bodiam.

Tory chose the long corridor that led to the round tower. On her hands and knees she mopped the flagstones, methodically moving her knee cushion backward as each section became clean.

When she reached the end, she sat back on her heels to admire her handiwork. Suddenly, she blinked and then rubbed her eyes. At the far end of the corridor she saw a leopard coming toward her. "Pandora!" Tory watched in amazement as the big cat turned and padded back the way she had come and then disappeared.

Tory got up off her knees and began to run. She climbed the spiral staircase of the round tower, calling Falcon's name.

Her husband was on a tall ladder cleaning the windows of their chamber. "What's amiss, sweetheart?"

"Falcon, you may not believe this, but I've just seen Pandora's ghost!"

He came down the ladder and stared at her intently. Tory was so fey and attuned to mystical impressions from the past that he believed the things she told him. "Where was she?"

"Pandora was in the long corridor on the ground floor. That was the exact same place that I first saw her, when she almost frightened me to death."

Falcon took Tory's hand and they descended the stairs together. "She padded toward me, then turned and went back, then vanished. Has she ever appeared to you?"

"Only in my dreams, I'm afraid."

"Why did she appear to me? There has to be a reason."

Falcon was alarmed. He hoped Victoria wasn't about to follow her back into the shadows of the past.

Tory's eyes widened. "The treasure! She guards a treasure!"

Falcon took her hands into his. "What do you mean?"

She gazed into his bold black eyes. "When you were dying, you told me you had hidden a treasure and that you wanted me to have it. Somewhere there is a large iron chest filled with solid gold reales that you marauded from a Spanish galleon!"

Falcon recoiled. "Did I sink the galleon?"

"No, no, I swear you did not, though you told me that sadly she sank on her return voyage. It is no wonder you felt compelled to equip the new ship with lifeboats."

"You think the treasure is hidden somewhere in this corridor?"

"I do! But I've just mopped the entire length. I cannot imagine where it could be hidden. Let's search."

They moved together slowly, looking closely at the floor and running their hands over the stone walls. When they found so sign of a hidden compartment, they turned around and searched the entire length again. They found nothing.

"Falcon, only you know where the treasure is hidden."

"Sweetheart, if there was ever gold hidden here, I fear it is long gone. You are speaking of events of a hundred years ago."

"Falcon, stop talking. Listen to your inner voice. All you have to do is open your mind."

He closed his eyes and concentrated. He stood there for long minutes as if he were in a deep trance. Eventually he opened his eyes and moved with purpose down the corridor. He paced off thirty-nine steps, then he halted and knelt down, placing his palms on the flagstone in front of him.

Victoria came up behind him. "Do you remember something?"

"Yes, the iron chest is buried beneath this flagstone."

"Falcon, that's amazing. I knew you had the knowledge."

"Stay right here. I'll get de Burgh and a crowbar."

It took the two men the better part of an hour to pry the huge flagstone loose and, using the iron crowbar as a lever, lift it from where it had lain for a hundred years.

All three of them tried to lift the iron chest from where it had been buried, but it was far too heavy. Finally, Falcon broke the lock with the long iron tool and he lifted the lid.

Tory sat cross-legged on the floor giddy with joy as Falcon scooped gold reales into her lap. "Please tell me it's real?"

"Its value is beyond your wildest dreams, my love."

"Will there be enough money to restore Bodiam?"

"Twice over, I warrant!"

"You mean there will be lots left over?"

De Burgh laughed. "You couldn't spend this in a lifetime."

"Can we send my brother Edmund to Paris, France, to study art?"

"Absolutely!"

"Oh dear, that would mean Mother wouldn't be able to stay at the priory, if Edmund was no longer the reverend."

Falcon grinned. "We'll buy the priory as a gift for her."

Tory jumped up and threw her arms about Falcon's neck and dozens of gold reales rolled across the flagstones. "This means we can go to London!"

"I thought you said London in winter wasn't very appealing."

"I've changed my mind! I can't think of anything more romantic than a honeymoon in London, buying antiques for Bodiam."

"Indeed, madam?" He masked his amusement and with a straight face demanded, "What makes you think you will decide how I spend my treasure?"

"Because it isn't your treasure, it's mine! You gave it to me a hundred years ago, you damned pirate!"

Laughing, he took her in his arms and kissed her soundly. "Have it, sweetheart. I don't need it. *You* are my treasure."

"And you are my Peregrine Falcon. I love you with all my heart."

# THE NAKED LAIRD

# SALLY MACKENZIE

# CHAPTER 1

Eleanor, Countess of Kilgorn, sank deeper into the copper slipper tub. After the long carriage ride, the hot water felt wonderful. The knot in her back began to loosen.

But not the knot in her stomach. That stayed hard and tight. She closed her eyes and tried to take a deep breath.

All the long ride from Scotland, she'd had this leaden knot in her belly. She'd wanted to turn back each mile they'd rolled farther into this flat, tame, unnatural land. She didn't belong here at this benighted house party, among the English ton. She belonged back home, amid the crags and lochs, safe at Pentforth Hall.

She gripped the sides of the tub. But the Hall wasn't safe anymore, thanks to that worm Pennington. That slimy bastard. Why had Ian hired him? Couldn't he have found a more suitable—a less randy—estate manager when sweet old Mr. Lawrence retired? Did he take some cruel delight in torturing her? Did he—

Good God. She jerked and some water sloshed over onto the floor. This was England, close to London.

Surely Ian . . . ? He wouldn't be at this gathering, would he? Was that why she'd been invited? So the Sassenach could snicker at her and watch the Earl of Kilgorn publicly discard his inconvenient wife?

She forced her fingers to release their death grip on the tub. No, of course not. Ian would decline any invitation that included her. He must have as little desire to see her as she did to see him.

"The footmen were right braw, weren't they, milady—for Sassenach, that is?" Annie, her young maid, grinned and handed her the soap. "Did ye see how the one with the blue eyes looked at me?"

"No, I didn't." Annie wasn't going to be chasing after Lord Motton's footmen, was she? This house party would be bad enough without that. "I'm not certain your mother would care to hear you taking note of Lord Motton's footmen, Annie."

"Oh, Ma wouldna mind. She kens I have eyes in my head." Annie snorted, wrinkling her nose as she looked around the room. "And right now I see this wee little mouse hole of a room. I'd have thought ye'd have a grander bedchamber, milady."

The room *was* . . . cozy. The four-poster bed took up most of the space. "It's perfectly adequate for me."

"But yer a countess. Ye deserve better."

"Don't be daft." A countess without an earl was more a figure of fun than respect. She only hoped everyone wouldn't gawk at her. Her stomach twisted. Perhaps it was hunger as much as nerves. It had been hours since they'd eaten. "Didn't you say you were going down to see about tea?"

"Aye, that I did." Annie glanced in the mirror and smoothed her skirt.

"Tea, Annie. *Only* tea. Don't be looking at the footmen."

Annie laughed. "Ye worry worse than my ma."

Nell sighed as the door closed and she turned back to face the hearth. She probably did worry more than Martha—the woman had raised five daughters, while Nell hadn't managed to birth even the one poor bairn she'd been gifted with.

She swirled her fingers through the bathwater. What would her life have been like if she hadn't lost the baby?

She'd have a daughter—or a son—now, a sturdy youth of ten, a child with quick strong limbs, a ready smile, and a sharp wit who'd spend hours climbing trees and swimming in Kilgorn Loch. She smiled. Surely she'd have other children as well—two or even three more. She and Ian—

What was she thinking? She detested the man. *He'd* never mourned their poor bairn—he'd just wanted to get busy making another. He certainly hadn't wasted any time after she'd left finding another female to warm his bed.

Well, all right—not his bed at the castle. He hadn't brought a woman into his home, but that was a distinction without a difference. He'd visited plenty of Sassenach beds in London. He was a man—he'd only one thing on his mind.

She rubbed the soap vigorously. He was just like Pennington. That cod's-head had had his arm around her waist when Mr. MacNeill had barged into the library. For once the butler had actually seen something of note—ha! The old man's eyes had just about popped out of his head. She'd wager an entire month's pin money he'd never run so fast as he did that night to send a message to Ian about her supposed flirtation.

Pennington wasn't the first amorous male she'd had to elude—Mr. MacNeill had had plenty of grist for his rumor mill over the years. Some men seemed to take her odd marital situation as a challenge—but Mr. Pennington? He owed his employment to the man he apparently wished to cuckold!

She glared at the soap cake. Not that Ian cared, of course. If the gossip in the newspapers were true, he'd already selected the Earl of Remington's widow as her replacement—and given the woman a thorough interview between his sheets.

Well, to be fair, he *had* just turned thirty. The succession must be on his mind. He needed an heir, and to get an heir he needed a wife—a real wife, not the girl he'd married too young.

She sunk lower in the tub. Oh, God, what a mess.

She should write him today. This had gone on long enough. They were adults now, even if they hadn't been when they'd married and then separated. Surely they could solve this . . . problem in a sensible fashion. He was not malicious.

The door opened and closed. Annie must be back with the tea. Nell splashed water on her face. If her eyes were red, the girl would only suppose she'd got a little soap in them.

"Did you see the blue-eyed footman, Annie?"

"Blue-eyed—what the hell?"

Her heart stopped.

Oh God, oh God. That voice. Even after ten years, it slid around her heart as no other ever had. After all the tears, all the pain, it reminded her of laughter, of lying on sun-warmed heather with a summer breeze blowing cool off the loch. Of twisted bedsheets, slick flesh, heat and damp and . . .

No, it couldn't be.

"I-Ian?" She struggled to her knees, turned to grasp the back of the tub. It *was* Ian. He'd changed, of course. The slender, wiry lad had broadened. His features were more chiseled; there were lines around his mouth and eyes that hadn't been there before. His eyes themselves were the same, though, the same turbulent green of a storm-whipped sea. They were staring at . . .

She looked down. Water dripped from her naked breasts.

"Ack!" She leaped for the towel, but it was a little too far and the tub was a little too slippery. She pitched forward. "Ow! Aaa!"

The edge of the tub smacked her knee and shin hard, but the floor was going to smack her face harder.

"Nell!" Strong hands grabbed her before she hit the ground and pulled her into a rock-hard embrace. The rough fabric of Ian's greatcoat rubbed against her breasts, her stomach, her . . . dear God.

She squeezed her eyes tightly shut. She would die of embarrassment. She was *naked* in Ian's arms.

"Are you all right, Nell? Can you stand?"

She felt cool air on her wet skin. He was holding her away from him and he was—she opened one eye to peek—yes, he was looking at her. She felt her nipples pebble—she was cold, that was all. Not hot. Her womb was *not* melting and the long-dead place between her legs was *not* throbbing and swelling.

They had married when she was seventeen. She had wanted him so wildly then, she could not wait to go to his bed.

She swallowed the sob, but not quickly enough.

"You're hurt."

"Nay, it's—"

"Aye, you're hurt, lass. I heard you cry." He pulled her up against him again, held her tight with one arm while he slid the other hand down her naked, wet back. Did he think to comfort her? It was not comfort he gave her. He was stoking the flames of a fire she'd thought so long dead even the embers were stone-cold.

"Tell me where you hurt. Is it your leg? Can you stand, love?"

She had been his love once, long ago, before she'd lost his babe. She choked back another sob. She felt his lips brush her forehead.

"Oh, sweetheart. Dinna cry. Let me see your leg."

"Nay, I—"

But Ian was already stooping, sliding his hand over her thigh, her knee, her calf. His face was level with—

Please let him think the wetness on her thighs was all from her bath.

"Hold on to my shoulders, Nell."

Was his voice huskier?

"Nay, I'm fine, Ian. Just get me that towel. I'm naked, ye ken."

He laughed then, though it was a short, choked sound.

"I ken, Nell." He ran his hands up her body, letting his thumbs skim her breasts, as he stood. He cupped her jaw and looked down into her face. His eyes were . . . hungry.

They'd been hungry when he was nineteen, too, but this was different. Were there pain and a hint of desperation there as well?

She certainly felt desperate. She moistened her lips; his eyes followed the sweep of her tongue. His head bent.

In a moment she would feel his lips again after so many, many years. She shivered with anticipation.

"Och, Nell, you're cold, and here I am . . . I am . . ." His head snapped up and he stepped back. "What the hell *am* I doing?"

Good God, he had just been about to kiss Nell. The need, the overwhelming lust, still hammered at him, like storm waves crashing against the shore. He'd never felt that intensity with any other woman. How had he stopped himself?

Thank God he had. If he hadn't, Nell would have done so for him. She hated him. She was glaring at him now.

He scowled. Would she put some damn clothes on? Did she not realize what a tease she was, standing there naked? The firelight glistened on her wet body—it was even more beautiful than it had been when she was younger—slightly rounder, a little fuller. Her breasts—

He jerked his eyes back to her face. He would *not* look at her breasts.

She finally wrapped the towel around herself. He should have handed it to her, but frankly, he didn't trust himself. He balled his fists. The damn lust was like a raging fever. If he moved, he'd fall on her like the rutting animal she thought he was.

She had made it very clear ten years ago that she never wanted him in her bed again. In all the years since, she had not once given him any indication she'd changed her mind, though MacNeill had told him time after time she was not averse to male companionship. Hell, just a fortnight ago, the man had sent word she was dallying with the damn estate manager. MacNeill had caught them in the library, apparently just moments before Pennington'd had Nell out of her gown and down on the rug.

Would she not put some clothes on?

There, finally she was reaching for her dressing gown. She was holding the damn thing in front of her like a shield. The sooner she put it on, the better.

He should just turn his back so she'd have the privacy to get the job done. If he turned, he wouldn't keep staring at her.

He couldn't move. He was worse than a randy schoolboy, hoping for another glimpse of her perfect . . .

Damn it all to hell, he was a thirty-year-old man.

He'd seen plenty of naked females. He should not be panting, almost mindless with desire, just because he was here in a bedroom alone with Nell. Naked Nell.

He was going to have an apoplexy if she didn't get some blasted clothes on right now. Perhaps speaking would help. Formulating words and even sentences would take some thought away from contemplating Nell, naked and—

"What the hell are you doing in my room?"

"Don't shout." Nell frowned. Ian was scowling at her now.

"All right." This time it sounded like he was talking through gritted teeth. "What the bloody hell are you doing in my room?"

"Don't curse." Did she actually hear his teeth grind? "And this isn't your room—it's mine." She turned away briefly to struggle into her dressing gown and then turned back, tying the gown's sash tight while she glared at him. "As you noted, I was in the middle of bathing. I suggest you leave me to my privacy and seek out the housekeeper. Obviously you have gone astray."

Yes, she'd been in the middle of bathing—and then in the middle of lusting after him.

What was the matter with her? Was the man a bloody conjuror? She hadn't felt these . . . urges in ten years. She didn't want to feel them. She was content the way she was. She didn't need any more heartbreak.

"This is *my* room." Ian's voice was hard—mulish.

*This* was the man she remembered. The man who'd insisted she come back to his bed once her courses had returned. The man who'd said it was her marital duty.

Perhaps by law he had been right, but she couldn't do it. If she'd submitted to him, something important would have died in her. Something besides the baby who was already dead . . .

"It's not your room."

"It is." His jaw jutted out. He could be incredibly stubborn. Everyone had used to say he was only stubborn with her because she was the only one who had the backbone to stand up to him.

"This is my room." She pointed to the tub and then flushed. She'd rather not bring his attention back to the tub, but it did prove her point. "Lord Motton's footmen would not have brought me up a bath if this were not my room."

Ian scowled at the tub. "They must have been confused. I tell you, the housekeeper was very clear. This is definitely my room. I did not make a mistake."

"Obviously, you did."

"No, I—" He grunted. "Wait here." He opened the door and stepped into the corridor.

Nell stepped closer to the fire. Of course she would wait here. Where else would she wait? She wasn't even dressed, for goodness' sake. She found her comb and attacked the tangles in her hair.

Five, ten minutes passed. What was taking so long? Had Ian left? But his bag was still here—

The door swung open and Ian ushered in Mrs. Gilbert, the housekeeper. He was scowling; Mrs. Gilbert was wringing her hands.

"I'm terribly sorry, milord."

"Just tell my—" Ian made an odd noise, sort of a cross between a cough and a growl. "Just tell Lady Kilgorn what you told me."

Nell hurried over to Mrs. Gilbert. The poor woman looked miserable.

"Mrs. Gilbert, please don't be distressed. Lord Kilgorn's bark is much worse than his bite, I assure you."

"Wait until you hear what she has to say, Nell."

"What?" Nell glared at Ian. Why was he being so fierce? Couldn't he see he was frightening Mrs. Gilbert? He hadn't used to vent his spleen on the servants. "Oh, stop it. You are giving poor Mrs. Gilbert heart palpitations." She turned back to pat Mrs. Gilbert's shoulder. "Now what is it? Surely it can't be as bad as all that."

"Oh, milady, I very much fear there has been a misunderstanding."

"A misunderstanding?" Nell's stomach clenched. "What kind of misunderstanding?"

"Miss Smyth, Lord Motton's aunt, is acting as his hostess, you know."

"No, I didn't know."

Mrs. Gilbert nodded. "She is. She assigned all the rooms. She usually doesn't make mistakes."

"Yes? Was there a mistake this time?"

"I—" Mrs. Gilbert sent a nervous glance at Ian. "Yes, milady, apparently there was."

So Ian was right. This *was* his room. Well, no matter. She didn't care, though she would insist on being given time to dress before she found her new chamber. "That's quite all right, Mrs. Gilbert. I don't mind."

"You don't?" Mrs. Gilbert looked as if she would fall on Nell's neck and weep tears of joy. The reaction seemed a trifle out of proportion to the situation.

"I don't believe you fully understand the nature of the error, Nell."

"No?" Nell glanced from Ian to the housekeeper. "Perhaps you'd best explain it to me more completely, Mrs. Gilbert."

Mrs. Gilbert paled. Her hands fluttered around her face and then fell, like dying sparrows, to her skirts. "Miss Smyth must not have understood . . . she must not have known that you and his lordship . . ."

She *and* his lordship? Nell felt a sudden flutter of nerves herself. "Just tell me, Mrs. Gilbert."

"Miss Smyth told me to put Lord *and* Lady Kilgorn—both of you, milady—in the Thistle Room." Mrs. Gilbert cleared her throat. She must have thought Nell's understanding was weak—not surprising as Nell definitely felt more than usually stupid at the moment—because she repeated herself. "Together, milady. In one room. Here."

"Oh." That was awkward, but surely no more than momentarily embarrassing. There was no need for Mrs. Gilbert to look so stricken. Nell smiled weakly. "But that's easily rectified, isn't it? You can just move one of us. And since Lord Kilgorn seems unwilling to change rooms, I don't mind being the one to move—just let me dress and get my things together."

Why Ian wasn't acting the gentleman and offering to take another room was odd, but he must have his reasons. Her stomach sank as the obvious reason immediately presented itself. He must already have arranged an assignation, most likely with Lady Remington.

Mrs. Gilbert's mouth flapped slightly, but it seemed the poor woman could not muster words. Ian spoke instead.

"The solution is not that simple, Nell."

"Oh? Why not?" Nell turned again to Mrs. Gilbert. The housekeeper truly looked as if she would swoon.

"The problem is . . ." Mrs. Gilbert swallowed so they could observe her throat moving. "The trouble . . . the difficulty is . . . well, you see . . ." She trailed off into silence, looking to Ian. Nell looked at him, too. His lips were twisted into an odd, almost desperate half smile.

"The difficulty is," Ian said, "there are no other bedchambers available."

# CHAPTER 2

Nell was still gaping at him as the door closed behind Mrs. Gilbert, but the click of the latch freed her from her stupor. She snapped her jaw shut, crossed her arms tightly, and stalked over to the hearth.

*Wonderful.* He studied her stiff back. She might as well be wearing a sign proclaiming in large letters: KEEP OUT.

What the hell was he going to do now? Ian looked around the tiny chamber. His eyes kept coming back to the bed. How could they not? It was just about the only damn stick of furniture in this little hole of a room.

He couldn't stay here. He certainly couldn't sleep here. Sleep? Ha! Sleeping was the last thing he wished to do on that bed.

He was an idiot, a complete and total idiot. One would think after all this time . . .

He glanced back at Nell. She was still staring into the fire, ignoring him exactly as she had these last ten years.

Bloody, bloody hell.

He wanted to shout, throw something, do something to make her acknowledge his existence.

When he'd followed her to Pentforth Hall—he'd waited a week or two, thinking she'd come back on her own—he'd been turned away at the door. He, the Earl of Kilgorn, the master of the estate, had been sent packing. Not by MacNeill, of course—the butler knew who paid his wages. Mrs. MacNeill was the one who'd told him Nell refused to see him.

Refused to see him! He clenched his hands into tight fists. The thought of it still had the power to infuriate him. Mrs. MacNeill had said a lot more, but he'd been too angry—well, and hurt, too—to hear it. Then he *had* thrown something—he'd been only twenty, after all, and new to such pain. He'd hurled some hideous knick-knack into the fireplace. It had made a lovely crash as it shattered into a hundred pieces.

He unbuttoned his greatcoat. Why had Nell turned him away? He still didn't understand it. She was his wife. She had vowed to obey him. She was compelled by the church and the state to submit to him—and she hadn't even had the courtesy to see him. It wasn't as if he were some reprobate. He hadn't caused her to miscarry. Damn it all, it wasn't his fault.

He shrugged out of his coat and threw it on the bed. And he'd loved her. She'd been his first, his only love. He'd been nineteen, little more than a boy, when they'd wed. A virgin still. He'd discovered heaven in Nell's arms. He'd been happy, proud—damn cocky, really—when his seed had taken root so quickly. Yes, he'd been disappointed when she'd lost the babe, but he'd thought they would just try again.

He shook his head. He couldn't understand why he'd had to lose his child *and* his wife. Had Nell never really loved him? Was that it?

Zeus, he had loved her. She'd taken his heart when she'd left. Nothing had ever been the same.

He started unbuttoning his waistcoat. He was hot,

tired, and dirty from his ride out from London. The bathwater was sitting there. He might as well use it. Nell couldn't care; she'd already had her bath. She was still standing in front of the fire, combing her long, black hair.

God, she was beautiful. He'd used to tell her some claptrap about how her hair was as dark as a moonless night. Silly cub—he'd fancied himself a bit of a poet when he was young. But it was true. Her hair *was* as black as a moonless night and her eyes as blue as Kilgorn Loch.

But it wasn't just her body that had wooed him. She'd been so full of life, so full of joy, when she'd been young.

He dropped the waistcoat on top of his coat. He'd been such a fool. He'd left Pentforth angry—livid—but the anger had faded quickly. He'd missed her so much her absence was almost a physical pain. So he'd written to her, letter after letter that first horrible year, sweating over each word—even, much as he cringed to admit it, crying over some. He'd never got one single word in reply.

How she must have laughed at him—*if* she'd even bothered to read what he'd written.

He'd sent her one last note on her nineteenth birthday. When that, too, was met with silence, he'd washed his hands of her.

Except he hadn't. She haunted him, even when he was in another woman's bed. And now the image of her naked in the tub, water streaming off her lovely, full breasts, was seared into his brain for all eternity.

Perhaps this was good, seeing her again. If he were lucky, the experience would be so painful he'd finally be cured of her.

"Has Lady Remington arrived yet?"

"What?" He looked up. Nell was still staring at the

fire. Her voice had been carefully devoid of emotion. Why? Did she know Caro was his mistress? Surely she didn't care.

"Lady Remington. Is she here yet?"

"Lady Remington is not coming." He untied his cravat. Caro had been a crashing bore about it, too. She'd tried to get him to procure an invitation for her, but he'd realized he liked the idea of being free of her for a few days—a definite sign it was time to give her her congé.

"Oh."

He stared at Nell. Her tone . . . she sounded pleased by Caro's absence. "Why do you care whether she is here or not?"

Nell shrugged. "I merely wished to know if I'd be sitting down to table with my husband's mistress."

"Ah." So she *did* know about Caro. He shouldn't be surprised. He hadn't tried terribly hard to be discreet. Caro was a widow, and he hadn't thought his wife would care if he fornicated on the floor of Almack's. Well, she shouldn't throw stones. "And I take it I won't be stumbling over Pennington?"

He tried to keep the venom from his voice. He didn't want Nell to think he was jealous, that he cared one iota what she did in her bed. He yanked his shirt out of his waistband.

"Mr. Pennington?" She finally turned to face him. "He's the Pentforth estate manager. Why would he be here?"

"MacNeill said the man's become slightly more than an employee." He couldn't stop himself. "Or that he's being employed to . . . manage more than the estate."

"How *dare* you?" Nell's eyes flashed and she stepped away from the fire. "And I do not appreciate you setting the servants to spy on me."

He grunted and grasped the hem of his shirt. "MacNeill isn't a spy—he's the butler."

"He's a spy, as you very well know and—*what* are you doing?"

"Isn't it obvious?" He pulled his shirt over his head. When he emerged from the linen he noticed Nell was eyeing his chest as if she was both appalled and fascinated. He glanced down. His chest looked exactly as it always did, but another part of his body was responding to her attention in a completely inappropriate manner. She'd best not let her gaze drop or she really would be horrified. He looked back up at her. "You're done with the water, aren't you?" His hands went to his fall. Nell squeaked.

"You're taking your clothes off!"

"One usually removes one's clothing before bathing." She was acting like a shy little virgin. What was Pennington doing—or, more to the point, not doing—with her? Surely the man didn't make love with his clothes on?

"But you can't . . . I mean . . . you shouldn't . . . You aren't really going to get into that tub, are you?"

She shouldn't be so nervous. It must be an act. Even if Pennington was an unexciting bedfellow, she'd entertained enough other men, according to MacNeill, not to be alarmed at seeing him naked.

"I did just arrive. The water is here, and I don't care to present myself to Motton's guests in all my dirt."

She looked around the room. "Aren't you going to wait for your man?"

Did she think he'd hidden his valet in his bag? He shrugged—and noticed how her eyes widened slightly at the movement. "Crandall wasn't feeling quite the thing, so I left him home. I can do fine by myself."

Damned if her eyes didn't keep coming back to his shoulders and chest.

He stepped a little closer to the tub and her tongue actually slipped out to moisten her bottom lip.

Her attention was definitely titillating. Part of him

was exceedingly stimulated. If he opened his fall now, she would get quite the eyeful.

Could he . . . was it possible . . . Should he try to seduce her? Likely he'd just be opening himself to more rejection, but it might be worth the risk. He was ten years older; his heart was now carefully guarded.

If he could get Nell into bed, perhaps he'd finally realize she was no different than any other woman. He'd be cured of her.

He smiled slightly. It was worth a try. As Nell pointed out, Caro wasn't here. And they were stuck in this small room with its small bed. "Crandall may not be here, but you are. You can help me."

"Oh, no, I—" She clutched her comb in her hands and backed toward the fire.

"Careful. You don't want to set that lovely dressing gown aflame."

"Ack." She jumped away from the hearth.

He sat in the chair and stuck out his legs. She was still darting glances at his chest. "Come help me get my boots off."

"Your boots?"

"Yes." He lifted a leg. "These leather things on my feet."

She frowned. "I know what boots are."

"I thought you did, but I was beginning to wonder." He tried to assume his most pitiful expression. "Please? I could get them off myself if I struggled, but it would be so much easier if you helped."

She glanced at the door. "Annie should be here any moment."

"I doubt it. I believe Mrs. Gilbert decided we needed our privacy."

"Privacy? Since when do servants affect one's privacy?"

"Since one has been estranged from one's wife for ten

years," he said softly. "I can act as your maid. I did so enough times when we were first married."

Nell flushed. "That was different. And we won't be doing anything that requires privacy."

The details of the action which most required privacy popped into her mind. She closed her eyes briefly. She had not considered that . . . activity in years. She did not want to think of it now, but it was as if a carefully built dam had burst. Memories flooded her, swamping rational thought. She could almost feel his fingers on her skin, his mouth on her breasts . . .

The fire must have caught a fresh log; the temperature had risen precipitously.

She glanced at his chest—and shoulders and arms—again. Had he had such sharply defined muscles when he was younger? Surely not. She would have remembered such sculpted curves.

But she did remember the feel of his arms holding her tight, keeping her safe. She remembered the comfort they'd given her when the midwife had told her she'd miscarried.

How could she have forgotten that? Ian had held her while she'd sobbed, her dreams—her trust in the world—gone with her child.

She blinked back tears. She didn't want to remember. Remembering hurt too much.

"No? We won't be needing privacy?" Ian half smiled at her, his eyes gleaming ever so slightly. "What a shame."

And that smile. It turned the hard, stern laird into a sly, beguiling man. It made him look years younger—too much like the lad she'd fallen in love with.

Ridiculous. That lad—and the lass she'd been—were long gone. If she were going to entertain memories, she should consider all the mistresses he'd had. She pulled her dressing gown's belt tighter and glared at him.

"Dinna frown so at me, Nell." His eyes seemed to invite her to share some secret with him.

"Then don't . . ." Don't what? Tease her? Mock her? Seduce her?

That was what she feared, wasn't it? But why? She could not be seduced; she had put all that behind her when her babe died. She closed her eyes, waiting for the familiar, terrible sadness to well up.

It didn't.

She was just tired and upset. Distracted. She'd not expected to see Ian.

She glanced at his chest again . . . and then forced her gaze down to his boots.

It would be childish not to help him. She would assist him now, and then go sit on the bed . . . well, perhaps not the bed. She would move the chair as far away as possible from the tub and read until he had bathed, dressed, and left, giving her the privacy to get dressed herself.

"Oh, very well." She stepped closer, grasped his boot, and jerked. It stuck for a moment and then slipped off more easily than she'd expected.

"Ack!" She toppled backward, sitting down hard on the floor.

"Are you all right?" Ian was obviously struggling not to laugh. He'd best not—if he did, she'd break his head with this blasted boot.

"I'm fine." She scrambled upright and grabbed the other boot, tugging it off more carefully. "There. Done."

"Thank you." He stood, not giving her a moment to retreat to a safer distance. She leaned back quickly and lost her balance again. He caught her, his grip strong but gentle.

His skin was so close now. She was tall, but he was taller. If she leaned forward ever so slightly her lips would brush his chest. If she stretched just a little she could kiss his collarbone. If she—

She stepped back and he let her go, but there was a light in his eyes that did unsettling things to her stomach.

"You're welcome." She spun away. Her disquiet was completely understandable. Seeing Ian—being in the same small room with him—was a shock. Once she adjusted to the situation, she would be fine.

Right. And she'd be just as fine sharing that very, *very* small bed with him. He'd used to spread out, taking over all the space. Did he still?

She was not about to find out. Mrs. Gilbert must be mistaken. There must be some other solution—some other room that he—or she—could move to. Perhaps she could share with one of the other women.

She would ask him to move the chair to the other side of the room now and then later, when she was dressed, she would seek out Mrs. Gilbert.

"Ian—" She turned without thinking and found herself staring at his naked back while he searched through his valise. At his narrow, muscled arse.

"What?" He shifted to face her and now she was staring at something else, something that blossomed under her gaze, growing thick and long and . . .

She wrenched her eyes to his face. His expression was stark and . . . hot. His lips curved into a half smile.

"Lass, ye can look as much as ye like."

She whirled back to the fire. "Don't be ridiculous." Ian had always been so comfortable in his body. He'd used to think nothing of walking naked around their room—

He'd best not be thinking he could do that here.

She *had* to get other accommodations. Being here with Ian—she felt unwell. Achy. Needy.

She didn't want this. She didn't want to feel anything. Feeling hurt too much.

She heard water splash against the sides of the tub.

"Can you hand me the soap, Nell?"

"Get it yourself." She was not going to look at him again. She should just walk out right now—but she wasn't dressed and she certainly wasn't going to get dressed with Ian in the room.

"I can't reach it. Please, Nell?"

Oh, for God's sake. "Where is it?"

"On the floor under the chair. It probably went flying when you did."

She felt herself flush. Could anything be more embarrassing than to go flopping naked toward the floor when seen by one's estranged husband for the first time in a decade? "Are you certain you can't get it yourself?"

"Aye. It's out of reach—and if you turned around, you'd see I'm already in the tub."

"I *know* you're in the tub. Can't you get out and get it?"

"I'd drip all over Motton's floor. It's not like I'm asking you to go to Glasgow, Nell."

"Oh, very well." She carefully averted her gaze, moved to pick up the soap, and thrust it in his direction. He chuckled.

"What, Nell, are ye shy? Ye dinna used to be. Ye used to look quite eagerly."

"Stop it!" She did look then. She was angry enough that she had no trouble focusing only on his face. "You can't walk back into my life—*by accident*—and act as if the last ten years never happened."

His face grew still, his eyes hard. "You're the one who walked out, Nell. I tried to see you; I wrote you letter after letter. You refused me at every turn."

She pressed her lips together. She had been mad

that first year—angry and crazy. But it didn't matter. Ian hadn't understood, would never understand why she'd mourned such a wee speck of a thing, a baby that had died before her belly had even begun to swell.

She could not talk about it now.

"I—" She shook her head. "It's . . . there's just too much time gone. The wound's too deep to heal, certainly by something as frivolous as this chance meeting—this accident of hospitality."

"Perhaps this accident is an opportunity."

He was not going to cut up her peace like this. She had worked too hard for too long to attain it.

"Could it be you are just looking for someone to warm your bed while Lady Remington is unavailable? Is that what this is about?"

Ian flushed. Ah, so she had hit the mark. She ignored the hollow feeling that thought provoked. Anger was what she wanted. Anger had always saved her in the past. "Where *is* Lady Remington, by the way? Did she have a prior commitment? I would have thought she'd break it to come here with you."

Ian's eyes narrowed. "Lady Remington was not invited."

"Oh? I'm surprised." She fanned the flames of her anger higher. She had perfected the art of sarcasm over the years. It was an excellent way to repel unwanted advances. "Does Lord Motton not read the society pages? Doesn't he know the identities of Lord K. and Lady R.?"

Ian's face grew stiffer and his voice sounded more English, precise and cold. "I have no idea what Lord Motton does and does not know. I didn't know you read that twaddle."

"Well, I do. I like to be *au courant*. It's so entertaining to keep up with your escapades." The anger felt good— and she could see she was infuriating him as well. "I would have thought you could have got her an invitation."

"Perhaps I could have, had I tried."

"Oh, so you didn't wish to be encumbered by your mistress? Did you hope to find her replacement at this house party, then—someone younger, more entertaining? Poor Lady Remington."

Ian's face was red with anger. It was a wonder he wasn't causing the bathwater to turn to steam.

She glanced down at the thought—and jerked her attention back to his face. The water was exceptionally clear. She could see . . . everything. At least that part of him had calmed down—unlike the rest of him. His jaw was tense—he must be gritting his teeth. His words certainly came out as though he were.

"Perhaps I shall look around. I don't usually have difficulty finding bed partners—and I suppose that would help our rather cramped situation here, wouldn't it? If you are certain you aren't interested? Though I suppose a wife can't be a mistress, can she?"

She wanted to slap him. "You conceited, arrogant—"

"Consider carefully. It would make sharing that bed so much more comfortable. As you point out, I am without Caro—and you are without Pennington—"

"Pennington?" She might be able to generate some steam herself. How dare he throw that disgusting, slimy . . . octopus in her face?

"MacNeill said the man was embracing you in the library."

"Exactly. *He* was embracing *me*—I was not embracing him. You are the one who sent the man to Pentforth. What were you thinking?"

"I certainly wasn't thinking to send my wife a paramour!"

"You really think . . . Pennington and I . . . you actually thought we . . ."

Ian shrugged. "You used to be a lusty girl. I'm not naive—I know women have needs. It's been ten years since we . . ." His voice softened. "I assume you've had lovers over the years, Nell—you've just managed to be discreet—and you've not presented me with another man's brat, for which I'm thankful, by the bye."

Her jaw was hanging open. She wanted to cry and scream at the same time. She wanted to drown the despicable, obnoxious, ignorant cur. Did he understand *nothing*?

She would hit him. She would strangle him. She would—

She was still holding the cake of soap in her hand. She wanted to throw it at his head; instead she flung it into the bath, sending water splashing.

She sincerely hoped she'd hit her target.

# CHAPTER 3

He'd certainly bungled that.

Ian opened the bedroom door and let Nell precede him into the corridor. She'd wanted him to leave as soon as he'd got his clothes on, but he'd pointed out she needed help dressing. *That* had been an uncomfortable exercise, akin to clothing a statue. They'd not exchanged a single unnecessary word since she'd tried to emasculate him with the soap cake. He winced. Thank God the water had slowed that missile. Her aim had been uncomfortably good.

"Will you take my arm?"

She spared him one cold look and started down the corridor alone. Wonderful. He lengthened his stride. He was not going to chase her all the way to Motton's drawing room. "Don't you think you are being a little childish?"

She glared at him again, eyes narrowed, nostrils flaring.

"If you clench your teeth any tighter, you'll break your jaw."

She made a short noise—a cross between a hiss and a growl—and moved faster.

Blast it. It wasn't his fault they'd been tossed into that wee room together. He was as much a victim of Miss Smyth's twisted sense of humor as she was.

He offered her his arm when they reached the stairs. She grabbed the banister.

Zeus! So he'd flirted with her. He was a man. Damn it, he was still legally her husband. He could have insisted she climb into that bed and fulfill her wifely duties. Not that he would have, of course. He had no need for an unwilling bed partner. . . .

But she *hadn't* been unwilling. Hell, she'd hardly been able to keep her eyes off him. He'd been holding his breath, waiting for her to touch him, to run her fingers over his naked—

He could have seduced her. She must know that—she'd never been a cabbage head. And she had no cause to get on her high horse. If he'd had mistresses, she'd had many male "friends."

He glanced at her. Her face could have been carved from stone. She still would not look at him.

He should divorce her. Caro had been teasing him to do so almost from the moment he'd first climbed into her bed. Her motivation was obvious, of course—she wanted to be his next countess. Hell would freeze over before *that* happened.

Truthfully, he'd used his married status as protection, to stave off husband-hunting mamas and their daughters. Any female choosing to dally with him knew from the outset a wedding ring was not in the cards. That suited him perfectly. He had absolutely no desire to step into the parson's mousetrap again.

But now he was thirty. He could no longer ignore the reality of his position—he needed an heir. He had no brothers or male cousins waiting in the wings. And to get an heir he needed a wife—a real wife. A woman who would—if not welcome, at least allow—him into her bed and into her body. Obviously Nell would do neither.

He would have Motton fix this infernal room situation and then he would avoid her for the rest of the house party. When he got back to London, he would see about ending his marriage.

Bloody hell, his stomach felt like lead. He'd love to hit something. Someone. Perhaps Motton—he couldn't very well hit Miss Smyth.

The footman took one look at them and flung open the door, almost jumping out of their way.

There was Motton, by the hearth, talking to two young women—twins. They could be trained monkeys for all he cared.

"Motton."

The man raised an eyebrow. The women actually stopped their bibble-babble to gape. He had not sounded particularly polite. Well, he did not feel polite.

"If I might have a moment of your time? We"—he gestured toward Nell—"have something of an urgent nature to discuss."

"Ah." Motton's smile remained in place, but his eyes turned watchful. He'd always been a downy one. "What—"

"Lord Kilgorn, Lady Kilgorn, how lovely to see you."

Ian was certain there was nothing lovely about him at the moment. He turned to see who had spoken. A short, gray-haired woman smiled up at him.

His frown deepened; her smile widened. Her blue eyes were actually twinkling.

"May I present my aunt, Miss Winifred Smyth?" Motton said. He treated the woman to a very pointed look. She patted him on the arm.

"Have a touch of indigestion, do you, Edmund?

Never fear. I have just the elixir for that. I'll give you some later, if you like."

"No, thank you." Motton smiled slightly. "The last time I tried one of your quack remedies, Aunt Winifred, I had to see a physician to be cured of your cure."

"Fiddle-faddle. You probably took too much—or not enough."

Miss Smyth turned back to Ian and smiled even more brightly, if that were possible. "I'm so sorry I wasn't there to welcome you when you arrived. I trust you found everything in order?"

Motton choked on his sherry.

"Actually, Miss Smyth, things are most certainly not in order."

"Oh? I'm sorry to hear that, Lord Kilgorn. What is amiss?"

Had he entered Bedlam? "Perhaps we could discuss this in a more private location? It is an issue of some delicacy." Not that the entire drawing room didn't already know he and Nell were estranged. Motton definitely knew or he wouldn't have that carefully blank expression pasted on his face. Miss Smyth must be the only woman in all of England and Scotland who was not fully aware of their marital situation—*if* she were truly in ignorance.

"Of course." Miss Smyth sounded as cheery as if they were chatting about a balmy spring day. "Let's step into the green parlor, shall we? Edmund, why don't you bring along the sherry?"

"A splendid idea." Motton grabbed a decanter and motioned Ian and the ladies to precede him.

The green parlor was a modest room with a settee, two upholstered chairs, a scattering of tables—and not a single hint of green.

"It used to be green," Motton said, pulling the door closed behind him, "but my mother hated the color.

Had it painted over the day after she married Father. Care for some sherry?"

"Please." Whisky would be preferable, but Ian would take anything alcoholic at this point.

He considered Miss Smyth. How did one vent one's spleen on an exceedingly cheerful woman who looked old enough to be one's mother? Nell was sitting on the gold-colored settee next to her. Perhaps she should handle the issue.

Or perhaps not. Miss Smyth was leaning over and patting Nell's hand.

"Don't say a word until you've had a glass of sherry, Lady Kilgorn. You poor thing! You do look like you could use a restorative."

"Yes, well—"

"And I shall have one, too, Edmund—a full glass, please."

"Of course." Motton handed the ladies their drinks.

Miss Smyth took a sip and smiled broadly at Nell. "You know, I'm so looking forward to you making Theo's acquaintance, Lady Kilgorn. You seem exactly like the merry sort who would enjoy him."

"Merry?" Ian blinked. Nell had been anything but merry recently.

"Not Theo, Aunt Winifred." Motton actually groaned.

"And Edmund!" Miss Smyth laughed. "Oh, not this Edmund—the other Edmund."

Motton groaned again, louder this time. "And not Edmund, either. Most certainly not Edmund. I had enough trouble with him earlier."

"Oh, pooh!" Miss Smyth waved a dismissive hand at Motton. "Where is your sense of adventure?"

"Not in a drawing room with a monkey on the loose."

"A monkey?" Nell choked on her sherry.

"Yes, indeed. A very sweet little, well-behaved—"

Motton snorted. Miss Smyth glared at him. "—very

nice monkey, though why I named him after my dull
nephew I will never know. *My* Edmund is not dull."

"And Theo?" Nell smiled. She looked as if she might
even laugh.

"Theo is Aunt Winifred's parrot." Motton rolled his
eyes. "Her *talking* parrot."

"Oh." Nell did giggle then.

Ian could think of a few things to say, but none of
them was appropriate for a lady's drawing room. Apparently they had landed in a zoo as well as an insane asy-
lum. But seeing Nell amused, his mood lifted as well.

Miss Smyth took a sip of her sherry. "But we didn't
come in here to discuss my pets, did we? You said you
had a problem. What seems to be the difficulty, Lady
Kilgorn?"

Any trace of mirth vanished from Nell's expression.
"It's our bedchamber, Miss Smyth," she said.

"You are in the Thistle Room, are you not?" Miss Smyth
smiled. "I thought that was rather clever, you being Scots
and all."

"Yes, but—"

Miss Smyth's brow wrinkled into a frown. "Is it too
small? I know it's probably not what you're used to. I do
apologize."

"It's not the size that is the problem, Miss Smyth,
it's . . . well . . . surely you know . . . ?" Nell shrugged
eloquently. Miss Smyth blinked at her.

"Surely I know what, Lady Kilgorn?"

"That Lord Kilgorn and I are . . ." Nell shrugged
again.

"I'm sorry. I'm not understanding." Miss Smyth
made the mistake of looking up at Ian.

Could the woman really not know? "Miss Smyth," he
said, "surely you are aware of the fact—the *well-known*
fact—that Lady Kilgorn and I have not lived together
for ten years."

"Oh." Miss Smyth frowned. "But you are still married, are you not?"

"Yes, technically we are, but—"

It was as if the sun had come out from behind a cloud. Miss Smyth beamed at him.

"Well, there you are, then. This will be an excellent time for you to become reacquainted."


Nell took another sip of tea and listened with half an ear to white-haired Lady Wordham, Lord Dawson's estranged grandmother, and Lady Oxbury, a delicate woman of about forty who was there with her niece, Lady Grace Belmont, the Earl of Standen's daughter. They were discussing people Nell had never heard of.

The men would enter the drawing room shortly, as soon as they finished their port. Could she slip out now and hide in her room?

No, it was not *her* room—it was hers and Ian's. It was more a trap than a refuge.

How was she going to survive this house party? Dinner had been torture, seated between Ian and Mr. Boland, a thin, balding man of indeterminate age who was far more interested in his mutton than his dinner partners. One would think the poor soul hadn't eaten in a month. She'd tried to engage him in conversation—even a discussion of the food on his plate—but he'd answered every one of her attempts with a grunt, a glare, and vigorous chewing.

She closed her eyes briefly. She'd been much too aware of Ian. She'd swear she'd felt the heat from his body. They *had* been seated very close together. Someone—Miss Smyth, most likely—had decided to squeeze in an extra chair on their side of the table. She couldn't move without brushing up against him.

She'd felt his thigh against her thigh. She'd watched

his broad, strong hand reach for his wineglass and his long fingers twist its stem, his heavy gold signet ring glowing in the candlelight. The sleeve of his tightly fitted coat—with his muscled arm inside, an arm she had viewed in all its naked glory just hours before—touched her arm more than once.

The first time it had happened, she'd tried to put more space between them by leaning toward Mr. Boland. Mr. Boland had glared at her as if he suspected she would snatch his buttered prawns from his plate.

"Would you like more tea, Lady Kilgorn?"

Nell jumped, splashing a few drops of liquid on her bodice. She hadn't seen Miss Smyth approach.

"No, thank you. I am quite content as I am."

"*Are* you, Lady Kilgorn?" Miss Smyth raised her eyebrows and gave her a very significant look.

"Am I . . . what?"

"Quite content as you are." She now wiggled her eyebrows. She clearly was not talking about tea.

"Well, I . . ."

"Perhaps it is time for a change." Miss Smyth leaned closer, her lips curving in a small smile. "One often finds opportunities in the most unexpected places, you know."

"What?"

"Think about it, dear Lady Kilgorn." She patted Nell's hand. "I do apologize for my . . . mistake. I will talk to Mrs. Gilbert in the morning and see what she can do. Now if you'll excuse me?"

"Yes, of course." Nell watched Miss Smyth slip out the door.

It was extremely difficult to believe a house this size didn't have plenty of spare bedchambers, but Miss Smyth had blamed leaky roofs, mold, mildew, smoking chimneys, even rodent infestations for the shortage. She glanced around the drawing room. It didn't *look* as if the viscount took such poor care of his estate, but he hadn't protested his aunt's story in the green parlor. He'd just calmly sipped his sherry and examined a black and gold vase on the immaculate surface of a small table.

"Here they come!" The two Misses Addison leaped from their seats as the door opened and the first unsuspecting male crossed the threshold.

Lady Oxbury frowned. "I don't understand why Mrs. Addison doesn't rein in her daughters."

"Probably because she is upstairs in her room with a brandy bottle." Lady Wordham shook her head. "I'm afraid she's given up even trying to control them. A pity. I cannot like the way they pursue my grandson."

Lord Dawson appeared quite adept at dodging the twins, however. He managed to keep Ian between him and the Addisons, then slipped behind the tea tray to reach Lady Grace.

"Well, if I had a daughter—" Lady Oxbury stopped abruptly. She turned bright red and then ghostly white.

"Are you all right?" Nell put a hand on Lady Oxbury's arm. Her skin felt almost clammy. Was she going to swoon?

"Y-yes. I'm fine."

"Pardon me, but you don't look fine. Shall I get you a glass of water?"

"Lady Kilgorn is right, my dear." Lady Wordham appeared as worried as Nell felt. "You look distinctly out of curl all of a sudden. Perhaps we should send for your hartshorn."

"No, no, really, I'm fine." Lady Oxbury mustered a weak smile. "Please, don't give it another thought."

Nell exchanged a glance with Lady Wordham. The elderly woman shrugged.

"Very well, but do be careful. I know I am ancient, but you are not as young as you once were. You need to take good care of yourself."

Lady Oxbury made an odd noise, something of a cross between a giggle and a sob. "Yes, I will. If you'll excuse me? I believe I'll get a fresh cup of tea."

Nell watched Lady Oxbury pour her tea and then wander over in Mr. Wilton's direction. Why had she reacted so oddly? They'd been talking about the Addisons and daughters . . .

"Do you suppose Lady Oxbury lost a baby?" Nell didn't realize she'd spoken aloud until Lady Wordham answered.

"You mean miscarried? Perhaps. It is a common occurrence, though I can't imagine her loss could be recent. Oxbury's been dead a while, sick longer than that."

"Miscarriage is common?"

Lady Wordham nodded. "Very common. I lost my first child—hardly knew I was pregnant. Went on to have a strapping son and three daughters."

"But Lady Oxbury doesn't have any children."

"True, but Lord Oxbury was thirty years her senior. I suspect that was the problem. Old man, old seed, you know."

"Oh."

"But a young man, like Lord Kilgorn . . ." Lady Wordham paused, turning a very penetrating gaze on Nell. She felt herself blushing and looked away.

"You and Lord Kilgorn are estranged, aren't you, Lady Kilgorn?"

"Yes, but I really do not wish to talk about it."

"And I will not pry. Believe me, I understand estrangement too well. I've not had the pleasure of knowing my grandson because of a falling-out with my youngest daughter." Lady Wordham leaned forward and grasped Nell's hand. "Believe me, Lady Kilgorn, when I tell you, most sincerely, only the most heinous transgressions are worth the pain of cutting yourself off from a loved one. Consider well Lord Kilgorn's sins. Are they really so evil you must suffer a solitary life? Or is forgiveness the better course?"

Nell was certain she would die of embarrassment. "Lady Wordham, I appreciate your—"

Thankfully she was interrupted by a commotion at the drawing room door. It was Miss Smyth with . . .

"Oh, my."

"What is it?" Lady Wordham twisted around and laughed. "Oh my, indeed."

Lord Motton's aunt had returned with a large gray parrot on one shoulder and a small brown monkey, dressed in black and silver livery just like Motton's servants, on the other.

Lord Motton did not look pleased. He left his conversation with Mr. Wilton and strode purposefully toward his aunt.

"Avast! Trouble on the portside!" The parrot flapped its wings, the monkey screeched, and the silly Addison twins screamed.

Nell slapped her hand over her mouth to muffle her laugh. "I've never heard a bird talk."

"You haven't?" Ian strolled over, teacup in hand. He nodded at Lady Wordham. "One of my schoolmates had a bird like that. They are very clever creatures."

"Really, Lord Kilgorn?" Lady Wordham smiled. "Please, sit with us."

Ian took the chair Lady Oxbury had vacated. Nell tried not to stare at him. She'd forgotten how his eyes sparkled when he thought of some wee bit o' mischief, how deeply his cheeks creased when he smiled. His hair glowed warm chestnut in the candlelight and, if she looked closely—which she must stop doing immediately before he noticed her interest—she could see the red-gold shadow of his beard tracing the strong line of his jaw.

"The fellow taught the bird to recite his Latin declensions," he was saying, "so the master would think he was studying, when he was actually out wh—" He flushed and cleared his throat. "Having some fun."

"I see. How . . . clever of him," Lady Wordham said dryly.

Nell studied her hands. What was the matter with men? They seemed to give no thought to climbing into any woman's bed. One woman would do as well as another. Love was irrelevant. Mr. Pennington certainly didn't love her, but he would have been happy to do . . . that with her. And Ian—

She glanced at him. Now he was frowning at the monkey, which had climbed onto the decorative lintel and was screeching down at the viscount.

"That silly leash is going to come loose," he said. "It's clearly not tied securely."

She looked at the red leather strap. "Don't you think Miss Smyth knows how to handle her pet?"

He looked at her, his eyebrows raised, his eyes incredulous. "Do you think the woman knows how to handle anything?"

"Well—"

Just then Miss Smyth pulled on her end of the leash. As Ian had predicted, the red leather fell off the monkey's leg. Freed, the creature screeched again and leaped for the curtains, scrambling up the twenty or more feet of gold fabric. Lord Motton glared at his aunt and then glared at the monkey.

Miss Smyth smiled brightly at the gathering. "Who would like to take a brisk turn about the terrace?"

Ian snorted. "I'll wager Motton would like to send his aunt for a brisk gallop back to London." He shook his head. "I'll see if I can help him capture the wee beastie. Perhaps in gratitude he'll find me an empty bedroom."

# CHAPTER 4

"Do ye suppose he'll be here soon?" Annie glanced at the door as she helped Nell out of her dress.

"Do I suppose who will be here?" As soon as the words left her mouth, Nell knew they sounded unbelievably stupid. There was only one gentleman expected in this bedchamber.

Annie rolled her eyes. "His lordship, of course." She grinned. "I caught a glimpse of him tonight. He's a wee bit old—"

"Old?" Was Annie blind? "He's just thirty."

"Aye, but ye'd hardly know it."

Nell pressed her lips together. Perhaps thirty did seem old to eighteen. . . . Of course it did. Eighteen certainly seemed young to her now.

She'd been only seventeen when she'd married Ian. So full of love. So certain life held only happiness for her. She glared at herself in the mirror.

So foolish. Well, she was indeed older now—and wiser.

"I passed him in the hall." Annie giggled. "And I'll grant ye, I waited for him to come by." She picked up

Nell's discarded clothes. "He was quite an eyeful. Ye can bet I'd not let him out o' my bed if he were my husband."

"Annie!" She didn't care to have her maid lusting after her husband, estranged or not.

"Och, I shouldn't be saying such things, I know. Looks can be deceiving. Did he beat ye, then?"

"No! Of course he didn't beat me."

Annie sent her a sidelong glance. "I know it's nae my place to ask, but we—the servants—always wondered why ye were at Pentforth. Even my ma dinna seem to ken the reason."

"It's . . ." She didn't owe Annie an explanation, but she had to say something. Ian was the laird, after all, and the problem rested as much with her as with him. But what could she say? "Things just didn't work out, Annie. Sometimes that's the way life is."

Annie snorted. "'Things' don't do anything, milady. Ye need to make things work. Ma always said it was a shame ye lived alone. And his lordship needs an heir. This may be yer golden opportunity." She grinned. "I know I'd see it that way if I had a husband as braw as yers."

Nell could not get any redder, she was quite certain of that. "Yes, well, um." She looked around. Where was Annie going to sleep? "I don't see a cot made up for you."

"Weel, ye couldna make much use of yer opportunity with me in the way, could ye?" The cheeky girl winked at her! "Dinna worry. Mrs. Gilbert has given me a snug wee room with Lady Oxbury's maid."

"But—"

Annie had already shut the door firmly behind her.

Nell sighed and glanced at the bed—the very narrow-looking bed. She'd certainly not get a wink of sleep tonight.

The memory of Ian, the very detailed memory of him standing naked by the bath, sprang into her mind.

Heat flooded her. She hadn't meant *that* would keep her awake. She'd only meant she'd be too nervous, too aware of him, to sleep.

She wrapped her arms around her waist and bit her lip. She hadn't thought about *that* in years. It was too tied up in the pain of her miscarriage, the shock and dread she'd felt when she'd first seen the blood trickling down her leg, the anguish and despair that had filled her when she'd finally admitted the baby was gone. She'd cried then until she'd had no more tears to shed, until her heart was exhausted and she couldn't feel anything at all.

That was how she'd decided—how she *wanted*—to go on—peaceful, even-tempered. No passion, no love, no pain. Tranquil.

Pentforth Hall had been her refuge. The neighbors had learned long ago to leave her alone. The servants were polite, but they kept the proper distance. All was calm.

Until now. Now Pennington had forced her out of Pentforth. Annie had started giving her advice. And Ian—

Dear God, what was she going to do about Ian?

He'd never cried, never shed one tear over their baby. No, he'd wanted to go back to bed as soon as they could and try again. He'd said something stupid about getting back on the horse right after you'd fallen off.

Mrs. MacNeill had told her he'd come after her, but she hadn't wanted to see him. She'd torn up all his letters until he'd stopped sending them. She'd counted all his mistresses over the years, each one evidence that he had no heart, had never loved her or the baby.

But now that she'd seen him . . .

She sat in the chair by the fire and tucked her feet up

under her. The flames flickered and leaped. A log snapped; she breathed in the scent of wood and ashes.

Seeing him was making her feel things again. She did not want to feel again . . . did she?

Her life was calm—and empty.

She glanced at the bed. Ian was here—would be very much here shortly. And Lady Remington was not.

What was she thinking? Was she completely daft? Of course she wouldn't . . . would she?

She lusted after him. There, she'd admitted it. Was that so evil? Men lusted for women—couldn't women return the favor?

Lust wasn't feeling, really. It was a response to an animal instinct—and apparently Ian could definitely stir animal instincts in her. And if Lady Wordham was correct . . . well, perhaps she could solve one of his pressing problems. Perhaps she could give him an heir.

They wouldn't have to go back to what they'd had. That was impossible. And they wouldn't even have to go back to living in the same house. Many married members of the ton didn't. But they could share this bed and see if anything came of it.

And if something did? If Ian gave her a child and she lost it again—No, she would not think about that. Just for tonight, she would try facing this as Ian must face all his bed play. As all men must.

And Ian was apparently very willing. Very apparently willing. She bit her lip, remembering exactly how willing he had looked. Very long and thick and eager.

She pressed her legs tightly together and shivered. She was damp and achy—and that was a minor miracle. Nell rested her cheek on her hand. Her skin was so hot—it must be because of the fire.

Ian had looked so funny chasing that wee monkey around Lord Motton's drawing room. He was so large, and the silly monkey was so small and noisy and, well,

cocky. It had shrieked and swung on the curtain rod
while Ian and Lord Motton had shed their coats and
discussed a plan of capture. She smiled. She hadn't
laughed like that in years.

He'd looked very nice in his shirtsleeves. He looked
even better with no shirt at all. Or breeches. Naked as
he'd been . . .

She fanned her hand in front of her face. The fire
was extremely hot this evening.

She should go to bed. It was late. She was tired.

Tired—but nervous. She looked at the bed. Her
stomach twisted into a tight knot. It was far too small,
too narrow, too . . . too bedlike.

Where was Ian? Had Lord Motton found him another room?

Her stomach sank.

And that just proved she was daft. She should not be
disappointed, she should be relieved. She *was* relieved.
She'd just been saved immeasurable embarrassment.
Ian would surely have laughed had she mentioned ba-
bies to him.

She jerked back the covers and climbed into bed. She
shivered. The sheets were cold. Ian had always warmed the
bed. . . .

Idiot! Ian had not been in her bed for years. She was
used to sleeping alone. She was being—

What was that? It sounded like . . . Oh, God, no, it
couldn't be.

It was. She stared in horror as the hallway door
began to open.


"Brandy?" Viscount Motton paused with the crystal decanter in his hand.

"You don't happen to have any whisky in that cabinet, do you?" Ian sat back in the large leather chair and

stretched his feet toward the study's fire. Everyone else had gone off to bed, including Nell. Damn and blast. He'd best get good and drunk if he hoped to survive the night.

"You're in luck." Motton grinned and moved a few other bottles, bringing out a flask labeled DR. MACLEAN'S SPECIAL TONIC. "I've a wee bit."

"I don't think a wee bit will be enough unless you can find me another bedchamber tonight." Thank God Motton poured with a heavy hand. Ian took the proffered glass.

"I am sorry about the confusion. Here." Motton put the flask on the table by Ian's elbow. "It's yours. I've got another one or two where that came from—and I might have a cask stored away in the cellar." He pulled out another bottle as he spoke and poured himself a hearty dose of tonic.

Ian swirled his glass and watched the golden whisky glow in the firelight. It smelled of the sea, of peat, of Scotland, of home. The first sip slid smooth and fiery over his tongue, down his throat to bloom into warmth throughout his chest. "Och, man, ye have some bonnie whisky here. Where did ye get it?"

Motton shrugged and sprawled in the chair across from him. "I have a few friends in Scotland."

Ian took another swallow and closed his eyes. Heaven. "Good friends. And have you friends among the gaugers as well?" He opened his eyes to regard the viscount. "Or shouldn't I ask?"

"I'm sure you shouldn't. You must know I support the efforts of our excise men wholeheartedly." Motton grinned. "Except when I don't."

"Hmm. I'm no lover of the gaugers, that's a fact. Just tell your Scots friends the Earl of Kilgorn sends his regards and thinks he might have a definite need for their tonic in future."

Motton nodded. "I believe they'd be happy to hear

that. I'm sure they wish you to remain healthy and vigorous."

"Aye." Vigorous. Damn, why did that make him think of Nell and the blasted bed upstairs? He took another swallow. "Seems odd an English viscount would know any Scottish distillers. Not that I'm complaining, you understand." He rolled a mouthful of whisky on his tongue. Mmm. "In fact, forget I even mentioned it."

Motton smiled slightly. "Let's just say I spent some time in Scotland when I wished to blend into the surroundings."

Ian sat up straight. "Spying for the crown?" He lived among the Sassenach—even counted many as friends—but he was a Scottish laird first and foremost. If Motton had betrayed—

"No, no. Nothing so organized, I assure you. And my interest was with Englishmen, not Scotsmen."

Ian grunted and studied Motton, then nodded. His gut told him the man wasn't lying, and he believed his gut. It had never before led him astray . . . except with Nell. God, Nell! What was he going to do about Nell?

He refilled his glass.

"Careful," Motton said. "The whisky's strong."

"Aye, and I need strong whisky to get me through this night."

Motton half smiled. "I've left all the arrangements to Aunt Winifred. Perhaps she'll find something in the morning."

"Perhaps she'll find some new way to torture me. I mean no disrespect, Motton, but your aunt is short a sheet, wouldn't you say?"

"Not at all. I think you'll find she's amazingly knowing."

"Knowing? How can you say that? Everyone kens Nell and I have lived apart these last ten years. I canna fathom how your aunt dinna know that, too."

Motton shrugged, his damn eyes gleaming, his lips curved into a smirk. "Maybe you should take advantage of the situation Aunt Winifred has placed you in. I didn't get the impression you hated Lady Kilgorn."

"Hate Nell? No, of course I don't hate Nell." Ian gulped the whisky left in his glass and picked up the flask to pour a drop or two more. Nothing came out. He turned the flask upside down. Still nothing.

"Here." Motton pushed his bottle toward him.

"I don't want to take your whisky, man."

"Please. I have plenty." He held up his glass as evidence. It was still half full. "And as I said, I have more if thirst overtakes me."

"Oh, well, then, thank you." Ian didn't need to be urged again. "This really is verra good whisky."

"I'm glad you like it." Motton smiled, then looked down as he swirled the golden liquid around his glass. "So you don't hate Nell?"

"Och, no. I love her. Have loved her forever. Never stopped loving her." Ian sniffed and swallowed his whisky. Spirits didn't usually make him maudlin. Maybe it was his age. Now that he was thirty, he had to face the fact that he wouldn't live forever.

"And I got the distinct impression that she cared for you."

"Nay, you're wrong there. She hates me. Walked out on me exactly ten years ago." Ian closed his eyes. God, he never wanted to relive that day. He'd come downstairs in the morning to see her standing in the front hall, a few portmanteaus and bandboxes on the floor around her, waiting for the carriage to take her out of his life.

They had argued the night before. He'd said so many things he hadn't meant. He'd been so frustrated—sexually, yes, but more than that. He'd had no idea how to bridge the chasm that yawned between them. He couldn't bring the baby back—and it had not been a baby, really. Her belly hadn't even begun to swell.

These things happened. She wasn't the only woman to lose a child early on. The only thing to do was to try again—but she wouldn't let him touch her.

He'd ended the argument by telling her if she wouldn't be a wife to him, she should leave. He'd regretted the words the moment they'd left his mouth, but he couldn't call them back. He'd seen how her eyes had hardened, how she'd drawn further into herself.

He'd thought she'd be better in the morning. Not over it—he was beginning to think she would never be over anything—but better. He'd never thought she'd actually leave.

She'd had no destination. His heart still clenched at what would have happened had he not come downstairs. Surely his coachman would never have dropped her at an inn—not and keep his employment. He'd tried to persuade her to stay, but when that failed, he'd told Seamus to take her to Pentforth.

He'd thought she'd be back in a few days, a week at the most.

"I don't think she hates you," Motton said.

"Och, man, she does. If ye'd seen the look in her eyes the day she left . . ." It had been as cold as the loch in the dead of winter. She'd looked straight through him, as though he weren't there—or as though he were the lowest sort of vermin.

"I saw the look in her eyes at dinner tonight. I wouldn't say it was hate; I'd say it was longing."

"Nay. Nay, ye're wrong." Ian studied his whisky. *Could* Motton be right? Was it possible Nell had softened toward him? Forgiven him?

Forgiven him for what? He'd done nothing wrong.

He hadn't caused her to lose the babe. If later he'd not kept his wedding vows, well, neither had she. She'd left him—and had taken up with Pennington and the rest.

No, he'd been faithful to her until she'd deserted him, but then, well, what could she expect? That he would live as a monk when she barred him from her bed? Not bloody likely.

"Do you wish to reconcile with Lady Kilgorn?"

"What?" Damn, he'd forgotten Motton was even in the room.

"Lady Kilgorn—do you wish to reconcile with her?" Motton met his eyes, then examined his own whisky. "Lady Remington has been putting it about that you are going to divorce your wife and wed her."

"Lady Remington is not in my confidence." And she damn well was not going to be in his bed ever again. "I have no idea where she would get such a ridiculous notion."

"No idea?"

Ian could feel his face flush. Yes, he'd gone to too many society events with Caro. He'd been bored, and it had been easier to let her attach herself to him than cut the connection. No more. If the damn harpy had the gall to approach him again, she would be in no doubt at all as to his sentiments.

"Lady Remington is of no interest to me. None."

Motton nodded. "Perhaps you should tell Lady Kilgorn that." Motton's gaze was steady. "Perhaps you could effect a reconciliation."

"N-nay." Could he make up with Nell? He would not have thought so before this damn house party, but now? Was Motton right? *Did* Nell care for him? Long for him, even?

She had certainly looked at him when he'd been naked in their room. She'd not been able to take her eyes off him. And she'd been jealous of Caro . . .

He should try. He *would* try.

He finished the last drops of whisky and staggered to his feet. "G'night, Motton."

Motton frowned up at him. "You're sure you haven't had a little too much whisky? Perhaps a spot of coffee—"

"I can hold my liquor."

"Yes, well, you are holding a rather great quantity at the moment. I'm not certain—"

"I am certain—and I'm certainly impatient to go to bed"—he waggled his eyebrows—"if you take my meaning."

"I'm afraid I do. Look, Kilgorn, you might want to be slightly less, um, elevated before you approach Lady Kilgorn."

Ian held up a hand to stop Motton—and then used it to brace himself against the bookcase. He spoke carefully. "I liked your earlier advice better, and I believe I shall act on it immediately."

"Oh, dear God."

Ian grinned. His melancholy had quite dissipated. "Prayer is very good, Motton. I'll leave you to continue your devotions." He turned carefully and headed for the door, taking advantage of the chairs, the desk, and the bookcases to guide and steady his path.

Would Nell be in bed already? Mmm, yes, certainly. In bed. Stretched out under the covers, hair down— surely she didn't braid it? Well, if she did, he would unbraid it and spread it out over his pillow.

He misjudged the height of a step and had to grab the banister to keep from tumbling up the stairs. See— his reflexes were splendid. He'd always been able to hold his liquor. Hell, he could drink many a man under the table. Of course he wasn't drunk. Maybe a little elevated, all right, he'd grant Motton that, but only a little. Just enough to take the edge off.

He reached the top of the stairs and turned down

the hall. Damn it, someone had carelessly placed a small table against the wall. Didn't they know people had to walk here? He caught the vase before it tumbled off, but the flowers in it cascaded to the ground. Well, that was easily fixed. Not all the water had escaped. Just scoop the flowers up and shove them back where they'd come from.

Ah, here was his room—their room. He fumbled with the doorknob, pushed the door open . . . Splendid! Nell was already in bed. He grinned.

"I'm here, lass, and I'm verra ready."

# CHAPTER 5

"Ian." Nell's heart slammed into her throat. She tried to swallow it back down where it belonged. It was not moving. She had to whisper the words around the lump. "Ready? Ready for what?"

He looked so . . . big. He filled the doorway. She pulled the coverlet up as a shield.

Were his eyes a little reckless? Had he been drinking?

"Ready for bed." He stepped all the way into the room and closed the door behind him. "And to sleep." He grinned. "Eventually."

She shivered in a most embarrassing place and pulled the coverlet higher. "What do you mean exactly?"

"Exactly?" He unbuttoned his waistcoat. "Hmm, what *do* I mean exactly?" The waistcoat hit the floor. "Let me think on it." He pulled his shirt out of his waistband and jerked it over his head.

Oh, dear God. She could only stare at him. Her mouth was dry—but another part of her anatomy was exceedingly wet. It shivered again, anxious, eager.

Her stomach shivered with . . . fear?

Should she really do this? Could she feel only physical sensations or would she feel more? Did she want to feel more? And if she . . . if his seed . . . if she became pregnant . . .

She couldn't think.

The firelight played over Ian's skin, revealing and then hiding. He was definitely larger than she remembered. Well, he'd been hardly more than a boy when they'd wed. Now he was every inch a man. Chiseled muscles bulged in his upper arms and his chest down to his flat stomach and—

Oh, my. His muscles were not the only part of him bulging. Had he always been so large there or had his . . . his . . . had *that* grown, too?

"Care to have a closer look, lass?"

"What?" She tore her eyes from his, um, well . . . she tore her eyes away to look up at his face. The blasted man was smirking. And he was coming in her direction.

She swung around to face him as he approached, her feet dangling over the side of the bed, the coverlet still held in front of her.

Ian laughed and twitched the cloth out of her fingers. He reeked of whisky.

"You're drunk."

"Nay." He smiled, the blasted dimple she hadn't seen in forever appearing in his right cheek. "Weel, maybe a wee bit bosky."

More than a wee bit. She'd get bosky herself just inhaling his fumes. This was a bad idea.

He took her hands and held them against his naked chest. His skin was warm; the hair, soft and springy under her fingers. She felt his heart beating.

"Your hair's like night; your skin like cream, so soft and smooth." He brushed her hair back from her face, his hands tangling in its length. She closed her eyes to concentrate on his touch.

His fingers skimmed over her forehead, her cheeks, down to her chin. He tilted her face up—dear Mother of God, was he going to kiss her? Her lips felt swollen; she parted them in anticipation. . . .

His mouth touched hers, his tongue slipped inside.

Mmm. He filled her with heat and whisky and a taste that was his alone. Desire pooled between her legs, hot and wet. Her lips felt swollen there, too. She spread her knees and Ian's leg came between hers. His fingers plucked at the skirt of her nightgown and pulled it up to her thighs so he could push her knees farther open. He stepped closer.

It was good. It felt good, the night air cooling her heat.

Now his fingers were brushing down her front, slipping her gown's buttons free. That was good, too. She was much, much too hot. She could hardly wait to feel the cool air on her skin there as well.

She slid her hands up the hard plane of his chest, over his broad shoulders, to his neck. Her fingers burrowed into his hair and she held his head steady.

Oh. He was pushing back the sides of her gown, exposing her—

Mmm. His palms slid over her breasts. His hands cradled them, lifting while his thumbs—

"Ahh." She broke free of his mouth. "Oh."

"Like that, do ye, Nell? Your breasts were always so sensitive. I loved to touch them, loved to hear you squeak." Ian nuzzled the spot on her neck just under her ear. "Do ye still squeak?"

"Uh, no, uh—eek!" Ian's thumb flicked over her nipple, which was budded hard and yearning. He chuckled and kissed her jaw.

"Aye, ye do." He rubbed both nipples.

"Ohh."

"And ye moan, too." He moved his hands to her jaw,

holding her face so he could look into her eyes. "God, Nell, how I've missed you."

His eyes were so . . . hot.

They hadn't changed. Oh, there might be a few wrinkles at the corners, but his gaze was as compelling as ever. He had looked at her this way before, when they were young and in love.

No, don't think of love. Don't think at all.

She moved her fingers from Ian's hair to his waistband. .

"Ah, that's it, lass." Ian rested his forehead against Nell's. He should not have had so much whisky. He knew it, in a vague sort of way. He was in a bit of a fog at present. He wished he weren't. He wanted to remember every single moment of this.

The lovely girl was unbuttoning his fall. Her fingers were so white against the black cloth of his breeches. So slim. They brushed against his belly. Ah, so soft. He sucked in his stomach to give her more room to work the buttons free. Thank God he dispensed with drawers when he traveled. Once she got the fall open—

Had she undone Pennington's breeches for him?

No, he would not think of that bastard.

Perhaps it was good he was drunk. The whisky-fog made the waiting less . . . agonizing. He could tear the thing open himself, couldn't he? But that wouldn't be very gent-gentlemanly.

No, it was good he was a bit fuzzy with drink. He didn't want to attack Nell like a satyr, did he?

No. No, he didn't. No satyrs. Just sex . . . sexual con . . . congress.

They'd been good together all those years ago, hadn't they? He remembered that they had, but how could he be certain? They'd both been so young. He'd been a virgin. . . .

Had she found Pennington more satisfying? Bloody

hell. Ah, but he'd learned a few tricks over the years. He'd make her forget Pennington.

If he weren't so drunk . . . but he'd still be sure to make it good for her.

He moistened his lips. Patience. They had the night before them. There was no hurry. The waiting was part of the delight . . .

Ah . . . delight. A dream come true.

The damn whisky made it seem too much like a dream.

Nell paused in her button struggles to cup his poor straining cock. Her touch was muffled by the damn cloth of his damn breeches, but he was grateful for it anyway. Once he was naked, once this damn cloud cleared from his head—and the blasted cloth from his cock—ah, that would be delightful.

Clever girl, she got another button free.

Zeus, how he'd missed her. He'd done this thing countless times—well, not countless, perhaps, but many times. Been in many different bedchambers over the long, lonely years—London was full of women willing to entertain a lonely lord—but it had never been like this. There had never been delight in it. Release, yes, but no delight and no real satisfaction. It had all been just bodies.

Well, that had been all he'd been looking for. Just physical release, not lo— not anything else.

But with Nell . . . with Nell it had never been just bodies. It had been hearts and souls, too. Not that he'd understood all that then.

Ah! Lovely Nell had finally got his fall open. She pushed his breeches down to his thighs. Cool air and her lovely, smooth hands touched him.

He shuddered with desire and delight. This was splendid. Beyond splendid. She cupped his cock and stroked it lightly as if it were a . . . lapdog.

Well, he certainly wished to lay it in her lap.

They'd married so young, been married such a short time. Not even a year before she'd conceived. They'd loved with such intensity, there'd been no need for skill or subtlety.

Ah—no need tonight either, at least for him. Her fingers traced his length and he'd swear he grew another inch. He hoped she felt the lust as strongly as he because skill and subtlety were beyond him at the moment.

Oh, Nell's clever fingers had moved to explore his ballocks. He bit his lip. Zeus, he'd never felt anything so wonderful.

He reached up and grabbed the bed curtain rail. She was rubbing her cheek against him now. Bliss. Bloody bliss.

Would she use her lips next? They had not played that game when they were married; he had learned it from his first lover, the Countess of Wexmore. She'd been lush, alluring, sinful—and very experienced. Well, she'd been ten years older than he and married to a very rich and very old man. She'd sampled most of the male members of the ton—pun intended. He'd learned many interesting bed tricks in her boudoir.

He frowned. Had Nell learned this trick from Pennington or one of the other men she'd dallied with?

Ah. He closed his eyes, biting his lip again. She was kissing him now. And now . . . yes . . . the tentative, wet sweep of her tongue . . .

"Do you like that?"

Did he *like* it? Couldn't she see he was just about bursting with enthusiasm? "Aye. It's wonderful." He reached to touch her hair. "Did Pennington teach you it?"

"*What?*"

That had obviously been an extremely stupid thing to say. *Extremely* stupid. He didn't need to hear the fury in Nell's voice—he felt it in her grasp. Her fingers tightened around the sensitive bit of flesh she was holding. Thankfully, she did not have the world's strongest grip, but it was strong enough. He gasped, pain surging up his body to lodge in his muddled brain.

At least she hadn't had him in her mouth. If she'd bitten down . . .

Perhaps she still would bite. She looked angry enough. He stepped back out of range. Unfortunately, his breeches were still at half mast. Fortunately he didn't hit anything *too* hard on his way down to the floor.

Unfortunately, the change in altitude didn't completely clear his drunken brain. "So you didn't do that with Pennington?"

A pillow hit him squarely in the face.


How could Ian have said such a thing? How could he have *thought* such a thing? *He* might have taken mistresses by the cartload, but *she* had kept her marriage vows.

Nell glared down at the man sprawled on the bedchamber floor. He was snoring, the coxcomb, had been snoring all night. She'd barely got a moment's sleep.

She'd taken pity on him during one of her many waking periods—why, she couldn't say—and had kicked one of her blankets down to him. Perhaps she'd hoped he'd sleep more soundly and stop his racket. He hadn't snored like this when he was younger—of course, he hadn't got so drunk when he was younger. And he used to sleep on his stomach. The floor did not make a very soft bed; perhaps that's why he was sprawled on his back.

The blanket had slipped to his waist, revealing his muscled arms and broad, naked chest. It was no wonder women lined up to climb into his bed. The man was a classical statue, a god come to life. Every inch of him—*every* inch—was impressive.

And she should not have been touching those inches last night. What had come over her? She'd never been that bold before.

"Snorkz."

Good heavens, he wasn't going to wake up now, was he? He couldn't find her staring at him like this. . . . No, he was just turning over—

Oh, my.

The blanket slipped off. Sometime during the night, Ian had divested himself of his breeches. His lovely muscled arse was displayed for her inspection, and if she peered over his hip, she could almost see—

She was not doing any peering. No, indeed.

She scrambled out of bed—on the side opposite from the sleeping devil—and splashed water on her face. The cool liquid felt very good on her heated skin. She took care of a few private tasks and then pulled on an old frock and cloak to slip outside for a brisk walk. She was used to exercise at Pentforth, and she most definitely needed to put some space between her and Lord Kilgorn.

She glanced at him—carefully keeping her eyes on his face . . . well, after a very small peek at—ahem. She glanced at his *face,* her hand on the doorknob. He looked so young, so innocent. Ha! He should be made to wear a placard proclaiming "womanizer." Well, and "drunkard." And "seducer."

That was redundant. He'd spent time in London, hadn't he? And been corrupted there. All the British ton were rakes and ravishers and harlots and whores. Mutton dressed as lamb, every last one of them.

She slipped out the door—and almost collided with Miss Smyth.

"Good morning, Lady Kilgorn." Miss Smyth gave her a sly look. "I trust you slept well?"

Slept well? Why did her face bloom with sudden

heat? She must look so guilty—but she was innocent. Completely innocent.

Well, perhaps not *completely* innocent. There had been those few brazen moments when she had actually touched Ian's . . .

Miss Smyth was smirking at her!

This would never do. She closed the door firmly behind her and straightened her spine. "Actually, Miss Smyth, I did not sleep well at all. It is most awkward having to share such a confined space with Lord Kilgorn. Have you made any progress in locating an empty room for one of us?"

Miss Smyth considered the bedroom door. "I am so sorry. It really is very difficult." She shrugged. "Awkward, don't you know."

"No, I don't know."

Miss Smyth frowned. "You're certain you didn't have a, er, pleasant night?" Was the woman waggling her eyebrows? What in the world was she implying?

Nothing, of course. "I am completely certain. In fact I slept hardly one wink." Did Miss Smyth's expression brighten? "I tossed and turned all night."

"That must have kept Lord Kilgorn awake."

There was no point in hiding the facts. Perhaps if the woman was aware of the extent of the problem, she would be more diligent in finding a solution.

"I couldn't say. Lord Kilgorn was a gentleman"—perhaps not the *entire* truth—"and slept on the floor."

"The floor!" Miss Smyth looked quite shocked and rather, well, crestfallen. Good. Perhaps she would be jolted into action. "That will never do."

"Exactly. So you see it is quite important that you locate a spare room for one of us. Perhaps another guest would not mind doubling up? Mr. Wilton, for example. Could he not share with his nephew, Lord Dawson?"

Miss Smyth shook her head so sharply her neat gray

bun looked in danger of tumbling free of its pins. "No, indeed. I'm afraid that would not work at all."

Nell pressed her lips together. A more forceful person would grab the woman by the shoulders and shake her, but she would not so far forget her breeding. She was sorely tempted to shout, but she swallowed that impulse, too. She might wake Ian, and she did not want to do that. And what would shouting accomplish, really? But why two related gentlemen could not share the same bedchamber—

She took a deep breath and forced a smile. "I'm sure you'll find a solution before tonight. Now if you'll excuse me? I was just going out for a walk."

"It's damp out, you know. Misty. Rainy even."

"Splendid. I shall feel quite at home. If you'll excuse me?" She stepped past Miss Smyth and proceeded down the corridor. She would not hurry. She was not running from Motton's aunt or, worse, Ian. She was just going out for some exercise, to clear her head.

She glanced back as she turned to go down the stairs. Miss Smyth was still standing where she'd left her, staring at the bedroom door, nodding her head and tapping her chin. Surely she wasn't going to enter the room to ascertain exactly where Ian was sleeping?

Nell paused. Should she say something? If the woman did venture inside, she was going to be exceedingly shocked. And Ian would be, if not embarrassed, then certainly startled. It would not be a pleasant scene. . . .

But it would also not be a scene that was any concern of hers. If Miss Smyth was going to barge into bedchambers, she needed to be prepared to face whatever she discovered there. And if Ian was going to be a cabbage-headed clod pole—a *naked* cabbage-headed clod pole—well, she didn't have any sympathy for him.

She grasped the banister firmly and proceeded down the stairs.

# CHAPTER 6

He was an idiot, a beef-witted, cabbage-headed clod pole, a great lobcock, a—

"Good morning, Kilgorn." Motton glanced up from his newspaper and the remnants of his breakfast. His eyes paused and then traveled the length of Ian's admittedly disheveled form. "Too much whisky last night?"

Ian grunted and turned to the sideboard. He captured a kidney and dumped it on his plate. Aye, he'd had too much whisky last night and it had led him to act the colossal ass. The truth was he'd been thinking with his cock, not his cock-loft.

"And how is Lady Kilgorn this morning? Better than you, I do hope."

Ian ground his teeth together and added a few kippers to his plate. He would like to upend the whole thing on Motton's head, but the man *was* his host. Still, the fellow was normally awake on every suit. He must know this teasing did not sit well.

"Feeling a bit peevish, are you?" Motton's right eyebrow rose.

Ian counted to ten. He would *not* dump his kippers and kidneys on the viscount, no matter how tempted he was.

"The sleeping"—damn, was he flushing?—"accommodations are not at all agreeable, as you know. Has Miss Smyth made any progress in finding me a separate room?"

"After you and I spoke last night, I got the distinct impression a change would not be required."

"Well, it *is* required. Lady Kilgorn does not find the current situation at all comfortable." Nor did he, of course. He did not care for sleeping on the floor.

Motton returned his attention to the paper. "I will speak to Aunt Winifred when I see her. I don't believe she has risen yet."

"There must be an empty bed somewhere in this vast pile." Ian snapped his teeth shut. Yelling at the viscount was not an inspired notion, but his temper was not at its best.

Motton shrugged and stood up. "One would think there would be, but Aunt Winifred was quite definite on the issue."

Ian kept his teeth clenched.

"If you'll excuse me," Motton was saying. "I have estate business to attend to." He held out the paper. "Care to peruse the *Post*?"

"Thank you." He'd rather roll the blasted paper up and hit someone with it—Miss Smyth came immediately to mind.

He sat down in blessed solitude and stared at his plate. His stomach had finally alerted him to the fact that a few corners of toast might have been a better selection. He poured himself some coffee.

Dawson arrived but had the good sense to remain mute, as did Wilton, who appeared not long afterward.

But then Miss Smyth entered and peace exited. She was so bloody cheerful. And talking to her—trying to get a sensible answer from her about a new bedchamber—was impossible. Like trying to converse with her demented parrot or silly wee monkey. He left as soon as he could, stepping out into the fresh, raw air. It was chill and damp and reminded him of home.

He headed off across the lawn, quickly lengthening his stride. He'd heard Motton had a lake somewhere on his estate. A plunge into clear, cold water would be just the thing to clear his head.

Nell walked and walked, but found no peace.

How could Ian think she'd done . . . *that* with Mr. Pennington? How could he think she'd done that with anyone? Surely he'd never credited Mr. MacNeill's daft tales that she was dallying with all the males around Pentforth Hall, had he?

No, Ian believed she'd been unfaithful because he'd been unfaithful. Many, many times, starting with the Countess of Wexmore. And while his current mistress was a widow, many of the women he'd gone to bed with had been married when he'd climbed between their sheets. Did he think she was like them? That she was as . . . soulless as those Sassenach whores? Did he know her so little?

Ian was welcome to the London women. She'd been beyond stupid to consider letting the man give her a child. Divorce was a very welcome solution to their problem. She could hardly wait to be free of him.

She followed a path through some trees and emerged by an ornamental lake. A swan glided along the water's surface. Beautiful—but swans could be quite nasty. Like many London ladies. She gave the creature a wide berth.

Had she been just a little nasty herself?

No, of course not. She'd had good reason to leave Ian. She'd—

She'd refused to see him when he'd come to Pentforth Hall—but the wound had still been too raw then. He hadn't come again. But had she given him any encouragement to come? She'd burned all his letters unread. She'd never written to him—the post did travel from Scotland to London. She could have written.

No, if she were honest—completely, painfully honest—she had to admit she was at least a little to blame. She'd been almost happy when she'd heard about the countess. Well, not *happy*, really. She'd felt betrayed, but she'd also felt just a little bit relieved. She'd not been willing to have Ian in her bed. She'd not been ready to be a wife to him again.

Had he really betrayed her, or had she abandoned him?

Did she hear splashing up ahead? What . . . oh. She ducked behind a large willow and peered out from behind its trunk. Someone—some man—was swimming. Ian. His arms flashed out of the water as he stroked across the lake. Then he dove beneath the surface, his back, buttocks, and legs flashing white before disappearing.

The water must be very cold, but that wouldn't bother Ian. He'd liked to swim at Kilgorn, where the loch was frigid. He'd try to lure her in to join him, but she'd only go if the day was very warm. Even then she could never last long.

She tilted her face to the sun, a smile curving her lips. Mmm. When she had gone swimming, Ian had been very, very good at warming her once they came out of the water. They'd lie on a blanket in the sun and heather, a slight breeze teasing their hot, entwined limbs, and make love till the chill of dusk finally sent them inside.

How she had loved him. He had been her life until she'd lost their baby. After that—well, her heart had been as cold as the loch, too cold for the sun or Ian to warm.

Was it still?

He was swimming toward the shore. He'd be getting out in just a few minutes. She would see—

What was that? A twig snapping? She looked to her left. A path climbed up through the trees and at its top, about twenty-five yards away, was Lady Grace.

The girl couldn't see Ian! Grace was unwed and, well, Nell did not want yet another woman seeing her husband—her estranged husband—naked.

Ian was still swimming. She had time to intercept Lady Grace. She darted out from behind the willow and hurried up to meet her.

"Lady Grace, how lovely to see you."

Lady Grace smiled. "Lady Kilgorn. I was looking for you."

"You were?" What could the woman want with her? She took her arm and directed her back the way she'd come. "You must call me Nell."

"Nell, then. I"—Lady Grace cleared her throat—"I was wondering . . . Well, I wanted to . . . You see, I thought perhaps . . ."

Nell frowned. What was this? "Yes? Is there something of a particular nature you wish to speak to me about?"

Grace looked distinctly relieved. "Yes. That is, if you don't mind . . . if you don't find me impertinent."

"Impertinent? Of course not." What could this be about? She was sure she'd exchanged no more than a handful of pleasantries with Lady Grace since they'd met yesterday. Why was she seeking her out?

"You see, I am struggling with an issue. I can't ask my aunt since she has problems of her own, but I need the advice of an older, experienced woman."

"Ah." That was all Nell could manage to say. Older and experienced? There could be only three or four years between them. She swallowed, trying to gather her scattered wits. "And this issue would be . . . ?"

"Love." Lady Grace blurted out the word and then turned bright red.

"Oh."

Apparently that little four-letter word was the plug that, ejected, opened the floodgates.

"Yes, love. I don't know what to do. Lord Dawson has been very attentive, and I lo—like him very much, but my father hates him."

Not a small problem. "Does your father have a good reason for his feelings?" Nell would not have thought Lord Dawson a blackguard, but then what did she know? "Sometimes men are more aware than we of another man's background and"—how to say this?—"unsavory habits."

Lady Grace shook her head. "I'm sure Papa knows nothing about Da—Lord Dawson. He's never met him."

"What?" Well, perhaps an actual meeting wasn't necessary. Reputations did precede people. "Why do you think your father hates the man? Perhaps you are mistaken."

"Oh, no, I am not mistaken. Papa would definitely hate Da—Lord Dawson if he knew about him. He hates all Wiltons on principle for something that happened years ago when Papa was young."

"Oh." A family feud à la Romeo and Juliet, perhaps. However entertaining the play might be, it would not act well in real life. "That doesn't seem particularly enlightened."

"No, it isn't, but Papa isn't particularly enlightened.

He's stubborn and opinionated and, well, somewhat overbearing. But he *is* my father. My mother died when I was very young, so it's been just the two of us for such a long time." Lady Grace's voice caught slightly. "I love him. I don't want to hurt him."

"Of course you don't."

Grace glanced at Nell and then looked away. "He's arranged for me to marry a neighbor." She might have been talking of darning socks, she sounded so unenthusiastic.

"Is the neighbor old and fat?"

Grace laughed. "Oh, no. John is perfectly presentable. Quite unexceptional. He would make someone an excellent husband."

"But not you."

"No, um, that is he would make me an excel— a suitable husband. I do like him when he's not prosing on about his plants."

"Hmm. Are you certain you can't discuss this with Lady Oxbury? She did bring you to London for the Season. She must have had in mind finding you a more appropriate husband."

Lady Grace shook her head vehemently. "Oh, no. Definitely not. As I said, Aunt Kate has troubles of her own, not that she has shared them with me. But something is amiss between her and Lord Dawson's uncle, Mr. Wilton."

"I see." They were almost back to the house and Nell still had no clue why Lady Grace was telling her any of this. "Well, you must know that I am not one to give advice of a marital nature."

"But that is exactly why I wanted to speak to you, Lady Kilgorn. I mean, I don't wish to pry, but, well, married love . . . it doesn't last, does it? It's not important for contentment?" Lady Grace frowned. "I don't have the experience of my parents to advise me since my mother died when I was so young, but from what I know of Aunt Kate's marriage, she rubbed along tolerably well with Lord Oxbury even though she didn't love him. And looking around the ton—there just aren't that many love matches."

"I wouldn't know. I've never been to London." The house was very close now. Could she break into a run and end this uncomfortable conversation?

"But—I know it is none of my concern, I am fully aware of that, but . . . was yours a love match, Lady Kilgorn?"

"Yes." There had been no question of that. She'd been completely, insanely in love with Ian as perhaps only a seventeen-year-old girl could be. He'd been almost a god to her—certainly a hero. She'd been blind to all his faults . . . as he'd been blind to hers. She'd never doubted he'd loved her. And if life had been different . . .

But life was as it was.

"And so love isn't enough." Lady Grace gave her a sad little smile. "I thought so."

"Perhaps." They were at the door now. Nell put her hand out to stop Grace. "But it is a lot. I still love my husband." It was true. The love was tangled with hurt and disappointment, but it was still there.

"And yet you have no real marriage." Grace touched Nell's hand lightly. "I don't mean to criticize. I thank you most sincerely for your candor. Only, I don't believe I could live your life. I would be too lonely."

Ah. Loneliness. Now *that* was something Nell could speak about with authority.


Ian cut his venison into precise pieces. The lake's ice-cold water had helped clarify his thinking. He had made his decision. He would get through this damn house party and then he would see about starting divorce proceedings.

He stared down at his dinner plate. He had no appetite. He slanted a look to his right. Nell appeared to be similarly afflicted. She was ignoring her meal entirely.

He glanced around the table. In fact, very little food was being consumed. Well, Motton and his aunt were doing a credible job on their dinners and the Addison twins were heaping their plates with second helpings—not to mention Mr. Boland's single-minded attention to his victuals—but Wilton and Lady Oxbury, Dawson and Lady Grace were exercising their forks much as he and Nell were—using them to push their food from one side of their dish to the other.

He took a sip of wine. He was not going to touch a drop of whisky tonight. He was going up to that bloody room stone sober. He brought a forkful of venison to his mouth—and then returned it to his plate. He felt like he had a rock in his stomach.

He didn't want to divorce Nell, but what could he do? He needed an heir. They had no real marriage—and now no hope of one. He'd trampled his chances good and well last night.

He sneered at his green beans. He hadn't thought he was so stupid.

"Is something amiss with your vegetables, Lord Kilgorn? I hope you didn't find a twig or other indigestible bit. The kitchen maids occasionally get to gossiping and don't pay as strict attention to their task as they should." Miss Smyth leaned forward, pointing her fork at his plate as if she intended to pick through his beans herself to ascertain that all was well.

He held his knife ready to beat back—or at least nudge away—her utensil if necessary. "No, no, there is nothing amiss. The beans are fine. Perfect." It certainly wasn't the kitchen's fault everything tasted like ashes tonight.

"Are you sure? You've hardly touched your dinner."

Good God, Miss Smyth sounded like his nursery maid. "I assure you, madam, the dinner is fine. I merely lack an appetite to do it justice."

"You aren't sickening, are you?"

He should say yes, but the woman actually looked concerned. "No, I am merely tired." He smiled. "I'm sure I'll sleep better and my appetite will return when you've been able to find me another bedchamber."

Damn. Miss Smyth's eyes lit up. Was that a sly gleam of mischief he discerned? Surely she wasn't going to make some salacious comment about lack of sleep and sharing a bed with Nell? It looked very much as if she was going to. She opened her mouth and horror gripped his soul.

"Miss Smyth, can I trouble you to pass the sweet-breads?"

Thank God for Miss Addison—whichever one it was. He would have sworn he'd never thank the Almighty for gracing the world with either of the annoying chits, but this one's request could not have come at a better moment. Miss Smyth paused, shrugged, and grasped the requested dish.

"Of course, Miss Addison. I'm so happy *someone* has a lusty appetite."

Nell started choking.

"Are you all right?" Should he pound her on the back? He lifted his hand, but she raised hers to deter him.

"I'm sorry," she whispered when she stopped gasping. "I'm afraid a mouthful of wine went down the wrong way. I'm fine now." She returned her attention to artfully arranging her French beans.

Damn. Her face was politely expressionless. She'd shut him out again.

If only he could turn back the clock. When she'd been young, she'd been so full of joy, of life, she couldn't hold it in. He'd been drawn to her—all the lads had. But he'd been the laird . . .

He speared another morsel of venison. No, it hadn't been his position that had given him her favor. Well, his position might have made the other lads back off when they'd seen he wanted her, but Nell herself had not cared, would not have cared had he been the lowest stable boy. She had loved him for himself.

He forced himself to chew the damn meat. It could have been shoe leather for all he knew.

When Nell had loved him, he'd felt stronger, smarter, quicker. Happier.

"Lord Kilgorn, would you care for some potatoes?"

"No, thank you, Miss Smyth."

Why in God's name had she lost the baby? She'd been young and healthy. She shouldn't have had any problems. There'd been no warning. Just the cramping and then the blood.

He reached for his wineglass and took a large swallow. That was a day he never wanted to relive. She'd cried and cried as if her heart had broken. He'd felt so damn helpless.

He shoved another tasteless bit of food in his mouth and chewed mechanically.

He'd been able to think of only one solution—to give her another child—and she'd rejected that. More than rejected. She'd screamed at him, sobbed . . . He'd felt like a complete monster.

And then last night . . .

He speared a bean and shoved it into his mouth.

She'd seemed interested at first—surely he'd not been so drunk as to be mistaken in that. More than interested. She'd taken his cock in her hand. . . . Zeus, that had felt good. Her tentative fingers, then the silky soft brush of her cheek, the delicate sweep of her tongue—

"Lord Kilgorn, would you like some sweetbreads?"

"Wha—?" Miss Smyth was blinking at him and holding a plate of . . . "No, no thank you, Miss Smyth. Really, I don't need anything else. I am quite satisfied."

The woman's damn eyebrow flew up and she looked pointedly at Nell. If there was a God in heaven, Nell would still be studying her plate. His faith was not strong enough to look.

"Oh, I doubt you're satisfied, my lord."

A certain part of his anatomy, thankfully hidden by the tabletop, agreed with her most vehemently.

# CHAPTER 7

She was hiding. All right, she admitted it. She was a coward.

Nell pulled the covers up higher and tried to find a comfortable position. The maids must have filled the mattress with rocks during the day.

She flopped onto her back and stared up at the canopy. She had to get to sleep—she did not want to be awake when Ian came up. With luck he'd be as late as last night—and not as drunk.

How many more days were left to this infernal house party? She could hardly wait to go home.

A sharp lump dug into the small of her back. She turned onto her side and tugged on the covers again.

Oh, why lie? She didn't want to go back to Pentforth Hall, and she surely did not want to go back to Mr. Pennington's amorous advances.

She turned over onto her stomach. If Ian truly thought she was engaging in such activities with the man, why had he allowed the disgusting toad to retain his position?

The answer was painfully obvious—he didn't care.

He was completely indifferent to the possibility that his estranged wife was trysting with his estate manager.

And she wasn't crying. She was angry, that was all.

She wiped her face on her pillow. She *had* to go to sleep before Ian arrived.

Perhaps he'd decided to keep Lord Dawson company. The baron had looked completely forlorn after Lady Grace left the drawing room. Was the girl right to marry her neighbor? She obviously loved Lord Dawson—and he loved her.

Yes, indeed. Without a doubt, Lady Grace was being very wise. Love didn't guarantee happiness. She had loved Ian beyond all reason, and here she was, in this hellish limbo, married, yet not. Love was far more trouble than it was worth.

She turned to her back once more. Surely she could find a position comfortable enough to let her drop off to sleep?

She closed her eyes and breathed deeply, but sleep still eluded her.

Perhaps the problem wasn't so much a lumpy mattress as a, well, lumpy conscience. Was it really love causing her misery—or was it fear? Was she afraid to let Ian back into her heart and risk the pain of conceiving and losing another child?

Yes. Yes, she was afraid. And it was too late now. If only she had reined in her temper last night, when lust had drowned out the terror—

Was that the doorknob turning? Dear God. She lifted her head to stare at the door. He couldn't be coming up this early, could he? It wasn't possible—

Yes, it was. The door creaked open. She shut her eyes, dropping her head onto the pillow. If she couldn't sleep, she'd pretend to. She heard some rustling . . .

"I know you're awake, Nell." The voice had come from very close by.

Her eyes flew open. "Ack!" The man was standing right next to the bed, his chest naked for all the world to see. Or at least for her to see. The candlelight turned his skin golden and gilded the fine hair curling over his chest, over his belly, down to—

At least he still had his breeches on.

"I *was* asleep."

His damn eyebrow arched up. She'd never been able to lie to him successfully.

"What are you doing here?"

He smiled slightly. "Isn't it obvious? Getting ready for bed."

"Bed?" Her voice squeaked. She tried to take a calming breath. "You don't really mean to . . . you aren't going to . . ." Another breath. "You don't plan to share this b-bed with me, do you?"

She should try for a little courage, but her heart was pounding too quickly for her to think.

"Actually, I do." He glanced away. "As I discovered last night, the floor is quite uncomfortable."

"Well—" Nell glanced at the other pillow. It was much, much too close. The bed was just too small.

"Unless you'd like to take a turn on the floor? I warn you, though, Motton desperately needs to replace the carpet. It is rather thin."

Nell looked down at the rug. "N-no . . ."

"I didn't think so." Ian shrugged. His muscles shifted in a very distracting fashion. She wanted to touch him exactly as she had last night.

Dear heavens. Well, it was his own fault, parading about without a stitch of cloth covering his chest. There were reasons men—polite men—kept their shirts on. Well, men like Ian. Pennington was a different case entirely. The thought of his scrawny chest stripped of shirt, waistcoat, and coat stirred the senses in a completely different—a completely unpleasant—manner.

What if she rolled over in the middle of the night and landed up against Ian? What if her face touched his warm chest; what if her bare hand found his smooth, strong back? What if—

What if she just threw herself at him right now?

How brazen could she be? She wanted to cradle the lovely organ she'd touched last night. She wanted to feel it deep inside her. She shivered.

"Are you cold, Nell?"

"N-no."

"Hmm. Actually, you look rather flushed. You aren't sickening, are you?"

Would he sleep on the floor if she said she was? "Yes, yes, I suppose I might be."

Dear God, he put his hand on her forehead and then on her cheeks. His fingers were large and slightly rough. "You don't feel hot."

She certainly did. It was a wonder his hand didn't burst into flame. "Uh." She should say something . . . what? "Um." She pulled her head back, breaking their contact.

She remembered with shocking clarity the feel of his fingers on her body, stroking over her arms, her breasts . . .

He'd used to sleep cuddled up—well, tangled up— naked, warm, and relaxed after coupling. Did he still?

She moistened her lips. Could he smell her desire? Could he hear it in the way her breath hitched?

He withdrew his hand. "Are you afraid, then?" His voice was harsh. "Are you worried I'll force myself on you?"

No, she was worried she'd force herself on *him*. But she couldn't say that. How mortifying. She simply shook her head and kept her eyes on her hands even when Ian made a short, disgusted sound.

"Will this make you sleep easier?" He went to the

hearth, picked up the poker, and laid it down the center of the bed. It was dark and hard; traces of ash smeared across the white sheets. "And I will keep my breeches on and stay on top of the sheets."

"Oh." Her disappointment was an egg-size lump in her throat, but she couldn't have Ian thinking she lusted for him like all the London women. "Splendid. Perhaps I shall be able to sleep tonight after all."

She glanced up. Ian's face looked like granite. His brows snapped down when his eyes met hers. "*You* had the bed last night. I would have thought you'd slept soundly."

She felt herself flushing. "It is difficult sharing a room with you."

His face grew even grimmer, if that were possible. "Well, with any luck, this will be the last time you'll be forced to do so. I intend to insist Miss Smyth find me other accommodations tomorrow."

"Good." The thought made her stomach sink. How was she going to go back to Pentforth Hall and ever find any contentment?

He was going to go bloody, raving mad.

Ian strode across Motton's well-manicured lawns. If he didn't get out of that damn bedchamber—that damn *bed*—he was going to start foaming at the mouth. Bedlam would not be large enough to contain his insanity.

Last night had been pure hell. He'd slept hardly at all. Every time he'd start to drop off, Nell would make some small noise. She'd tossed and turned constantly. He almost suspected her of purposely trying to torment him. She hadn't been such a restless sleeper when they'd been young.

He glared at an innocent squirrel that had had the

audacity to dart across his path. Any closer and he'd have stepped on the brainless rodent.

When they were young, if she'd been restless, he'd had a very efficient—a very pleasant—way of calming her. A thorough bout of lovemaking had always made them both wonderfully relaxed. But obviously that solution had not been available to him last night, damn it all to hell.

The bloody poker was not the only hard object in that bed.

He reached a large oak tree and turned back toward the house. This was ridiculous. He'd already taken his horse out for an hour ride, yet he was still as . . . tense as hell.

His horse was not what—whom—he wished to be riding.

Should he try the inn? Surely he could find a woman to cure his problem there—

No, damn it. He didn't want a whore, he wanted Nell. Zeus, did he want her. But she didn't want him.

It was a damnable coil. Seeing her again—smelling her, hearing her, touching her—had brought all the old longing back. That was why he hadn't visited Pentforth again. He'd known the only way he could live without her was to try to forget she existed. He'd never been completely successful, even after all these years, but he'd been able to keep the need to a manageable level of discontent.

Now it was a damn, raging fever. He might not survive this blasted house party.

He had to divorce her. It was the uncertainty of the situation—yes, the *hope*—that was the problem. Once he took steps to end their marriage . . . well, it would be final. Like death.

If he didn't get his own room today, he *would* die.

He approached the house. Hmm. There was a traveling carriage on the drive. How was Miss Smyth going to handle this? She would have to rearrange sleeping accommodations now or magically find an empty room. He smiled slightly. This should be interesting.

A knot of people clogged the entry hall—Dawson, Lady Grace, Miss Smyth, Motton . . . Nell. His eyes were drawn to her like iron to a magnet. Damn. He forced himself to study the scene instead. There was a good bit of brangling going on.

The Earl of Standen had arrived to drag his daughter home. Why he was doing so remained a bit of a mystery and, frankly, Ian didn't care what the man's reasons were. If Lady Grace departed, her room was suddenly free for him, though he wouldn't be at all surprised if Miss Smyth concocted some asinine reason why he couldn't take it. Well, he was not going to be hoodwinked again. He would insist, most strenuously.

"But the house party isn't over yet," Motton was saying. He smiled at Standen. "Why don't you join us? I'm sure we can find you a room."

Find Standen a room? Bloody hell!

"Ah, so there *are* extra rooms?"


Ian was finally going to get his own room. She was delighted, of course. It had been exceedingly awkward and uncomfortable sharing such a small space—such a small bed—with the man. She had hardly got a moment's sleep since she arrived. She—

She didn't feel delighted. She felt tired and depressed.

Nell closed her eyes and leaned back slightly on the garden bench, turning her face up to the sun. Bees buzzed nearby; the jumbled scents of flowers hung in the air. The day was full of life . . .

Life that was passing her by. She squeezed her eyes

more tightly shut. This was the end. She could feel it. When Ian left this house party, he was going to begin divorce proceedings. She tried to swallow the large lump that had suddenly appeared in her throat.

Stupid! This was what she wanted, wasn't it? It was *good* Ian would finally be taking steps to end their sham of a marriage. It was time she finally got on with her life.

A life that extended, gray and solitary, year after year, for as long as she could imagine—

"Are you all right, Lady Kilgorn?"

"Wha—?" Nell jerked open her eyes. Lady Oxbury stood before her, a look of concern on her face.

"Are you quite all right? I don't mean to pry, but, well, I see you've been crying."

"Crying?" Nell put her hands to her face. Her cheeks *were* damp. "Oh, no. I am just . . . overly warm. It's a sunny day, after all, and I've been sitting here. . . ."

"Lady Kilgorn . . ." Lady Oxbury sighed and shook her head slightly as if shedding reservations about whatever she was going to say. "Do you mind if I join you?"

Nell did mind, of course. She was not eager to be gifted with some unsolicited advice, but she couldn't find the tact—or energy—to politely decline Lady Oxbury's company. And the woman had already settled herself on the bench next to her.

"I wouldn't normally . . . I don't usually . . . oh, fiddle!" Lady Oxbury looked Nell straight in the eye.

Nell dropped her gaze like a frightened rabbit to stare at her hands clasped in her lap. This was *most* uncomfortable.

"You must know everyone—even Miss Smyth, I dare say—is aware of your unconventional—your *unfortunate*—situation."

"I'm not certain what you me—"

"Of course you know what I mean. You have lived apart from your husband for a decade."

"That is not so unusual. Many couples of the ton live apart, don't they?"

"Yes, but not many of those couples married so young—and for love."

"Er . . ." She really, really did not wish to discuss this, especially with a virtual stranger. "We *were* very young, too young to—"

Lady Oxbury made a disparaging sound. "And you were very much in love, were you not?"

There was no point in lying. "Yes. But as you say, we were young, too young to know better. Too young to sustain—"

Lady Oxbury actually snorted her disgust this time. "Balderdash! You are still in love."

Nell gaped at the older woman. Was she to be allowed no pride? "How can you say such a thing?"

"Because it's true." Lady Oxbury pinned her with a gaze that brooked no nonsense. "Don't bother to dissemble. I've seen the way you look at your husband. Your feelings are not a secret—except, apparently, from him."

"Ohh." She closed her eyes. She was going to expire from embarrassment.

"And he loves you."

"*What?*" Nell's eyes flew back open—truthfully, they almost started from her head. "You must be—you are—mistaken."

"No, I am not." Lady Oxbury leaned forward. Nell thought for a moment she would grab her shoulders and shake her. The woman's gloved hands did rise from her skirts briefly.

What did one say to such a statement? "Oh?" A weak response but the only one Nell could manage.

"Indeed." Lady Oxbury shook her head decisively. "But, like most men, he will probably refuse to acknowledge his feelings unless forced to do so."

"Oh?" She felt as mindless as Miss Smyth's parrot. More mindless. At least Theo was always definite in his pronouncements.

"Yes." Lady Oxbury rested her hands on Nell's. "Please understand, Lady Kilgorn, I am not normally so bold, but this time I feel I must speak plainly. I cannot let you make the same mistake I did."

"Mistake? I don't—"

"Of course you don't know what I am talking about. You are too young, and the . . . situation never rose to the level of a scandal." She frowned. "If I had been braver—if I'd had the courage to follow my heart . . ."

Did Lady Oxbury actually regret not causing a scandal? That was hard to fathom. "I really don't—"

The older woman tightened her grip. "Twenty-three years ago I met and fell in love with Mr. Wilton."

"Mr. Wilton? But you married . . ."

"Exactly. I married Lord Oxbury. The whys and wherefores aren't important. What *is* important is that I loved Alex and I didn't fight for that love. I let circumstances sweep me along, and I have regretted that— I've regretted my cowardice—every moment of every year we've been apart." She sighed and looked down at her hands where they still rested on Nell's. "Not that I wasn't . . . fond of my husband, but . . ." She met Nell's eyes. "I will just say regret colored every happiness."

"I see." Regret. Yes, that was all too familiar an emotion.

Lady Oxbury smiled. "Fortunately, I am getting a second chance. We are finally marrying as soon as may be."

"Ah. My sincere felicitations." Nell tried to repress a pang of jealousy.

Lady Oxbury waved aside her good wishes. "Thank you, but the important issue here is you. Do not make the same mistake I did. Be brave. Be resolute. If you love Lord Kilgorn, fight for him. You may not be as lucky as I—this may be your last chance. Don't let it slip through your fingers."

Lady Oxbury was very impassioned, but she didn't know the details of their separation. "I do appreciate your concern, Lady Oxbury, but I really believe you are laboring under a misapprehension. Ian doesn't love me."

"Have you asked him?"

"Of course not!" Lady Oxbury wasn't impassioned; she was mad—utterly and completely mad.

"And more to the point—and the question you *can* answer—do you love him?"

"I-I . . . there is no possible way I could—"

"Be brave, Lady Kilgorn. What have you got to lose? And isn't it better to know for certain how Lord Kilgorn feels than spend the rest of your life wondering what would have happened if you'd had more courage?"

Lady Oxbury glanced away—and suddenly smiled so broadly her face almost glowed. Nell was not surprised to see Mr. Wilton had stepped onto the terrace.

"If you'll excuse me?" Lady Oxbury was two steps down the path to the house before she paused and turned back for a moment. "Do think about what I've said, Lady Kilgorn. Believe me, regret is not a pleasant companion."

Nell nodded politely and watched the woman hurry to reach Mr. Wilton.

"She's completely correct, you know."

"Ack!" Nell whirled around. Miss Smyth was standing in the shade just a few feet away. "How long have you been there?"

"Not long. I came up as Lady Oxbury was exhorting you to find some backbone—and I do hope you find it soon. Lord Kilgorn will be moving to his own bedchamber this afternoon. I couldn't stall him any longer."

"Oh." So Lord Motton's aunt *had* had ulterior motives in arranging the sleeping accommodations. She should be incensed.

She was just more depressed.

"Oh, indeed." Miss Smyth snorted. "Here I thought you had some bottom. I gave you the perfect opportunity to smooth things over with your husband and, as far as I can tell, you've totally bungled it. Don't you know how to seduce a man, Lady Kilgorn?"

"Uh . . ."

Miss Smyth rolled her eyes. "Well, I hope you figure it out quickly, because you've run out of time. It's now or never. As Lady Oxbury said, regret is not a pleasant companion—and it's a damn disagreeable bedmate."

# CHAPTER 8

What should she do?

Nell sat alone on the garden bench. Miss Smyth had gone inside, clearly washing her hands of such a cork-brained pudding-heart.

She sighed. She had come into the garden for peace. She'd spent many an afternoon in the calm of Pent-forth's gardens, enjoying the quiet, the solitude, the . . . loneliness.

Was that Lady Oxbury's laughter she heard through the trees? And then the lower murmur of a male voice and sudden silence—

Damn it. She could imagine in painful detail exactly what Mr. Wilton and Lady Oxbury were doing in Vis-count Motton's bushes. She should be horrified. She was not. She was jealous, agonizingly jealous.

She pressed the heels of her hands hard against her forehead. She wanted—she *craved*—the sound of Ian's voice, the touch of his hands, the taste of his—

Damn, damn, *damn*.

If she pushed any harder on her forehead, her skull

would collapse. She was giving herself a blinding headache.

She clasped her hands together instead.

It was all Miss Smyth's fault. Her life had been going along just fine until that woman had invited her to this dreadful gathering. Why did Lord Motton's aunt feel the need to meddle in strangers' lives? One would think she'd have the sense—the decorum—to limit her officiousness to her own relatives. The viscount was past his majority and unmarried. Shouldn't Miss Smyth be busy selecting an appropriate wife for him?

Well, she couldn't linger in the garden any longer. There was no peace to be had here now, not with Lady Oxbury and Mr. Wilton lurking in the shrubbery. Hearing them was bad enough—actually encountering them would be beyond embarrassing. She would just have to go inside.

And do what? Read a book? She did not feel like reading. Do some needlework? No. She was far too agitated. She'd impale herself with the needle. If only she were back at Pentforth Hall . . . but then she'd be dodging the annoying attentions of persistent, pestilent Mr. Pennington.

Oh, who was she trying to fool? Her life most certainly had *not* been going along just fine before she'd got Miss Smyth's missive. It had not been going along at all. She'd been as frozen as the loch in winter.

For the last ten years her days had been a monotonous procession of mindless duty. Not even duty. No one depended on her. No one would miss any of the small tasks she did to fill her time.

She had been given this last chance to choose a new path. She could continue to be fearful and live—exist— as she had. Or she could be brave and risk finding the happiness she'd once known.

Lady Oxbury and Miss Smyth were right. She had nothing to lose.

Ian looked around the small room. How the hell had he survived the last two days? More to the point, how the bloody hell had he survived the last two *nights?* He eyed the narrow bed. It was a miracle he hadn't gone mad. Every time Nell had stirred, he'd felt it; every time she'd made the slightest noise, he'd heard it. He'd wanted her so badly he'd ached.

He shifted position, adjusting his fall. He still ached, but it was time to get over it. Past time. He'd spent a decade in longing and regret, and those useless emotions had not brought him one iota closer to happiness. Or contentment. Or even resignation. He was done with wishing the past could be undone. It could not be. It was time to move on.

And damn to hell and back the sinking feeling that thought brought to the pit of his stomach.

At least he'd got Miss Smyth to admit the obvious. With Lady Grace's departure only the world's greatest dunderhead would believe there were no empty rooms, and he was not quite that yet. Oh, the woman had tried to fob him off with some Banbury tale about it taking several days to get a room ready, but he was having none of it. Then she'd tried to lecture him about Nell, but he was most certainly having none of *that*. He'd cut her off before she'd got three words out.

He picked up his valise. So he was finally moving. At last he would have some peace. At last—

He heard the rustle of fabric behind him, the scrape of a shoe on carpet. He turned.

Nell stood in the doorway.

God. He felt as if he'd been kicked in the stomach . . . or lower.

He gritted his teeth. So he'd been lying to himself. He did still wish the past could be undone. No matter. Nell was done with him.

"Nell." Surely his voice sounded properly remote? He'd had years of practice hiding his emotions.

She stepped—lurched, really—into the room and jerked the door shut. Did she square her shoulders? Surely her jaw looked very determined. He had a sudden memory of her as a girl, insisting she could climb the big tree by the loch, even though he knew she was deathly afraid of heights.

What was this about?

"Are you changing rooms, Ian?"

He shrugged. "Miss Smyth finally agreed to give me my own"—he cleared his throat—"bed." Damn. Why hadn't he said "room"? No, it had to be bed. He was as bad as a lust-crazed schoolboy. Had she noticed? She didn't appear to have done so. "She couldn't very well deny me, with Lady Grace leaving."

Nell bit her lip. "No. No, I don't suppose she could." She glanced at the bed. "You'll be more comfortable." She blushed.

"The bed"—good God. Surely he wasn't blushing as well? "I mean, this room is rather cramped."

She nodded. She was chewing her lip now. Her hands twisted her skirt. He should go. They would both be more comfortable when this interview—this exceedingly awkward interview—was over.

Once he went out that door, he'd be leaving part of his past behind. His youth.

His heart.

Ridiculous. He sounded like an actor in a bad farce. If he did feel as if he were cutting off a part of himself, well, sometimes amputation was necessary to save the patient. He took a step toward the door.

Nell didn't move. If anything, she looked more determined. Her hands stopped twisting and instead clutched her gown in two fists. Her dress was going to be sadly wrinkled.

She frowned at him, her jaw now like granite. Was he going to have to push her aside to get out of this room?

"Did you want the baby, Ian?"

His stomach lurched. "What?" The baby? Why was she talking about the baby now? They had never spoken about the topic before.

"Did you want the baby?" Her voice was thin, tense, teetering on the edge of tears.

He felt as if he were teetering, too. As if he were blindfolded, forced to cross over an abyss with only a thin rope as a bridge. One wrong step and he would plunge into a morass of emotion, of pain and regret.

"Of course. Of course I wanted the baby, Nell."

She was still standing stiffly, blocking the door.

"You never said so."

"I—" *Had* he never said so? Surely he'd told her. Well, perhaps not. That time was such a dark, confused memory. He'd been sad when it was clear Nell would lose their child. He'd been so proud he'd got her pregnant, cocky young cub that he'd been. But he'd thought they would just try again.

It was true, he'd not felt the loss as intensely as Nell. He'd been more upset by her pain. He'd hated seeing her so distraught. He'd wanted desperately to fix things, to make her whole and happy again.

Nell was crying finally, tears streaming down her cheeks, her hands still gripping her skirts, her body stiff.

"Of course I wanted the baby, Nell." Perhaps this was

as it should be. They should share this truth before they parted. "But I wanted you more. You shut me out." He heard the pain in his own voice. He sniffed; his eyes were wet. Stupid. He was not some sensitive dandy to be crying over the past. "I didn't understand—I still don't understand—why I had to lose you, too."

She shook her head, her hands now fluttering at her waist. "You didn't lose me."

"I did. You closed me out—out of your bed, out of your life, out of your heart."

"No. I-I just hurt too much. And I was so afraid." She was crying hard now, her words all broken. "It was all my fault. I'm so sorry, Ian."

He dropped his valise and stepped closer. He still couldn't bear to see her hurting. "Nell, it wasn't your fault."

"It was. I lost our baby, Ian."

"No."

"Yes. I failed you, your clan—everyone."

"No." He wanted to comfort her, but he would wait for her to close the distance between them. It was her choice. "You didn't fail. It was just bad luck or fate or . . ." Or what? How could he explain the tragedies of life? God's will? God's curse? No, he'd never thought God so cruel. "Things happen, Nell. Sometimes things just happen."

"But I lost our baby."

Their child, born of their love—their young, blissfully hopeful, wildly romantic love. Had they had only enough love for one child? He'd not thought so.

"Our baby died, Nell. You didn't lose him. Something went wrong. It was not your fault." He paused, swallowed. "What I never understood was why we couldn't have tried again?"

She shook her head as if she could shake the memories away. "I wasn't ready."

"And I pushed you?" Would things have been different if he'd waited longer to come to her bed? But he had waited for what had seemed like forever . . . at least to a twenty-year-old boy.

"No. Yes. I don't know. I—I was just so afraid." She shook her head. "I was wrong."

"You were young. We were both young. You should— we should—forgive ourselves."

They had probably wed too young. Many of his friends had told him he was making a mistake, that he should sow some wild oats first. But he had been so certain.

He ran his hand through his hair. "I came after you, Nell, but you wouldn't see me. That hurt. I wrote you, but you wouldn't answer, and that hurt, too. I didn't know what else to do."

"I know, I know. I'm sorry." Nell wiped her cheeks with her fingers. "I was so miserable, so wrapped up in my pain. I couldn't think of anything—anyone—but me." She sniffed, straightened. The odd, determined look was back in her eyes. "But if you are willing—if you can forgive me—I would like to try again."

Was he understanding her? "You'd like to try what again?"

"Making a baby."

"Ah." His knees were going to give out. He was going to collapse in a heap at her feet. She'd like to try making a baby again. All right. He was certainly eager to do that. More than eager. If only she would come closer. He'd vowed to let her be the one to close the gap between them, but if she didn't do so very soon, he might break that vow.

A very insistent part of him was trying to leap the gap on its own.

She did move, then—to place one hand flat against his chest, holding him away.

"But you must understand a few things, Ian."

"Yes." He kept his hands at his sides through an extreme exercise of will. "What things?"

"I never had anything—*anything*—to do with Mr. Pennington or anyone else. You are the only man ever to have come to my bed."

"All right." This was important. He could tell it was important. He told his impatient organ to be patient. He was delighted he'd been Nell's only lover, but he really, really wanted to stop talking and start doing the lover part. "I believe you."

"And from this day on I must be the only woman in your bed. There can be no more mistresses."

"Ah."

"Do you promise?" She was frowning at him, but she looked uncertain, too. "Do you swear it?"

Perhaps he had a demand as well. Much as he'd like to fall into that bed with Nell, maybe something else was more important.

"Do you mean to be a wife to me, then? This is not only about having a child, is it? It's about having a life together as well? Because I will tell you, losing you once was enough. I cannot go through that again. I would not survive it."

Her other hand joined the first, and she took the last step to bring her body against his. "Yes. I want to be your wife, Ian—and the mother of your children, God willing."

"And if God doesn't will, Nell? If we aren't blessed with bairns, will ye still be my wife?"

"Yes. Yes, Ian, I will."

"Then I can swear there will be no other women. It is an easy oath, Nell. I never wanted anyone but you. When I did go to other women's beds—and I did, but only after you left me—I always wanted them to be you. I never stopped loving you. Never."

She closed her eyes briefly. She believed him. She

truly did believe him. "And I never stopped loving you, Ian." She moved a hand from his chest to his cheek. "I've missed you so much. For the longest time, I couldn't feel anything. Nothing at all. I was as frozen as Kilgorn Loch in winter. But now . . . seeing you again has melted the ice around my heart."

He smiled slightly, but his eyes were intent, almost strained. "I would like to try to melt more, Nell. I would really like . . . I am really very anxious . . . do you think we might go to bed now?"

"Now?" She flushed. "It's barely past noon."

His hand covered hers. "That never stopped us before."

"No." She felt her flush deepen. The low throbbing had started again. "But we are older now."

"Older, but not old. Not decrepit."

She laughed. "No, not decrepit."

"And it has been so long since I've really touched you. These last two nights have driven me to the edge of madness. And now you are here. You say you wish to"— his voice dropped, grew huskier, deeper—"try to make a child."

Heat and dampness pooled low in her belly and between her legs. She was suddenly very hot. Her clothes were too tight, too confining.

Why *should* they wait?

"Please, Nell? Please let me make love to you now."

She smiled then. She had vowed to be brave; now she would be daring. He was her husband and he was right. It had been far too long since he'd been a true husband to her. She dropped her hands and started working open his waistcoat buttons.

"Very well, if you insist." Her fingers paused. They'd been young and inexperienced when last they'd done this; she was still inexperienced, but he . . . "It has been ten years. You will be disappointed."

"How can I be disappointed, Nell? I am finally with my wife whom I love."

"But I know nothing; I've learned nothing—"

He put his fingers over her lips. "You were very inventive the night before last."

Was he referring to—? She flushed.

He smiled. "We have thought and talked and discussed enough, Nell. Now let's just feel." He replaced his fingers with his lips. They were warm and firm and . . . comforting. Welcoming. "Remember," he murmured as his lips moved to her eyelids, "we have this afternoon and tonight to learn together. We have a lifetime. There is no hurry."

His lips trailed down to her jaw and then to a very sensitive spot behind her ear. Her knees melted; she had to cling to him or collapse.

His mouth came back to hers and his tongue swept inside. His touch was urgent, consuming.

She pressed against him. She *wanted* to be consumed. She wanted to be so much a part of him no one could tell where she ended and he began. She never, never wanted to be separated from him again.

They were separated by far too much clothing.

Ian must have read her mind. "This is a very lovely frock, Nell, but it would be much lovelier on the floor," he whispered as his hands moved to deal with her buttons.

"Mmm." His fingers were exceedingly nimble. Had he learned—no, she would not think about the other women. And truthfully he'd been equally fast getting her out of her clothes when they were first married.

The frock fell to the ground, quickly followed by her stays and shift. The room's cool air slid over her skin, pebbling her nipples.

"Nell!" Ian reached for her, but she stopped him

with a hand on his chest again—rather, on his waistcoat. His very stylish, still very-much-in-the-way waistcoat. She'd only got one button open when she'd been distracted.

He frowned. "Wha—?"

She smiled up at him, liking the hot, smoky look in his eyes. "My turn." She slipped the second button from its hole.

"I can do that quicker."

"Oh, is speed the object then? I seem to remember . . . very faintly, you understand . . . you once telling me that faster wasn't always better."

He gave a short, breathless laugh. "Did I say that? I dinna think I had that much sense when I was just a lad."

"You were more than a lad."

He shook his head, inhaling sharply as her hands, freeing the last button on his waistcoat, brushed over the sizable bulge under the fall on his breeches. "Nay, I was hardly more than a boy."

He traced a circle around one of her nipples as she pulled his shirt free of his waistband. It was her turn to inhale sharply. Damp heat flooded the part of her that was most eager for his touch. Perhaps slow wasn't possible this time, but she would try to wait as long as she could.

"Take off your shirt."

"My pleasure." Ian shrugged out of his waistcoat and grabbed the hem of his shirt, jerking it over his head and flinging it into a corner. Then he reached for her, bringing her up against him. His hands slid all over her, from her shoulders down her back along her waist to her rounded buttocks and back up to skim the sides of her breasts where they were pressed against his chest.

Her hands were busy, too, exploring. His skin was

soft, but his muscles were hard. She buried her face in his chest and breathed deeply. He smelled like . . . home. Not Pentforth or even Kilgorn Castle, but like heather and sun and Scotland. Like Ian.

Ian, who still had his breeches on. They were scratchy against her skin, and the hard ridge hidden in them pressed urgently into her belly.

She moved, and Ian let her go just far enough to reach his buttons.

"Ah, lass, I was hoping ye'd get to that."

"I couldn't very well forget, could I? You were pressing rather insistently against me."

"Aye. I'm verra, verra"—he sucked his breath in as she freed the last button—"eager. Oh, Nell . . ."

She cradled him in her hand. He was long and thick. Hot. She rubbed a drop of moisture over his tip.

"Nell." His voice sounded very strained now. He was panting. Well, she was panting, too. "This game is lovely, but 'tis time to end it. I canna wait any longer."

She stretched, rubbing her breasts against him. "I was just waiting for you to take charge, Ian, as ye always used to."

He growled low in his throat. "And here I thought I was being a gentleman, deferring to a lady's wishes."

"Oh." She kissed his jaw. "Well, this lady wishes to be taken to bed immediately."

"I see." He grinned. "Then I shall be delighted to obey." He scooped her up and deposited her on the narrow bed.

He stopped just to look at her. He'd never thought to see her like this again—her black hair spread over his pillow, her creamy white shoulders on his sheets. He loved her mind and her heart, but he also very much loved her body—the graceful mounds of her breasts with their lovely rosy nipples, the delicate curve of her waist sliding into her hips' generous flare, the beautiful dark curls marking the place he would enter in just a little while.

He bent to slip off her shoes, to peel off her stockings, running his hands slowly over her knees and calves. He breathed in the musky scent of her need.

He couldn't resist. He bent quickly and kissed her there, drank—

"Ack!" Nell grabbed his hair and tried to tug him away. "What are you doing?"

He swirled his tongue over her. "Don't you like this, Nell?" He slid his hands under her hips, lifting her so he could drink more deeply, lapping over the hard little point of flesh hidden there.

"Oh. Ah. *Ohh.*"

"Does it feel good?"

"Yes."

She was hot, panting, twisting on the sheets. She smelled of woman, passion, and Nell. He could not remember ever being so happy.

A particularly insistent organ reminded him he would be even happier soon. Sooner if he would just get on with it.

Nell, wise girl, apparently agreed. "Ian." She tugged on his hair again. "Now. Please. I don't want to be alone any longer."

He put her hips down and leaned over her. "And I don't want to be alone any longer, either." He kissed her mouth slowly, then moved to her breasts, her nipples. Mmm. He suckled one while he slid his finger back over the wet, sensitive flesh at the opening of her passage.

Her hips jerked up and she squeaked. "Ian, get your breeches off *now.* I canna wait any longer."

"Yes, milady. As ye wish." He scrambled off the bed and out of the rest of his clothing.

Nell watched him through a haze of desire. She literally ached for him. The past, the present—everything came down to this room, this bed, the small opening between her thighs that cried for him. She was mad with lust—and with love.

He came to her and she spread her legs to welcome him. Ah. The moment he touched her there, she began to come apart. As he slid into her, her body shivered and clenched around him. He moved once, twice . . . and then she felt his warm seed fill her.

Had he given her life? Had they started a child?

They had started their love, their marriage again. If children came, that would be an extra blessing. She sighed and ran her hands down his sweat-slicked back. She felt she would burst with the love that filled her.

He chuckled. "That was quick."

"Mmm."

"I'm not usually so fast, you know."

"Mmm. I was fast, too."

"God, Nell." He rested his forehead against hers, his eyes closed. "I've missed you."

She cupped his jaw. "And I've missed you."

"You won't change your mind, will you? You won't leave me again? I couldna bear it if ye did." His words whispered over her mouth.

"Nay, Ian, I've learned my lesson well." She threaded her fingers through his hair. "I intend to stick to ye like a burr."

The corner of his mouth curved up and he flexed his hips. "A burr? Are ye close enough now, then? Shall I keep you stuck to me like this?"

She giggled. She felt him growing thicker inside her. "Yes, please."

"Mmm." He kissed her again—and then raised his head. "What's this?" He frowned, touching her tears with his fingers. "You're crying."

"Tears of joy." She wiped her cheeks. "I've been so fashed since I got here—since before I got here." She giggled again. "I haven't been sleeping well, ye know."

"Aye." The other corner of his mouth slid up. "I weel know that. I've not been sleeping much myself." He leaned down to kiss her nose and flexed his hips again. "Shall we—" He paused, and then slid quickly out of her body, pulling the coverlet up over them.

"Don't—"

He put his finger on her lips and grinned. "I've got sharp ears—the result of my ill-spent time away from you, Nell. We're about to have company."

*"What?"* Nell's gaze swiveled to the door. Sure enough, it was opening. Nell dove farther under the coverlet as Annie came in with an armful of clothes.

"Miss Smyth said ye'd be here, milady, so I—" Annie finally looked over at the bed. Her jaw dropped—and then she grinned. "Weel, what do ye know?"

Nell was certain she would expire of embarrassment. She looked at Ian—the man was shaking with laughter! It was obvious he'd be no help at all. She cleared her throat.

"Yes, Annie? Lord Kilgorn and I were—" Ian was still laughing. She was certainly not going to say what they'd been doing—though only an idiot would not be able to surmise the answer. "Well, did you need something?"

Annie was laughing as well. "No, milady. I'll just be going. I'll tell Mrs. Gilbert she needn't worry about getting a room ready for milord." She opened the door. "Ma will be so pleased."

Nell flopped back on the pillows the moment the door clicked shut. Ian was now laughing so hard tears ran down his cheeks and he gasped for breath.

"Oh, stop it. In minutes the entire house party will know exactly what we were doing."

That cured him. He stopped laughing to put his large hand on her breast. "Splendid. Let's be certain to live up to even the most lurid gossip."

"But—oh. Um. Mmm."

Nell decided she did not really feel like arguing.

# LESSONS IN PLEASURE

## VICTORIA DAHL

For my sister, Danielle

# CHAPTER 1

*London, 1875*

Sarah Rose Hood was in love with her husband. She was almost sure of it.

James was kind and handsome. Considerate and smart. He'd taken good care of her in the two months they'd been married, providing a home and servants and new dresses. She loved him. Surely.

And she feared him. Just a tiny bit.

"I'll be late, I'm afraid," he said, picking up his gloves from the parlor table. He smiled as he tugged them on. "Hanover will want to discuss the provisions of the new bill, and you know how he tends to go on."

Sarah nodded as if she did.

"You needn't wait up." His rich voice traveled in waves over her skin as he leaned down to brush a kiss against her cheek. "Good night, Sarah."

She had to hide a shiver at his touch. "Good night," she returned, still breathing in the strange spice of his soap.

*Strange.* That was the best word to describe her feelings of late. It was decidedly strange to live in such intimate proximity with a man. Strange to be so abruptly picked up from a life sheltered from the attentions of gentlemen and then simply plopped down into a marriage and everything that entailed.

Not that she hadn't wanted to marry James. She had *craved* it, but . . .

When she heard the front door close, Sarah shook her head and rose to her feet to ring for dinner. The meal would be a solitary affair, as it always was on the nights James spent at his club. She didn't mind. James encouraged her to invite friends over to keep her company; he worried she was lonely. But these evenings alone gave her time to breathe, time free of worrying if she were behaving the way a wife ought to and filling her time with appropriate activities.

The meal of boiled beef and pudding ticked by in peaceful silence, and Sarah spent the rest of her evening curled in a chair in the cozy parlor, sipping wine as she soaked up the drama of the new novel she'd purchased that day. Reading was her greatest indulgence, and James encouraged her to spend as much as she pleased at her favorite bookshop. Another reason she was certain she must love him.

The new novel proved far too delicious, and the wine as well. When Sarah looked up from the story of highseas adventure and frightening storms, she realized that it was after ten and past time to ready for bed. When she rose too quickly, her head swam with wooziness.

"Oh, my," she breathed, pressing her palm to her forehead. One glass of wine too many. Or two.

She wobbled a bit as she made her way carefully across the room and headed straight for the stairs. Thank God James hadn't come home early to find her drunk. And thank God he'd hired her a quick and capable lady's maid. Sarah felt a sudden urge to hug the girl when a few tugs freed Sarah from the tight embrace of her corset. The deep breath she drew sent sparks floating before her eyes.

"Oh, thank you, Mary!"

"You're welcome, ma'am," the maid responded, her Irish brogue soothing as a whisper.

Each unrestricted breath felt better than the last. An ache took over her ribs and then faded into a pleasant warmth. Sarah smiled at the wall. "Where did you work before you came to us, Mary?"

The girl's fingers froze for a bare second on Sarah's leg before she continued unfastening the stockings. Sarah immediately regretted the question. She did not speak to Mary about personal things. The wine had loosened her tongue.

"I worked for a Mrs. Albertson, ma'am. I was maid to her and her two daughters. They were sixteen and eighteen."

"Ah. I hope I am easier work then. Simpler, at least."

"Yes, ma'am."

"Girls of that age can be difficult." But of course, she herself was only twenty. Another strange thought.

Most of her friends had held secret fantasies of marrying up. A gentleman of the ton, perhaps, who would sweep a girl into that sparkling swirl of society parties and elegant country retreats. But Sarah had never wanted that. She had wanted love and friendship. Comfort and compatibility. A man of her father's station in life.

When she'd met James, a young barrister who'd just acquired a seat in the commons, her heart had turned over and then beat so hard she'd wondered if he could see the pulse in her neck. He was tall and handsome, his dark hair a fascinating contrast to pale green eyes. And then he'd smiled.

Sarah pressed a hand to her chest as her heart jumped to life at the memory.

"Ma'am?"

Blinking, she found that Mary was standing before her, holding a gown of delicate muslin. "Oh, so sorry." Sarah dutifully held her arms up and let Mary pull her chemise off over her head. Her body was exposed for a moment, pale and vulnerable. She closed her eyes until Mary pulled the sleeveless nightgown into place.

They were nearly done. She would sit in her chair for a few moments while Mary took down the hair she'd braided that morning. She would brush it out and then tidy up before lowering the lamps and leaving her mistress to herself.

Sarah felt the pins in her hair loosen. "Do you have family?" she blurted out, wanting to continue the conversation for reasons she could not fathom. There was that infinitesimal pause in the maid's hands again, but Sarah looked into the mirror and saw Mary nod. "Aye, ma'am. Two brothers, two sisters. A father. Me mum died when I was young."

"Oh. Mine also."

Mary nodded, subsiding into silence. Sarah could not fault her. She had valued the girl's silence all these weeks. It was not Mary's fault that Sarah felt so odd and restless tonight. The wine should have left her exhausted, but while she felt sleepy, her muscles were buzzing beneath her skin, her mind falling over itself with too many thoughts. But she let Mary be, and soon found herself tucked into bed and staring wide-eyed into the dark.

James would join her soon. They shared a bed, and that was, without a doubt, the very strangest part of being a married woman. She, who before marriage had never even seen a man's bare arms, slept in a man's bed every night. Felt his skin and his muscle against her. Breathed in the scent of his body. Eased him with her own.

Kicking her legs restlessly beneath the covers, Sarah flipped over and buried her face in the pillow. Sleep felt so far away, despite her weariness. And each minute that passed, a new thought of James spun through her mind.

Their wedding night. Lying alone in this very bed, awaiting him. His first careful touches. The strange texture of the hair on his body. The warmth of his mouth, his hands. The knowledge that he could do as he pleased.

Her absolute mortification.

But he'd been gentle and patient and kind, and she'd tried very hard not to be afraid.

She'd grown accustomed to the idea now, but it still did not feel natural. It still felt . . . strange.

But not as strange as her body felt tonight.

Her mind could not rest. Anxious thoughts skittered through her head, frightening sleep away. She loved him, or wanted to, and the more fond she grew of him, the more worried she became.

She had a secret. A secret she should have revealed to James before they'd married, before she'd even accepted his suit. Now her lie of omission sat between them like a fence, and Sarah was on one side, pacing and alone.

All she wanted now was to throw herself over that fence and into his strong arms, but fear kept her feet glued to the ground.

Sighing, Sarah squeezed her eyes shut and tried to will herself to relax enough to sleep.


James Hood handed his coat and hat to the butler and rolled his weary shoulders. By God, he was tired. The hours he'd spent fighting for this damned agricultural measure over the past weeks had finally caught up with him. But it was done for now, and the next fight wouldn't start for . . . oh, probably three or four days.

He headed straight for his library, then paused at the threshold. Normally, he'd spend another hour there, gathering his thoughts, taking notes, and writing letters. But tonight . . . tonight his neck ached and his throat felt raw from too many days spent breathing in the cigar smoke of his colleagues. Tonight he wanted sleep.

Or . . . perhaps not just sleep. His gaze shifted toward the dark oak of the wide stairway. His wife was upstairs. His sweet, shy wife. Sarah had likely retired hours ago, and he wasn't brutish enough to wake her just to sate his needs.

He'd always thought himself practical and decent. He'd known that when he took a wife he would honor and care for her. Still, he hadn't really expected that he'd spend whole days thinking of her.

There was something about Sarah. Something serene and soft that drew him close, though he never quite reached her. She was inscrutable. A mysterious feminine creature. Surely time would change that. Time to know her and let himself be known. Time to ease into the comfort of marriage.

A spark of recognition had struck him at their first meeting. And what a relief to find that the pretty girl with the peaceful smile was not only fair but also generous and keen-witted. Now that they were married, he loved to watch her read in the evenings in front of the fire. Loved to watch the emotions flit across her face as she sped through the pages.

Her soft brown hair seemed always to choose that moment to start escaping its knot, her brown eyes would sparkle with excitement, and James would watch her. He could not observe her enough during the day, when she would notice and blush and grow flustered. But when she read, she forgot his gaze.

Perhaps someday she would let him stare whenever he liked.

Smiling, James turned and took the stairs two at a time, though he slowed his step at the door to their chambers and slipped quietly into his dressing room. Once undressed, he started to reach for a nightshirt, but even in the nude the June air felt heavy tonight. Warm and humid.

No nightshirt. Sarah was too reserved to say a word even if she did notice, and it would only get hotter in July. He'd be damned if he'd sleep in a nightshirt during the hottest part of summer. She would get past it.

Decision made, he opened the door to the bedchamber and eased into bed as carefully as he could. The mattress absorbed him, the feathers easing his tired muscles even as they surrounded his skin with heat. Tossing off the covers, he spread out and closed his eyes, but a soft sound floated to his ears.

A sigh. Sarah shifted and sighed again as she settled into a new position.

Perhaps she wasn't asleep after all.

Feeling a cad, James reached slowly out until he touched bare flesh. Her arm, probably. He rolled toward her, rising up to his elbow to see her better.

Yes, her arm, pale and bare, curved back toward her body, her fingers twisted into the fabric of her gown. Shifting, she frowned, her fist tightening in the muslin.

"Sarah?" he breathed. She sighed again. A bad dream, perhaps.

Her skin was cream silk beneath his fingers when he stroked her arm to calm her. He stroked again.

"James?" Her eyes opened and found him.

"You were dreaming."

"Mm." Her eyelids drifted shut. "You look like the shadow of a giant."

"Do I?" Her skin enticed him still. He dragged the

pad of his thumb farther, dipping into the crook of her elbow, feeling her pulse. When he moved higher, he felt chill bumps rise on her arm, but there wasn't even a hint of cold in the air. "*You* look like an angel."

Her soft laugh swirled through the room. "Do angels ever have too much wine after dinner?"

"Did you have too much wine, cheeky girl?"

"I did," she groaned. "But the room has finally ceased its spinning. I hope you are not horrified."

He smiled down at his tipsy wife. "Not horrified at all. But perhaps I should drag the chamber pot close?"

"Hush."

So he did, and watched her body relax and settle, her lips maintaining their soft smile. His hand continued its path to her shoulder. He dipped his fingers beneath the strap of her gown, spread them over her skin. So soft. His little finger ventured lower.

Time seemed to freeze for a moment as her body went still, but then her deep breath raised his hand, and he could no longer resist the temptation to lower his mouth to the bare curve of her shoulder.

Sarah did not respond at first. He felt a familiar guilt press his heart. He wanted her. He wanted her even when she held her breath and waited for him to be done with it. So he wasn't surprised when her muscles turned to stone beneath him.

But when he opened his mouth and touched his tongue to her flesh, Sarah sighed, her muscles relaxed, and James's heartbeat thundered.

His mouth was on her, heat and wetness. Nothing more than that quiet, simple kiss on her shoulder. But the warmth spread out from there when he drew slightly at her skin. He'd put his mouth to her flesh in the past, had even licked her breasts, her nipples. Somehow, the thought of that affected her more on this night than the actual sensations had before. She breathed and waited.

His hand slipped over her gown, as if he'd read her mind, and his palm cupped her breast as his tongue licked at her shoulder. The two feelings somehow tangled up and made her gasp.

Horrified, she shut her mouth and held her breath. She needn't have bothered. He seemed not to notice at all, just kept licking her skin in little whips of fire, kept his hot palm curved over her breast. His tongue trailed closer to the wide strap of her nightgown. Then he skipped over it entirely, and that wet heat was on her neck.

"Oh." That felt lovely. Lovely. So very wicked. Or perhaps the wickedness was his thumb moving like butterfly wings over her breast. Her nipple pushed up to meet the attention, and suddenly the butterfly wings disappeared under sizzling sparks.

Startled, she flung her hand out . . . and found that sparks were not the only startling thing about the night. Her knuckles met up with something hot and hard and surrounded by crisp hair.

They both gasped, James perhaps a little more loudly.

She had never touched him there, had never . . . "I'm sorry," she whispered in horror. "I didn't mean to. Did I hurt you?"

"No." But he sounded hurt. Sounded as if he were holding his breath. "Sarah?"

"Y-yes?" His hand tightened on her breast, his thumb and finger pinched her nipple, and brightness trailed through her body. When she recovered from that, she realized she arched up, pressing herself boldly into his grip, mewling a little. Whatever James had been about to say, he forgot it, and his mouth covered hers.

She'd never thought him a poor kisser, but these kinds of kisses had always seemed a bit . . . sloppy. Too intimate. But tonight when his tongue slipped against hers, it was the exact right thing. Somehow appeasing and inflaming at once. Enough and not nearly enough.

Sarah turned toward him and kissed him back. That was the end of conscious thought for her. All further sensation tangled up in a great mess of mouths and hands and fingers. He caressed her breasts and stroked her belly, then pulled her nightgown up and off. Then his mouth was on one nipple and his hand on the other and the whole of his hard body pressed against her side. She could feel his shaft snug against her thigh, and his mouth sucking and his fingers exploring lower, until all she could think was, please, please, please.

He was so slow, so gentle, and by the time his fingers snuck into the dark curls between her thighs, Sarah was beside herself. Whimpering and writhing, wanting so much what she had hoped to avoid on other nights. She wanted to be *had*. Taken. Entered.

His hand stroked her, and Sarah had to hold her breath lest she scream. His fingers slipped easily against her, lubricated by her body, and he ceased to kiss her breasts and merely panted against her damp skin.

*"Sarah."*

She clenched her eyes shut, horrified by the flagrant wetness of her sex, wishing he would simply get on with it and not notice. Her prayers were answered. James eased between her thighs and pressed his maleness to her. When he thrust in, Sarah gulped for air.

*My God.* My God, it felt so right. So necessary. How had she only thought this tolerable? Tonight when he sank deep, she wanted him deeper. When he stretched her flesh with his startling girth, she shuddered for more.

Lungs straining, she clasped her hands around his

sweat-damp back and held him close until he rose to his arms and began to move. His hips thrust. In and out. Sarah had found the in rather uncomfortable before, but now it seemed the entire point. The *in*. Yes. The *in*.

Her fingernails dug into his back. James groaned and thrust harder. Her breath tripped out of her lungs as if forced by a bellows. She strained up, up, to meet him. To make the *in* more and better. And when she lifted her knees higher, it was.

"Ah, Christ," James gasped. "Sarah. Yes."

*Yes.* He felt it, too. Something. Something tight and empty in her belly. The place his seed would go, perhaps. A hollow only he could fill. "James," she begged. He must know what to do. He must.

His body turned to stone. He froze. And Sarah nearly wept.

It was over, but her sex was still stretched and needing. Her belly still empty.

But he didn't collapse on her. His chest still heaved for air, and his shaft did not diminish in the least. After a few more deep breaths, James shifted his weight onto one arm and slid one hand between their bodies.

Wide-eyed, she waited in complete confusion. And then she cried out.

His fingers had found that spot. That place he often stroked before he took her. The place that had, heretofore, made her wriggle a bit at the sensation. But tonight, that place sang like an instrument under James's stroking fingertips. *She* sang. She moaned and gasped and strained her head back into the pillow.

Despite what she'd suspected, James had not finished. Still stroking, he thrust again. And again. And what she'd thought was glorious before had been nothing to this. Friction and tightness and the perfect amount of pleasure.

Gritting her teeth, she arched to meet him.

"Yes, Sarah. My sweet. Yes."

Yes, she thought. *Yes.* And then her body turned in on itself, a snake writhing into a knot. Everything tightened to an impossible tension, and then . . . then she was set free, sobbing, gasping.

James shouted something, stiffened above her for a long moment before he shuddered hard against her.

Before she slept, she felt him press a dozen kisses to her neck, and then she was falling deep into blackness.

# CHAPTER 2

Every time a step sounded outside the breakfast-room door, James tensed and stared, cold toast and kipper forgotten. After the fifth time the footsteps of the industrious maid passed, James rose, opened the door, and propped it open with the nearest vase.

There. Now he would look less like a hound anticipating his generous mistress and her pocketful of treats. Sarah would not enter to find him all agape. Instead, she'd enter to find him only stunned and eager.

Last night had been . . . Well, frankly, it had been the most shocking night of his life. Not the most debauched. Not the least dignified. Just the most surprising.

He'd had lovers. The widow of a prosperous merchant. A brief affair with a rather lusty governess. And a long affair with a slightly older woman whose husband had moved to France fifteen years before and refused to send for her. He'd had pleasant affairs, and had pleasured those women.

But he'd mistakenly assumed that Sarah wasn't quite like them. She was so dignified. Innocent and reserved.

Measured. A woman of a higher class, perhaps not geared toward the carnal.

Not that he'd given her no pleasure at all. He'd always been sure to caress her until her body made itself ready. He'd been slow and careful, especially on their wedding night. Sure to make her wet and ease his way. But stroking the little pearl that made other women scream had only made Sarah a bit more relaxed.

Until last night.

Shifting, James looked again toward the open doorway, but she wasn't there. A quick glance at his watch revealed the sad truth that he could tarry no longer. A meeting with this new incarnation of his wife would have to wait.

"Damn," he cursed as he folded his paper and snapped it shut. He'd wanted to see her. Kiss her goodbye. See if her eyes shone a little more brightly when she spied him. But he'd not wake her. After last night, she needed her sleep.

James couldn't help his smile as he took his hat from the butler—more slowly than strictly necessary— checked the stairway one last time, and reluctantly took his leave.


Sarah didn't wake fully aware of the night before. No, her head felt a bit achy and her throat raw with thirst when sunlight finally woke her. She was snuggling into her pillow to escape the discomfort when the first inkling of what she'd done hit her. Hand pressed to her chest, she sat bolt upright and inhaled as much air as would fit in her lungs.

She was stark naked.

"Oh, good Lord."

The memories weren't exactly crisp, but they were vivid nonetheless. She'd moaned and writhed. Shuddered and scratched. A stray cat howling for a tom. And then . . . then she'd had some sort of fit. A screaming, jerking fit.

"Oh no," Sarah sobbed, pressing both hands to her mouth. What must her husband think? Eyes rolling, she scanned the room, but saw no sign of him. When her gaze caught sight of the small clock on the mantel, her shoulders collapsed. It was nearly ten. He'd left for work long before. She would not see him for hours, and she couldn't help but be thankful, disloyal as that seemed.

She fell back to the pillows and pulled the coverlet up to her nose. What in the world had happened to her? The wine perhaps, except her strange mood had started earlier, so much worry and restlessness. And then . . . when her husband had touched her, something had . . . come to life inside her body. Something hot and trembling. Something almost *hungry*.

A groan escaped her throat, scaring her almost as much as her thoughts. If there was a beast inside her, lurking in her deepest soul, she knew what it must be. Her secret. Her family's secret.

Sarah set her teeth and swallowed hard. She wasn't a woman prone to dramatics. James had hardly seemed alarmed, from what she could recall. He had seemed . . . What? *Encouraging?* But he did not know the truth. She had not *told* him the truth. So she could not depend upon him to know whether her paroxysms were a normal phenomenon or a sign of worse to come.

In truth, she had heard her own mother cry out like that on occasion. Usually when the doctor would go in and shut the door for her treatments. Then, afterward, her mother would weep, sometimes for days.

Knowing full well that time spent lying in bed would only mean more worry, she dug her nightgown from beneath the sheets and twisted and wiggled until she had it on. Then she rang for a bath. By the time the clock struck eleven and she found herself staring down at the congealing breakfast on her plate, Sarah knew what she must do.

Though the housekeeper was a slightly terrifying presence, Sarah forced herself to calmly request the woman's attention in the morning room. It took her approximately two minutes to quench her suddenly dry mouth, wipe her fingers, and rise to make her way to the morning room. The housekeeper was already there, awaiting her.

"Oh, Mrs. Baylor. Such a prompt response." Sarah could not understand how Mrs. Baylor could be quite so round and still move more swiftly than a startled mouse.

"Yes, ma'am. Would you care to review the menus this morning, then?"

"No, I think the schedule is going splendidly. You run this house with great efficiency."

Mrs. Baylor waited, eyes darting toward the door as if she'd like to be off to see to other duties.

"Well, then," Sarah chirped. "I am running a few errands today, and I should like to steal one of the maids away. Could you spare Betsy, do you think?"

"Betsy? Which Betsy, ma'am? There are two."

Sarah blinked. Two? Lord, she thought she had planned so well. One of those Betsys couldn't read even the simplest words. Sarah knew this because she'd heard the girl explain to Mrs. Baylor why she couldn't fetch a certain spice from the larder one evening when Sarah had been trying to teach them the recipe for her grandmother's spiced cakes. Sarah needed *that* girl.

She cleared her throat. "The, um, the Betsy with the curly brown hair that sneaks from her cap?"

"Aye, I've spoken to her about that, ma'am. I'll—"

"The hair is fine. Only can you spare her?"

"Of course."

Sarah nodded and smiled past her pounding heart. "Wonderful. I shall be ready in half an hour. Please notify the footman that I will require a hack."

The moment Mrs. Baylor quit the room, Sarah rushed to the writing table and drew a piece of paper from the drawer. After staring at the blank page for at least ten minutes, she took the pen into one shaking hand and scratched out three lines. She did not sign it, only dried it carefully and folded it into a tight, neat square.

The rest of her preparations took no time at all, and before the half hour was up, she and Betsy were in the coach and on their way.

The shop was less than a mile from the house, but Sarah rarely patronized it. The owner was her least favorite of the nearby book merchants, he being more interested in science and politics than "those dreadful novels," as he called them. An arrogant bore in Sarah's opinion, but he might prove useful today.

As soon as the hack creaked to a halt before the store, Sarah pressed the note into Betsy's hand, along with a generous fistful of coins. A few simple instructions later, and she was alone in the coach, still rocking from Betsy's jarring descent.

She stared at the opposite cushion, hands clenched tight together, and waited. Minutes dragged by. She thought about James. Wondered if he was thinking about her. Perhaps the night had meant nothing to him. Perhaps it had been like any other. Nodding to reassure herself, Sarah took a look at the door of the shop.

Nothing.

Had the bookseller grown suspicious? Was he even now questioning the maid? Surely he couldn't object to the request.

*Please remand, to the bearer of this note, three or four of your most popular texts on the subject of female health and marital relations.*

Could he know it was from a woman? Would he report her to her husband?

A flutter of panic was just beginning to rise in her throat when the door to the shop flew inward. Pressing her fingers to her mouth, Sarah held her breath until a familiar skirt appeared above the threshold.

Betsy stepped out, mouth set in a serious line as befit a kitchen maid elevated to a temporarily important status. She didn't look scandalized or titillated, only determined. When she saw Sarah watching, she broke into a smile, then remembered herself and smothered it.

"'E drove a hard bargain, ma'am, but I got him down to four quid!" She was proud of herself, regardless that she had no idea how much her package should have cost, but Sarah thought four quid a good bargain and told her so.

The maid kept the paper-wrapped bundle close as she alighted, and though Sarah wanted to snatch it from her, there could be no reasonable excuse to do so. Still, she stared anxiously at the brown paper as Betsy settled it on her lap and wrapped her chapped fingers around the string.

Sarah's answer might be inside that brown paper, just inches from her hands. Had last night been a fit? A sign that her mother's tainted blood had been passed to her? If so, she would have to tell James a truth too horrible to consider . . . that she might pass on the illness she'd hidden to his children.

The palms of her white gloves were soaked with perspiration by the time the hack delivered them back to the Hood door. When they entered, Betsy moved to carry the books to the library, but Sarah touched her elbow.

"I will take those," she said too loudly, then managed

a smile when Betsy jumped in shock. "Thank you, Betsy. You were a great help to me today." Heart beating too hard to hear the maid's reply, Sarah wrapped her arms around the books and spun to run up the stairs.

"Sarah?" a deep voice called, interrupting her retreat. The tone and timbre of that voice spread icy fingers over the skin of her back. Her knees locked and she nearly pitched forward onto her face.

"Sarah?" James's voice repeated from only a few feet behind her. Clutching her guilt tighter to her chest, Sarah tried hard to breathe.

She was caught.


When his wife turned toward him, James felt no small amount of alarm at her pallor. He was actually reaching out to catch her when her lips trembled into a smile.

"James, you surprised me. Whatever are you doing home at this hour?"

He frowned. "Are you quite well, my dear?" He started to ease his hand beneath her elbow, but she shifted away, drawing his eye to the package she held.

"I am fine. I was only out to . . . I only just . . ."

He smiled. "More books, darling?"

"I . . ." Her eyes fell. "Yes," she whispered. "Books."

"Come." He slid his hand over her shoulder and curled his fingers to touch the back of her neck, shocked at the way her skin played havoc with his nerves. But shock didn't stop him from lowering his mouth to her forehead. He let himself breathe her in for a bare second before he pulled away. "You may buy as many novels as you like. We have a library to fill, after all."

Her eyes filled with tears.

"Sarah," he said on a nervous laugh. "Pray do not look at me as if I were a monster." As soon as he said the word "monster" it occurred to him that maybe her upset had nothing to do with books and everything to do with last night. Horror froze his blood to a sluggish crawl. Had he hurt her? Frightened her? His stomach fell to his feet.

His wife shook her head and tried to blink the tears away. "Of course not. You are so good to me. Always."

Helpless and confused, he dropped his hand from her neck, though he clenched his fingers to hold her warmth captive. "I thought perhaps we could take luncheon together. Have I upset you too much to join me?" What he'd actually thought was that they might use luncheon as an excuse to flirt. He'd hoped to tease a blush to her cheeks, hoped that the memory would keep him company for the rest of this interminable day. Now he only hoped not to hurt her tender feelings.

Sarah took a deep breath and squared her shoulders. Against him?

"I would love to dine with you, James. I was only overset by a headache this morning. Please forgive me."

"Of course!" he answered. Of course, she'd suffered a headache. His wife did not often indulge in too many glasses of wine. "If you are ill, I will leave you to your rest."

"No, stay! Please stay. I only need a moment."

Before he could offer even a small bow, she'd whirled away and started up the stairs, arms still clutching her package. James watched her go, tracing her small waist with his eyes.

Her delicate femininity had inspired his protectiveness from the moment they'd met. Whenever she was near, he felt larger. Stronger, somehow. But today, for the first time, he felt like a clumsy oaf with hands far too big to handle a creature as beautifully fragile as his wife.

# CHAPTER 3

Luncheon had been a miserable affair, though Sarah had tried her best to be bright and lively. Her husband rarely returned home during the day, and on any previous day, she would have been nervously excited at his unexpected appearance. But today, guilt had eaten at her, devouring bits of her slowly. When it had finished its feast, she'd been left hollow, but at least it had been done.

Then she'd remembered that she should be embarrassed as well as guilty. Had he been thinking about the previous night when he'd watched her so closely? She had blushed at the thought, and the burn had stayed through the rest of the meal.

But James had been lovely, as always, trying his best to coax a laugh from her lips. She had laughed for him, and wished she were not such a fraud.

When he'd gone, he hadn't pressed his customary kiss to her cheek. Instead, he'd kissed her lips, and the taste of his mouth made her heart tumble and fall, made her breath hitch. James's eyes had widened at that small sound, and he'd stared at her for a long moment before taking his leave.

Pulse thumping at the memory, Sarah pressed her fingertips to her mouth and curled tighter into the chair. Sunlight streamed through the bedroom window, warming the corner where she hid and lighting up the pile of books she'd unwrapped.

Another secret kept from him.

Hand trembling, she reached for the smallest book. *A Physician's Wisdom Pursuant to the Fruitful Marriage.* Well, she had certainly felt ripe as a peach last night in the dark.

After one last, deep breath, Sarah cracked open the book and began to read.

The first two chapters were so decidedly *un*-scandalous that Sarah actually began to feel sleepy. Complementary temperaments that would make for a good marriage. Physical attributes that might normally be considered attractive to a mate. She would've called for tea if the thought of packing up the books and hiding them didn't seem too tremendous a feat. So she read on, and soon felt her sleepiness dissipate like fog before a hard wind.

*Here.* Here was information that would prove useful.

Frequency of marital relations will be determined by the husband's spirit and humours. The wife should, of course, accommodate the enthusiasm of his masculine needs but should never be bullied or cowed into acquiescence. Despite that her body does not rise in demand as a man's does, it is not the impassive vessel it seems. Her own seed must be called if the marriage is to result in healthy progeny. Even from the time of Aristotle it has been known that the wife's womb will not quicken unless she experiences her own feminine climax.

"Climax," Sarah breathed. At the sound of that word, her body bloomed into chill bumps that tightened her nipples. *Climax.* That seemed exactly what it had been. A culmination of the sensations her husband had encouraged.

Could it be that her fit had been a good thing? She wanted children, badly. Perhaps this was only a harbinger of fertility?

Feeling more hopeful by the moment, Sarah read on, wide-eyed at the information printed on the pages. The author provided fascinating details of pregnancy and childbirth and admonitions against "self-pollution," whatever that might be. Further assertion that pleasure between a man and his wife was vitally important to the health of both. And, most interesting of all, a *drawing* of how the male and female bodies in their entirety were designed by God himself to complement each other.

Sarah studied the picture closely, trying in vain to picture James's body opposite her own. She could not. She'd tried hard not to glimpse any bits of him that might be . . . frightening. It seemed odd now, that something had been deep inside her own body and she'd never even peeked at it. Surely she should be acquainted with the thing.

The hum that had been slowly building in her body over the past hours began to center itself in a very specific spot. She recognized both the hum and the spot now. After reading such enlightening text, the sensations felt rather friendly instead of frightening.

Perhaps James would touch her again tonight. Perhaps he would stroke her and urge her on.

By the time her maid knocked and asked if she'd like to dress for dinner, Sarah's skin felt too tight, her clothing too stiff. The idea of putting on a heavier gown for the evening made her cringe, but she rose anyway, care-

fully repacked the books in their paper, then hid the
bundle under the bed.

James would be home soon, and she must be dressed
to receive him, whether he stayed for dinner or not.

"Ma'am," Mary greeted her, already removing a dress
from the wardrobe.

Sarah stared at the moss-green cotton that spilled
over her maid's arms. Glancing into the jumble of colors in the wardrobe, she shook her head. "I shall wear the
yellow silk tonight."

Mary only nodded and switched the dresses.

"And my hair . . . perhaps in a fall down my back?"

"Yes, ma'am."

Mary seemed completely unfazed by her mistress's
requests, but Sarah felt so different she wondered that
it wasn't visible. Surely her lips were pinker, her breasts
fuller? But if her own maid didn't notice, likely no one
would, perhaps not even James. He might simply come
home, relax with a brandy and the newspaper, then
head out for an evening at his club. The thought
caused a flutter of relief along with mortification.

She could not wait for him to be home. And she was
scared half to death.


The sun was still high in the sky when James found himself mounting his front steps that evening. Not that he
could see the sun past the thick clouds that had gathered above London, but the day still felt too bright for
the kinds of thoughts crowding his head.

After that disastrous luncheon this afternoon, James
had been perfectly sure that he would flee to his club
for the evening and avoid the discomfort he'd forced
between him and his wife. Sarah simply wasn't that kind
of woman. He'd proved he could coax pleasure from
her beautiful body, but in the process, he'd frightened

and disturbed her, forced her to a place she did not wish to go. She was a wife, not a doxy.

That had been his thinking all through the meal, while Sarah avoided his eyes and asked pleasant questions.

But then he'd kissed her.

Knowing he should leave it be, he'd still kissed her. And thank God he had.

She'd drawn in a sharp breath just before her lips offered their own fleeting pressure. When he'd looked into her eyes, they'd gone black, dilated with pleasure. Her lips remained slightly parted as if she might welcome another kiss.

After that, James hadn't known what to think, but he'd come home early with great hopes of puzzling it out.

"Mr. Hood," Crawford murmured, offering a bow even as he took James's hat and gloves. "The evening paper awaits you in the library. May I bring a refreshment as well?"

"Ah . . . I'm not sure. Is Mrs. Hood in?"

"I believe she is in her chambers, sir. Shall I send word that you are home?"

James glanced toward the stairs, weighing his options. He thought of that kiss. "Yes, please do. And can Cook have dinner prepared in half an hour?" He hadn't managed to choke down much of the cold beef on his plate this afternoon.

Waiting in the library, he paced from the window to the fireplace and back again. And again. His heart had broken today when her eyes had filled with tears. The thought that he might have hurt her was almost as bad as on their wedding night, when he'd known he must. He'd had to choke down three fingers of whisky that night before going to her. He was beginning to think he might need the same tonight.

Except that he hadn't imagined the way she'd responded to him in the dark. Surely he hadn't. Her whimpers of desire. Her body arching into his, *needing*.

The click of the door latch stopped his pacing. Sarah's voice stopped his heart.

"James?" she whispered, so tentative.

But when he turned and saw her there, his fears tumbled away like brittle leaves.

Self-conscious at the intensity of his stare, Sarah smoothed a hand down the side of her gown. His eyes followed, making her anxiety worse.

She looked foolish, wearing a dress more appropriate for a dinner party than an evening at home. Far too much of her bosom was revealed, as if she *wanted* him to stare there. And her hair . . . tumbling down her back like an opera singer's. She'd thought that putting effort into her appearance would be a subtle way of inviting her husband to seduce her. But now she was too exposed. Stripped of any pretense of innocence in this game.

"You are so beautiful," James said simply. His eyes did not leer; they glowed, and her heart swelled in response.

"Thank you." Her voice seemed to disappear in the large room, but it did not matter. Her husband was drawing closer.

He whispered her name, touched his hand to her cheek, and when she raised her head to look at him, he kissed her. Her eyelids fluttered closed at the first soft brush of his mouth. Then his tongue grazed her bottom lip and she opened for him, welcomed him into her body. The kiss was soft and slow. Not a promise of more to come, but an act in and of itself. As if they had a lifetime to explore each other's bodies. And they did.

James broke the kiss first, and she was forced to lean against him for support. "I have been dreaming of kissing you all day," he murmured.

Sarah tried to hide her pride. "But we only just kissed a few hours ago."

"Yes. And however short a time before we kiss again tonight, I'm certain it will feel an eternity. Men are quite cursed. When a man desires a certain woman, he can think of little else."

She blushed and put a little distance between them, unable to flirt and look him in the face at the same time. "Mm? And what of women?" From the corner of her eye, she watched him follow her progress as she strolled from the doorway toward the window.

"I'm not sure," he finally answered. "Have you ever found yourself consumed with thoughts of kisses?"

Sarah curled her fingers into the drapery and squeezed hard to push some courage into her veins. The curtain rod gave a small creak, so she forced herself to loosen her hold. Then she took a deep breath and turned toward her husband, though she couldn't manage to raise her gaze from the carpet. "Yes," she admitted to the reds and golds of the Oriental tapestry, "even more than kisses . . . sometimes."

They both held their breath after that. Only the ticking of the clock, suddenly loud, pierced the silence for a few torturous moments. Her heart struggled in desperate panic.

James finally inhaled, then breathed out one soft word. "More?"

She'd forced out all the bold talk she could, so Sarah only nodded.

"I was afraid . . ." he started, then shook his head. "I was afraid I had frightened you."

That made her smile, and she managed to glance up for a brief moment. "I was afraid *I* had frightened *you*."

The unbearable tension broke on the wave of his laughter. "Never think that. You please me to no end, my love."

"Will you . . . ?" She cleared her throat. "Will you stay for dinner, then?"

His smile changed subtly, shifting from amusement to satisfaction. "Yes." His eyes drifted down her yellow gown. "I had no plans to go anywhere at all." Then he met her gaze.

*Oh, mercy.* Now James was changed, too. A different creature than when he'd first returned from work. Instead of joviality, his green eyes glinted something dangerous. His jaw was harder, etched from a material more ruthless than flesh.

The new mood in the room reminded her of the countryside in the fall, when buck deer would suddenly transform from gentle, pretty animals to fierce creatures bunched with muscle. The males wanted something, and they seemed mad with that want. But the doe responded, just as Sarah was responding to her husband's possessive gaze.

It was frightening to be wanted so. Frightening and stunningly exciting.

When he stepped toward her, Sarah tensed with the impulse to flee. She was too new to this to respond any other way, regardless of her intentions. But a shadow fell into the room, and Crawford bowed from the doorway. "Sir, madam, if it pleases you, dinner will be served when you are seated."

James stared at her a moment longer, but when he blinked, the spell was broken. "Madam," he said, offering a little bow before he held out his arm.

The imagined danger had passed and, with a sigh of mild relief, Sarah went to him and took his arm. The simple touch made her burn.

* * *

*My wife thinks of more than kissing.*

James clutched his glass of port and stared daggers at the library clock.

*My wife,* he repeated to himself, *thinks of* more.

When this change had started, he had no idea. Had there been new signs of passion he'd missed? Was it only that she'd begun to trust him? Perhaps it simply took time for a restrained gentlewoman like Sarah to become accustomed to a man's touch. Whatever the reason, he could think of nothing else now.

The second hand of the clock had become weighted down, too heavy to keep the right time, he was sure of it. According to that blasted clock, Sarah had excused herself only five minutes before to prepare for bed.

Dinner had been enjoyable, despite the fact that James had been in a painful state for most of it. And at the end, Sarah had stood, hands still clutching her serviette, and announced that she was quite worn out. "I must call Mary to help me ready for bed. Please enjoy your port." She'd practically run from the room, and left James standing there alone, still caught up in the lovely memory of the pale rise of her breasts above the neckline of her gown.

He knew she wasn't readying for sleep; sunset was barely upon them. No, she was readying for *him.*

Six minutes. Was six minutes enough? It would have to be.

James set his drink down with a purposeful clink and headed for the stairs.

When he reached his dressing room, he paused to listen. Not a sound from their bedchamber. Was she lying in bed, waiting for him? Thinking about *more?* James tugged off his tie, slipped out of his jacket, and turned the door handle.

"Oh!" a female voice gasped. His wife or her maid. He couldn't be sure. They'd both turned to gape at him. The maid's hands had frozen over the ties of Sarah's corset. Her dress was gone, her bustle and petticoats as well.

"I . . ." James tried to think what to say, but his mind was occupied with sending up a prayer of thanks that he hadn't strolled through the door in the buff. "I apologize," he finally managed. "I see I did not give you enough time."

Sarah shook her head. "No, it is just that Mary wasn't expecting me so early and—"

"I'm sorry, sir," Mary murmured, bobbing a curtsy. "Ma'am." She hovered for a moment, clearly uncertain if she should continue with her task.

James cleared his throat. "Shall I . . . ?"

His wife looked from him to the maid and back again. "I'm sure we can . . . Um, Mary, if you could only unknot the strings?"

Mary's fingers sprang to action and worked at the laces as if her life depended upon it. A few moments later, the knot gave way to her determination. Before the ties fluttered to rest against Sarah's back, the maid had dropped her curtsy and spun toward the opposite dressing room door. The door closed, and they were alone.

The skin of her shoulders gleamed in the lamplight. Her cheeks were soft pink when she started to turn toward him, but then she paused and turned her back again, and James watched the blush creep toward the nape of her neck. The combination of her modesty and her bare skin twined together and dug deep into his body. She was so innocent, and still she wanted him.

Trying to tamp down the need that already throbbed through him, James slowly crossed the room. He paused a foot from her, taking in the sight of her cinched waist and gauzy chemise. He'd never seen her thus: fully covered, but completely indecent. When he reached for her stays, his hands trembled.

Her gasp echoed through the room when he moved his fingers beneath the crossed strings and tugged. A few more pulls, and her ribs expanded as she inhaled a deep breath. Something about the breath rushing past her lips made him even harder.

She pressed both hands to her waist to unlatch the front hooks, and the corset fell to the floor to land at her feet. They stared at it together, but when James noticed the way she rolled her shoulders, he put a hand to her back to rub the tension away.

Reveling in the surprising heat of the slightly damp linen, James pressed his thumb along the edge of her spine.

"Ah," she sighed.

"It must be a relief to take that thing off."

"Yes."

He put his other hand to work on the left side of her spine.

"Oh, James. That feels so good." Her head bowed, stretching her neck out for his view, only inches away. Tempted, he lifted the heavy fall of her hair and pushed it over one shoulder. Now her spine was exposed from the middle of her back to her hairline. His thumbs crept up to bare skin and elicited a soft whimper with each circle he pressed to her muscles. The sounds vibrated through the pads of his fingers and chased along his nerves until his cock throbbed.

As soon as he reached her shoulders, he stepped closer and put his mouth to the side of her neck, finally tasting her. This new, wanton Sarah let her head fall to the side so that he could nibble to his heart's content. Even more surprising, she pressed her backside to his erection.

"Will you . . . ?" She took a breath and tried again. "Will you douse the lamps?"

James didn't bother answering; he simply let go of her shoulders and moved toward the closest lamp. But it made no difference. The faint light of the lowering sun still exposed her to his view. He did not volunteer to close the thicker drapes. Instead, he began unbuttoning his shirt.

Eyes wide, she watched, gaze lowering as each button slid free. When he shrugged the shirt off entirely, her eyes closed.

"Does my body disturb you?" He tried to ignore the sharp hurt that caused.

"Of course not." Her eyelids rose, her gaze darted frantically over his chest, then to the floor, back to his body and then his eyes. "I should not like to stare."

Honest relief made him smile. "You wouldn't *like* to or you are trying to be all that is proper?"

Her attempt to answer his smile did not quite succeed, so he only took her hand and led her across the room to their bed. "Close your eyes, Sarah," he murmured.

Facing him, she stood still and closed her eyes, not offering a protest when he reached for the hem of her chemise and slowly dragged it up. First her drawers were revealed, stark white against her ivory skin. Then her belly, soft and smooth.

James averted his eyes when he pulled the chemise over her head. He wanted to see all of her, needed that, so before taking her in, he reached for the tie of her drawers and freed her from every stitch of fabric.

Then . . . By God. The moonlight views he'd stolen of his wife were nothing to this. Her rose-tipped breasts a bit too small to fill his hand. Her waist where it nipped in just before flaring out to succulent hips. Her sex, the dark curls of her mound. James held back a hum of approval.

Though her hands fisted at her sides, Sarah did not cover herself. She only stood, eyes closed, and let him look.

James went to his knees. His fingers felt too thick as he fumbled at the clasps of her stockings. All his coordination had been stolen by the shock of the view. He could see past her curls from this vantage to the beckoning pink beneath. He could smell her heat, the musky scent of feminine arousal. His mouth watering, he thought of kissing her there. Would she cringe in horror? Would she sob in pleasure?

The idea of shocking her proved impossibly tempting. He wanted her shocked. Scandalized. By him.

He pushed the stockings down, one at a time, then smoothed his palms back up her bare legs, slowly, slowly. When he reached her outer thighs, he pushed farther around, so that his hands slipped up to the perfect roundness of her buttocks. Sarah gasped, and her hips jumped forward just a bit, offering a more generous peek of glistening pink.

His mouth watered for a taste. Just a taste. How could she know if he didn't show her?

James spread his fingers out, taking a firmer grip on her round bottom. Then he pressed one chaste kiss to the triangle of dark curls that tempted him.

"Oh!" she gasped. But she did not pull away.

He kissed again, lower, and let the tip of his tongue delve in to graze her plump flesh.

"James, don't!"

Cursing himself for a beast, he ignored her and slid his tongue lower, feeling her lips part just the tiniest bit at his thrust. He'd finally found the taste of her, pleasure on his tongue.

"You can't . . ." she protested, finally touching him. Her hand curled into his hair and pulled. "Please don't."

James looked up her body, past the curve of her belly and the jut of her breasts. "Open your eyes," he urged. Sarah shook her head. "Open your eyes," he said more firmly, telling himself he'd stop now if she didn't. He'd stop and apologize and tuck her beneath the sheets. But Sarah opened her eyes.

Willing her to yield, James darted his tongue against her slit. When he looked back to her, her whole face had tightened. He held her with his eyes and shifted his hands lower to tug her legs apart. She slid her feet only a few inches, but it was enough. This time his tongue parted her lips and he was sliding over that pearl of hard tissue.

Her hand clenched in his hair and she gasped. He knew it felt good to her, because he could taste her pleasure. He licked again, flicked his tongue over her bud, and when her thighs began to shake, he eased her to the bed. Yes, now she was spread before him, deep and pink and wet, and James could hardly think.

He'd done this before, only a few times. But this was his *wife*, letting him suck at her, letting him push his tongue into her center, and he almost could not bear it.

"James?" she gasped. "James, is this all right? Can we . . . ?"

"Yes," he groaned. When she thought of *more*, he wanted her picturing *this*. He would never stop thinking of it, surely. Never.

James dragged his tongue down as far as he could, then back up to circle her clitoris.

"Oh, it feels so . . . I don't think I should . . ."

Some wretched animal inside him swelled with dominance. No, she shouldn't. He shouldn't. But he would, because he wanted this with her. His sweet, innocent wife. He wanted to create a world where she was something else in private. His secret lover.

So James closed his lips around her tight bud and sucked gently.

"James! Oh, God, oh, no! Please. Please."

*Yes, please,* he thought, as her soft thighs tightened, squeezing him, shaking. Her hips jerked, she screamed, and his mouth was full of the taste of Sarah.

Listening to her ragged panting, James sat back on his heels and wiped his lips. He could spend his seed right now with only the barest touch of his own hand, he was sure of it. Best to take a few deep breaths himself.

Sarah's knees closed with a slap as she sat straight up. "What did you do?" she demanded. Her nipples were even pinker now, tipped with deep, hard rose.

"I kissed you."

"Yes, but . . . Do men . . . ? Is that something that people *do?*"

"Yes."

She stared him down for a long moment. "Are you quite sure?"

"I'm certain. But if you ask me not to, I'll never do it again."

"Oh." Her eyelids fluttered, and he thought she was looking down to the place he'd just tongued. "I can't imagine that it brought you any pleasure. Surely—"

"On the contrary. I'm sure I've never enjoyed anything more. Did you like it, Sarah?"

She swallowed hard.

"It's all right to say yes." He added, "Or no," though his throat tried to cut off the words.

"Yes," she finally whispered, and the animal raged back to life in his chest, greedy with lust.

"You liked it?"

"Yes."

"And . . . tomorrow, Sarah? Tomorrow, would you like it again?"

"Oh. I . . . y-yes." Her eyes filled with tears, shaming him.

An ache in his chest briefly overcame the one in his groin. "Ah, love. I'm sorry. Men are beasts when they're overcome with lust, and I seem to be no exception." Chastened, he rose to his feet and lifted her from the bed to turn back the sheets. "Here."

Though he grieved the loss, he covered her naked body in crisp white, then sat on the edge of the bed and let his head fall to his hands.

By God, he might have ruined everything. All her awakening desire and tentative curiosity. What kind of man couldn't control himself with his own wife? What kind of husband would hope to make her feel dirty?

When Sarah's hand brushed his back with a butterfly touch, he cringed.

"James," she breathed. "Are you overcome with lust?"

"I was, but I can control it. You needn't worry." Perhaps he should excuse himself to the dressing room and take care of the problem in private.

Her voice interrupted his brooding. "For me?" she asked.

"Hm?"

"You were overcome with lust for me?"

He froze. Her warm hand settled flat against his spine. "Of course for you, Sarah."

"I . . ." Her fingers curled into his back. "I like that, too." His heart stopped as her hand stroked down to tease along the waistband of his trousers. "I'm sorry I'm so nervous. I do not mean to be."

He turned to face her, clasping her hand in his. "No, I'm to blame. There's no need to rush. We have a lifetime together. Thousands of nights."

She looked startled for a moment, then her mouth bloomed into a wide smile. "Thousands? My word."

"Too melodramatic?"

"No, but you remind me that perhaps . . ." Blushing, she hesitated until James arched an eyebrow. "Um, perhaps I should see exactly what it is I've committed myself to."

He frowned in confusion. "But we have already done that. Many times."

She turned from pink to red in a fascinating suffusion of color. "Yes, but . . ." Clutching the sheet to her breasts, she leaned close. "I have never seen your instrument."

James suffered a brief, disorienting thought of the violin he kept on the top shelf of his wardrobe, but then her meaning burst over his mind with startling clarity. He should not have laughed, but he did. Thank God, Sarah did not seem to mind, though she put her hands over her eyes and peeked through her fingers.

"I'm sorry," he chuckled. "Of course you would wish to view the beast that hunts you every night."

"James!" she scolded, voice full of laughter, then she squeaked when he stood and reached for the buttons of his remaining clothing. But when he slipped off his trousers and unfastened his drawers, Sarah's hands fell away, and she watched with not a glimmer of humor in her eyes.

# CHAPTER 4

The next morning Sarah woke very differently than she had the day before. She remembered everything she'd done immediately. Before the room had even come into focus, the night was acting itself out in her mind in vivid colors. Finally, she'd seen his body . . . nude.

James had blushed a bit. Or perhaps it had only been blood rushing to his skin, because he'd met her gaze unflinchingly as he'd divested himself of every stitch of clothing.

His boldness had sent shivers through her body. Not just over her skin, but everywhere, into her stomach and her sex, even her soul. That shivering had been nothing to do with modesty, so Sarah had let her hands fall from her face and offered the same honesty he was offering her.

His body was so different from hers. The same structure, perhaps, but a different architecture altogether. Straight planes where her body curved, texture where she was smooth. And, of course, his sex . . . proudly exposed while hers hid itself in shyness.

Though, as she'd looked him over from head to toe,

her sex had felt decidedly less shy than it had in days past. She'd even dared to run a quizzical finger down his shaft . . . and back up. He had held still, like granite despite the shocking heat that emanated from his flesh. Her courage had seen her through one more touch, a slower slide of her fingers down his length, a quick caress of the tight testicles beneath. Then she'd dropped her hand, nodded, and tossed back the bedsheets to invite him in.

Smiling at the bright morning sunlight that stole over those very sheets, Sarah sighed with joy. A little of the strangeness of her life had washed away during the night. Her husband's body now seemed a mystery to be explored with enthusiasm. And her own body, too. James had shown her just this morning that she had many things to learn about her own flesh as well.

He'd awakened her with strokes and kisses, then entered her body from *behind,* like a stallion covering a mare. At the very thought of it, Sarah blushed and hid her smile. The shock of it, along with the attention of James's gentle fingers, had pushed her to her climax with scandalous speed.

Sarah Rose Hood was *definitely* in love with her husband.

She laughed aloud at the happy thought, then shut her mouth with a snap when footsteps hurried toward her from the dressing room.

"Good morning, ma'am," Mary said, heading straight for the curtains to throw them wide. "Shall I call for tea?"

"Please. And I should like a bath this morning."

"Of course, ma'am."

After she tugged the bellpull to signal for tea, Mary bent down to retrieve something from the floor. Sarah's thoughts flashed immediately to the packet of books she'd hidden beneath the bed, but Mary rose with evidence even more mortifying than the books. James's trousers. The maid bent once more and retrieved one of Sarah's stockings.

The trail of clothing continued to the pile heaped in the middle of the room. Sarah's corset and shift. Her drawers. James's shirt.

*Oh, God.* Sarah took the easy way out and drew the sheets up to her nose as she closed her eyes and pretended to curl back into sleep for a few more moments. But instead of sleeping, she murmured a silent prayer that Mary was not the type to gossip with the maids next door. *Why, they must have gone at it like beasts. And her so proper and missish!*

Not that it mattered. Sarah wouldn't take it back for the world.

Her tea arrived, and then the tub. She heard the metal thud of it being set in place in the dressing room and the first loud swish of water. James had promised they would build a bathing room next year, but Sarah felt thankful for the slow preparation this morning.

"Mary, will you knock when the bath is ready?"

Mary nodded and closed the door to the dressing room.

As soon as the door clicked shut, Sarah set the tea tray aside and jumped—naked!—from the bed to reach beneath it for the books. She wanted to know more, wanted to know *everything*. She scrambled back beneath the bedcovers and tore open the packaging to pull the second book from the pile. Cup of hot tea in hand, she began to read.

A quarter hour later a knock on the door relieved her from her boredom. This book was nothing like the first. In fact, the author seemed dedicated to writing a whole book on only the most boring topics of marriage. Frugal meal planning. Economic use of servants. The proper way to address one's spouse in public and pri-

vate. When he finally got to the bedroom, the writer's
language became so circumspect that Sarah could not
begin to puzzle out his meaning.

Happy to be interrupted, she haphazardly retied the
books and stowed them under the bed after pulling on
the wrap Mary had left.

She sank into the hot bathwater with a deep sigh,
noticing every caress of the little waves she created. Her
sex stung a bit at the touch of the heat. Perhaps James
had used her too roughly. The delightful idea made her
chuckle, and the steam jumped and stirred at her
breath.

Not until later did she realize that, for the first time
in her life, she'd stepped into the tub with not one moment of shame at her nudity.

She'd dressed carefully again, choosing her clothing
with an eye toward the view she'd provide her husband.
Then she'd tinkered with next week's menu a bit, avoiding any of the foods mentioned in that horridly practical book. She hadn't gone out on any of her usual
excursions; instead, she'd waited to see if her husband
would join her for luncheon.

In the end, he hadn't come. She might have sulked,
but he'd sent an extravagant bouquet of flowers with an
errand boy, as well as a slightly risqué note of apology,
so Sarah only pouted for a few minutes before deciding
to make the most of it.

"Send a tray to my room!" she called to the maid
sweeping the parlor and rushed up the stairs to pull a
new book from the pile.

She hadn't known that James could—or would—
take her from behind. She hadn't known he would put
his mouth *there* and make her shudder and cry. What

else must there be? What more could they do together? Her sex felt warm and tight as she pondered the thought.

Waiting for her meal—and squirming a bit on her chair—Sarah flipped idly through the book, hoping to find some interesting pictures. Unfortunately, this author showed more interest in charts than drawings. She crinkled her nose in disappointment as she hid the book in her skirts at the sound of approaching footsteps.

Despite her brief hope that it might be James, it was only Betsy, the kitchen maid, lugging the heavy tray. Sarah had nibbled half a piece of buttered bread by the time the girl stopped pouring tea and puttering around. As soon as the door clicked shut behind her, Sarah slipped the book onto the table.

*Women in Marriage: A Treatise on the Peculiar Health of Wives and Mothers.*

*Peculiar.* Well, that might be the word to describe her. Sarah's lips were just rising into a smile when she saw the author's name.

*Dr. C. Malcolm Whitcomb.*

Her lungs froze, body reacting before her brain could generate a thought. *Whitcomb.* Brow furrowed, she stared at the name imprinted into the cover in gold ink. The name was familiar, but why did it make her muscles tighten to the point of pain?

"Doctor Whitcomb," she said aloud, and the words left a bright trail of recognition in their wake. The bread fell from her hand, landing on the carpet with a *plop.*

Her mother's doctor. The very man who had treated her mother in the years before her death. He'd been an elegant man, polite and handsome, and very somberly concerned about his patient's deterioration.

The anticipation with which Sarah had approached her reading vanished like paper tossed into a fire. In the space of one short day, she'd forgotten her original purpose in acquiring the books. It hadn't been titillation or curiosity, but true fear that had driven her to that bookshop. That fear was back.

Tray of food forgotten, Sarah rose with the book in her hand and rushed to the door to lock it. This would be far more than idle reading. She curled into the large chair nearest the fireplace and opened the book.

She tried to read slowly, but the words rushed at her. Whitcomb seemed to believe that women's natural modesty often protected them from their own inherent weaknesses. Their sheltered lives provided protection and insulation from the realities of life. He theorized that the very delicacy that so attracted a man to clasp his wife to his bosom also left her susceptible to being traumatized by that attention.

> A woman is not a sexual creature. The scabbard is designed only to embrace the sword, not to take action. The wife receives the husband's attentions because she was made to do so, not because she is compelled by desire. But her delicate psyche, previously innocent of all idea of lust and copulation, can be damaged by this male assault. She cannot make sense of it. It holds no meaning for her. And so, if already predisposed to pitiful weakness, her brain may suffer peculiar maladies that lead to mental destruction.

Pitiful weakness? She hoped that wasn't true, but the rest of it . . . The rest of it made her hands tremble. Marital relations *had* been strange and startling to her, even frightening in the beginning. She certainly hadn't been compelled by desire.

Sarah glanced at the bellpull, tempted to call for a glass of sherry to steel her nerves against the rest of it.

But she was already putting on an odd show for the servants. They might be inclined to report to her husband if she began drinking wine in the middle of the afternoon.

After taking one long, deep breath, Sarah bent her head back to the book. She read quickly, emotionlessly. Pages and pages of information.

According to Doctor Whitcomb, there were several different manifestations of this mental damage. Paranoia. Hypochondria. Exhaustion. Painful spasms and rictus of the birth canal.

Despite the terrible nature of the afflictions, Sarah began to relax. She was fine. These diseases had nothing to do with her.

But she breathed a sigh of relief too soon.

*Nymphomania,* the chapter heading screamed in dark script. *An ungovernable desire for sexual contact and congress.*

Well. It was possible there was a hint of familiarity in that. Though she smiled at the thought, her amusement faded as her eyes crept over the page.

Nymphomania, sometimes known as erotomania, is the most insidious of all the feminine disorders. It begins with restlessness and creeping warmth. Insomnia. Confusion. Then the building desire for physical stimulation which becomes a preoccupation with thoughts of marital relations.

"Oh, no," Sarah breathed. "Oh, my Lord." She pressed her fingertips to her lips, hard. Nymphomania? Was that the strangeness that had been crawling under her skin for days?

Though marital relations may occasionally occur more often than once a week in a healthy relationship, a nymphomaniac may encourage sexual congress every night, perhaps even multiple times in the same twenty-four-hour period. Morning or midnight, it makes no difference to this pitiful creature. Her obsession has nothing to do with duty or even procreation, and her affliction endangers the husband's health as well. Without the natural damper of expected wifely modesty, a man will succumb to his basest lusts. Her insatiable demands force him to engage in unnatural acts involving alternative stimulation of the genitals as he cannot otherwise satisfy her urges.

She dropped the book, threw it, almost, so that it bounced off the wall before landing back at her feet. Despite that she could see it lying on the rug, the feel of it lingered on her fingers. Sarah rubbed her hand against her skirts, desperate to remove the phantom stain.

Unnatural acts. Yes, she had done that, had tempted her husband into it. Not only that, but she had reached her climax three times in the space of a few short hours. She *was* insatiable. What had seemed so pleasurable now seemed fraught with danger.

What did it mean? If this was her illness, could it be cured? Would it worsen?

Heart pounding, she stared at the blue cover as if the cloth had suddenly begun to ripple with dark life. Her symptoms were laid out so clearly, so vividly. Whatever else she would read seemed certain to be just as true. The very reason she needed to read more, and yet her hand would not obey the order to reach down and grasp the book.

"Do not be so cowardly," Sarah whispered to herself. But it seemed as if her marriage—indeed her whole life—might hang in the balance, teetering on the delicate edge of one page in a book. "Coward," she said again but still could not lean down. Instead, she leapt to her feet and began to pace.

There was no reason to think this particular physician was right where others were wrong. Hadn't she just read a book asserting that women should feel pleasure and desire? Indeed, that author claimed that female climax was *necessary* for conception and marital harmony. She'd stopped feeling ill about her desires after that. In fact, just moments ago she'd been happy.

Sarah scrubbed her hands over her face, hoping the pressure would rub away her confusion, but nothing changed. Nothing but the shifting view of the rug as she paced back and forth.

Yes, this doctor had treated her mother, and perhaps that lent his words a certain weight, but her mother hadn't improved. She'd declined. Dr. Whitcomb was no demigod.

Sarah stopped and turned slowly toward the book. She stared it down.

She'd deceived James into this marriage. She owed him at least the courage to discover if her deception had been harmless . . . or horrendous.

# CHAPTER 5

Figures rushed past her, dark masses in the gloomy light. The fog thickened around her, viscous, putrid-gray as cold porridge. Sarah pushed through it, nearly running, darting through the packs of people making their way toward home or market or their favorite tavern. Her maid called out in alarm, and Sarah slowed her pace to allow the girl to catch up.

"Ma'am," Betsy panted. "Is something wrong?"

There was nothing about this trip that called for an illiterate companion, but Sarah felt secure with Betsy now, as if the maid were part of keeping this secret safe.

She didn't bother answering the question, just waved at her to move faster.

Sarah's father and stepmother lived nearly a mile from her new home, but despite the weather, Sarah had been determined to walk. The idea of being shut in a hack in creeping traffic had made her hands tremble.

Too many words were crawling through her, too many terrors. *The condition is most often hereditary....* *Weakness leading to hysteria ... slow descent into lunacy ...* *confinement to an institution ...*

Sarah pressed her handkerchief to her mouth to cover her quiet sob. If she had inherited her mother's disease, then she'd cursed James to misery. Her father had lived through it, but had lost so much of himself in the process. She could remember him in her early childhood, still garrulous and cheerful. But each month had added a new crease to his once-smooth brow. Each year had darkened his eyes. In the end . . . in the end, his grief had been more like hatred for his wife.

They had never once spoken of Sarah's mother after her death. She did not expect he would speak of it now, but perhaps he had talked with his new wife about it. Not likely, but perhaps.

Finally, she reached her old street. She started to turn the corner, but made herself pause and wait for Betsy to catch up again. Without giving the girl time to slow her breath, Sarah rushed on. "You may rest in the kitchen while I take tea with my stepmother," she said over her shoulder. The girl's red cheeks wobbled when she nodded.

"Wait!" she cried when Sarah put her foot on the first step.

Sarah was so startled that she actually stopped, providing Betsy the time to rush past her and clank the knocker herself. Here was a girl with ambitions and the determination to do things right. Before her descent into madness, Sarah would have to remember to recommend her for promotion.

She actually managed a smile for that morbid thought just before the door swung open.

"Mrs. Hood!" the butler cried with far too much unseemly fondness when he spied her. But Sarah was supremely grateful for the show of affection.

"MacNeal, it is so good to see you. Is my stepmother in? I am sorry for not sending word, but I was in the neighborhood, you see, and . . ."

"Let's just see if she's receiving," he offered with a wink as he waved them in. But he didn't have to check after all, as Lorelei rushed out of the drawing room at just that moment.

"Oh, Sarah! What a lovely surprise. I've just poured myself a cup of tea. Will you join me?"

"I'm not intruding?"

"Of course not," her stepmother laughed, motioning her forward.

It was still strange to think of her as a mother. Lorelei was only seven years older than Sarah and had been married to Sarah's father for a mere five months.

Still, Sarah liked Lorelei. How could she not? Her warm smile bloomed with an ease that bespoke her kindness. Her eyes shone with calm joy. There was no doubt in Sarah's mind why her father had chosen this new bride after so many years. Sarah couldn't imagine anyone less inclined to melancholia or instability.

"We must have you and James over for dinner soon," Lorelei chattered as she took a seat. "I daresay it's been two weeks since we've seen you."

"It's my fault, of course. I keep meaning to have a small dinner party. I promise to speak with Cook as soon as I get home."

Lorelei handed her a cup of tea, already sweetened with two lumps of sugar just as Sarah liked it. "Forgetful? Why, don't tell me you're feeling ill in the mornings as well?" Her eyes darted quickly to Sarah's middle.

"Oh, no!" she protested. "Not at all."

A moment passed. Lorelei's smile blossomed. Her cheeks went pink. "I am!" she suddenly blurted out. "I mean . . . that is to say that I am feeling unwell in the mornings!"

"Oh?"

"We can talk about these things now, can we not? We are both old married women, after all. Oh, Sarah!" Her delighted laugh finally drove home the point that Sarah had missed.

"You are expecting?" She looked with disbelief at Lorelei's flat stomach.

"Yes! I am so happy, and your father as well. And you, Sarah! You will be a sister!"

"A sister," she repeated, stunned. Despite her shock, she had to grin, if only in response to Lorelei's joy. Still, she couldn't help but reel at the thought that her father and Lorelei had been doing the same kinds of things that Sarah and James had. And if she'd conceived, did this mean that Lorelei *enjoyed* the marriage bed as well? Sarah blinked and shoved the thought away. It didn't bear thinking about.

To hide her shock, she pulled her stepmother into a tight hug. "I am so happy for you."

"I have always wanted to be a mother," she whispered into Sarah's shoulder. "Always."

"You will be wonderful." And she would be. Nothing like Sarah's own mother, who had spent so much time in her bed that she'd hardly seemed real.

Sarah cleared her throat as she sat back and straightened her skirts. "Have you . . . ?" She reached for her tea and took a bracing sip before she tried again. "Has my father ever spoken to you of my mother?"

Her smile faded into a look of surprise. "Oh, Sarah. I'm so sorry. I did not mean to be insensitive."

"Nonsense," Sarah said immediately. "Your words only brought her to mind. I find I have been thinking of her lately, being newly married. It is quite a change of circumstance."

"Oh, it is wonderful, is it not? I thought I should never marry, but your father seemed relieved that I was firmly on the shelf. Silly man."

Yes, Sarah's mother had been seventeen at their marriage, so Lorelei's age could only have been an asset in his mind.

"But what was it you wanted to know?" she asked.

"My father, does he ever speak of her?"

"No, but you know how quiet he can be. I do know that she died, of course, after a long illness." She clasped Sarah's hand. "It must have been so hard for you."

"I was only seven. I remember very little," she lied.

"Still." Lorelei sniffed, and wiped a tear from her eye. "Oh, look at me! They say a baby makes you fretful, and I fear it is true. I will ask your father about her, if you like."

"No, I don't wish to distress him."

Lorelei nodded. "When he mentioned her illness, he seemed very subdued. I think he must have loved her very much."

"I'm sure."

"Well, do have a treat," Lorelei urged, reaching for a plate. "It will give me an excuse to eat more. And I'm sure you need your strength, too. No doubt you will also be enjoying motherhood soon if James is doing his duty."

Though she hadn't yet taken a bite of sweetmeat, Sarah choked.

Her dry throat seemed to send Lorelei into a swell of giggles. "The last time you were here, I was talking with your husband when you laughed at some ridiculous thing my cousin said. James's eyes were drawn to you like a magnet. The man watched you laughing from across the room and completely lost track of our conversation! I wondered if you might not get pregnant that very night."

"Lorelei!"

"Oh, pshaw. We are wives now, Sarah. What is the

point of being married except to enjoy it? Do you not feel so . . . whole?"

"Whole?"

"Yes! For so many years I was led about with blinders on, always aware of the hushed conversations that ended when I stepped into a room of women my own age. They had all married years before, and I was not one of them. I was some sort of bizarrely overgrown child to be patted on the head and guided back toward the younger girls so that the adults could talk. And unmarried women were even worse. How many conversations can one have about bonnets before one goes mad? And to be treated as if my circumstance might rub off and curse them to spinsterhood as well . . ."

"Lorelei," Sarah sighed. "I had no idea."

"I do not mind now, for I have your father and he is wonderful. Forty-two is not so old a man, I've found." Her grin nearly split her face. "Not very old at all." Her hand went to her belly, and Sarah watched her fingers curl gently over the treasure there.

If only Lorelei wasn't married to Sarah's father, she could answer so many questions. *Do you enjoy your husband's attentions? If so, how often? Does his touch make you shake and sob? Has he ever approached you in the morning?*

But she could not ask those questions of her father's wife, so she didn't. And when she left an hour later, Sarah knew nothing more than she had when she'd arrived, except that there would be one more life affected by any disease she might eventually succumb to.


James Hood scowled at the man on the opposite seat of the carriage. "If that piece of rubbish imagines he can convince me to support his measure over Harding's, he's clearly picked up more than bad manners at that whorehouse he frequents."

Montgomery snorted. "Syphilitic or not, he has high hopes for that bill."

"I'd rather cross the aisle than throw my support behind him."

"Come now, the bill simply expands—"

"He not only wants to send women of 'doubtful morals' to the workhouse but also he wishes to confiscate their children for factory work? *He,* who refers to the Priory as his London home? That level of hypocrisy begs a beating."

Montgomery arched an eyebrow. "Have you ever *been* to the Priory? I wouldn't say those girls' morals are in any doubt at all. I'd say they are quite delightfully irredeemable. No need to send them to a workhouse; it wouldn't take."

"Christ," James muttered as Montgomery laughed.

"Come, James. You've been married for weeks now. Time to get back to the hunting grounds. I'd planned a trip to the Priory myself tonight. Come along and I'll give you a tour."

James glanced out the window to see how close they were to his house.

"Good man." Montgomery slapped his shoulder and leaned forward conspiratorially. "Listen, they're a bit pricey, but there are a pair of twins—rather fleshy, but they're identical twins, you understand—and they will absolutely devour your—"

"No."

"I'll treat. Consider it a belated wedding gift."

"Bugger yourself, Monty."

"What?"

"I'm in love with my wife."

Montgomery's hand froze on James's shoulder, then dropped back to his side of the hack as if he feared contagion. "Pardon?"

James glanced up to find his friend watching him as

if he'd just announced that he was running off to Timbuktu with a stable hand. He couldn't help but laugh. "I'm in love with Sarah."

"Since when?" Monty scoffed.

*Since the day I met her,* he wanted to say, but didn't. "None of your business. Just watch your mouth if she ever deigns to invite you to dinner."

He scowled. "I can't imagine when that will be. I don't think she likes me."

"Hard to fathom."

His friend's confusion wasn't feigned. He'd flirted with Sarah the way he flirted with every woman and grew more dumbfounded each time she responded with annoyance. Most women loved Montgomery. Sarah did not. James felt inordinately pleased.

"Well, this is intolerable," Monty complained. "You were enough of a stick-in-the-mud before."

"Then it's not much of a loss, is it?" When James saw familiar doorways begin to pass by the window, he smiled. He'd had no choice but to attend this dinner meeting, but now he was home and his pretty, surprising wife awaited within. He had the door open before the carriage rocked to a stop. "Good evening, Monty."

His friend snorted in disgust as the hack pulled away, but James only grinned wider. Half an hour, tops, and he planned to have the taste of Sarah on his tongue. He'd spent a good quarter of the day hard. At every opportunity, his mind turned to the image of her sex spread wide for his enjoyment. How pretty and delicate she was down there, how perfect as she shuddered against his lips.

His mouth watering, he inclined his head at Crawford's greeting, then contemplated holding on to his hat to avoid embarrassing the servant.

"Sir?" the butler intoned.

James gave in and turned over the hat, spinning quickly toward the parlor in an attempt to flee with his pride intact. "Is Mrs. Hood still up?"

"No, sir. She retired a half hour ago."

"Ah. Wonderful." He'd already made it halfway up the stairs when Crawford's next words reached him. "Madam was suffering from the headache and decided to retire early."

"Oh." He froze, one foot already on the next step. Was she sick or was she laid out naked in anticipation of his arrival? He thought of the blush that so easily overtook her, and revised his fantasy. Not naked, perhaps, but still anticipating his return? "Thank you, Crawford." He continued on, hopeful.

There was no hint awaiting him in his dressing room. Tugging off his tie, he dropped it on a table as he passed through to the dark bedroom beyond. His cock throbbed in anticipation as he moved toward the bed.

"Sarah?" he murmured.

"Hm?"

"Are you unwell?"

"Yes," she whispered. "A bit."

"Oh, I see." He tried not to indulge the disappointment that flooded his veins. The disappointment had no effect on his erection, unfortunately, but it also did not dull his need to breathe her in after a full day away from her side. Whether they made love or not, he wanted to be in bed with her.

He looked toward the pale smudge of her face in the dark. "Can I get you anything, sweetheart?"

"No, Mary has already brought a glass of wine to help me sleep."

"Very well." He walked slowly back to the dressing room, wondering if she was really sick or only suffering a guilty conscience as she had the day before. Or, he supposed, it was possible she was miffed over his long absence today. Regardless, he meant to join her in their bed.

A few minutes later, he slid beneath the cool sheets, startling a little jerk from her side of the mattress. "James?"

"Shh. I didn't mean to wake you."

"Oh." That one little sound seemed full of relief, forcing James to push down his wounded pride.

"Go back to sleep, Sarah." He felt her nod and reached to smooth a hand over her brow. No fever, at any rate. When he repeated the motion, she sighed. "A headache?"

"Yes," she whispered. "I'm sorry."

"Come." He tucked her into his shoulder, meaning to offer comfort, but the seconds dragged into minutes before her body relaxed into his. "Go to sleep, love."

Her nod stirred up the scent of her soap as she finally lay an arm across his naked chest. She was thoroughly clothed in a long-sleeved gown far too hot for the night. Staring at the blackness above him, James wondered what that meant. His chest ached with the answer.

He could not be so greedy next time. As he'd said himself, they had a lifetime of nights together. Sarah had lived nineteen of her twenty years knowing nothing of her own body, much less her husband's. He could not resent her nervousness . . . even if it did thrust a knife through his gut.

"I'm so sorry," Sarah whispered again, as if she could feel the sorrow churning inside him. Her hand stroked his chest, smoothing away some of the pain.

When he pulled her tighter and pressed a kiss to her forehead, Sarah's arm wrapped farther around him. She rolled her whole body against his side, moved one flannel-covered knee up over his thigh, and the rest of his worry flowed away like a receding tide.

She'd never lain like this before, pressed so comfortably against his naked flesh. She'd never sighed into his skin and rubbed her cheek against his shoulder like a settling cat. This was a headache, nothing more.

She was his wife and he loved her. All would be well, or he would make it so.

# CHAPTER 6

The nondescript door gave no indication of what Sarah would find within. It looked neither seedy nor stately. The blue painted wood wasn't scarred, but neither was it ornate. A tiny sign hung above the lintel, naming the occupant of the space and his credentials, but again, that offered her no help. She already knew who Dr. Whitcomb was and why she was here.

Sarah clutched her reticule tighter and eyed his doorstep from the opposite side of the narrow street. She needed answers. She could not go through one more day of lies and subterfuge. Of course, her head really had been pounding the night before, but she knew that wasn't why she'd apologized to her husband. She'd apologized for bringing this curse into his house, for lying, for failing to live up to the promises she'd made at their wedding. For pretending to be a whole woman, when it seemed more clear every day that she was not.

She needed to know.

Her foot had just touched the first cobblestone in the street when that dreaded door swung open. Sarah leaped back, nearly tumbling to her backside when her heel caught on the curb.

A lady emerged. A real lady, not a shopgirl or seamstress. The feather in her hat bobbed jauntily as she descended the steps. Her cheeks glowed with good health. Her smile looked soft and sleepy, relieved even. Was this woman under his care? Impossible to think she could be ill, but in his book Dr. Whitcomb promised an 85 percent success rate with his specialized battery of treatments.

Sarah watched the woman touch a lace-edged handkerchief to her brow before a shiny carriage pulled up to take her away.

Bolstered by the innocuous scene, she stepped off the curb again and rushed across the street. If Dr. Whitcomb could save her and her marriage, Sarah would risk anything. She knocked before she could lose her nerve, and a thin maid in an oversized mobcap opened the door.

"I need to see Doctor Whitcomb, please."

"Do you have an appointment?"

"No, but it's an emergency. I'm sure he'll see me. He treated my mother."

The maid looked doubtful, but she opened the door wide, revealing a small entry. "Doctor Whitcomb is a busy man, of course, but I'll convey your message."

Sarah gave her name and her mother's name, then stood rigid as the woman plodded up a short set of polished stairs. The maid knocked on the first door and waited until a male voice called out before she disappeared inside.

She'd been afraid of the doctor as a girl. Would he frighten her now? Would he even see her? Perhaps her mother's name meant nothing to him.

All her doubts spun around her, weaving a tight net

that slowly squeezed the air from her lungs. The room seemed to recede until all she could see was a wide square of sunlight where it struck the landing.

"Mrs. Hood?"

She blinked, and he was there, at the top of the stairs. He smiled as he descended, and she was relieved to see that he grew smaller with each step. He'd seemed a giant for a moment, but when he stood before her, her eyes were even with his.

"Mrs. Hood, I'm honored that you've come to see me." His gaze seemed to devour her. "Why, you are the very image of your mother." His smile widened until she could see his back teeth. She had expected someone older; he had seemed so intimidating in her youth. But in truth he must have been a very young man then, for he looked only a few years older than her husband.

"Doctor Whitcomb," she finally managed to say.

"Please come up to my office. I'd imagine that you didn't stop by simply to chat about the weather."

"No." She drew a deep breath before she took his arm.

His office was very much like the man himself, clean, simple, attractive. Not the least bit intimidating. A large desk sat in front of the window, faced by two delicate chairs. A chaise longue dominated the rest of the room, remarkable only because of the linen sheets folded at the foot of it and the chair snug against its side.

"Please," he said, indicating the desk area. "Have a seat."

He held a chair out for her before rounding the desk and taking his place behind it. His short blond hair gleamed in the sunlight. "What can I help you with today, Mrs. Hood?"

Sarah cleared her throat, shocked to find that she actually *wanted* to talk to him. "I've read your book."

He nodded and rubbed a hand over his close-clipped beard.

"My mother . . . I suspect that her illness was described there?"

"Yes, of course. She was one of my most tragic cases."

"It was . . . It was nymphomania."

He dipped his head in assent. "Yes, and hysteria leading to dementia, of course. I tried my very best to help her rise from those depths, but her illness . . ." He sighed. "It was too severe. I'm sorry."

Her heart thumped hard against her throat, and she felt startlingly ill for a moment but pressed on. "If it had been caught earlier, do you think that would have helped?"

"It's very possible. Her symptoms began after your birth. As I stated in the book, I believe that the very same illnesses that can be brought on by the shock of a female's introduction to intercourse can also be brought on by the brutality of childbirth. With slightly different manifestations, of course."

He leaned back in his chair and stared thoughtfully at a little ceramic figure. Sarah realized with a start that it was a nude female form.

"Your mother became quite listless after giving birth. She was lethargic and morose for nearly a year. When she emerged from that melancholia and resumed her marital duties, the mania began to set in. Restlessness. An interest in conjugal relations that superseded the fact that she wanted to avoid another pregnancy. Over-arousal. Her husband—your father—did not recognize any danger, as most men do not. This went on for nearly four years between bouts of sadness and depression before she happened into my office."

Stunned, Sarah sat staring at him for several heartbeats before he raised his gaze to her and blinked.

"I apologize. Perhaps I was too graphic."

"No." She had wanted honesty and it seemed she'd come to the right place.

"When I confronted her with her symptoms and made my diagnosis, she became obstinate, but I continued asking questions." He leaned forward now, eyes locked with Sarah's. "Did she have trouble sleeping? Did she encourage unusual acts in the bedroom? Did she find that her . . ." His gaze flickered down and then up again, "feminine parts became congested at the mere thought of marital relations?"

"Congested?" Sarah breathed.

"Swollen," he answered. "Wet."

*Oh, God.*

She wanted to leave, but Dr. Whitcomb's eyes held her frozen.

"Mrs. Hood," he said gently. "This disease is very often hereditary. Medical science has proven the familial connection with no doubt at all. Did you come to me because you are suffering these same symptoms?"

"I . . ." She couldn't think what to say, much less force it from her throat.

"By the time she came to me, your mother was very ill. It had gone on too long. When confronted with the truth, she sank into another depression. Her maid realized that she was suffering and sent for me. I started intensive treatment right away, but despite the many months she was under my care, you know what happened. She grew irritable, then inconsolable. She vacillated between restlessness and lethargy. When she decided she could not be helped, she went to the river and threw herself in."

Sarah had known this. She'd always known how her mother's life had ended, with stones weighing down her pockets as she sank to the bottom of the Thames. Still, she shuddered to hear it said aloud.

"But yes," he continued, voice so soft it barely crossed the distance between them. "I believe I could have saved her if she had come to me earlier. Are you suffering, Mrs. Hood?"

Tears clogged her throat. She dragged a handkerchief from her reticule and pressed it to her lips. She couldn't help but think of the woman she'd seen leaving, the woman who had looked so calm and happy as she wiped a touch of perspiration from her brow.

Dr. Whitcomb offered a sympathetic smile. "We shall do an exam. I can see you're clear-eyed and that's an excellent sign that you have not let this go too far."

Nodding in relief, she stood and moved toward the chaise to perch on the very edge of it while Dr. Whitcomb stood above her.

"First, your pulse." He took her wrist in his hands and watched the clock on the wall. "Tell me about your symptoms."

"I've been restless. Nervous. Sometimes I have difficulty sleeping."

"When were you married?"

"Two months ago."

"And you were a virgin?"

She jerked a little at the word. "Of course."

"When your husband took you, was it painful?"

"Yes, but—"

"How often do you engage in sexual congress?" He dropped her wrist and indicated she should recline against the back of the couch. His fingers pressed against the sides of her throat.

"Um, three or four times a week until recently."

His hands froze on her skin. "Recently?" He crouched down to look into one eye, then the other.

"Recently, yes. It's become more, um, frequent."

"How frequent?" One of his hands pressed her stomach, just below her breasts.

She closed her eyes. "More than once a day."

"I see." The hand moved lower, to her belly. "And do you become congested when he touches you?"

A tear leaked from the corner of her eye, but she admitted the truth. "Yes."

Dr. Whitcomb stood. "I will leave you alone to undress. My maid will be in to provide assistance. She will cover you with the sheet before calling me."

"Pardon? No! No, I cannot . . . My husband . . ."

"Mrs. Hood, I am a physician. How am I to examine you past whalebone and petticoats?"

"Can you not . . . ?" Her tears started in earnest. "Can you not simply give me the medicine to try?"

He sat in the chair and took her hand. "Mrs. Hood, there is no medicine, there is a physical treatment. Your pulse is elevated, and I suspect from your description that your uterus is inflamed and congested. The treatment involves manual relief of the congestion and pressure. We do not need to begin treatment today, but I must palpate the uterus to be sure of diagnosis."

They were at an impasse then. She simply could not remove her clothing in front of this man, doctor or not. When she shook her head, he sighed.

"Well, your modesty is another good sign, at any rate. Lie back and I'll do my best."

She lay back awkwardly, her bustle pressing into her lower back, arching her body up as he felt along her skirts at the bottom edge of her corset.

"The next time you visit, please wear your stays a bit looser, if you will."

"All right." He pressed so hard against her belly that she winced.

"Ah, yes. Definitely full and inflamed." Before she realized what he was doing, Dr. Whitcomb had reached for the hem of her skirts and slid his hand beneath it.

Quick and methodical in his movements, his hand was on her thigh before she could respond.

"Sir!" Sarah snapped up, nearly hitting her head against his chin.

His fingers spread over her thigh, holding her. "Calm yourself, Mrs. Hood. I only need to do a quick internal exam. Nothing more than what you can expect during pregnancy." His hand crept up toward the slit in her drawers, the slide of his skin burning her like acid.

"No!" When she pushed his arm away, he let her, but his fingers smoothed down her leg as she shoved.

"Very well. But your skin is flushed and very hot, and I'd imagine that your vulva is hotter still. Until our next visit, please refrain from eating any rich foods. In fact, I advise a daily dose of barley water to calm the humors. Of course, you should refrain from any marital relations with your husband and from reading novels. Do you read novels, Mrs. Hood?"

Panicked, she didn't answer, but simply pushed to her feet. "Thank you, Doctor."

He stood as well, and took her fisted hand in his. "I understand that this is difficult, Mrs. Hood. But I am very hopeful for you and for the future of your marriage."

*James,* she thought. I can do this for James.

He placed a small pot into her hands. "Camphor. Please rub it thoroughly into your labia once each day."

She had no idea what a labia was, but she nodded anyway.

"It will start to relieve the congestion in preparation for your treatment. Would you prefer to take treatment here, or shall I come to your home?"

"I'll . . . I'll come here."

"Excellent. Please return at the same time next week."

As soon as the words left his mouth, Sarah rushed for the door. She flew down the stairs and clawed the front door open before the maid could reach it. Desperate to get away as quickly as possible, Sarah stepped into the street and nearly stumbled right in front of a dray wagon pulled by four massive horses. The driver scowled and whipped them faster as he passed her by.

She needed a hack. She needed to get home and bathe. She shouldn't have allowed him to touch her. She felt soiled by the questions. If she felt so awful just from the examination, how could she bear to return for treatment at his hands?

And yet that other woman, that perfectly respectable lady, had left Dr. Whitcomb's office with a smile on her face.

Sarah wanted that, too. Serenity. Happiness. And she wanted that for James.

When she spied a hack she nearly jumped in front of it to make it stop. The driver eyed her warily, but when she handed over a coin along with her direction, his scowl turned to a grin.

"Right-o, madam. Let me help ye in."

But she didn't want him near, so she scrambled in herself and shut the door on the hem of her skirt. The wheels seemed to seek out ruts in the road as they turned. Sarah closed her eyes and braced herself against the back of the seat.

She did not feel hysterical. She hadn't felt deranged even as he asked those awful questions. And though she wanted to be home, she did not feel as if she might crawl into bed and stay there for days, crying and sleeping and staring at the ceiling as her mother had once done.

The doctor's hands on her body had felt wrong, wrong, wrong. But when James touched her, it felt real and good.

Was she sick, as Dr. Whitcomb suggested, or was she normal, as the other book seemed to imply?

Sarah moved to wipe a tear from her eye, and realized her cheeks were wet with them. She wanted to talk to James, tell him her worries, but because of her own dishonesty, she could say nothing. He would hate her if she told him. How could he not? At the very least he would watch her always with a wary eye, wondering if she might descend into madness at any moment.

Despite her desperate need to be home, when the carriage stopped, Sarah held her breath. She swiped both hands across her cheeks. She could not pass the servants like this. She needed to calm down.

The door snapped open. "Home, madam."

She made herself take his gloved hand—*calm, calm*—and stepped heavily to the street. She held herself straight as an arrow as she climbed the steps to her house and opened the door. She maintained her calm facade until she saw that she and Crawford were not alone in the entry. James stood frozen in mid-pace, eyes narrowed at her.

"Sarah, where have you been? I've been worried sick."

"James!" *Oh, no. Oh, God. Why was he home?*

"You told no one where you'd gone and didn't even take a maid with you!"

"I . . ." She stepped back, away from her husband.

He stepped closer. "My God, Sarah. Have you been crying?"

She'd have to tell him the truth: that she'd lied, that she'd endangered him and any future children. That she was a disturbed woman.

Sarah felt the world receding, turning gray and then black at the edges. Lights sparkled in the middle of her vision. She could see James mouthing her name as he rushed forward, but couldn't hear the sound of it.

Sarah Rose Hood was fainting for the first time in her life, and she was supremely grateful for the opportunity.

"Sarah!" He held his wife tight to his body in an awkward grasp. "Call for the doctor, Crawford." She began to slide down, so he scooped her up and hurried into the parlor to lay her on the settee. "Sarah, darling, wake up, please."

She didn't stir. Her lips were pale against the alarming white of her face. At least her forehead was cool, though he didn't like the clammy feel of it. He touched her all over—her shoulders and chest, her arms and belly and legs—as if he could sense any injury just by the feel of her.

When he saw her torn skirt, he stared at it, struck dumb with horror. Surely she hadn't been attacked?

*Where the hell had she been?*

To make up for the day before, he'd come home in the middle of the day expecting another quiet luncheon with his bride. Instead he'd spent a half hour pacing the hall, trying to figure out where the hell she could have gone without even a maid as an escort. He'd been frightened and angry. And sadly, even suspicious. Just two days before he'd come home and found her gone, and when she'd returned she'd behaved so strangely.

Damn it, what the hell was going on?

"Sarah," he tried again, and this time her eyelids stirred. "Sarah!"

Her eyes blinked open, brown eyes darker than ever against her pallid skin as they slowly focused on his face.

"Sarah, are you hurt?"

Eyes growing wider still, she shook her head.

"I've sent for the doctor. He should be here any moment."

"No!" She threw her hands to the cushions beneath her and pushed up. "No, please don't."

"You're unwell. You need—"

"I'm fine. I promise. I wasn't ill, only frightened."

He rocked back on his heels. "Frightened of *what*, Sarah?"

Her mouth closed, literally snapping shut.

"Of *me*?"

"No, of course not."

"Did someone hurt you? Your skirt is torn."

She looked down and brushed at the blackened fabric. She brushed and brushed until he realized she was crying. "No one has hurt me," she sobbed. "I am fine."

James collapsed onto the seat beside her and pulled her to his chest. "You must tell me what is wrong before I go mad, Sarah. Please, you're scaring me."

Nodding, she sniffed into his jacket. "I'll tell you. I must. I should never have hidden it from you in the first place. Only call off the doctor, please, and I'll tell you the truth."

Reeling at her words—what could they mean?—James nodded and went to speak with Crawford before shutting the parlor door. He stood there for a moment, head bowed, hand pressed to the door, and tried to calm his heart. What had she done? Could there possibly be another man? Some secret love she'd have preferred to marry eight weeks ago?

If so . . . if so, James would murder him and toss his body into the river. Or perhaps just have him pressed into Her Majesty's navy. Yes, that would be a more reasonable solution. And then he'd convince Sarah that she could love him just as well as this other man.

He heard her rise and walk toward him, and turned

to meet her gaze. As he watched, she put her shoulders back and straightened her spine. She would have looked regal if not for her torn skirt and disheveled hair. Instead, she looked even more vulnerable.

"There's something I should have told you before we married, James."

*Christ.* Whatever terrible thing she was about to say, he wanted to stop her.

She nodded as if he'd spoken. "I should have told you and now I cannot live with it."

"Go on," he ground out.

"I . . . My mother was not a well woman."

James blinked. "Pardon?"

"My mother. She was ill for many years before she died." She paused to take a deep, shaky breath. "And there's a possibility I could have inherited her illness."

He cocked his head, totally confused. "Her illness? Sarah, have you been unwell? Does this have to do with your headaches?"

"No. At least I don't think so. My mother . . . You must understand, it went on for years. It was quite mild at first. I saw her doctor today, and he says I'm exhibiting some of her symptoms." Her fingers twisted her skirts.

"I don't understand. Are you speaking of something other than your mother's lunacy?"

Sarah drew back as if he'd slapped her. Her face faded to the colorless white it had been only moments before. "What?"

James reached for her elbow. "Why don't you sit down?" Actually, he needed to sit down himself. This had nothing to do with her loving another man, and his knees wanted him to drop down and say a quick prayer of thanks.

But she didn't move toward the chair, she only

looked down at his hand and then back at his face. "You *knew?*"

"About your mother? Of course."

"But how?"

"Your father told me when I asked for your hand."

"You knew she was mad? You knew she took her own life?"

"Yes." When she only gaped up at him, he touched her cheek, stroking the line of the bone beneath. "And I'm sorry for it. You were so young. It must have broken your heart."

"But . . . but I thought you didn't know. I thought I should have told you."

"Well, I have never revealed how my father died. Apoplexy, by the way."

"James," she gasped. "You knew? And you still married me?"

"What in the world have you been thinking? And you still haven't explained what happened today."

"As I said, I went to see my mother's doctor." She finally headed toward the chairs nearest the fireplace and James followed gratefully. He needed to sit down.

"I've been worried," she continued. "And I found a book written by Doctor Whitcomb. It detailed some of my symptoms—"

"What symptoms?"

Her cheeks flamed to scarlet at the question. "I've been recently overcome with . . . feelings and . . . urges."

"Urges?"

"I'm sure you've noticed," she added in a rush.

"Your urges?" His mind finally latched on to an impossible thought. "Ah, Sarah? Are you speaking of our recent lovemaking?"

"Yes! I don't wish to speak of it, James, but you have seen the changes. Doctor Whitcomb says it is one of the

first signs of hysteria. I don't want to go mad, James.
You have no idea the destruction it brings. He is willing
to treat me, but—"

"Sarah, stop! You are not mad. You are the most
serene person I know."

"But I do not feel serene!" she cried. "I feel restless
and hot and *hungry*, and it only gets worse every day! Doctor Whitcomb says that treatment will help me to control these thoughts, but—"

"I can't believe this," he muttered, finally dropping
into a chair, unable to wait a moment longer for her to
be seated.

"Oh, James, I never ever meant to—"

"A doctor actually means to treat you for wanting to
make love with your husband? Perhaps you *are* mad."

"James!"

"Did he hurt you?"

Sarah shook her head. "Who?"

"The doctor. Did he hurt you or frighten you or—"

"No!" Sarah interrupted. "I only went to ask him a
few questions. There was a quick examination, and . . .
but I never should have kept this from you. If I become
like my mother . . ."

"Come here."

She frowned at his firm tone.

"Come here, Sarah."

"Why?" Though she'd started off so vulnerable,
Sarah now looked angry and strong as she took only
one step closer to him.

As soon as she was within reach, James snagged her
waist. She struggled when he pulled her to his lap, and
James's body appreciated the fight.

"What are you doing?" she demanded. "This is serious."

He wrapped his arms around her to keep her still.

"Hush. Do you know what I thought the first time I saw you?"

She glared at him. "No."

"Have I never told you?"

"No."

"It was at the Worthings' party, do you remember? And before I saw you, I was thinking, 'My God, Beatrice Worthing has a terrifically bad singing voice.' But when she finished that song, *you* were there, Sarah. My first glimpse of such a lovely stranger. You clapped as you approached Beatrice, smiling as if she'd just performed a beautiful aria. And I heard you ask if she knew your very favorite song in the world. I noticed, because I thought you *were* mad, volunteering your favorite song to be butchered.

"But then she began to sing, and I realized what you had done."

"What?" Sarah breathed.

He stroked her back. "You had given her a song in a lower key, in her natural voice, and it was almost lovely. You saved her from humiliating herself."

She shook her head.

"And I watched you smiling over Beatrice as she sang, and something in my heart twisted so hard I thought everyone must have noticed. But the evening went on; everyone else was unchanged, but I was a different man."

Her face turned up to him, eyes swimming with shock.

"I thought in that one moment that I might love you, Sarah."

"You did?" When she blinked, two fat tears escaped and slipped down her face.

"I did. But that is very near an insult. I didn't know you. We had not even been introduced. I knew nothing of your quick mind and sly sense of humor. I had no idea that you were kind not only to your friends but also to strangers, even those beneath your notice. I could not know that your shyness would slowly blossom into this fascinating passion.

"And I could not have known that you held such foolish bravery in your quiet soul. That hint of a feeling I had was a shadow compared to how I feel for you now, love."

"But . . . the doctor. My mother."

"Nonsense. You are as steady and lovely as the moon. When your father explained the circumstances, he made a point of saying that you had never shown any of your mother's tendencies to be melodramatic and over-emotional, but I did not need to be told that."

"But it was so clear when I read the book . . ."

"Come. Let's see it." He could see obstinacy creeping back into her face, so he simply stood and set her on her feet. "Where is it?"

Five minutes later, he was staring, slack jawed, at the unbelievable nonsense that had been tormenting his poor wife. "This is ridiculous!"

Sarah stopped her pacing and set her jaw. "How could you know that? I have experienced *everything* listed there. Who are you to say that it doesn't signify?"

"I . . ." There was no decent way to broach this subject. "I do not wish to offend you."

She threw her hands in the air. "That is the least of my worries, James!"

*Damn.* "All right . . . before I knew you . . . That is . . . I had, um, *experiences*. With other women. Just a few."

Her expression didn't budge.

"They all enjoyed themselves. They all experienced pleasure, Sarah. That is rather the point of it. Only the most worthless of men can enjoy himself without regard for his partner."

Her jaw edged out. She crossed her arms. "But these were harlots, were they not?"

"Um . . ." *Ah, Jesus,* there was no way around this. "I am not a man who feels comfortable paying for the use of a woman's body."

"What does that *mean?*"

"They were not harlots. They were normal women. Respectable."

"They could hardly have been respectable, James!"

"Sarah . . . When a woman's husband dies or leaves her or . . . her need does not fade away, just as a man's does not. Your body is designed to feel pleasure, and that would not change if I were to die tomorrow."

"But . . ." Her face twisted in confusion. "The doctor was clear."

"Damn it," he growled, sorry that he made her jump, but not willing to back down. "Did he do anything to help your mother? Did she improve? Did she recover?"

"No."

"Your father made clear to me that she had been under treatment for many years. He said that in the end it made no difference. The doctor did nothing for her. He is a charlatan. A hack."

"He said she was already too far gone—"

"Damn it, I am your husband, and I am telling you that sexual desire has nothing to do with madness, Sarah. Do you believe me?"

Her mouth opened, then closed. She clenched her arms tighter over her chest. "Those other women? They . . . they reached climax with you?"

James ignored the heat that climbed up his face. "Yes."

"Perhaps you are only humoring me."

"By God, I would hardly classify throwing other women in your face as humoring you!"

Sarah rubbed her arms and bit her lip, but she did not respond.

"I love you, Sarah." Her eyes flew wide at the words, and James realized he had never said them out loud. "I love you, and if I thought you were in danger, you must believe I would do everything I could to make you well again. But there is nothing wrong with you. You are perfect."

James was known as a fierce negotiator in the Commons, and there was a reason for that. He could read people, and the signs of capitulation were clear on Sarah's face. She wanted to give in, wanted to believe him. Finally, he knew exactly what to say to end her distress.

"When we married you made me a promise, Sarah."

Her eyebrows rose in surprise. "I did?"

"Before God and our family, you promised to love and obey."

"I-I did."

"Then let me make this clear. If there is anything you need to learn about your body or my own, I will be the one to teach you. Do you understand?"

She stared, teetering on the edge of giving in to him.

"If you have questions about desire, we will find the answers together. We will discover your pleasure *together*. No more books by idiotic quacks. And if you become worried over your health, we will find the best doctor in London. Are we agreed?"

His wife took a deep breath and let her arms fall, so that only her hands stayed clasped together. One finger worked over the ring he'd placed on her hand a few weeks before. "Yes," she whispered.

"Pardon?"

"Yes, I will come to you, James."

The sound of his name on her lips combined with sheer relief and rolled through him like a wave. But she needed his strength, not his gratitude. "Good," he said quietly. "Now I believe that your last lesson was quite inadequate."

Her lips parted in question.

"We just barely touched on male anatomy."

Sarah's gaze trailed down his body before it jerked back to meet his. "James, it is the middle of the day."

"So it is."

A flush touched her lips, then deepened.

"You have clearly been in search of answers today," he pressed. "What is it you wish to know, wife?"

When her tongue darted out to wet her lips, James knew that victory was his. And hers.

He unknotted his tie and locked the door . . . and the lesson began.

# Chapter 7

Sarah stretched her legs beneath the sheets, seeking out a cooler spot. How strange it felt to be so thoroughly naked in her own bed. Strange and very wicked. She stretched even longer, letting her body sink into the fine linen.

It wasn't even dinnertime yet. She should rise and dress. James had been up for nearly an hour, though he'd kissed her after he'd dressed, and ordered her to stay abed.

Smiling at the memory, Sarah set aside thoughts of getting up. Her husband had told her to stay and relax, and she had vowed to obey him.

Despite the heaviness of her limbs, Sarah felt amazingly light. She'd told him the truth—he'd *known* the truth—and James had not rejected her. In fact, he'd assured her she was normal.

When he'd spoken of other women, Sarah should have been hurt. Perhaps one day the idea would wound her, but today she could only be grateful for those women. She was like *them*; she was not like her mother.

She was not anxious and nervous and morose, she was *happy*.

Touching his body had made her happy. Making him groan with her touch had brought her joy. Sarah snuggled into the pillow with a grin.

"What has you purring like a kitten?" her husband's voice asked from the other side of the bed.

"James!" Sarah popped up, dragging the sheets with her.

"Such modesty all of a sudden."

"Hush." Her blush seemed to make him smile as he sat on the edge of the bed. He brushed a lock of hair from her cheek.

"Shall I call for dinner? I thought perhaps we could dine here."

Sarah thought of the servants and what they would think . . . and found that she no longer cared. "I'd like that."

When he reached for the bellpull, Sarah gasped. Dark bruises covered his knuckles. One of them was scraped. "What have you done to your hand?"

His arm froze for a moment before he grasped the cord and tugged. "You needn't concern yourself with your appointment next week. The doctor understands that you have no need of his care."

"All right. But what has that to do with your hand?"

His gaze slid to hers.

"James, you didn't!"

"When we married, I vowed to love and *protect* you."

"What can beating a man of science have to do with protecting me?"

Her husband did not look the least bit chastened when he shrugged. "All right. I'll concede the point. Consider it part of loving you then."

"James!" she scolded, though she couldn't manage

to put much heat into her voice, perhaps because he had mentioned love again. He loved her. He knew all her secrets and still he loved her.

When he took her hand and stroked his thumb over her palm, they both watched. Once again, Sarah marveled at the contrast of his skin against hers. His fingers were long and bronzed and dusted with hair, and the sight of his scraped knuckles thrilled her in a way that didn't bear examination. Ladies were not bloodthirsty, after all.

"James?" she whispered.

"Hm?"

She turned her hand around and threaded her fingers through his. "I have one last confession."

His thumb froze against her hand. "Another?"

"Yes. I think . . . that is, I am quite sure that I am terribly in love with you."

"Ah, I see. Terribly?"

"Yes, horribly."

Slowly, he raised her hand to his mouth for a long, lingering kiss that turned into a smile against her skin. "Good. I would hate to think myself alone in this misery. But I detect that you were recently in doubt."

She swallowed the thickness from her throat. "Not doubt. Not of you. I have only felt so . . . confused. My life changed so completely. A new home, a new role, a new life. I was Mrs. Hood, and I did not know who she was."

When she dared a look at James's face, she found his brow falling into a deep frown. "I never thought . . ." he murmured. "That sounds horrid, Sarah."

"No, it wasn't horrid! It was only a change, and you have been lovely and patient and kind. And if it hadn't been you . . . if it hadn't been *you*, James, I would've been afraid and lost.

"But it *was* you," she said when he looked as if he

would interrupt. "And now I know who I am again. I am Sarah. I am your wife. And I love you."

James did not answer. He only stared down at their clasped hands, with his mouth set in a flat line.

Love and fear pulsed through Sarah's veins. She had said too much, revealed something that might hurt him. "James?"

"I am thinking what I could do to help you adjust. I am trying to imagine how it would feel to give up my home and family and habits and start anew with a virtual stranger."

Sarah could not help but smile at that. He was hardly a stranger anymore. The fear left her, dissipating through her skin and disappearing entirely.

She kissed his shoulder, but he didn't look up. "The strangest thing was that I had never been allowed to even be alone with a man, and suddenly . . ." She smiled at him when he glanced up, a pained expression on his face. "Suddenly I was expected to be *very* alone with a man, if you understand my meaning."

James cringed. "I think I do."

"But I have come to realize that the best solution for strangeness is complete immersion."

"Immersion?"

"Yes. If you truly wish to help me adjust . . . ?"

His eyes grew warmer at her tone and flickered down the sheet that hid her body. "Oh, I most certainly do."

"Then I believe if you would focus your attentions on only my most pressing anxieties . . ."

James leaned a little closer and idly wrapped one hand into a trailing edge of the sheet. "My God, Mrs. Hood. You are a genius. Pray tell, what is your most aching concern?"

Sarah nodded, trying to look solemn even as she blushed to the roots of her hair. "I am wondering . . ."

"Yes?" When he shifted, the sheet wrapped around her bosom became precariously loose.

"I understand that a husband has certain needs . . ."

His hand moved beneath the edge of the linen, and his fingers spread wide over her naked knee. "Oh, yes," he answered, voice a little lower than it had been. "Definite needs."

"But I've read several books on the subject, and it's not clear . . ."

"Hm?" His thumb slipped higher, feathering against her thigh.

"Just how often"—she had to pause to draw a breath—"those needs might *arise.*"

"Ah," James sighed sympathetically. "Poor wife, kept so thoroughly in the dark. Perhaps a demonstration would make it most clear?"

When he nuzzled her shoulder, the sheet finally gave up its hold and fell away. He bent his head immediately to his task.

"Oh, yes," Sarah gasped. "A demonstration."

He proved over the next few hours that a man's needs might arise quite often between husband and wife. And Sarah proved herself a quick student of her new role.

# SWEPT AWAY

## KRISTI ASTOR

# CHAPTER 1

"He's like Mr. Rochester and . . . and"—Christobel searched her mind for a proper literary example—"and Mr. Darcy, all rolled into one brooding, supercilious parcel." *Yes, that was it. Precisely.* "Without the redeeming characteristics, of course," she added with a sigh.

"Come now, Christobel," her mother scolded. "Don't be so dramatic. Mr. Leyden isn't as bad as that." She paused, chewing on her lower lip as she often did when dissembling.

Christobel gave her mother a knowing look. "Isn't he?"

"Well, even if he is," she relented, "he's Jasper's cousin and you must endure his company with good grace. I won't have you acting childish and snippy—"

"I've never been anything but pleasant to Mr. Leyden, Mother. But goodness, you must admit he's a terrible bore."

In all the years they'd been acquainted, she'd tried to see past his deficiencies—his brooding silences and arrogant attitude coupled with his common birth and an ever-so-slight yet discernible limp—to find something to admire. Yet for all her trying, she'd found nothing in his character to merit more than a passing interest.

This never failed to puzzle her, as he was exactly the type of specimen she was often drawn to. Never could she walk past a starved dog or a bird with a broken wing and not take such a creature into her heart, to see to its care and comfort as best she could. Yet for Mr. Leyden, her brother-in-law's most devoted cousin, she felt nothing more than a vague annoyance.

Perhaps, Christobel realized, it was because Mr. Leyden made his disapproval of *her* so very evident. How many evenings had she suffered beneath his stare, his brow raised in censure as he watched her across the room while she laughed and coquetted? As if such activities—laughing and coquetting—were inappropriate behaviors for a young lady of her situation.

Christobel sighed heavily as she glanced out the train's sooty window, the autumn colors blurring into a glorious canvas of reds and golds. What else was an unmarried girl to do at a house party but flirt and enjoy herself? She shook her head, plucking absently at the folds of her skirt, wishing the train were taking her anywhere but to Edith and Jasper's home—and Mr. Leyden's unavoidable company.

"Don't frown, dear. It isn't good for your complexion."

Christobel shifted her gaze from the window back to her mother, seated directly across from her in the train's compartment. Beside her mother sat Simpson, her head tilted at an awkward angle as she dozed, snoring softly.

"How does she sleep so soundly, with all this noise and activity?" her mother asked with a smile.

Dear, dear Mother, who never frowned despite the misfortune that had plagued them since Father's death. Indeed, the woman had smiled in the face of the insurmountable debt and near financial ruin her husband had left behind.

Her mother's smile hadn't faded as they'd been forced to sell off their furnishings and leave the only homes Christobel had ever known—their lovely country estate in Surrey and their town house in Wickham Road.

And now they were reduced to *this*—rented flats in London during the summer season, and traveling from one of Christobel's three sisters' homes to the next for the remainder of the year.

The only servant they'd been able to keep on was the ever-loyal Simpson, who had been their housekeeper but now served as lady's maid, housekeeper, and sometimes cook, at least when they were in London.

The situation was mortifying at best, almost enough to make Christobel wish to marry, simply to have a place to call home. Of course, it wasn't as if she had many options, as far as her future was concerned. She could either marry or continue to remain the spinster sister, forced to rely on the charity of her siblings and their husbands.

She wasn't entirely opposed to marriage, of course. It was just that their funds had been limited, especially after Father's death. They'd not been able to afford a true season for her, not after the expense of putting out three girls before her. By now she'd become almost complacent, used to her mother's companionship. They'd fallen into a comfortable routine, the two of them. No man of her acquaintance had inspired her to change her course, not yet.

"Whom do you suppose Edith has invited this year?" asked her mother. "She's always so clever with her guest list."

"Clever?" Christobel couldn't help but laugh. "She's shrewd, is what she is. Almost mercenary."

Her mother nodded, a smile of satisfaction on her face. "Successful matches that led to marriages three years in a row now, isn't it? Your sister is becoming a legend."

"There must be a better use for such talents," Christobel muttered uncharitably, then instantly regretted it.

After all, with what else had her sister to occupy herself, living so far north where genteel company was hard to come by? Poor Edith.

Of course, she could not blame Jasper for the misfortune of his place of birth. After all, Hadley Hall was a nice enough estate and would be more than tolerable were it located in, say, Kent or Surrey or Dorset rather than Lancashire.

Dull, gloomy Lancashire, where mills and factories often dulled the sky to gray. Part of Jasper's family's fortune had been made in the mills—cotton mills, to be precise. Unfortunate, yes, but there had been enough good breeding in Jasper Hadley's lineage to make him an acceptable groom for Edith, nonetheless.

Indeed, Jasper was a dear, a worthy match for Edith. *If only* . . . Christobel let the thought trail off. No use wishing the impossible. Her mother had done the best she could after Father's death. A wave of guilt washed over her, shaming her. She should be grateful for her sister and brother-in-law's generosity. Yet she could not help the feeling of unease that crept into her heart as the train chugged northward.

She glanced at the watch she wore on a thin gold chain around her neck, then dropped it back against her blouse.

Across the train's compartment, her mother smiled at her—a warm, fond smile. "Why don't you sleep, dear? We've still a ways to go before we reach Manchester."

A weary Christobel nodded. Indeed, hours of travel

still lay ahead. Nearly two hours remained till they reached Manchester, and then they must change for the Oldham Loop to Cranford, where Jasper would fetch them and drive them the short distance to Hadley Hall.

Too tired to read the volume of poetry that lay on the seat beside her, she closed her eyes and allowed the train's rhythmic movements to lull her into a dreamless sleep.

"And Mr. Godey has requested a room next to Lady Margaret's, so I'll put him here."

"Good heavens, Edith! However can you keep it all straight?" Christobel shook her head in amazement as Edith laid down the last of the cards on the table before them—each card representing one of her expected houseguests. Later, the cards would be placed in special holders on each guest's door.

Edith just shrugged. "It's been much less difficult this year. Except for the complication with Mr. Aberforth, that is."

Apparently a Mrs. Lovelace had requested a room beside Mr. Aberforth, which wouldn't be a problem except that a Mrs. Roth had requested easy proximity to Mr. Aberforth's room, too. Had Edith known that Mr. Aberforth was currently keeping company with two ladies, she would never have invited them both.

How could Edith look so calm and serene, Christobel wondered, dealing with such arrangements as this? But as usual, Edith looked entirely unruffled, her warm brown eyes as tranquil as ever. Edith had always been the great beauty of the family, the one on whose shoulders the greatest responsibility of marrying well had lain.

After all, everything about Edith was the height of fashion—the feminine ideal—from her dark, glossy hair to her porcelain-hued skin and deep brown eyes lined in kohl.

Christobel, on the other hand, had never been a beauty. Oh, she was perfectly attractive enough, she reasoned, just nothing as extraordinary as her sisters were, all doe-eyed beauties like their mother. She'd inherited her father's green eyes, eyes that were too sharp, too expressive to be fashionable.

And though Christobel spent far too much time out-of-doors, she refused to paint her face with enamel before brushing it with rice or pearl powder. Thus, her skin was noticeably tanned, with a dusting of freckles that were hard to conceal and gave her mother much to fret about.

It wasn't that she eschewed cosmetics altogether— she enjoyed visiting Madame Rachel's salon in Bond Street as much as any other young lady. She had pots of face and lip rouge, bottles of Jordan Water. Still, her looks would never rate above average, a fact that didn't bother her in the least.

With a shrug, Christobel turned her attention back to the cards spread on the table. "What of these?" she asked, tapping two cards with unfamiliar names written in Edith's precise script. "I don't believe I'm acquainted with either."

"They're new acquaintances, both. Miss Bartlett is a lovely girl, quite fair of face. Bookish, I suppose, and somewhat solemn." Edith raised her brows, a mischievous twinkle in her eyes. "I was hoping that she and John Leyden might suit."

"No!" Christobel exclaimed, laying a hand on Edith's wrist. "You're actually hoping to make a match for Mr. Leyden?"

Edith nodded. "It's high time, don't you think? He spends far too much time at the mill. He'll never meet the proper sort there."

Christobel couldn't help but smile as she reached for her teacup and took a sip. Knowing Edith as she did, she was certain that much time and consideration went into selecting this Miss Bartlett. She likely *was* a good match for Mr. Leyden, and Edith would no doubt make her intentions quite clear on the matter. How fascinating it was going to be, watching Mr. Leyden squirm under such machinations.

"Shall I ring for more sandwiches?" Edith asked, picking up the cards from the table and placing them in a neat stack beside her saucer.

A feeling of unease skittered across Christobel's consciousness. Wait a minute . . . "What about the other? Sir Edmund Blake, it says."

"What about him?" Edith asked, busy neatening the stack of already-neat cards. "He's a fine gentleman, charming and full of life. A baronet of some means, with a country house in Kent."

Christobel could barely credit it, but Edith positively refused to meet her eyes. *No, Edith wouldn't dare.* "Indeed? Single, I presume?"

"What good fortune that he is," Edith said brightly.

"With whom were you hoping he would suit?" Christobel asked crisply, though her sister's uncomfortable demeanor was answer enough. "Either of the Misses Allen, perhaps?"

"Perhaps," she answered with a shrug.

"Edith Hadley!" Christobel rose from the table, her hands clenched into fists by her sides. "Tell me you did not invite this Sir Edmund on my account, or I'll get right back on that train and return to London at once."

At last Edith met her gaze, her dark eyes flashing. "With no chaperone, and no home to return to? Of course you won't."

Christobel could only huff indignantly, so flummoxed was she by Edith's impertinence.

"Sir Edmund went to Eton with Jasper. He's a charming man, one with whom I'd like to get better acquainted. And if the thought did cross my mind that perhaps the two of you might suit, well, what of it?"

"I do not need you playing matchmaker on my behalf, Edith. I've told you so on more than one occasion."

"And before now, I've always heeded your protestations. Can't you at least allow me *one* attempt? I *am* such a good matchmaker, after all. And where is Mrs. Gardner? I must have more sandwiches."

"You've already eaten a plateful," Christobel muttered, feeling churlish. "Besides, you're looking rather plump, if you ask me."

"And perhaps there's good reason for that," Edith shot back, a smile playing on her lips.

Realization dawned on Christobel at once. "Edith, dear! But I thought . . . after the last time . . ." Christobel trailed off miserably. Edith had already suffered two miscarriages, though the doctor had assured her that, physically, there was no reason she could not carry a child to term.

"I can't help but try again. Anyway, the doctor said I'm perfectly well as long as I'm not vexed—"

"You wouldn't dare use this to . . . to convince me to go along with your meddling," Christobel sputtered.

"But of course I would," Edith answered with an angelic smile. "However could I resist? Now please, sit back down and enjoy your tea. Ah, there's Mrs. Gardner now with more sandwiches."

The portly woman carried in a silver tiered tray laden with sandwiches and scones, then whisked away the empty one.

Christobel reached for a cucumber sandwich so thin you could almost see straight through it, then slumped back in her chair with a scowl. "I'll never forgive you this, you know."

"Of course you will. And you'll be nice to Sir Edmund, else you might vex me." Edith's smile was triumphant. "And if a gentleman compliments you, you will smile sweetly and accept it graciously. You'll hold your tongue, too, and keep your suffragist notions to yourself."

"But you agree with—"

"Of course I do. Privately. But everyone knows that speaking of such things will not land you a husband. At least, not a suitable one."

"Very well. Anything else?" Christobel asked tartly.

"Yes, try and be nice to John, too," she added. "I need him in good humor if I'm to make a match for him. Lord knows he can be disagreeable enough without any help from you."

Christobel merely glared at her in reply.

At the sound of footfalls, both women turned toward the doorway.

"There's Mother," Edith said, effectively ending the argument. "Shall we tell her my good news?"

At once Christobel's ill temper was replaced by fear—fear for Edith's health, her happiness. How badly she must want a baby, to risk heartbreak once more. Tears burned behind her eyelids, and she averted her gaze from her smiling sister to the window and the gray skies beyond.

*It's this blasted northern air,* she thought, anger joining her fear, further fraying her nerves. She'd only been in Lancashire one day and already she longed for Surrey's tidy green pastures and neat hedgerows, for the lazy, languid days so typical of Christobel's youth.

Why ever hadn't Edith stopped to consider what it would mean, living in the industrial north where everything moved far too briskly, where the winters were severe and unforgiving, where smokestacks belched and obscured the horizon?

"Christobel, dear, did you hear the news?" her mother called out cheerily. "We'll take good care of her, won't we?"

"Of course we will," Christobel said, forcing her lips to form a smile. "But are you sure it's prudent to host a house party at a time like this? I worry about you overtaxing yourself."

"Don't be silly," Edith said with a smile. "The doctor says I'm the model of good health. The other two times . . . well, it was just bad luck, nothing more."

Christobel nodded silently, hoping that her sister was correct. Forcing away her misgivings, she hurried to Edith's side, reaching for her hand and clasping it tightly in her own. "Still, I'll make sure you get plenty of rest and pampering, beginning straightaway. Sit, and let me pour you some more tea. Shall I pour for you, too, Mother?"

Her mother nodded. "That would be lovely, dear. Come, now, let's all sit, and Edith can tell me about the guests."

"Don't fret, Edie," Christobel whispered into her sister's ear as she leaned over to pour the fragrant brew into the cup set before her. "I'll behave; I promise."

At the very least, she would try.

# CHAPTER 2

John heaved a sigh as he turned the car into his cousin's long drive. A cloud of dust billowed up around the vehicle, clouding his goggles and nearly making him choke.

Dust or no, he was excessively fond of his motorcar, a 1906 Darracq speedster that had set him back nearly three hundred pounds—well worth every quid, in his opinion.

In fact, at that very moment he longed to be racing his motor through the countryside, the scenery blurring like an impressionist painting as the wind whistled in his ears.

Instead, he was sedately motoring up Hadley Hall's drive at a snail's pace, the house looming larger as he approached. He'd promised Jasper and Edith he'd attend their annual autumn Saturday-to-Monday, as he always had.

And, as always, Jasper had convinced him to arrive early. His mother- and sister-in-law would be there helping Edith prepare for the guests, and Jasper had insisted that he'd go mad listening to the hens cluck about, if left to his own company. Indeed, Jasper was never content to suffer alone.

So, here he was—arriving several days early, as promised. The drive curved sharply to the left, toward the house. Dead ahead, beyond a roughly hewn fence, the lawn stretched out before him. There, beneath the drooping branches of a yew, a lone figure stood, shielding herself from the sun with a parasol. John's hands gripped the wheel as he turned it.

Though he hadn't been able to make out the woman's face, he knew with certainty that it was Christobel Smyth standing there, the hem of her virginal white skirts aflutter in the breeze. Damn it all, but every inch of his traitorous body sensed her presence.

Lovely, intelligent, sweet-smelling Christobel, who never failed to make him feel like an ugly, clumsy oaf. If only she knew how he suffered, mentally undressing her while he chastised himself for doing so, for wanting a woman he could never have, who despised him and pitied him without even taking the pains to conceal it.

Insufferable, snobbish girl! And what a fool he was, drawn to her like a moth to a flame. A low growl of self-loathing rumbled from his throat as he pulled up in front of the great house and cut the motor.

At once Edith burst forth from the house, the housekeeper trailing behind her. "Mr. Leyden!" she called out, waving gaily.

John removed his goggles and fixed a smile upon his cousin's wife as he tugged off his thick leather driving gloves. "Good afternoon, Edith," he called out in return, striving to sound more jovial than he felt. He tossed his gloves to the driver's seat and made his way up Hadley Hall's front steps, ever conscious of his limp.

Just then a pair of footmen appeared from the side of the house and saw to unstrapping his luggage from the back of the motorcar.

"You're just in time for tea, Mr. Leyden," Edith said, reaching for his elbow and allowing him to escort her back inside. "The weather is so lovely we thought to take it on the patio. I hope you won't object."

"Not at all," he answered, wishing they could dispense with the pleasantries.

"And how was the drive over?" she pressed on.

"Splendid. Only managed to puncture one tire."

Releasing Edith's arm, he shrugged out of his Norfolk tweed duster coat and handed it to the housekeeper. "Might want to take it outside and beat it."

"Of course, Mr. Leyden." The housekeeper bobbed a curtsy, then disappeared with the garment folded across one arm.

John followed Edith out to the patio, where a wrought-iron table was set for tea.

"Jasper went down to the train station to retrieve a parcel, but he should be home directly. Would you care to sit?" Edith asked, motioning toward the table. "Or perhaps you'd prefer to stretch your legs while we wait for him?"

"I think I'll take a turn about the garden, if you don't mind."

"Not at all. In fact, Christobel is out there, ambling about aimlessly as she always does. You might see if you can find her and fetch her back in time for tea." Edith smiled sweetly at him, but John detected a hint of mischief in her eyes, as if she were enjoying a private joke.

"Very well," he said, bowing sharply before turning and striding off in the opposite direction from where he'd seen Christobel standing beneath the tree.

Let them play their feminine games, whatever they were. He would not be an active participant.

Despite all efforts to the contrary, he found her not ten minutes later, sitting on the grass before the ornamental pond with her arms wrapped around her knees.

Her chestnut hair was piled on her head beneath a large straw boater, but loose tendrils had escaped the arrangement and danced in the breeze, brushing against the lace of her high-necked collar.

How he longed to curl the silky hair around his finger, to brush his hand across her flushed cheek—and how he hated himself for such thoughts.

As if she sensed his presence, she turned, one hand raised to the brooch at her throat. "You near enough frightened me half to death, Mr. Leyden," she said, shaking her head. "You might have called out a greeting or something, you know. A simple 'good afternoon' would have sufficed."

"My apologies," he said, his tongue suddenly thick and awkward.

She smiled then, her rose-colored lips curving upward. "You needn't look so stricken," she said, tilting her head to one side. Her clear green eyes shone like polished glass beneath a fringe of dark lashes. "Now that you're here, you might as well join me. Would you care to sit?"

"I was instructed to fetch you back to tea, should we cross paths." He spoke more sharply than he'd intended, as he often did in her company.

"And here I was, thinking you meant to be sociable. Come now, can't you sit for a minute? Would it pain you so very much to simply sit and admire the way the afternoon sun plays upon the water's surface? Just look—it's lovely this time of day."

Christobel fought the urge to roll her eyes as she watched Mr. Leyden stand there stiffly, considering her offer. Why she'd extended it in the first place, she had no idea.

But she had, and now he simply stood there watching her warily, his pale blue eyes narrowed in displeasure. Indignation washed over her. Was her company so very abhorrent to him?

"Very well," he conceded at last. As solemn as a bishop, he made his way toward her, his gait slightly uneven. Despite that, she could not deny that Mr. Leyden was pleasant enough to look at.

He was tall, at least six feet, and broad of shoulder. The closely cropped hair beneath his bowler hat was as black as midnight, his pale blue eyes direct—piercing, even. His nose was slightly long, though not unpleasantly so, and his lips surprisingly full. If only the man would ever smile!

Christobel continued her examination as he lowered himself to the grass beside her—rather gracefully, considering his height. He looked out of place in his somber black suit—well cut, though not terribly fashionable. Still, he was decidedly handsome, in a rough, fierce sort of way. Perhaps this Miss Bartlett would find him agreeable, particularly if she weren't the vivacious sort herself.

She turned her attention back to the pond, watching a fat green frog hoist himself upon a lily pad where he sat puffing out his throat as he croaked loudly. A cocky, proud fellow, just like the man sitting beside her.

"There, now, Mr. Leyden." Christobel favored him with a sunny smile. "This isn't so terribly unpleasant now, is it?"

"I suppose not," he answered, his gaze fixed on the pond.

"How is your family's mill faring?" she asked, simply trying to make conversation. "Is business well these days?"

"Well enough, thank you."

Would he say nothing unless prompted? At the very least he could comment upon the weather. Blast it, if only Edith hadn't made her promise to be nice. "Do you find yourself quite occupied, then?" she asked lamely.

"To the contrary. Lately I've been less involved in the day-to-day operation of the mill."

"Oh? And how do you occupy yourself, then? Have you taken up fishing and shooting?"

"I've mostly occupied myself with books, hoping to fill the gaps in my education. I'm well aware of my deficiencies, Miss Smyth," he added somewhat coldly, plucking a blade of grass from the ground and twisting it between his fingers. Long, elegant fingers, she realized with a start. Why ever did that surprise her so?

A prickle of guilt niggled her conscience, and Christobel dropped her gaze. It was this blasted gap in their social status, making things so uncomfortable. After all, if it weren't for the fact that he was Jasper's cousin, their paths would never have crossed. Still, she hadn't meant to insult him—she simply hadn't been able to think of anything else to say. What *did* one discuss with a man who made his living in the cotton mills?

"Perhaps we should head back to the house," she offered instead. "I didn't mean to keep you from your tea."

Mr. Leyden stood, reaching a hand down to assist her up. "I'll go on ahead and tell them you will be there shortly."

"Nonsense. You shall escort me back." She rose to her knees and retrieved her mackintosh square, folding it into fourths before reaching for her discarded parasol. Tucking it under her arm, she took Mr. Leyden's proffered hand.

He tugged her to her feet with too much force, causing her to lose her balance and fall forward against him, her breasts pressed firmly against the rock-solid hardness of his chest. For a single, horrified moment, Christobel feared they might both fall in a tangled heap of limbs on the grass. Instead, Mr. Leyden reached for her shoulders, steadying her.

"Goodness!" she exclaimed a bit breathlessly, undone by the frisson of awareness that shot through her body. He was so close that she could smell his scent—soap and leather, perhaps a hint of tobacco. It was an entirely male scent, and a pleasing one, at that.

For a moment their eyes met and held, Christobel's widening with surprise at the sudden, inexplicable heat she saw there in his gaze. "I . . . I'm so clumsy," she stuttered.

At once he released her, inhaling sharply as he did so. Balling his hands into fists by his sides, he stepped away, a muscle in his jaw flexing perceptibly.

For several seconds, neither of them spoke. Christobel struggled to regain her composure, feeling oddly flustered.

"Shall we?" he said at last. He offered his arm, the fleeting warmth in his eyes replaced with the usual coolness.

Christobel could only nod in reply as she laid her hand in the crook of his elbow, thinking that perhaps she was far more exhausted than she'd imagined.

"Thank you, Mr. Leyden," she managed to say. *A nap,* she promised herself. Right after tea.

As he led her back to the house in silence, she couldn't help but recall the heated look she'd seen in his eyes, if only for a moment.

Perhaps there was more to Mr. Leyden than she'd supposed—something lurking just beneath that quiet exterior, something far more complex, far more . . . alive.

No, she concluded with a shake of her head. It was

just her overactive imagination making her see things that weren't there, nothing more.

And with that, Christobel put Mr. John Leyden entirely out of her thoughts.

# CHAPTER 3

As was her custom, Christobel rose early the next morning, just as the first silvery light of dawn cast shadows across her coverlet. She liked to greet the day, to walk about the garden while the morning dew still glistened upon the lawn.

There was nothing she cherished more than her quiet morning walks, the rising sun piercing the shadows and causing the countryside to come alive. If only she had a way with words like that clever Miss Potter or the scandalous Elinor Glyn.

If she had, she would sit in the ethereal light of dawn, pen and journal in hand, and describe the sights, the sounds, the smells. Yet she dared not try, knowing she would fail abysmally. Instead, she simply observed.

Slipping out of bed, she hurried to the clothespress and dressed quickly, her gown a simple one—one her mother claimed far too closely resembled a dressing gown, but had the advantage of allowing Christobel to manage without Simpson's aid.

As quiet as a mouse, she made her way downstairs

and threw on her heavy woolen cloak. Tiptoeing across the hall, she let herself out the French doors and skimmed down the back stairs, sighing happily as she stepped onto the soft, springy lawn below.

Mist rose from the ground, swirling about her ankles in dark, atmospheric wisps. Walking slowly, leisurely, she left the quiet house behind. So much to see before the others awoke, before voices broke her reverie, before the day's activity stole away her solitude.

Nearly an hour later, she made her way back toward the house clutching a colorful bunch of chrysanthemums—yellow, gold, orange, red—and humming quietly to herself. The hem of her skirt was soaked straight through, her hair escaping the simple ribbon with which she'd tied it back and falling about her shoulders in disarray. Time for a steaming bath, she thought, and then perhaps a spot of tea.

But as she drew closer to the house, she became aware of voices—loud, angry voices—coming from the direction of the service door. Likely just a servants' dispute, she realized. Still, she quickened her pace and hurried off in that direction.

What she saw when she came around the bend beside the patio made her breath catch in her throat. A line of servants stood against the house watching one man—a gentleman, judging by his attire—hold another man, clearly a servant, by the lapels, landing blow after blow upon the poor soul's face.

When the servant crumpled to the ground, the gentleman advanced . . . Dear Lord in heaven, with a limp. Christobel inhaled sharply, one hand rising to cover her mouth in horror. The man was Mr. Leyden, beating the life out of some poor, wretched servant boy.

"Not very tough now, are you?" Mr. Leyden snarled, aiming a kick at the prone man's abdomen. "Get out of here, you filthy piece of horseshit, and don't ever return."

The smaller man staggered to his feet, straightening his jacket as he did so. "I'm owed two weeks' wages, and I'll get 'em before I go, ye bastard—"

"You'll not get a dime." Mr. Leyden landed another blow, this time to the man's nose. Blood spurted from the wound, a flood of bright red that stained his muddy shirt. Christobel felt her stomach lurch at the sight. Still, her anger propelled her into motion. Dropping the flowers, she picked up her skirts and ran.

"Let him go, Mr. Leyden!" she called out, placing herself between the two men. "Good God, he's just a boy!"

"Get out of here, Miss Smyth. This is no business of yours." Mr. Leyden's face was livid, his eyes wild with rage. For a moment, Christobel felt a stab of fear, but her fear was soon replaced with righteous indignation.

"It *is* my business when I see a . . . a gentleman abusing a servant in such a fashion. Haven't you any sense at all? Why, what would Jasper say?"

"I demand you take yourself inside at once, Miss Smyth." His hands—swollen and covered with blood, she realized—were balled into fists, ready to continue the abuse.

"I won't let you kill him, you . . . you barbarian! You base, brutish man," she sputtered.

For the briefest of moments, he looked slightly taken aback. Dazed, almost. "And this is what you think of me?" he finally said.

The housekeeper hurried to Christobel's side, clutching at her sleeve. "Please, miss. I beg of you to do as he says and go in at once. This is no sight for a lady."

She met Mr. Leyden's steely gaze. "I will go inside. I'll find Jasper at once and tell him what you've done."

But as soon as she stepped in the door, Edith intercepted her. "Heavens, Christobel. You must stay inside. There's been some . . . some unpleasantness with the servants, and—"

"Unpleasantness? Is that what you call it? Why, he was beating the man senseless!"

"No more than he deserves," Edith muttered, causing Christobel to gasp in surprise. Her sister did not condone violence of any sort, particularly a man of Mr. Leyden's station picking on someone so far beneath him. It just wasn't done.

"I'm told the girl is in terrible shape, cut and bleeding, violated in the worst sort of way," Edith whispered. "Jasper just phoned the doctor. I only hope he arrives quickly."

The girl? Whatever was Edith talking about? Christobel shook her head in confusion. "What girl?"

"I thought you heard. I thought that's why you came racing in, that look of fury on your face. Come, sit down." She led Christobel to a settee beside the fireplace.

"One of the housemaids, a young girl, very pretty. Marie is her name. She was attacked and"—Edith cleared her throat loudly—"viciously attacked early this morning by one of the new footmen."

"Attacked?" Christobel could barely believe it.

"Yes, and she stumbled out for help, her dress in tatters. Thank God Mr. Leyden is an early riser and happened upon her when he did. She told him what happened and . . ." Edith trailed off, covering her mouth with a trembling hand. "It's dreadful, isn't it? His references were sterling; there was no hint of it, or we'd never have engaged him. I feel so . . . so responsible. The poor girl's mother." A fat tear rolled down Edith's cheek.

Christobel clutched her sister's hands in her own. "Please don't cry, Edie. It can't be good for you, not in your condition. Come, you must go lie down. Where's Mother?"

"Not yet arisen, thank goodness. I . . . perhaps I *should* go lie down. The doctor should be here any moment. Perhaps after he sees to Marie, he'll look in on me."

"Of course," Christobel said, rising from the settee and leading Edith toward the stairs.

"I hope Mr. Leyden has taken care of the . . . the situation with the footman," Edith said, her voice tremulous.

"I think he has." And dear Lord, how she'd wronged him. The things she'd said . . . Christobel shook her head, her cheeks burning with mortification. How would she ever apologize? If only she'd known, if only she'd minded her own business and hurried inside like any proper lady would have done when faced with such a scene.

But no, she had to champion what appeared to be an injured party, as was her habit. Only in this case, the injured party was some poor girl named Marie, not the servant boy.

Christobel let out her breath in a rush, feeling like a fool. "Come, Edith. Let me help you upstairs. Shall I call for some tea?"

"No, I already had my tea in bed."

Edith looked entirely discomposed, slightly dazed as Christobel escorted her up the stairs and down the corridor toward her bedchamber.

Once they stepped inside, Edith's maid helped her undress and settled her into bed.

"Shall I read to you?" Christobel offered, reaching for the slim, leather-bound book that sat on the commode beside the bed.

"If you don't mind. Anything to take my mind off the situation belowstairs."

And so Christobel opened the book and began to read aloud.


Hours later, Christobel sat on the bench in the front hall, waiting for Mr. Leyden to appear. After she'd left her sister's bedside and had her bath, she'd changed into a simple lawn skirt and blouse and had her hair put in proper order by Simpson. Still, she felt anything but orderly as she sat waiting for what felt like an eternity.

At last Mr. Leyden stepped out of Jasper's study and closed the door, headed down the corridor toward her. Twisting the handkerchief she held in her lap, Christobel rose to face him.

Mr. Leyden stopped short when he saw her there. "Miss Smyth," he said coldly.

Gathering her courage, she spoke quickly. "Mr. Leyden, I must have a word with you."

"No need," he said sharply, pushing past her.

Impulsively, she reached out and plucked at his sleeve. "I beg to differ, sir. I . . . I behaved most inexcusably this morning, and you must allow me to apologize. I had no idea of the situation, and I had no right—"

"Indeed, you hadn't." He stared down at her in his usual supercilious manner, only this time Christobel could not resent it. Truly, she deserved it.

"I . . . I'm ashamed of the things I said to you. You must think me an unbearable fool."

He said nothing in reply, neither denying nor confirming the accusation. Instead, he rubbed his chin with one hand, and Christobel winced at the sight of his bruised, swollen knuckles.

"I could find some bandages and wrap your hand," she offered. "With some liniment, perhaps, and—"

"That won't be necessary," he said, cutting her off.

Nodding, Christobel dropped her gaze to the floor.

"Miss Smyth, I . . ." He cleared his throat. "Your words weren't so very far off the mark. The idea of a man raising a hand to a woman tends to blind me with rage. I'm only sorry that you saw me in such a state."

Christobel couldn't hide her astonishment.

"I apologize for speaking so frankly, Miss Smyth. If you'll excuse me." He made to quit her company once more.

Christobel shook her head. "I insist you let me take a look at that hand, Mr. Leyden. Please. It's the least I can do."

He relented, the barest hint of a smile on his lips. "If it will ease your conscience," he quipped.

"Mother always travels with her special liniment. If you'll just let me fetch a tube and some bandages, I'll see to it straightaway."

He flexed his hand, wincing as he did so. "Hurts like the devil."

"Wait right here," she said. "No, better yet, wait for me in the library. The light's so much better in there. Go on; I'll be there directly."

Not five minutes later she found him in the library, sprawled in a worn leather chair, his long legs stretched out before him, a glass of brandy clutched in his good hand. Nothing but his familiar brooding silence greeted her, the glimmer of good humor entirely gone.

Steeling herself, she hurried across the room and knelt before him, uncapping the tube of her mother's liniment. "Let me see it," she said, leaning across his lap to take his hand in her own. He visibly flinched as she did so, as if repulsed by her touch, her very nearness.

She couldn't help but bristle. After all, she was just trying to help, to make amends. "Perhaps I should send in my maid, instead."

He looked startled. "If you'd prefer, Miss Smyth. I wouldn't want to make you uncomfortable."

Christobel sat back on her heels, trying not to laugh at the absurdity of the situation. Truth be told, she hadn't the slightest idea what she was doing. It wasn't as if she'd ever treated an injury like this before—his knuckles might be broken for all she knew.

"I don't quite see the humor in the situation," he muttered.

"I'm only laughing at my own ineptitude. But must we always quarrel?" she asked, shaking her head. "We're nearly family, you and I. Some sort of cousin-in-law, I suppose, if such a relation exists. Would it be so very wrong for you to call me Christobel? Miss Christobel, perhaps, if it felt more comfortable?"

John shifted uneasily in his seat, taking a sip of brandy to avoid replying. Christobel remained at his feet, looking up at him hopefully. Her skin was flushed a delicious shade of pink, the sooty lashes above her green eyes fluttering prettily as she awaited his reply. Devil take it, how lovely she was. How he longed to call her by her Christian name; how he wanted that intimacy.

But damn it, the rational part of him must prevail. She did not desire such intimacy with him, of all people. No matter his money, his success, nothing could give him the breeding that she was born to, that his cousin Jasper was born to. She thought him uneducated, uncultured, uncouth—

"Mr. Leyden?" Christobel asked, peering up at him with drawn brows. "You must let me see your hand."

"Go on, then," he grunted, giving himself up to her ministrations.

He ordered himself to ignore the feel of her bare fingers against his; to ignore the way his skin warmed to her touch; to ignore the fact that his cock swelled and pressed painfully against his trousers—proof that he was every bit as coarse, as base as she believed him to be. *Bloody hell.*

It was no use; the battle was lost. In one swift motion, he reached for Christobel's wrist and dragged her into his lap.

# CHAPTER 4

Mr. Leyden's mouth muffled her gasp of surprise, his lips hard and unyielding against hers. For a moment she thought to scream; instead, she pressed her fists against his chest, trying to push him away. As if fueled by her protests, his tongue sought entrance to her mouth, dancing along her lower lip—teasing, testing.

She could have bit him then. Should have. It was no less than he deserved, the brute. Instead, she yielded. God help her, but her lips parted and her own tongue met his, warm and alive. Next thing she knew she was kissing him back, as roughly and thoroughly as he was kissing her. A soft moan escaped her lips and his grasp on her wrist tightened in reply.

For a fleeting moment she thought he might be punishing her, yet she didn't care. She couldn't care. Couldn't think. Couldn't feel anything but the warmth that spread through her body, making her heart beat a wild rhythm, her limbs suddenly weak.

And then she *did* bite him, just a nip on his lower lip. A low growl tore from his throat and his body tensed beneath hers, but he did not push her away. Instead his kiss deepened, his body straining against hers, her breasts now pressed flat against his coat.

Her nipples had stiffened, her undergarments abrading them, the sensation both wicked and welcome. Beneath her, she felt his arousal, hard and firm, pressing against her bottom.

*I should stop this,* her mind screamed in protest. Now, before it was too late, before—

Mr. Leyden abruptly released her wrist and struggled to stand, nearly toppling her over in the process. "Good God, I—"

"No," she choked out, humiliated beyond belief. "Don't . . . don't say anything. Please." Not till she got her wits back—not till she could think clearly and rationally.

"Devil take it, your wrist," he said, his voice hoarse.

Shaking her head in confusion, she glanced down at the wrist he'd held captive just moments before. The marks his fingers had left behind were faintly visible on her skin. "It's . . . it's nothing," she stammered.

He raked a hand through his hair, a muscle in his jaw throbbing as he did so. She'd never before seen him so discomposed, so thoroughly vexed. "You must forgive me," he said, his voice wavering slightly. "Damn it all, I've no excuse—"

"Please, Mr. Leyden. I . . . I must go." Without waiting for his reply, she turned and fled from the library, her vision blurred by the unexpected nuisance of tears.

Christobel stepped into the drawing room and found Edith standing by the window, gazing out on the lawn below.

"Have all your guests arrived?" Christobel asked.

She'd been out in the garden sitting by the pond, listening to the steady procession of carriages and the occasional motorcar in the drive.

"They have. Everyone is settling into their rooms at present, but I expect them all to assemble outside before the hour is out. I thought we'd enjoy some lawn games before tea."

"That sounds like great fun."

Edith looked toward the hall with a frown. "Have you by any chance seen Mr. Leyden today? I vow, I've seen neither hide nor hair of the man since Wednesday. Odd, isn't it?"

Christobel felt the heat rise in her cheeks. He was avoiding her, hiding from her, and she knew exactly why. *That damnable kiss.* Meant to punish and humiliate her, and it had done exactly that. How could she ever forgive herself for succumbing to it, for kissing him back the way she had?

She'd thought of nothing else since that day in the library, her mind reduced to a muddled, confounded mess. Even Edith had commented once or twice that Christobel had seemed distracted, and how on earth could she answer that charge?

*Why, it's just that John Leyden kissed me, you see. A hard, punishing kiss that I somehow enjoyed. He despises me, and yet . . . and yet he was clearly aroused. So was I, if truth be told.*

Never in a million years could she speak such words to her sister!

"Miss Bartlett does not usually participate in lawn games," Edith continued on, "and I was hoping Mr. Leyden might escort her on a stroll about the gardens, instead. Oh, there's Jasper now! I must go ask him if he's seen him. Go and change into your tennis costume, won't you? That lovely striped flannel one; it'll do nicely." Edith hurried off without waiting for Christobel's reply.

It turned out Miss Bartlett *did* play lawn tennis. Quite badly, Christobel decided as she stood across the net from the woman, waiting patiently for her serve. As much as Christobel would have liked to claim exhaustion and quit the match, that would mean rejoining Sir Edmund there on the patio, and she'd already had enough of the man's attentions. Not that he was disagreeable; in fact, he was quite jolly. Too jolly, perhaps. And the way he looked at her . . . well, it was as if he were judging livestock at the county fair.

At last, Miss Bartlett took her serve. The ball flew through the air, over Christobel's head and beyond the hedgerow behind her. A resounding *thunk* could be heard in the distance as the ball hit a structure, likely her sister's greenhouse.

"I'm hopeless!" Miss Bartlett cried out, laughing at her own ineptitude with a good grace that Christobel admired greatly. "I hope you'll forgive me if I retire to the patio for some lemonade, Miss Smyth. I'm sure you can find a more worthy opponent."

"I've had quite enough of the game myself," Christobel called out cheerily, reaching up to adjust her cap. "Just let me fetch the ball and I'll join you."

Dropping her racquet to the lawn, she headed off in search of the errant ball, poking around the bushes surrounding the greenhouse with no luck. The door was slightly ajar, so she hurried inside, inhaling the sweet, heady fragrance. She closed the door to peer behind it, then began to search the floor beneath the many pots and trellises. Wherever could it have gone?

"Looking for this?" a voice called out, startling her so badly that she bumped her head on a clay pot that held a lemon tree.

"Oh! Good heavens, I think I've cracked my skull." Christobel straightened, rubbing her head as she looked about for the voice's owner.

Mr. Leyden stood scowling near a potted jasmine, the tennis ball clutched in one hand.

She couldn't help but sigh in exasperation. "Pray tell, Mr. Leyden, do you always skulk about, hoping to frighten me half to death? Whatever are you doing, hiding in here? Edith has been looking for you all afternoon."

"Which is precisely why I'm here," he answered. "Are you injured?" He closed the distance that separated them in several long strides.

"It's nothing mortal, I assure you."

He only nodded in reply, his eyes cool and guarded— an entirely different man from the one who'd pulled her into his lap and kissed her with a fierce cruelty. He showed no remorse, nor any desire to repeat such behavior.

At the very least, he should beg her forgiveness. She was a lady, after all, and . . . She let the thought trail off. She did not wish for an apology, not really. Instead, she wished for a hint of longing, of yearning in his eyes; for some indication that the kiss had affected him the same way it had affected her.

Yet there was nothing in his countenance to suggest such a thing. Tamping down her humiliation, she boldly met his gaze. "You're meant to be entertaining Miss Bartlett, you know. Have you made her acquaintance yet?"

"Briefly."

"Well, then, you must satisfy my curiosity," she said, endeavoring to keep her voice light and teasing. She would play the part of coquette, and play it well. "Is it Miss Bartlett you're hiding from, or is it me?"

"And you must satisfy mine, Miss Smyth," he countered. "Was there no servant to be spared to look for this"—he held up the ball—"or were you, too, hoping to escape your sister's meddling?"

"Oh!" Christobel gasped in outrage.

"No? Jasper tells me that Edith was particularly looking forward to introducing you to Sir Edmund Blake. A fine catch, Jasper called him."

Christobel reached for the ball with a sigh of defeat, wondering just why she *had* come after it. They had an entire basket of balls, after all. There was nothing special about this one. "It would seem we're both victims of Edith's matchmaking efforts," she said with a shrug. "I have not yet formed an opinion of Sir Edmund, though Miss Bartlett does seem quite pleasant, does she not? Perhaps there's some merit to—"

"I do not need your sister's assistance where women are concerned."

"Oh? Well, then. Is there a particular lady with whom you—"

"No," he interrupted, but said no more.

"Pray, forgive me," Christobel said. "I didn't mean to pry."

A moment of uncomfortable silence ensued, and yet neither made to leave.

"I'm somewhat acquainted with Sir Edmund Blake," Mr. Leyden said at last. "He is a gentleman, and one with whom I can find no fault. Perhaps you will find his company more pleasant than mine."

"Like you, I do not require my sister's assistance in matters of the heart," Christobel said. "Besides, if I *were* hanging out for a husband, I certainly wouldn't be looking for one in these parts."

"Of course you wouldn't," he said, his voice suddenly cold.

Heat flooded Christobel's cheeks, and she instantly regretted her candor. *Time to change the subject, and quickly.* "Tell me, how is your hand? Has the bruising gone down?"

John reached for his injured hand, absently massaging the still-sore knuckles that were now an odd shade of greenish-yellow. "It no longer pains me," he lied.

"I . . . I hope the liniment helped," she continued on, her cheeks deepening to scarlet. No doubt she was thinking of the liberties he'd taken while she'd seen to his hand—that thoughtless, reckless kiss that had haunted him, taunting him endlessly with the memory. Her warm body atop his, her breasts pressed against his coat; her soft, sweet mouth, more delicious than he'd ever imagined.

*What a bloody, damnable fool I am.* "Miss Symth," he began, rubbing his cheek with the palm of one hand, "I fear I proved myself to be exactly what you thought of me. Unmannered, un—"

"Please don't," she interrupted, dropping her gaze to her feet. "We mustn't speak of it."

"To the contrary, we must. You must allow me to apologize, though I've no excuse for my behavior." How he longed to reach for her chin, to tip her face up to meet his gaze. How he wished himself more a gentleman, so he wouldn't be in this predicament. How he wished himself less a gentleman, so that he might have done more than just kiss her.

*Damn it all.* "I can assure you, Miss Smyth, that it will never happen again."

In light of his apology, she only looked annoyed. Disappointed, perhaps.

"Didn't I give you permission to call me Christobel, Cousin John?" she snapped. "Really, is your memory so very faulty—"

"Miss Smyth?" a male voice called out. "Wherever has

she gone to?" It was Sir Edmund, of course, searching
for Christobel in a proprietary fashion, though he'd
only made her acquaintance that very day.

Christobel whirled toward the closed door of the
greenhouse, fluttering the hem of her skirt. He
watched as indecision played across her features, her
brow drawn in thought. At any moment, he fully expected her to hurry toward the door and dash out into
the sunshine, calling gaily to her new suitor while he
shrunk back in the shadows.

Instead, she did something wholly and completely
unexpected—she put a finger to her lips, her eyes dancing merrily. "Shh," she whispered.

Grasping his sleeve, she silently pulled him back
against the wall, behind the door. She stood beside him,
so close that he could feel her warmth, smell the lilac
scent of her hair, the spicy scent of her perfume.

The door opened, squealing loudly on its hinges.
"Miss Smyth?" the tenacious Sir Edmund called out. He
peered inside, standing mere inches from where they
cowered. "Are you in here, Miss Smyth? Hullo?"

The door opened a fraction more, and Christobel
pressed against John. He felt the fluttering of her heart,
felt his own pounding relentlessly against his ribs as she
buried her face in his coat. Her hands were seemingly
everywhere, one clutching his arm, the other pressing
the blasted tennis ball into his groin, mere inches from
his far-too-eager cock.

His own hands were trapped against the small of her
back, resting against the belt that cinched her tiny
waist. All he could think about was taking her, right
there on the dusty floor, Sir Edmund be damned.

What in God's name was she doing, taking such a
risk as this? If they were discovered, alone and unchap-
eroned, hiding behind a door . . .

He held his breath as the door creaked shut. The sound of Sir Edmund's footsteps grew fainter, then mercifully disappeared altogether.

He suddenly became aware of tinkling laughter, muffled against his coat. They'd almost been discovered in what would have surely seemed a compromising position, and she was *laughing*? All he could do was shake his head. He'd never understand women, least of all this one.

At last she released him and stepped away, her face flushed. Escaped from their careful arrangement, tendrils of dark hair fell against her collar.

"Why, Cousin John!" she said, still laughing softly as she attempted to straighten her blouse and tidy her hair beneath her cap. "Who knew you had such mischief in you?"

Completely bewildered and more than a little aroused, John watched in stunned silence as Christobel strode out, her head held high, a look of triumph gleaming in her eyes.

Only then did he let out his breath in a rush, swearing violently as he did so.

# CHAPTER 5

Christobel took a sip of sherry, hoping it would calm her nerves. After all, Sir Edmund had gotten on every last one of them. She stepped around her sister's pianoforte, hoping to hide herself behind it.

Somehow, Mrs. Lovelace found her. "A shame that Mrs. Roth had to depart this morning, isn't it?" she said, a vicious smile on her face. "And so hastily, too."

"Indeed," Christobel murmured, searching wildly for Edith among her guests.

She found her, wringing her hands as she whispered something into the housekeeper's ear. Poor Edith. Last night—the very first evening of her party—had been dreadful. Both Misses Allen had taken ill with a stomach ailment just after dinner, and then Mrs. Lovelace and Mrs. Roth, both widows, had had a terrible row, right there in the drawing room.

The fickle Mr. Aberforth was to blame, of course, but the man had done nothing to intercede, leaving that unpleasant duty to Edith, who'd managed to smooth their ruffled feathers, at least temporarily.

But then something had happened in the dead of

night to prompt Mrs. Roth to pack up her belongings at daybreak. Edith wouldn't say, but Christobel suspected that one woman had found her lover in the other's bed, and chaos had ensued. Long before the other guests had breakfasted, Jasper had been forced to drive a tearful Mrs. Roth to the train station.

Now it would seem that Mrs. Lovelace would spend the remainder of the house party crowing in victory. As if Mr. Aberforth were such a prize, Christobel thought, shaking her head. She turned toward the balding, portly man in question, who sat at the card table twirling his moustache as he regarded the cards in his hand. He was rich, she supposed, but beyond that she could find nothing to recommend him. Across from Mr. Aberforth sat Sir Edmund, a good ten years and two score lighter than his opponent.

"I see you have your eye on Sir Edmund," Mrs. Lovelace said, startling her. "If you don't mind my saying so, I think you could do far worse. He's quite the gentleman, and handsome, too."

"I suppose he is," Christobel conceded. Tall and ginger-haired with an athletic build, he cut a fine form, indeed. His disposition seemed perpetually sunny and bright, and he was polite to a fault. Despite all that, he left Christobel's emotions positively unmoved.

"If I were you, I'd make it known straightaway that you are receptive to his intentions. After all, he's made them clear enough."

Christobel attempted to laugh. "My dear Mrs. Lovelace, you must be mistaken. After all, my acquaintance with Sir Edmund only spans the length of a day."

"Time enough to know the size of his fortune," Mrs. Lovelace said with a toss of her curls. "What else is there to know?"

"Indeed, if one were considering becoming chattel," Christobel murmured between clenched teeth. She watched as Mr. Leyden entered the room and accepted a glass of sherry from a serving maid.

"That one there," Mrs. Lovelace said, following the direction of her gaze, "the tall, dour-looking one. Have you any idea why he walks as he does? Do you suppose he's trying to imitate the Queen?"

"You must excuse me," Christobel said, smiling sweetly. "There is Miss Bartlett, and I promised her that I would show her the library."

Anything to escape the horrid woman's company.

"Miss Bartlett," she called out, hurrying across the room. "Shall I show you the library now?"

Miss Barlett's pretty heart-shaped face lit up at once. "Oh, I should so love that, but I've promised a game of whist to Lady Margaret. Afterward, perhaps?"

Christobel nodded, feeling ridiculous. "Of course," she said, watching as Miss Bartlett deftly shuffled a deck of cards and took her place at the baize table opposite Lady Margaret.

*Perhaps I'll find Mother,* she thought. Trying her best to avoid Mrs. Lovelace, she looked furtively around the room where all of Edith's guests were happily occupied in one diversion or another, enjoying the morning sunshine that cast a warm, golden glow through the drawing room's windows.

"Miss Smyth," a voice called out, and Christobel turned to see Sir Edmund rise from the card table and head toward her, smiling broadly with his hands clasped behind his back.

Feeling like a cornered fox, she looked about wildly for an escape. From across the width of the room, Edith caught her eye and winked. Oh, how very unfair of Edith to manipulate her so, leaving her with no means of retaliation, thanks to her sister's delicate condition.

In seconds Sir Edmund was beside her. "You look lovely today, Miss Smyth. A vision, one might say."

"Why, aren't you full of flattery this morning, Sir Edmund," she replied lightly. "I suppose you've said as much to all the ladies present."

"Indeed not. Suffice it to say that no one shines as brightly as you do on this fine day," he said rather loudly. Enthusiastic, as always.

Christobel laughed, amazed at his audacity. "Be careful, sir, or I'll develop airs with such grand compliments as that. You would not want me to become insufferable now, would you?"

"You, insufferable? Never! Why, I have it from Mrs. Hadley that you are the model of humility and—"

"Humility?" she interrupted with a laugh. "Dear me, Sir Edmund, you mustn't trust a word my sister says about me. I can assure you, whatever she's said, I'm likely the exact opposite."

As Sir Edmund's easy laughter joined hers, Christobel noticed several pairs of eyes suddenly turned their way, including Mr. Leyden's. As always, his eyes appeared narrowed in disapproval, his nostrils slightly flared as he regarded her with obvious disdain.

Why did he have to look at her so, as if she were a naughty child caught sticking her fingers in the tea cakes? For the briefest of moments, their eyes met across the room, and then he turned and left without a backward glance.

Heat flooded her cheeks, no doubt staining them red. She turned her gaze back to Sir Edmund, forcing a tight smile. "If you'll excuse me, I'm suddenly feeling a trifle unwell."

"Hmm, you do look rather flushed, if you don't mind my saying so." He examined her from head to toe with a scowl on his face. "Perhaps you should go lie down. I would hate for you to take ill like the Misses Allen, poor souls. *La grippe*, I'm told."

Christobel nodded, drawing the back of one hand across her forehead for effect. "I think I will go lie down. How kind of you to suggest it."

She had no intention of lying down, of course. Instead, she retrieved her hat, which hung by the front door, and slipped out, trying to decide how she could make her way to the ornamental pond without being spotted through the drawing-room windows.

Perhaps if she went out the front gate and walked along the road for a bit, then cut back through the woods toward the park—

A loud, sputtering noise nearly made her jump out of her skin. Good heavens, it was Mr. Leyden's motor-car, she realized. It materialized in a cloud of dust, its motor now a steady hum as it chugged down the long drive toward her. She stood watching the car's approach, the sun glinting off its dark green exterior and brass fittings. In seconds, he pulled up alongside her, braking hard.

"Where are you going?" he called out over the engine's roar. His driving goggles were in place, though his tweed duster was not to be seen.

"For a walk," she yelled back, cupping her hands around her mouth. "Where are you going?"

"For a drive," he yelled back.

Christobel just nodded, eyeing the empty, red-tufted leather seat beside him. Suddenly she wanted nothing more than to go for a drive in the sleek, shiny motorcar.

"Good day, Miss Smyth." He reached over the door to release the brake.

"Wait!" she cried out. "May I come with you?"

He did not conceal his surprise as he turned toward her. For a moment, he said nothing. Even behind the goggles, she could see the indecision flit across his features. "Have you a hat?" he asked at last.

Christobel produced her wide straw hat and placed it on her head, hurriedly tying the ribbons beneath her chin.

"Without a veil or coat, you're going to be covered in dust—"

"I don't care," Christobel said with a shrug, hurrying around the car to the passenger side before he could argue further. In seconds, she'd climbed inside and settled beside him.

"Don't say I didn't warn you," he said with a shake of his head.

Christobel just nodded, grasping the side of the car with a squeal of delight as they set off.

Once John turned the car onto the road, he accelerated, picking up speed as Miss Smyth clutched the leather squabs so tightly that her knuckles turned white. Occasionally he'd steal a glance at her, wondering just how it was that she came to be sitting beside him, laughing gaily as the wind whipped stray tendrils of hair about her face.

Her cheeks were stained pink, her eyes bright as she shielded them from the ubiquitous cloud of dust.

"Faster?" he asked, shouting to be heard over the engine's roar.

"Oh, yes!"

He obliged her, smiling inwardly as she leaned into him, clutching at his sleeve. Entirely content, he drove on aimlessly for a quarter hour, headed vaguely toward the Pennines in the distance.

There was a lovely spot ahead, he realized, a bluff with excellent views of Cranford down below. Minutes later, he guided the car off the main road and turned onto a narrow lane.

"Are we stopping?" she asked, releasing her death grip on his forearm.

"I thought you might like to catch your breath for a

moment." He cut the motor and removed his driving gloves and goggles before climbing out and hastening around the car to hand her down.

"Goodness, I am rather breathless," she said, taking his hand and stepping down. "I don't remember when I've had so much fun."

He was acutely aware that he still held her small hand in his. Suddenly self-conscious, he released it and stepped away, attempting to brush the dust from his coat.

"Look at me!" She reached up to tuck her hair back under her hat, laughing softly as she did so. "I'm a fright. Whatever am I going to tell Edith when we return?"

She did look rather like a chimney sweep, he thought, suppressing a smile. "You've got . . . ahem, right there." He indicated her left cheek. "A smudge of some sort. Here." He reached for his handkerchief and handed it to her. "Right there, on your cheek."

"Here?" she asked. She swiped at it, entirely missing it.

"No, higher." He shifted his feet uncomfortably. "There," he said, resisting the urge to run the pad of his thumb over her smooth, rosy skin.

Her second attempt was no more successful. "Better?"

"Not quite."

"Here," she said, handing him back the handkerchief. "You do it."

John took a deep, fortifying breath, then nodded.

"I don't bite," she teased. "At least, not often."

Taking the square of linen, he firmly wiped away the smudge, noticing for the first time a smattering of freckles across the bridge of her nose. "There," he said gruffly, feeling foolish as he stuffed the handkerchief back into his pocket. How he longed to trace the freckles with his fingertip, to trail kisses in their wake.

"It's a lovely day, isn't it?" she asked brightly.

John leaned back against the motorcar, one boot resting upon the running board, his hands thrust into his pockets. "Indeed it is."

"I had to escape the house for a bit. Do you think they've noticed my absence yet?"

He nodded. "Likely so."

"And how are you enjoying Edith's party so far, Mr. Leyden?"

"Tolerably well, I suppose."

He heard her sigh. "That's progress. Four words," she muttered.

"Pardon?"

"Four words, Mr. Leyden. That seems to be your limit today. I'm only trying to make conversation. You could put a bit more effort into it. After all, you were nearly chatty last time we met. In the greenhouse," she added, as if he had forgotten.

For a moment he simply stared at her, entirely bewildered. "You must excuse me, Miss Symth." If only he didn't become so damned tongue-tied around her. If only he could converse easily and charmingly, as Sir Edmund did.

When he glanced back at her, he was surprised to see the color had risen in her cheeks, and her eyes, once so merry, were now flashing angrily. "That's it? I must excuse you? Really, Mr. Leyden, you might try harder."

"I don't always find idle talk . . . comfortable, Miss Smyth. I did not mean to offend—"

She advanced on him. "Yet I offend *you,* don't I? What is it about me that you find so distasteful?"

*What the devil was she talking about?* "You misunderstand, Miss Smyth."

"Is your good opinion so very hard to come by? Heaven knows why I should care what you think of me. Perhaps it's the challenge; I'm not quite certain." She shook her head, then raised her flashing gaze to meet his. "All I know is, all these years I've had to suffer beneath your disapproving stare, and I've no idea what I've done to earn it. Pray, enlighten me."

Did she not realize the double standard? All these years, she'd looked down her pretty nose at him, perhaps pitied him, yet she expected him to behave like a lapdog, panting after her like Sir Edmund did? Like all the young gentlemen of her acquaintance did?

And why would he? While she coquetted with every other man about, he might as well have been invisible to her.

"I realize that I'm no gentleman, Miss Smyth," he said angrily, his blood thrumming hotly through his veins. "That I lack the education and good breeding of the men you're used to associating with."

She tipped her chin into the air. "I've always treated you as an equal."

"Have you?" he asked harshly, unable to keep the accusatory tone out of his voice.

"I always supposed I did."

"How very charitable of you," he bit out.

Tears gathered in the corners of her eyes, clinging to the dark fringe of her lashes. "I suppose that explains why you despise my company, then."

At the sight of her stricken expression, his temper vanished at once. Bloody hell, he hadn't meant to hurt her. "I admit I am often uncomfortable in your company," he said softly, "but not because I find you lacking in any respect. Besides, you have an army of gentlemen like Sir Edmund to do your bidding—"

"Sir Edmund is a silly fool. You think I wish to have men like him pawing—" She stopped short, one hand rising to cover her mouth. "Forgive me," she said at last. "Perhaps we should head back to Hadley Hall."

He swore under his breath, pushing off the side of the

motorcar and moving toward her before he could reconsider what he was about to do.

In seconds he reached her side and placed his hands on either side of her face, his thumbs gently stroking her silky skin. "I'm uncomfortable in your presence not because I have an ill opinion of you, Christobel, but because I'm constantly fighting the urge to do this," he said roughly, his mouth slanting toward her trembling lips.

At first she stood motionless, her arms stiff by her sides. As his mouth opened against hers, her hands rose, sliding sensuously up the back of his coat, to his neck. With a small moan, she pulled him closer, her own hot, wet mouth soft and inviting.

He kissed her hungrily, his mouth hard and insistent as she pressed her body against his, her fingers digging into the corded muscles in his neck, her stomach firm against his rock-hard cock.

At last he retreated, his mouth moving down the column of her neck, to her throat. "And this," he added, pressing his lips against her collar, where her pulse fluttered wildly. He inhaled her sweet, familiar scent, unable to bear meeting her gaze, to risk seeing displeasure there in her face.

"I had no idea," she said at last, breathlessly. "I thought . . . I thought you despised me."

Emboldened, he met her gaze. "I only despised myself for wanting something I could not have—something I can never have."

"Except twice now . . . good heavens, if anyone were to see us!"

"No one can see us. We're well off the main road, Christobel."

"You called me 'Christobel,'" she said softly, a smile tipping the corners of her mouth.

"Such a lovely name."

"Goodness, Mr. Leyden, I think you've made my knees go weak. I need to sit down."

He led her back to the motorcar and handed her up to the seat. For a moment, neither spoke. John looked off toward the bluff, toward the town in the valley below. Cranford—his home. He could see Leyden Mills in the distance, their smokestacks rising toward the sky, reigning over the bustling town.

"What do you think of the view from here?" he asked, unable to disguise the pride in his voice.

"It's dreadful, isn't it?" came her reply. "So . . . so crowded and dirty and . . ." Her voice trailed off as she met his gaze. "And you love it, don't you? You must forgive me. I did not mean to offend—"

"Don't apologize for speaking your mind, Miss Smyth." He reached for his gloves and goggles and climbed in beside her. He must have been mad to ever think that he and Christobel . . . no. *No.* He would not allow his thoughts to travel that route.

"You're right, we should head back to Hadley Hall," he said. Without waiting for her reply, he reached for the plunger pump on the dash and quickly pumped air pressure into the fuel tank. When that was done, he set the throttle and climbed out to turn the crank on the front of the car. In seconds, the engine roared to life, and John climbed back in and unlatched the hand brake.

Their return to Hadley Hall was accomplished in utter silence.

# CHAPTER 6

"Wherever have you been?" Edith asked with a scowl. Sir Edmund trailed behind her.

Christobel did her best to school her features into a pleasant expression. "I was sitting with Marie. I fear I let the time slip away from me."

It was true, after all. As soon as she and Mr. Leyden had returned, she'd hurried in and had Simpson return her clothing and hair to their proper order. She'd immediately gone belowstairs to check on the recuperating housemaid, as she'd done each and every day since the girl's assault. Unused to such idleness, poor Marie was going mad with boredom.

Edith just shook her head. "I should have known."

"Marie?" Sir Edmund asked, his ginger-colored brows drawn over bright blue eyes.

"One of my housemaids," Edith supplied. "She was . . . er . . . recently injured."

Christobel nodded. "And while she's abed, I'm teaching her to read." Indeed, she'd found an old primer in the library and started with the basics, and Marie had shown a quick, sharp mind.

Sir Edmund looked at her as if she'd gone mad. "Teaching her to read? A housemaid? Why would a maid need to read?"

Christobel bristled. "And why not? Such a dull, dreary life, the life of a maid. Should she not be able to escape into the worlds created by the Brontës or Miss Austen? Or perhaps you'd think Mr. Dickens more appropriate?"

Sir Edmund rocked back on his heels, looking entirely flummoxed. "Well, er, perhaps. Still, I don't think it's your place—"

"Come, Sir Edmund," Edith interrupted, casting her a scathing look. "Everyone is gathering in the drawing room. I've got a delightful entertainment planned for this afternoon."

Looking suitably repentant for her outburst, Christobel followed the pair out and into the drawing room, eager to see what diversion Edith had in store for them. Anything to take her mind off John Leyden.

*Hide-and-seek.* Not what Christobel would have hoped for, even though it had become all the rage of late. Even now, Edith was drawing names from two hats, one holding the ladies' names, one the men's. Once everyone was paired up, one couple would be designated the seekers, and everyone else would head out in search of hiding places, either indoors or out in the park. The game could go on for hours, as those "found" joined in the search.

Christobel generally found the game tedious at best— she did not enjoy sitting still, just hanging about waiting to be discovered. But now, as she eyed the hats filled with folded slips of paper, her mind raced. *Not Sir Edmund. Please, anyone but him.* Silly, of course, as he was the perfect gentleman. Still, she had no wish to be alone with him. What if he were to attempt to take liberties? Thank God Mr. Leyden was nowhere to be seen, because if she were to—

"Miss Christobel Smyth," Edith's voice called out gaily. She reached into the dark gray bowler hat that Jasper held aloft. "And Mr. John Leyden."

Christobel's heart skipped a beat. She saw the confusion on Edith's face. Clearly this was not the outcome her sister had hoped for, either.

"I told my cousin I would not take 'no' for an answer," Jasper said in reply to Edith's questioning gaze. "It shall be great fun, won't it, John?"

Christobel's gaze darted about the room, and then she saw him, tucked into the shadows by the door, looking every bit as uncomfortable as she felt.

Still, there was no way to beg off without publicly insulting him. She had no choice but to go off with him, alone, for God knows how long.

Minutes later, the boundaries of play had been set and Edith and Jasper were named seekers. *Time to pair up with one's partner.* Christobel took a deep, fortifying breath and made her way toward Mr. Leyden, who still stood where she'd seen him last, as immobile as a statue, leaning against her sister's William Morris–papered wall, watching her approach.

She swallowed hard as she continued to pick her way across the room toward him, his icy gaze bold and unwavering. His arms were folded across his chest, one knee bent, the sole of one boot pressed flat against the wall in an insolent pose. He looked rakish, almost dangerous . . . nothing at all like the bland, boring John Leyden she remembered.

Heat pooled in her belly; excitement raced through her veins. Dear God, whatever had come over her? Over him? This was madness—her and John Leyden, of all people.

Christobel was nearly breathless by the time she reached his side, though she could not credit why. "I suppose we shall have to make the best of it," she said before she'd thought better of it.

Instantly, his eyes darkened a hue. A muscle in his jaw flickered, and she realized that, once again, she'd insulted him. Blast it, but her wits seemed to abandon her whenever she was in his presence.

She'd been seventeen when she'd first met Mr. Leyden, when Edith had become engaged to Jasper. Nearly eight years ago, she realized. So many days spent in his company, and yet he'd never before affected her as he did now. Whatever had changed, and in so short a time?

After an uncomfortable pause, Mr. Leyden pushed off the wall and offered his arm. "Shall we?"

Christobel glanced back over her shoulder. Edith leaned toward Jasper with a furrowed brow and whispered in his ear; he nodded in reply, then cocked his head toward the door.

Her legs trembling, Christobel turned back toward Mr. Leyden and tucked her hand into the crook of his arm. "I know just the place," she said.

*The old gristmill.* It sat abandoned, not far from the ornamental pond. She'd seen a cat dart inside just yesterday. A female cat, she'd determined, and dubbed her Clementine. Fearful and skittish, Clementine was clearly not used to human interaction, but Christobel was determined to tame her. She'd asked Jasper's groundskeeper to bring food and water to the mill each day. Going there now would give her a chance to check on the poor cat and see that the groundskeeper was heeding her request.

Mr. Leyden allowed Christobel to lead him out without comment. Other pairs were dashing this way and that, whispering among themselves, but she and Mr. Leyden walked in silence.

"Might you tell me where we're headed?" he said at

last, startling Christobel as they ducked under a cottonwood's low branches.

"The old gristmill. There"—she pointed to a clearing just ahead and to the left—"beyond that maple."

"You're sure that's within bounds?"

Christobel nodded. "Quite sure. Come, let's hurry."

Minutes later, they stepped inside and closed the door on rusted hinges behind them.

"Here, Clementine!" Christobel called out. "Here, kitty, kitty."

"Clementine?" Mr. Leyden asked, looking about with a scowl.

"A lovely gray and white cat. I found her here just yesterday. Oh, good—I see Mr. Carter has brought food for the poor beast." There were two dishes in the corner beside a wooden trestle table and bench, one containing water, the other a half-eaten piece of fish. "I wonder where she's gone off to?"

Mr. Leyden resumed his previous pose, leaning against the mill's dusty planked wall. "Jasper tells me that you're teaching Marie to read," he said, folding his arms across his broad chest. He'd finally abandoned his somber black dress and was attired more appropriately today in a buff-colored pinstriped suit with a gold-striped waistcoat and matching four-in-hand cravat. His tan oxfords looked freshly shined, his gold cufflinks buffed to perfection.

"Indeed, I am teaching her to read," Christobel said. "And I suppose you're going to scold me about it, too?"

His brows drew together. "Why would I do that?"

Christobel wiped her damp palms across her skirt. "I don't know. Sir Edmund seemed to think it folly to teach a servant such a skill."

"I would think that someone in her position would welcome the escape afforded by the ability to read."

"Precisely!" Christobel said, her cheeks warming with

pleasure. At last, someone understood her way of thinking on the matter. "The poor girl is perishing from boredom right now, forced to remain abed. The reading lessons are giving her pleasure, and she's catching on so quickly, too."

"I'm glad to hear it. I've recently started a free school at our mill for the workers' children. In most cases, it's their only chance for an education. At first my father and brother scoffed at the notion. The children will be put to work soon enough, they said, and book learning will be of no use to them. But now I think they're coming around to my way of thinking."

"What a lovely thing to do," Christobel said. "How very generous of you."

Mr. Leyden suddenly seemed uncomfortable. "Yes, well," he muttered, unable to meet her gaze.

Christobel's breath hitched uncomfortably in her chest as she realized how wrong she'd been about him, how vastly she'd underestimated him. Traits she'd seen as weaknesses were actually signs of his good character—his brooding silence hid a deep sensitivity; his supercilious nature a response to what he saw as snobbery. She'd dared to fault his quiet sensibility, when in fact she should have applauded his inability to indulge in empty, meaningless talk and mindless flattery. "Perhaps we're more alike than we believed ourselves to be," she said at last.

She was right, John realized with a start. All these years they'd been acquainted, and he'd never really known her—never known that she was the type to teach a servant girl to read, to make sure that a stray cat was fed and cared for. Instead, he'd thought her vain, selfish, even. How far off the mark he'd been, and how his heart—among other organs—swelled with the knowledge.

Desire coursing hotly through his veins, he watched

her, mentally measuring the distance between them. Three yards, perhaps? No more than five. How he wanted to close that distance, to take her in his arms.

"Your limp," she said, so softly he could barely make out the words. "I . . . I know it's horribly rude of me to ask, but, well, considering what we've shared these past few days . . ." She trailed off, her cheeks suddenly red.

He didn't wish to speak of it, not now. The last thing he wanted was a reminder of his weakness, his physical imperfection. "I'd rather not discuss it," he bit out.

"Of course," she murmured. "I should not have presumed—"

"Pray, forgive me, Miss Smyth." *Damn it.* Why had he spoken so sharply? It was a legitimate question, he realized, and she deserved an answer.

"Christobel," she corrected. "Please."

He nodded, rubbing his chin. "Christobel, then. I was a boy, no more than ten or eleven at the time, and—"

"Don't," she interrupted. "You've no need to speak of it if it makes you uncomfortable."

"My mother sent me around to some of the workers' homes to deliver baskets of fruit," he continued, not heeding her protestation. Suddenly he wanted to tell her; needed to. "Fruit was scarce, you see, and rickets common in the poorer homes. As I was just about to knock upon a door, I heard a baby wailing, a woman screaming, crockery breaking. For some stupid reason, I pushed open the door. Inside, I found one of my father's foremen laying a horsewhip upon his cowering wife, a baby crying in the cradle. The man reeked of spirits; the entire house stunk of it.

"Like a fool, I charged in, taking on a man twice my size. I was no match for him, of course. He flayed open the skin on my arms, broke my leg in three places. I was lucky to get out of there alive."

The color drained from her face. "Dear God! That's dreadful. I hope he paid for his crime."

"Two years in jail. Not six months after his release, he killed his wife. An accident, he claimed, but I knew it was a lie. I'd seen the hate in his eyes. Less than a year later, he took his own life, the cowardly lout."

"Good riddance," Christobel said hotly.

"Anyway, to answer your question, my leg never healed properly. I've been lame ever since."

She took two steps toward him, closing the gap. "It's a badge of honor, then. You should be proud. You were brave and righteous and—"

"Foolish," he supplied with a wince. "Had I not been in such bad shape, my father would have taken a whip to me himself."

She tipped her chin in the air, the same defiant pose he'd seen her strike so many times over the past few days. "Then he would be the fool, not you."

Two more tentative steps. Another two, perhaps three, and she would be an arm's reach away. If she came any closer, he'd have no choice but to take her in his arms. Devil take it, he'd ravish her, right here, right now, given an ounce of encouragement.

"Cousin John?" she said breathlessly, moving on silent feet to stand directly before him.

"Just 'John.' We're no blood relation." As his cock swelled painfully against his trousers, all rational thought fled his mind. Call him base, call him coarse and ungentlemanly, but he was suddenly consumed with the idea of getting her naked. *Now.*

Christobel's tongue darted out to moisten her lips. "No, we're not blood relations, are we?" She was close now; so close he could smell her sweet scent. "Dear God, I . . . I want . . ." She trailed off, shaking her head, confusion playing out upon her features.

"You want what?" he urged, reaching for her hand

and drawing her closer still. His heart pounded against his ribs; his blood roared through his veins. "Say it, Christobel." *Want me,* his mind urged silently. *Want me, as I want you.*

She was so close now that her breasts grazed his coat. Summoning every ounce of strength he possessed, he released her hand and balled his own into fists by his sides. He could not touch her till he knew her mind, till he had her permission. *Naked,* his mind screamed. God help him, but he wanted her naked. How many years had he imagined her naked, lying on his bed, her glorious hair spread out around her.

"John, I . . ."

He closed his eyes, waiting for more, steeling himself for disappointment. He felt a rush of air and opened his eyes, only to find her moving quickly across the room, away from him, toward the door. Good God, he was going to die of sexual frustration, right then and there. She didn't want him, she was leaving, she was—

*Locking the door.* The heavy bolt slid into place with a squeal of protesting metal.

That was all the encouragement he needed. He met her halfway, lifting her off her feet and carrying her toward the room's darkest corner, away from the windows. As soon as he set her back on her feet, their lips met, hot and hungry. He pressed her back against the wall as her hands moved over his chest, tugging at his coat. He shrugged out of it, dropping it to the dusty floor without care.

"Please, John," she murmured, tearing her mouth from his. "Please. Now."

Damn it to hell, but he was going to oblige her, before she changed her mind. He found the fastening on her belt and tugged it free, then pulled her blouse from her skirt's waistband. Seconds later, his hands slid up her belly, over her corset and whatever undergarments she wore, cursing them all the while.

When his fingers reached the top of her corset, he felt skin at last—skin as smooth and satiny as the finest silk. With a groan, he tugged at the coarse fabric of her corset, dragging it downward, ripping seams as he did so. At last his fingers found his prize, her nipples pebbling to his touch.

He heard her gasp at the intimate contact. "Oh, God, John . . . what . . . oh!"

Without thinking, he raised her blouse, fighting with the fabric as his tongue captured one firm, rosy peak. With a soft moan, she arched against him as he suckled her, his hands cupping her breasts. They were round and full, exactly as he'd imagined them all these years. *Perfect.*

Devil take it, she was exquisite. He was going to spill his seed right then and there if he kept on. A growl of frustration tore from his throat as he forced himself to retreat.

But soon her fingers were unbuttoning his waistcoat, then moving on to his shirt and cravat. He stood, motionless, allowing her to undress him, barely able to believe it. At last his shirt was open, his waistcoat and cravat tossed carelessly aside.

"You're beautiful," she said breathlessly. "Like . . . like the finest sculpture." Her fingers trailed up his torso, drawing gooseflesh in their wake.

Christobel let out her breath in a rush, unable to believe how perfect, how sculpted his chest was. Never had she imagined . . . She let the thought trail off. She couldn't think, couldn't breathe, couldn't do anything but reach for his trousers with trembling fingers. Dear lord, but she'd never wanted anything this badly. Her entire body ached with it—her legs trembled violently, her thighs were damp with need. She fumbled with his trousers, silently urging him to complete the task.

Mercifully, he did. Next thing she knew, he was reaching beneath her skirts, tugging down her drawers. Silently, she said a prayer of thanks that she'd decided to don plain drawers that day rather than her ungainly combination. She heard John curse under his breath as he fought with her skirts, finally bunching them up around her waist as he pressed her back against the wall. Instinctively, she raised one leg and wrapped it around his hips.

"Have you any idea how long I've wanted this, Christobel?" he asked, his voice so filled with need that her heart accelerated dangerously, thumping noisily against her rib cage. "How I've dreamt of this?"

"Now!" she urged breathlessly. "Please."

His eyes met hers—his gaze steady and unblinking, full of heat and lust and wanting. "I don't want to hurt you," he said gruffly.

"Then do it quickly!" she said, unable to stand the wait a second longer.

She felt the tip of him, tentatively probing her entrance. Soft and silky, yet hard and insistent all at once. In one sharp motion, he plunged inside, clutching her buttocks hard as he buried his face in her neck. She bit her lip, fighting the urge to cry out.

"Oh, God, Christobel," he ground out. "I can't . . . I can't stop."

"Don't, John. Don't stop." The pain was exquisite, sharp and burning, yet it began to subside almost as quickly as it had appeared. She felt herself stretch as he filled her, inch by glorious inch.

Tilting her hips, she urged him on, urged him into a rhythm, one she quickly matched, thrust for thrust. She felt wild, wicked, wanton. *Wonderful.*

"Your cunny's so tight, so wet," he murmured, his lips hot against her neck.

Heaven help her, she'd never heard such coarse words spoken aloud. She knew she should be shocked—outraged, even. And yet . . . and yet she'd never heard anything so erotic, so sinfully arousing.

"Look at me, John," she demanded, suddenly desperate to see his face, to look into those piercing eyes, so full of longing, while he said such wicked things to her.

His gaze rose to meet hers, their lips just inches apart, their heavy breaths mingling as their bodies moved as one. His eyes were heavy-lidded, the pupils nearly fully dilated. "You're so very lovely, Christobel. Christ," he swore, the corded muscles in his neck standing out.

She ran her fingers through his hair, damp now from perspiration. Sighing with pleasure, she trailed a finger down his temple, across his whiskers, over the curve of his lips. Into his mouth her finger dipped, and soon he was sucking it, sucking her finger with a firm pressure that made her gasp, her entire body beginning to buck against his as the speed of his thrusts increased. Nothing had prepared her for this—this overload of pleasure, this complete and total surrender of her senses.

At once, everything began to quiver inside her, to tingle as she hovered over some unknown precipice, just waiting to tumble over into . . . something. "Good God, John, harder. Oh!" She bit her lip till she tasted blood.

And then everything seemed to explode, pinpoints of light nearly blinding her as she closed her eyes in ecstasy, her insides pulsing against his shaft, which was still buried deep inside her.

He called out her name, his voice breaking on the last syllable as he roughly withdrew himself and pressed his still-erect organ against her. A hot, sticky wetness pumped out onto her thigh, warming her bare skin as she attempted to catch her breath.

"Oh, John," she murmured, wanting to cry as a vast emptiness tore through her. Oh, how she wanted him back inside her, wanted him to hold her in his arms until she stopped trembling.

Grasping her chin with his thumb and forefinger, he raised her face, forcing her gaze to meet his. "Christobel, I"—he swallowed hard, and all she could think was that if he apologized, she would scream.

And then she heard a peal of laughter, coming from outside. "Shall we try in here?" a voice called out.

*Edith.*

"Dear God, no!" she whispered, shoving down her skirts and attempting to tug up her drawers, all at once.

Any moment now, Edith would discover them. And when she did . . .

*No.* It was simply unthinkable.

# CHAPTER 7

The next moments were a blur of frenzied activity as both John and Christobel set about righting their clothing. Any moment now, Edith would be at the door—the locked door. However would they explain it?

Not a minute later, the door rattled loudly. "It's locked," she heard Edith say. "Can you look through the window there?"

Christobel shrank back against the wall, John beside her, his breath coming as fast as hers. *Please, God, don't let us be discovered. Not like this.*

Not two years past, her sister Miriam had been caught in a compromising position with a young army officer. Miriam had married him straightaway, though the gossip had taken months to die down. At the time, Christobel's mother had begged her to never put her in such an embarrassing situation as Miriam had, and Christobel had been indignant. She would never do anything of the sort, she'd sworn. And now here she was, breaking her promise in the worst way possible. Why, this would be the scandal of the year!

"There's no one inside," Jasper called out. "Come on, let's keep searching."

Had Jasper seen them? She couldn't be sure. Her eyes began to fill with tears, but she willed them to remain at bay.

John reached for her hand. "I'm so sorry, Christobel," he said, his voice soft and gentle.

She squeezed her eyes shut and shook her head. "Don't apologize. Just don't . . . don't say anything."

"They're gone now. Follow me out, and we'll make our way back around the pond. We can claim we were hiding in the grove and grew tired of the game."

"But the grove's out of bounds," she said, her throat constricting uncomfortably. Blast it, if only her heart would slow down. It felt like it was about to burst.

"Better out of bounds than admitting we were here."

"Of course," she said with a nod. "You're right. I . . . I don't know what I was thinking."

"Follow me." He reached for her hand. "And don't say a word."

"I'm sorry, Sir Edmund," Christobel said brightly. "You were saying?" She set her wineglass down on the table, horrified to see that her hand shook as she did so.

"I was just saying that you haven't touched a bite of your supper. Are you feeling unwell?"

Ever since both Miss Allens had come down with a touch of *la grippe,* everyone worried over the slightest digestive twinge, though Beatrice and Grace seemed entirely recovered. In fact, Beatrice sat on the opposite side of Sir Edmund now, as vivacious as ever.

Christobel had done everything possible to direct the man's attention toward Beatrice rather than herself throughout the interminable meal, with very little success. It would seem that Sir Edmund would not be deterred on his mission to flatter her as excessively as possible, the ninny.

Could he not take a hint?

"I'm feeling perfectly well, thank you." She pushed away her plate of champagne-and-primrose jelly, forcing her lips to curve into a smile. "I vow, I must have overindulged in tea cakes this afternoon. I suppose they ruined my appetite."

"But not your figure," he answered cheerfully. "It remains as lovely as ever."

She resisted the urge to roll her eyes. Instead, she retrieved her wineglass and took a sip of the scarlet-colored liquid. It took an amazing amount of restraint to keep from tossing back the entire contents of the glass at once. *I'd like to be tipsy,* she thought. *So tipsy that I cannot think or feel or remember.*

John sat mere inches away, on her left. He'd spent most of the meal engaged in quiet conversation with Miss Bartlett, who sat to his left, looking lovely in a gauzy, soft mauve gown.

Christobel's mouth went suddenly dry. She took yet another sip of sweet wine, wishing beyond hope that it would soothe her nerves.

"May I pour you some more?" Sir Edmund asked, reaching for the cut-glass decanter that sat before them.

She examined her glass, surprised to find it almost empty. She'd need more, if she were to get through this night—thankfully the last night of Edith's party.

"Yes, thank you," she said, pushing the glass toward him.

"You must come and visit us at Longberry, Miss Smyth," he said as he poured. "You and Mrs. Smyth both. My sister Josephine acts as my hostess, and she'd delight in your company."

"Longberry?" Her tongue felt strangely thick in her mouth.

"Indeed. My estate in Kent, near Tunbridge Wells. It's particularly lovely in the springtime—rolling green pastures carpeted with bluebells, the magnolias coming into flower, wisteria climbing the back of the house. If Kent is the Garden of England, then Longberry is its crown jewel. You simply must see it."

"It does sound charming," she murmured.

"I believe you'd feel right at home there, Miss Smyth," he said, a bit too pointedly.

Christobel took another sip of wine. He was waiting for a response, no doubt, but she could think of nothing to say that would not offer encouragement.

Mercifully, Beatrice asked him a question about his gardens, temporarily diverting his attention. Taking a deep, fortifying breath, she placed her hands in her lap, twisting her napkin between her fingers. Every fiber of her being was painfully aware of John's presence there beside her. For perhaps, oh, the tenth time in the past hour, the sleeve of his coat brushed her bare arm, sending shivers down her spine.

If anyone knew . . . if anyone found out what they'd done, she'd be ruined. *Ruined.* However could she have been so foolish? *No one knows,* she assured herself. Just as they'd planned, they'd left the old mill and made their way around the pond, and then back to the house. They'd been scolded for abandoning the game, but if anyone had noticed anything was amiss, they gave no indication of it, not even Edith.

And now she was forced to sit, hurting in places she'd never before hurt, and make polite conversation with Sir Edmund while her stomach pitched queerly and her whole body ached for the other man beside her, who was seemingly oblivious to her presence—a fact that bothered her far more than she liked to admit.

Beneath the table she clutched her skirts, wishing desperately to stop her hands from trembling so.

And then she felt it—a finger, not her own, grazing her thigh. John's hand, searching for hers. She swallowed hard, ordering her features to remain impassive as he stroked her wrist with featherlight touches. His skin was hot, his own fingers trembling as he laced them with hers.

Her body responded intuitively, dampening her drawers with need. She trained her gaze on the plate changer before her, refusing to turn toward him though she was exquisitely aware of him watching her with a sidelong, furtive glance.

Oh, how she wanted him! She knew it was wrong—dangerous, even. And yet she could not help herself. The events of the day had changed her irrevocably and nothing in her life would ever be the same again.

At the far end of the table, Edith caught her eye. "Heavens, Christobel, you're dreadfully flushed!" she called out, her voice rising in alarm.

"Am I?" she managed, her hand still joined with John's beneath the table.

"Indeed, Miss Smyth," Sir Edmund offered.

John cleared his throat. "Perhaps she's only sunburnt. She was out in the grove without a parasol this afternoon for nearly an hour."

"And I suppose she refused to stay beneath the shade of a tree," Edith said with a laugh. "That sounds just like Christobel."

John released her hand and trailed his fingers across her thigh. Somehow, despite the layers of clothing and undergarments, his thumb managed to find the sensitive nub of flesh between her legs, and Christobel could not help but gasp as he stroked her, right there at the supper table.

"I say, Miss Smyth," Sir Edmund said sotto voce, "I shall be very sorry to take my leave tomorrow."

"I . . . oh! I shall be sorry, too," she said hurriedly. Anything to shut him up.

Dear God, this had to stop. John had gone mad, behaving like this at her sister's supper table! Worse still, she was allowing it, enjoying it. Of course, after what they'd done in the abandoned mill—

"If you'll excuse me," she said abruptly, rising on wobbly legs. She nearly knocked over her wineglass with her elbow, but caught it just in time, clasping her fingers tightly around the stem. "I . . . I think perhaps I *am* unwell. If you'll excuse me."

"Poor Miss Smyth," she heard Sir Edmund say as she rushed out of the room. "I do hope it isn't *la grippe.*"

A quarter hour later, Christobel lay tucked into bed, staring up at the ceiling. Her stomach pitched and railed, but not from *la grippe. I'm a coward,* she realized as confusion and indecision rattled her brain.

It was the second time in so many days that she'd falsely claimed a malady and run off with her tail between her legs. An unusual occurrence, as Christobel had never before lacked the fortitude to face her troubles head-on, no matter what form they took.

But this . . . this was beyond the pale. She'd allowed a man—John Leyden, at that—to touch her in ways no other man had ever touched her. She'd given up her virtue without the slightest hesitation, without even considering the consequences of her actions. No man had ever tempted her as John had—in fact, no other man had ever come close.

In just a matter of days, she'd gone from almost complete indifference toward him to . . . to this. Just what *this* was, she wasn't entirely sure. Admiration? Lust? Love? All three, perhaps?

The sound of laughter drifted up from the drawing room below. Any moment now, the musicians would begin tuning their instruments, readying for the concert Edith had planned for the evening's entertainment.

Her heart racing, Christobel turned over on her side to face the window where a faint sliver of moonlight shone through the gap between the heavy drapes and the window sash. A frisson of fear shot through her belly as she clutched at the linens.

*Whatever is going through John's mind right now?* She could only wonder what his feelings were toward her, what his intentions were. As was his fashion, he'd said very little. *I must speak with him,* she resolved. *Alone.* First thing in the morning, she would seek him out. She would speak frankly, openly, honestly.

Of course, exactly *what* she'd say, she had no idea. She could only hope that, by the morn, everything would at last be crystal clear.

Until then, well . . . what was the harm in reliving every touch, every wicked sensation? Burying her face in the pillow, she muffled a groan. Surely it wasn't at all proper for her to have enjoyed it as much as she had.

Still, she couldn't help but reach down, under her silk nightgown, to the place that John had so expertly stroked at the supper table. Where he learned such skills, she did not wish to know—but that didn't mean she couldn't appreciate them.

A moment later, a knock sounded upon the door. Startled, she sat up, clutching the bedclothes around her. "Simpson?" she called out, her heart thumping noisily.

The door opened, a dark figure slipping inside. "Shh," someone whispered, then turned the key in the lock.

Downstairs, the musicians began to play. "John?" she whispered. "Dear God, please say it's you."

"We must be quiet," he said, moving toward her in the darkness.

Christobel could barely make out his face. "Are you mad? Surely we'll get caught."

"No, we won't." He sat down beside her, cupping her face in his hands. "Everyone is downstairs, enjoying the concert. I'll be gone before the last note is played."

Christobel shook her head wildly, trying to clear away the cobwebs. "I'm imagining this. I must be drunk—too much wine."

"Do you want me to go?" he asked. "Just say the word and—"

"No!" she breathed, laying a palm against his cheek, now rough with stubble. "Don't go. Stay."

She felt him nod, and she sighed in relief. "I was just . . . just thinking about you," she whispered, inhaling his now-familiar masculine scent.

The music below grew louder, more lively, though she could not name the piece.

"Don't speak," he said, his mouth drawing closer to hers, his breath warm on her cheek. "Just let me show you"—his lips brushed tantalizingly against hers—"what *I* was just thinking about," he finished before his mouth crushed hers.

They kissed deeply, hungrily. Her senses reeled, the room seeming to tip on its axis as she gave herself up to every sensation, every touch, every smell, every taste. An electric current raced over her skin as he pressed her back against the pillows, his body held rigid above hers.

"Your hair is so soft, so beautiful," he said, curling one lock around his finger. "I've never before seen it down."

Laughing softly, Christobel took a tendril and drew it across his cheek—tempting, teasing.

With a groan, he reached for the hem of her night-gown, tugging it out from beneath her hips. In one quick motion, he slipped it over her head, leaving her entirely bare. Despite the heat running through her veins, she shivered.

"All these years you've tortured me," he growled. "Now you must let me torture you."

His mouth was on her skin now, warming it, trailing hot kisses from the curve of her shoulder down to her breasts, her belly. Desire pooled in the pit of her stomach, making her breath come faster as he made lazy circles with his tongue just below her navel.

She writhed beneath him, nearly crazed with lust. "John," she whimpered, arching up off the mattress, instinctively knowing where his mouth was going next before it happened, before she felt his tongue *there*.

His breath hot and ragged against her, he parted her with his tongue, did things she could not name to her tender flesh, things that made her entire body quiver.

As if on cue, the music swelled to a crescendo in the drawing room below as he brought her closer and closer to release. Her hips began to buck as she gave herself up to the wondrous sensations.

This was torture, yes. Delicious, wonderful torture. For a split second she teetered there on the edge of ecstasy. And then, just as the last plaintive notes sounded from below, she tumbled headlong into the abyss, turning her face to the pillow to muffle her cries of pleasure.

Applause rang out as Christobel struggled to catch her breath. She felt John move away, a rush of cold air replacing his body's warmth. "Don't go," she murmured, reaching for his hand.

"I must," he said, his voice a hoarse whisper. "Though it's near enough killing me."

Their fingers met, then slipped apart as he moved away, toward the door.

Still panting, she fell back against the pillows, her damp hair fanning out around her. "John?" she whispered dazedly, wondering if perhaps this had been a lovely dream.

"Tomorrow, Christobel," he said, then slipped out.

Not five minutes later, she fell into a deep, restful sleep, a smile still playing upon her lips.

# CHAPTER 8

Christobel didn't get to speak with John first thing in the morning, after all.

*Tomorrow, Christobel,* he'd said. Yet tomorrow was here, and he was gone. Had she dreamed it? She'd overslept, thanks to the wine she'd drunk at dinner, and John had apparently left in his motorcar just after dawn with no word of where he'd gone off to, or when he would return.

Instead, she spent the first few hours of her day helping Edith bid farewell to her guests, trying all the while not to look over her shoulder, toward the road, at five-minute intervals.

The last to go was Sir Edmund, who had kissed her hand and begged her to consider a visit to Longberry come springtime, appealing to her mother when Christobel had answered as noncommittally as possible. Of course they would, Mother had assured him, nudging her in her ribs as she did so.

With a sigh of relief, Christobel watched his enormous Mercedes touring car rumble off down the road.

As soon as he was gone, Christobel hurried inside and summoned Simpson to help her change into her cycling suit and knickerbockers.

The day was sunny and mild, only the faintest hint of an autumn chill in the air. She'd borrow Edith's bicycle and ride down the well-worn path that led off the main road toward the river. The fresh air would clear her head, give her time to think. Besides, it was better than staring at the drive, watching for the dark green motorcar.

An hour later, she returned, her skin dewy and covered with dust. *I must have a bath,* she thought, hurrying up the front stairs and across the marble-tiled front hall.

"Thank goodness, Christobel!" Edith called out, hurrying in with her hands clasped to her breasts. "I thought you'd never return!"

"I wasn't gone more than an hour," she said with a shrug.

Her sister just stood there, smiling broadly.

"Well, don't you look like the cat who swallowed the canary," Christobel teased, wiping her forehead with the back of one hand. She really *did* need a bath. "I should think you'd be ready to collapse with exhaustion by now."

Edith shook her head, her mysterious smile widening. "Come, dearest. Follow me into my sitting room. I have the most wonderful news!"

Entirely baffled as to what sort of news could make Edith grin so, she followed her sister down the corridor and into the sunlit room with pale green walls.

"So tell me your news," she said, taking a seat on the embroidered sofa beside Edith.

Edith took her hand and patted it. "Did you not see Sir Edmund's motorcar, back by the stables?"

"No, I came in the front. Besides, he left over an hour ago. Why ever would he come back?"

Edith positively beamed. "To speak to Jasper, it would seem. He's asked for your hand, dearest!"

Christobel rose, dropping Edith's hand. "Asked for my hand? Whatever do you mean?"

"He said that as soon as he drove away, he realized he was entirely sure of his heart. So he turned right back around and asked for your hand. In marriage, you goose!"

"Whatever did you tell him?" she asked, horrified. Edith thought this *good* news? Had she gone mad?

"Why, Jasper gave his approval, of course. As did Mother. Now's he waiting to speak with you himself. I've asked him to stay on a day or two more while we settle this. His valet is upstairs unpacking his things now."

"No," Christobel cried out. "You must tell him to leave. I cannot . . . I have no intention of marrying him, Edith. You cannot make me!"

"Of course I can't make you." Again, Edith reached for her hand and urged her to sit back down. "I know it's sudden," she said soothingly, as if she were speaking to a child. "After all, you've only known him a matter of days. Still, it's time enough to know that he's just the sort for you, isn't it? Tell him you require a long engagement to get better acquainted first, that's all."

Christobel's stomach lurched uncomfortably. "I'm not marrying him, Edith."

Edith's brows drew together. "I don't understand. Why, he's everything you could want in a husband. He's a baronet, after all, and he's accepted you with no dowry. Have you any idea—"

"I shouldn't care if he was the Prince of Wales," Christobel interjected hotly.

"Don't be foolish, Christobel. He's a gentleman, handsome, kind—"

"You needn't go on, Edith. You must go find Jasper at once and have him tell Sir Edmund that there's been a mistake, that I will not consider him."

Edith looked at her queerly. "I vow, Christobel, you sound almost as if . . . as if you're in love with someone else."

She *was* in love with someone else, she realized with a start—with John. She loved him, with all her heart. He was like nothing she'd imagined in a husband, and yet he was everything she wanted.

If only he wanted her, too. She thought he did, but she could not be sure. "I . . . I am in love with someone else," she stammered, warmth flooding her veins, making her flush uncomfortably.

"But . . . but who? Mother didn't mention—"

"Because Mother doesn't know. I didn't know myself, till now. Oh, Edith! I can barely believe it, but I'm in love with John Leyden." Just saying the words aloud filled her with pleasure, made her heart sing a joyful song.

Edith snatched back her hand. "That's not at all funny, Christobel. I realize you don't care for him—"

"Oh, but I do care for him. Truly, Edith. I love him desperately. Haven't you noticed, did you not see—"

"I've seen nothing but your usual quarreling," Edith snapped. "Dashing off to avoid him, claiming headaches and what have you, just because you were paired with him yesterday."

Christobel shook her head. "You've no idea how wrong you are. If I was dashing off anywhere, it was to avoid Sir Edmund, not John."

For a moment, Edith simply stared at her, her mouth slightly agape. "Do you mean this?" she asked at last. "I don't understand. You've always disliked him. Always, from the first moment you met."

"I did not know him, Edith. I thought he disliked *me*, and I suppose that pricked my pride."

"And now you know him? Come now, Christobel. It's been, what? Seven days? Eight, perhaps? You expect me to believe that you've gone from loathing to loving in a week's time?"

"I can barely credit it myself. But I know that I love him, Edith."

"And . . . and what of his feelings for you?" Edith asked delicately. "Has he given you any reason to think he has formed an attachment, as well?"

Christobel swallowed hard. "I cannot speak for him, of course. But yes, I have reason to believe that he . . . he cares for me in return."

Edith looked entirely perplexed, as if Christobel had just told her that the sky was red, the sun blue. "Even if it's true, you must realize that you can't possibly marry him. I mean, come now, Christobel. I know he's Jasper's cousin, but . . . but you must see the differences. Jasper's father was a landed gentleman, while John's owns a textile mill!"

"What difference does that make?" Christobel asked sharply.

"You know exactly what difference it makes! Besides, what will you do? Live in town, the wife of an industrialist, socializing with other . . . other people in trade? You hate the mill towns, you hate the northern provinces altogether. Whatever can you be thinking? Especially when you've got a gentleman like Sir Edmund—yes, a *gentleman*," she repeated with added emphasis, "asking for your hand."

Christobel folded her arms across her breasts. "Are you quite finished?"

Edith rose to face her, her hands planted firmly on her hips. "If you will not see reason, then I suppose I am. What an awkward position you've put us in!"

"If only someone had first asked my thoughts on the matter, there would be no awkward position at all."

Tears gathered in Edith's soft brown eyes. "Please don't think I'm criticizing John. He's a good man, and I *am* quite fond of him. It's just that I want to see you happy, Christobel—as happy as I am with Jasper. I was so sure that Sir Edmund . . . well, I thought you two so perfectly matched."

"Oh, Edith, please don't cry." This time, it was Christobel who reached for her sister's hand. "I *am* happy, don't you see? With John. I know you meant well, and in theory you were entirely correct. On paper, I suppose Sir Edmund and I *are* well matched. Only it turns out my heart knew better, that's all."

Edith gave her hand a squeeze. "You're certain?"

Christobel nodded. "Entirely so."

"I'll go speak with Jasper straightaway, then."

"And please, do everything you can to spare Sir Edmund any embarrassment. Do you think it would be better if I spoke to him myself?"

"No, I think it better if Jasper tells him. They're old chums, after all. Besides, you look like a tinker—look at you, covered in dust from head to toe. I think it best if you go have a bath."

Christobel let out a sigh of relief. Cowardly of her, she realized. Sir Edmund was a kind man, a generous man. Truly, he did not deserve this. If only Edith hadn't encouraged him so!

"Thank you, Edie," she said, holding her tongue for once in her life. "I will go have a bath. I'm quite sure I smell of *eau de corsage.*"

"Some gentlemen find the scent intoxicating, I'm told," Edith said, wrinkling her nose.

*Some gentlemen don't have the sense God gave a goat,* Christobel thought rather uncharitably. But of course, she couldn't say that. The last thing she wanted to do was vex her sister any more than she'd already done.

"Do they?" she said, instead. "How very interesting, indeed."

She glanced at the clock—it was nearly noon. Wherever was John?

# CHAPTER 9

Just as he expected, John found Christobel sitting on a mackintosh square beside the ornamental pond, a lacy parasol shading her from the sun's rays.

She must have heard his approach, yet she gave no indication of it as she stared straight ahead, watching a frog hop from one lily pad to the next as if it were the most fascinating thing in the world.

She was as elegantly attired as always, her pale, rose-colored gown trimmed in lace, the high collar ending in a row of ruffles just beneath her chin. Wide, puffy sleeves tapered at her elbows, narrowing down to her delicate wrists.

A row of bows a shade darker than the rest of her gown adorned the front of her bodice, matching the sash that tied about her waist and ended in silver tassels that fluttered on the breeze. Several strands of pearls lay across her breasts, and a wide straw hat with enormous silk flowers sat at an angle upon her head.

As always, the sight of her took his breath away, making him feel awkward, oafish. How could he ever have thought himself her equal?

Without a word, he joined her there on the grassy knoll, lowering himself to the ground beside her. For a full minute they sat there in silence, till John could stand it no more.

"You were right," he said. "It *is* lovely here this time of day."

Still, she stared straight ahead. "I've been waiting for you for hours," she said at last, her voice barely above a whisper. "It's nearly time for tea."

"I apologize. I had to . . . had some business to attend to at home. It took the better part of the day."

"I see," was all she said in reply, her gaze still trained on the pond ahead.

He cleared his throat before continuing, thankful that she refused to meet his eyes. For if she had, he couldn't have borne what he was about to say. "I heard about your marriage proposal. From Jasper's groom, just as I drove up."

Her head snapped toward him at once. "Oh? Good news travels fast, doesn't it?"

*So it was true, then.* "As soon as I heard, I came looking for you. To offer my congratulations."

"Congratulations? Surely you didn't think—"

"I realize that I've acted coarse and common," he interrupted, anxious to speak his piece. "What I've done to you . . . I've no excuse for it. I cannot claim to be a gentleman. Sir Edmund is a fine man, and I deeply regret that I have taken what was rightfully his—"

"You stupid, stupid man!" Christobel dropped her parasol and scrambled to her feet, her cheeks stained an angry red. "Do you honestly think that I accepted Sir Edmund's offer?"

John rose to face her, jamming his hands into his pockets. His fingers closed around the ring he'd planned to give her, right up until he'd leaped out of his car, his heart near to bursting with joy, and heard about Sir Edmund's proposal. Right then and there, all his happiness had evaporated, leaving him empty, bereft.

Thank God he'd had the fortitude to withdraw himself yesterday before he'd spilled his seed inside her. It was bad enough that he'd stolen her virginity so roughly, so impatiently. He'd taken her up against a wall, for God's sake. But at least he hadn't risked impregnating her. And after what he'd done to her last night . . .

"How could I expect otherwise? I'm not a fool, Christobel," he said. "I know well enough that I'm not of your class, not of your world."

Before he realized what was happening, her hand flew out and struck him across one cheek. "You *are* a fool, John Leyden. My only regret is that I was a worse one."

He reached up to rub his smarting cheek, inadvertently dropping the ring to the grass below as he did so. It bounced off his shoe and landed mere inches from Christobel's dainty slippers, the sun glinting off the gold setting.

"What's this?" she asked, bending down to retrieve it. He saw her eyes widen a fraction as she clasped it between her finger and thumb and raised it to examine it more closely, her dark brows knitted in confusion.

"It was my grandmother's," he said, his voice suddenly thick as he stared at the jewel. It was exquisite, not a flashy bauble like his father's friends' wives favored, but a simple, understated piece—an heirloom that had been passed down through the generations on his late mother's side. An enormous emerald, square cut and without a single flaw, flanked by two triangular diamonds, both of which were equally flawless.

"Why on earth are you carrying it around, then? A piece like this . . . well, it should be locked in a safe somewhere, John." As she held it aloft, he saw that the gem perfectly matched her eyes, just as he supposed it would.

"I visited her just this morning. My grandmother," he clarified. "A grand old woman, nearly ninety and still full of life. I had to go see her, to tell her about you and to ask for the ring—"

"This ring was meant for me?" she interjected, her voice rising a pitch. "Why? Why, John?"

What the bloody hell, he might as well tell her— might as well expose himself for what he was. "I meant to ask you to marry *me*, Christobel. I damn well know it was foolish of me, but I couldn't help but—"

"Oh, John!" she cried out, launching herself into his arms. Her hands went round his neck, her fingers tangling in his hair as she buried her face in his coat. "I thought you didn't . . . thought it was just me—"

"Never," he said hoarsely. "By God, Christobel, I've loved you for so long. I never dared to hope you'd feel the same. But after yesterday—"

"Kiss me, John. Please!"

So he did—long and hard.

Christobel's head began to swim as she clutched John more tightly, her legs growing strangely weak beneath her. Heavens, but his kisses always seemed to have that effect on her.

She pulled away, breathlessly. "You've gone and made my knees weak again, John. I really must sit."

"What if I hold you, instead?" he offered, sweeping her up into his arms as if she were as light as a feather.

Oh, but it felt so right in his arms. So perfect! She couldn't explain it, but he'd swept her away entirely— body and soul. Swept away everything she'd thought she'd known about him—every prejudice, every supposition—and replaced it with a wonderful truth, instead.

"Have you any idea how much I adore you?" she asked, laying her cheek against his heart.

"No, but marry me, and—wait, I'm not doing this properly. This, at least, I'll do as a gentleman would," he said, setting her back on her feet and reaching for one hand.

"You're every inch a gentleman, John. The finest gentleman I've ever known," she said, meaning every word of it.

He didn't reply. Instead, he dropped to one knee, her hand still clasped in both of his. "Marry me, Christobel Smyth?"

She would have laughed, but he looked so earnest, so solemn. *Solemn as a bishop,* she thought, smiling inwardly. That was her John, the kindest, most honest man she knew.

"Of course I will," she said softly, her heart near to bursting with happiness.

For perhaps the first time in all the years she'd known him, his entire face lit with a smile—the most glorious smile she'd ever seen. "It's a perfect fit," he said, slipping the heavy ring onto her finger.

She held up her hand and admired it, turning it this way and that so the waning sun reflected off the precious gems. "Truly, I've never owned such a lovely piece as this."

His smile vanished almost as quickly as it had appeared. "You realize my home is in Cranford—a town house. I haven't a country house like Jasper; nothing like this," he said, gesturing toward the manicured gardens behind them. "And you so fond of the outdoors. It will never do."

"Dear John, don't you see? My home is wherever you are. I'm sure I'll come to appreciate Cranford as time goes on. It'll just take some getting used to, that's all."

"Milne Abbey," he said, nodding to himself. "Of course. Why didn't I think of it before?"

"Milne Abbey?" Christobel had never heard of the place.

"It's not more than a half hour's drive from here, by motorcar. It's an old, rambling farmhouse in need of some work, but the grounds are immense. They've been looking for a buyer for quite some time, so I can get it for a fair price, no doubt."

"No, John." Christobel shook her head. "It's not necessary. I'm sure your house in town is perfectly satisfactory, and—"

"It'll be my wedding gift to you." He reached for her hand and began leading her toward the path, abandoning her mackintosh square and parasol. "Let's drive out there now, and I'll show you."

Christobel hurried to keep up with him, matching her gait to his slightly uneven one. "Goodness, don't you think we should go back to the house and tell them our news first? I'm quite sure they're all staring out the windows right now, wondering just what's going on."

He favored her with yet another dazzling smile. "Won't they be surprised?"

"Not terribly so," Christobel said with a shrug. "I already told them I was in love with you. At least, I told Edith I was. I'm sure everyone from the housekeeper down to the groom knows by now. If only you'd waited in the stables a little longer, you might have heard that particular part of the tale."

Slowing his pace, he wrapped one arm about her shoulders. "You know, I've never much cared for house parties. But I believe this was the best Saturday-to-Monday I've ever attended. I'll have to express my appreciation to your sister."

"Don't you dare! She'll be swelled enough with pride

as it is. Four years in a row now, with successful matches, even if ours wasn't one she expected. Still, she's quite the little matchmaker, isn't she?"

John paused, wrapping his arms about her and burying his face in her neck. "She is, indeed," he murmured.

Her pulse leapt as a wave of desire washed over her. "Do you think perhaps we can find a place to be alone while we're out visiting Milne Abbey? Is there, for instance, an old, abandoned sawmill on the property somewhere?"

His eyes gleamed wickedly as he met her heated gaze. "Oh? And just what would we do there?"

"I can think of several things. Several naughty things, in fact."

"I'm afraid an old mill won't do this time. When I next make love to you, Christobel, I'll do it right."

"Are you saying that what we did yesterday wasn't done right, John? For it felt right enough to me. Both times," she added.

"I'm saying that next time we'll both remove every piece of our clothing first. Two, there will be a bed involved, or a cushioned chaise at the very least, and there will be light enough to see. And three—"

"There they are!" a voice called out, and Christobel turned to see Edith waving gaily from the edge of the garden, their mother there beside her.

"Later, then," John whispered as he returned the ladies' friendly wave.

"Not too much later," Christobel whispered back.

John laughed then, a deep, hearty laugh. "Who would have thought you had such mischief in you?"

*Her own words, thrown back at her.*

Little did he know, she had plenty more mischief in her, and all the time in the world to show him.

A lifetime, in fact.

*Five months later*

"Goodness, Edith, but he's beautiful." Christobel peered down at the squirming bundle that her sister held tightly to her breast. "Have you settled on a name?"

"Jasper wants to call him Ezekiel," Edith answered, glancing down at the sleeping babe with obvious pride.

"Such a mouthful for so small a boy. Will you call him Zeke?"

"I hadn't thought of it. Zeke," Edith tested. "Yes, that will do nicely."

Still sleeping, the baby made a snuffling noise, raising one tiny fist in the air and waving it about like a prize-fighter might.

"Do you suppose that means he approves?" Christobel asked with a laugh.

"He hasn't much choice, has he?" Edith reached down to stroke his soft, dark hair.

Christobel rose, one arm wrapped about the bedpost as she stared down at the pair. "You look exhausted, Edie. Shall I leave you both to get some rest before supper?"

"Don't be silly! I've done nothing but rest for the past two days. Stay." Edith patted the mattress beside her. "Tell me, how is Marie settling in?"

"Very well. She's got a room in Mrs. Sharp's house, not very large, but safe and respectable. I vow, you'd barely recognize her, she's grown so confident and assured! She's a natural teacher—the children adore her."

"From what John tells Jasper, the children adore you, too. I hope you are not running yourself ragged. Managing Milne Abbey is enough of an occupation in itself without spending time at the school, too."

"But I love it, Edith. Truly, I do. The school is a marvelous place; I'm so proud of John. Besides, I only go once or twice a week now that we've moved out to the Abbey. John's teaching me to drive and he says he'll buy me my own motorcar soon. That will make it so much easier to get back and forth."

"Your own motorcar? Surely you jest!"

"Indeed not," Christobel said indignantly. "I'm a perfectly able driver."

Edith just shook her head. "Honestly, you never cease to amaze me. Why, you make me feel so . . . so old-fashioned. Now that I think about it, you're quite like the town of Cranford, aren't you?"

"Are you saying I'm brash and ill-mannered?" Christobel teased. Truth be told, Cranford was beginning to grow on her.

"No, just that you're forward-thinking and capable. I think perhaps you—and Cranford, too—represent the future of England, while people like me, well . . ." She trailed off, shaking her head. "I fear we're more suited to the past. The world is changing so quickly, isn't it? I can only wonder what it will be like for little Ezekiel here."

Christobel shook her head. "Goodness, I've never known you to be so contemplative. Is that what motherhood does to you? Anyway," she continued, "I'll settle down soon enough with a babe of my own, and—"

"Do you mean that you're already—"

"Heavens, no!" she cut her off. "We've only been married two months, after all."

"Yes, but I'm fairly certain the pair of you got a head start on such matters," Edith said, a mischievous twinkle in her eyes.

"Edith!" she scolded, though of course it was true. Still, she hoped to have the renovations entirely complete at the Abbey before setting up a nursery. If only she could keep her hands off her husband. Her cheeks warmed at the thought.

"Why, you're blushing, Christobel."

"Oh, shut up! Besides, it's your own fault. You're the one who not only insisted we play hide-and-seek that day, but who also paired us up."

"If I'd had my way on that particular day, I'd have paired you with Sir Edmund, instead. What a ninny I was!" She shook her head with a smile.

"Speaking of Sir Edmund, did you hear that he and Miss Bartlett are engaged?"

"No! Wherever did you hear that?"

Christobel folded her arms across her breasts, feeling smug. "I had it from Miss Bartlett herself, just last week. We've been corresponding, you know. I quite like her. You *do* realize this means that you made not one, but *two* successful matches this year?"

"Why, I suppose you're right, though the couples got a bit mixed up. Still, I expect I can take credit."

"Unmarried ladies and gentlemen from all over are going to be clamoring for your invitation come autumn. It shall be quite a spectacle, I think. Look, Zeke is waking up." He'd begun to make soft mewling noises as he rooted around. "He must be hungry."

Edith smiled warmly as she readjusted her bed jacket and placed the baby at her breast. "It hasn't even been two hours, greedy little bugger."

At the sound of a motor, Christobel rose and hurried to the window, drawing aside the drapes and craning her neck to make out the familiar sight of the shiny green motorcar chugging up the drive in a cloud of dust.

"There's John!" she said, her heart racing in anticipation. "I'm glad he made it in time for supper. He's so looking forward to meeting his nephew." Dropping the drapes back into place, she turned back toward her sister. "Wait, not just his nephew—little Zeke is also John's first cousin once removed, isn't he? Goodness, I didn't think of that before now."

Edith cocked her head to one side. "Why, I suppose you're right. Imagine that, some sort of double relation. Well, go on, I know you're dying to run down there and greet him. There's still time before supper; go off to the pond, or wherever it is you two lovebirds always go off to."

Christobel couldn't help but laugh. It was true; they *did* favor the ornamental pond. After all, John had proposed to her there. *But not as much as we favor the old abandoned gristmill,* she thought, smiling wickedly to herself.

Not *half* as much.